Seductive Scoundrels

SERIES BOOKS 1-3

COLLETTE CAMERON

Blue Rose Romance®
Portland, Oregon

Sweet-to-Spicy Timeless Romance®

Check out Collette's Other Series

Daughters of Desire (Scandalous Ladies)

Highland Heather Romancing a Scot

The Blue Rose Regency Romances: The Culpepper Misses

Castle Brides

The Honorable Rogues®

Heart of a Scot

Collections

Lords in Love

The Honorable Rogues® Books 1-3

The Honorable Rogues® Books 4-6

Seductive Scoundrels Series Books 1-3

Seductive Scoundrels Series Books 4-6

The Blue Rose Regency Romances- The Culpepper Misses Series 1-2

Contents

A Diamond for a Duke

Introduction

"A Diamond for a Duke" is loosely based on Charles Perrault's 1697 French fairytale, "Les Fées" or "The Fairies," also known as "Toads and Diamonds" or "Diamonds and Toads." I'd never heard of this tale until I began research for an unusual fable to base a Regency novella upon.

As in Perrault's tale, there are two sisters, Adelinda Dament, the eldest—contentious, self-centered, rude, and who values all things related to the socially elite. Metaphorically speaking, because of her inner ugliness, her words manifest as vipers and toads. The sisters' mother, Belinda, blatantly favors Adelinda, who resembles her in looks, attitude, and behavior.

Jemmah, the younger sister, is portrayed as gentler, kinder, and as someone who cares more about people than their status. She possesses a beautiful soul, and when she speaks, her words spill forth as jewels and flowers. She, too, is banished from her home, as is the younger daughter in "Diamonds and Toads."

The fairy takes the form of two feisty characters, Faye, the Dowager Viscountess Lockhart, and the Viscountess Theodora Lockhart. Theodora is Adelinda and Jemmah's aunt, and godmother to Jules, the sixth Duke of Dandridge. He plays the role of the hero and has his own nemesis to contend with in the form of Phryne Milbourne.

My quirky humor worked overtime when I selected the characters' names. Several of them were chosen specifically for their meanings:

Adelinda - noble snake

Belinda - beautiful snake

Charmont - charming

Dament - diamond

Jasper - bringer of treasure

Jemmah - gem

Jules - well, it sounds like jewels!

Faye - Fairy

Phryne - toad

A final thought about "A Diamond for a Duke"...

In today's culture, Belinda would be considered an abusive parent—unfortunately, a common and often accepted motif threaded throughout fairytales of old, as was parental partiality. The authenticity of my tale required both of these unpleasant themes.

I want to encourage everyone who has experienced or is experiencing abuse that, as in the fairytale and my novella, there is hope for you.

Help is available in many forms.

Please ... please, don't wait another day to seek it.

1

April 1809

London, England

A *pox on duty.*
  A plague on the pesky dukedom too.

Not the tiniest speck of remorse troubled Jules, Duke of Dandridge as he bolted from the crush of his godmother, Theodora, Viscountess Lockhart's fiftieth birthday ball—without bidding the dear lady a proper farewell, at that.

She'd forgive his discourtesy; his early departure too.

Unlike his mother, his uncles, and the majority of *le beau monde*, Theo understood him.

To honor her, he'd put in a rare social appearance and even stood up for the obligatory dances expected of someone of his station. Through sheer doggedness, he'd also forced his mouth to curve upward—good God, his face ached from the effort—and suffered the toady posturing of husband-stalking mamas and their bevy of pretty, wide-eyed offspring eager to snare an unattached duke.

Noteworthy, considering not so very long ago, Jules scarcely merited a passing glance from the same *tonnish* females now so keen to garner his favor. His perpetual scowl might be attributed to their disinterest.

Tonight's worst offender?

Theo's irksome sister-in-law, Mrs. Dament.

The tenacious woman had neatly maneuvered her admittedly stunning elder daughter, Adelinda, to his side multiple times, and only the Daments' intimate connection to Theo had kept him from turning on his heel at the fourth instance instead of graciously fetching mother and daughter the ratafia they'd requested.

A rather uncouth mental dialogue accompanied his march to the refreshment table, nonetheless.

Where was the other daughter—the sweet-tempered one, Miss Jemmah Dament?

Twiddling her thumbs at home again? Poor, kind, neglected sparrow of a thing.

As children and adolescents, he and Jemmah had been comfortable friends, made so by their similar distressing circumstances. But as must be, they'd grown up, and destiny or fate had placed multiple obstacles between them. He trotted off to university—shortly afterward becoming betrothed to Annabel—and for a time, the Daments simply faded from his and society's notice.

Oh, on occasion, Jules had spied Jemmah in passing. But she'd ducked her shiny honey-colored head and averted her acute sky-blue gaze. Almost as if she was discomfited or he'd somehow offended her.

Yet, after wracking his brain, he couldn't deduce what his transgression might've been.

At those times, recalling their prior relaxed companionship, his ability to talk to her about anything—or simply remain in compatible silence, an odd twinge pinged behind his ribs. Not regret exactly, though he hardly knew what to label the disquieting sensation.

Quite simply, he missed her friendship and company.

Since Theo's brother, Jasper, died two years ago, Jules had seen little of the Daments.

According to tattle, their circumstances had been drastically reduced. But even so, Jemmah's absence at routs, soirees, and other *ton* gatherings, which her mother and sister often attended, raised questions and eyebrows.

At least arced Jules's brow and stirred his curiosity.

If Jemmah were present at more assemblies, perhaps he'd make more of an effort to put in an appearance.

Or perhaps not.

He held no illusions about his lack of social acumen. A deficiency he had no desire to remedy.

Ever.

A trio of ladies rounded the corner, and he dove into a niche beside a vase-topped table.

The Chinese urn tottered, and he clamped the blue and white china between both hands, lest it crash to the floor and expose him.

He needn't have worried.

So engrossed in their titillating gossip about whether Lord Bacon wore stays, none of the women was the least aware of his presence as they sailed past.

Mentally patting himself on the back for his exceptionally civil behavior for the past pair of vexing hours, Jules permitted a self-satisfied smirk and stepped back into the corridor. He nearly collided with Theo's aged mother-in-law, the Dowager Viscountess Lockhart, come to town for her daughter-in-law's birthday.

A tuft of glossy black ostrich feathers adorned her hair, the tallest of which poked him in the eye.

Hell's bells.

"I beg your pardon, my lady."

Eye watering, Jules grasped her frail elbow, steadying her before she toppled over, such did she sway.

She chuckled, a soft crackle like delicate old lace, and squinted up at him, her faded eyes, the color of weak tea, snapping with mirth.

"Bolting, are you, Dandridge?"

Saucy, astute old bird.

Nothing much escaped Faye, Dowager Viscountess Lockhart's notice.

"I prefer to call it making a prudently-timed departure."

Which he'd be forced to abandon in order to assist the tottering dame back to her preferred throne—*er, seat*—in the ballroom.

He'd congratulated himself prematurely, blast it.

"Allow me to escort you, Lady Lockhart."

He daren't imply she needed his help, or she'd turn her tart tongue, and likely her china-handled cane, on him too.

"Flim flam. Don't be an utter nincompoop. You mightn't have

another opportunity to flee. Go on with you now." She pointed her cane down the deserted passageway. "I'll contrive some drivel to explain your disappearance."

"I don't need a justification."

Beyond that he was bored to his polished shoes, he'd rather munch fresh horse manure than carry on anymore inane conversation, and crowds made him nervous as hell.

Always had.

Hence his infrequent appearances.

Pure naughtiness sparked in the dowager's eyes as she put a bony finger to her chin as if seriously contemplating what shocking tale she'd spin.

"What excuse should I use? Perhaps an abduction? *Hmph*. Not believable." She shook her head, and the ostrich feather danced in agreement. "An elopement? No, no. Won't do at all. Too dull and predictable."

She jutted her finger skyward, nearly poking his other eye.

"Ah, ha! I have just the thing. A scandalous assignation. With a secret love. Oh, yes, that'll do nicely."

A decidedly teasing smile tipped her thin lips.

Jules vacillated.

She was right, of course.

If he didn't make good his escape now, he mightn't be able to for hours. Still, his conscience chafed at leaving her to hobble her way to the ballroom alone. For all of his darkling countenance and brusque comportment, he was still a gentleman first.

Lady Lockhart extracted her arm, and then poked him in the bicep with her pointy nail.

Hard.

"Go, I said, young scamp." Only she would dare call a duke a scamp. "I assure you, I'm not so infirm that I'm incapable of walking the distance without tumbling onto my face."

Maybe not her face, but what about the rest of her feeble form?

Her crepey features softened, and the beauty she'd once been peeked through the ravages of age. "It was good of you to come, Dandridge, and I know it meant the world to Theodora." The imp returned full on, and she bumped her cane's tip against his instep. "Now git yourself gone."

"Thank you, my lady." Jules lifted her hand, and after kissing the back, waited a few moments to assess her progress. If she struggled the least, he'd lay aside his plans and disregard her command.

A few feet along the corridor, she paused, half-turning toward him. Starchy silvery eyebrow raised, she mouthed, "Move your arse."

With a sharp salute, Jules complied and continued to reflect on his most successful venture into society in a great while.

Somehow—multiple glasses of superb champagne might be attributed to helping—he'd even managed to converse—perhaps a little less courteously than the majority of attendees, but certainly not as tersely as he was generally wont to—with the young bucks, dandies, and past-their-prime decrepitudes whose trivial interests consisted of horseflesh, the preposterous wagers on Whites's books, and the next bit of feminine fluff they might sample.

Or, in the older, less virile coves' cases, the unfortunate woman subjected to their lusty ogling since the aged chaps' softer parts were wont to stay that way.

Only the welcome presence of the two men whom Jules might truly call 'friend,' Maxwell, Duke of Pennington, and Victor, Duke of Sutcliffe, had made the evening, if not pleasant, undoubtedly more interesting with their barbed humor and ongoing litany of drolly murmured sarcastic observations.

Compared to that acerbic pair, Jules, renowned for his acute intellect and grave mien, seemed quite the epitome of frivolous jollity.

But, by spitting camels, when his uncles, Leopold and Darius—from whom his middle names had been derived—had cornered him in the card room and demanded to know for the third time this month when he intended to do his *ducal duty*?

Marry and produce an heir...

Damn their interfering eyes!

Jules's rigidly controlled temper had slipped loose of its moorings, and he'd told them—ever so calmly, but also enunciating each syllable most carefully lest the mulish, bacon-brained pair misunderstand a single word—"go bugger yourselves and leave me be!"

He'd been officially betrothed once and nearly so a second time in his five-and-twenty years. Never again.

Never?

Fine, maybe someday. But not to a Society damsel and not for many, *many* years or before *he* had concluded the parson's mousetrap was both necessary and convenient. Should that fateful day never come to pass, well, best his Charmont uncles get busy producing male heirs themselves instead of dallying with actresses and opera singers.

Marching along the corridor, Jules tipped his mouth into his first genuine smile since alighting from his coach, other than the one he'd bestowed upon Theo when he arrived. Since his affianced, Annabel's death five years ago, Theo was one of the few people he felt any degree of true affection for.

Must be a character flaw—an inadequacy in his emotional reservoir, this inability to feel earnest emotions. In any event, he wanted to return home early enough to bid his niece and ward, Lady Sabrina Remington, good-night as he'd promised.

They'd celebrated her tenth birthday earlier today, too.

Jules truly enjoyed Sabrina's company.

Possibly because he could simply be himself, not Duke of Dandridge, or a peer, or a member of the House of Lords. Not quarry for eager-to-wed chits, a tolerant listener of friends' ribald jokes, or a wise counselor to troubled acquaintances. Not even a dutiful nephew, a less-favored son, a preferred godson, or at one time, a loving brother and wholly-devoted intended.

Anticipation of fleeing the crowd lengthening his strides, he cut a swift glance behind him, and his gut plummeted, arse over chin, to his shiny shoes.

Blisters and ballocks.

Who the devil invited *her*?

2

Jules's brusque sound of annoyance echoed in the corridor.

Miss Phryne Milbourne, the only other woman he'd considered marrying—for all of a few brief hours—had espied him. Given the determined look on her lovely face, she again intended to broach his crying off.

London's perpetually foggy and sooty skies would rain jewels and flowers before he ever took up with the likes of that vixen again, no matter how beautiful, blue-blooded, or perfectly suited to the position of duchess others—namely, Mother and The Uncles—believed she might be.

Within mere hours of his uncles and his mother taking it upon themselves to broach a *possible* match between Miss Milbourne and him, which she'd bandied about with the recklessness of a farmwife tossing chickens table scraps—Jules had observed her true character, quite by chance.

And thank God, he had, or she might well be his duchess by now.

The notion curdled the two servings of *crème brûlée* he'd indulged in at luncheon.

Truth to tell, he would've been hard put to decide which rankled more: Miss Milbourne's callousness or her promiscuousness. Or perhaps, her ceaseless, nigh on to obsessive, pursuit of him was what abraded worse than boots three sizes too small. In any event, he had neither the time nor the inclination to discuss the issue with her tonight.

Or ever, for that matter.

Familiar with the manor's architecture, he ducked into the nearest doorway and sidled into an elegant, unlit parlor situated between dual sets of ornate double doors. Doors which provided him with another, less obvious, route from the house through an adjacent passageway.

Unaccustomed to the room's darkness, he blindly groped until he found what he searched for. With the merest scrape of metal, he turned the key, and chuckled softly, if perhaps a might wickedly, to himself.

He truly was a social misfit, and that he rather liked the peculiarity made him more so.

Staid, abrupt, off-putting, somber, reticent, taciturn, reserved...

He knew full well what others thought of him and, for the most part, their descriptions were accurate. What they didn't know was why.

Jemmah Dament knew.

As timid, overlooked children, they'd sought refuge in each other's company and whispered their secret fears to one another, too.

Peculiar that twice in a matter of minutes Jemmah had popped to mind. Must've been encountering her bothersome family that caused the dual intrusions.

Feminine footsteps accompanied by a heavier, uneven tread echoed on the corridor's Arenberg parquet floor as Miss Milbourne neared.

"I'm positive I saw Dandridge a moment ago, Papa." A hint of petulance flavored her words. "He's still avoiding me, though I've repeatedly explained that he misunderstood what he thought he saw and heard."

The devil I did.

Keaton's arm had been elbow deep inside her bodice, and his tongue halfway that distance down her throat too.

Far worse, in Jules estimation, was Miss Milbourne's treatment of sweet, crippled Sabrina. Whorish behavior was repugnant, but cruelty to an unfortunate, doubly so.

Intolerable and unforgivable in his view.

There and then, he'd told Miss Milbourne as much and that she'd best cease entertaining notions of a match between them. His ire raised, he may have suggested he'd welcome starved chartreuse tigers at the dining table with more enthusiasm than continuing their acquaintance.

"Why, the stubborn man dared return the perfumed note I sent him last week, Papa. Unopened too, the obstinate wretch," she fumed, her footsteps taking on a distinct stomping rhythm. "How many times must I apologize before Dandridge forgives me?"

"Tut, m'dear. I wish you'd let me sue the knave for breaking the betrothal," Milbourne wheezed, great gasping rattles that threatened to dislodge the artwork displayed above the passage's mahogany raised panel wainscoting.

If wishes were food, beggars would eat cake, old chap.

There'd have to have been an actual proposal and a formal agreement, including a signed contract.

Not a mere wishful suggestion in passing, which Miss Milbourne latched onto like a barnacle to rock.

She'd led her father on a deuced merry chase the past two years, setting her cap for, and then tossing aside, one peer after another, each ranking higher and with fuller coffers than the last. Served him and the late Mrs. Milbourne right for naming her Phryne after a Greek courtesan.

Dotty business, that.

Whatever could they have been thinking?

Breathing heavily, Milbourne grumbled from what must be directly outside the door, "Would do the arrogant whelp good to be taken down a peg. He'd be lucky to have you, my pet, he would. I can pull some strings—"

"No, Papa! That would only anger Dandridge further. He must be made to see reason. I'm confident he'll come 'round in time. His uncles and her grace are easily enough manipulated, and they want me at his side. I shan't be denied my duchy because of a prudish misunderstanding. I'd remain faithful to him until an heir was produced. Perhaps even a spare. Surely, he must know that."

How very obliging.

The door handle rattled, kicking Jules's pulse into a gallop.

An unladylike snort carried through the walnut.

"Locked. I suppose Lady Lockhart, the pretentious tabby, is afraid the guests will make off with her vulgar oddities."

Jules drew in a prolonged, grateful breath. By discovering Miss Milbourne's vices early on, he'd been spared a lifetime of misery.

"Papa, did you see her expression when we entered with the

Wakefields tonight? Looked like she'd swallowed newly-sharpened needles." Miss Milbourne's scornful laugh faded as she and her father explored the rest of the passageway.

Jules remained still, listening as doors swished open and clicked close as they snooped in room after room in their search for him.

And here he cowered, like an errant child, his temper growing blacker by the minute. However, an ugly confrontation was the last thing Theo warranted at her birthday celebration. Hence her decision, no doubt, not to send the Milbournes packing when they showed up uninvited on the Wakefields' coat strings.

Zounds, Jules loathed manipulators.

A stunning beauty—a diamond of the first water according to the *haut ton*'s standards— Miss Milbourne was intelligent, accomplished, versed in politics, a gracious hostess, and popular among the social set. In short, she possessed all the trivial qualifications Mother and The Uncles deemed necessary for the next Duchess of Dandridge, and of as much value and importance to Jules as a hangnail or pernicious boil on his bum.

Naturally, his mother would approve of Miss Milbourne.

She was cut from the same calculating, mercenary fabric, after all.

Plato had it right, by Jove. Like does indeed attract like.

Jules didn't much care one way or the other who the next duchess was. Or, for that matter, if there was another while he lived. Young and smitten, he'd dared gamble on love once, and when Annabel—always petite and frail—died from influenza a mere month prior to their wedding, his ability to love must've been buried with her. For no sentiment stronger than warm regard or affection ever stirred him again.

Except for where Sabrina was concerned.

And long, long ago, Miss Jemmah Dament too.

Contemplating a match with Miss Milbourne had nothing to do with affection and everything to do with benefiting the dukedom. More fool he for not having listened to Theo's blunt warnings against such a hair-brained notion.

Jules was capable of finding a diamond of his own choosing, thank you very much.

One whose multi-faceted inner beauty glowed far more brilliantly than Miss Milbourne's exquisite outward countenance.

Shaking his head, he rubbed his brow against the slight twinge tapping there and glanced around the lavish parlor. The undrawn draperies permitted moonlight to stream through the emerald-and-gold brocade-festooned windows and cast a silvery, iridescent glow over the gilded, carved furnishings. Muted music filtered into the peaceful chamber even as the Sevres mantel clock lazily chimed ten o'clock.

He'd best hurry or Sabrina would think he'd decided to remain at the ball longer and she'd retire for the night. She'd only been permitted to stay up so late because she'd obediently taken an afternoon nap. To disappoint the child after she'd already endured so much tragedy in her short life was unthinkable.

Jules didn't make promises he didn't mean to keep.

Should he unlock the door before taking his leave through the other pair?

No. Theo's servants would see to the matter.

She really ought to consider securing unused rooms when she

entertained, especially with the likes of Miss Milbourne prowling about.

He'd mention the subject when next he saw his godmother.

Wending between the numerous pieces of furniture in the moon's half-light, he smacked his shin into the settee. Pain spiraling from calf to knee, he softly cursed and bent to rub the offended limb.

"Dammit. Must Theo constantly rearrange the furniture? Two hell-fired times since December."

A startled gasp, swiftly stifled, had him jerking upright, whacking his shoulder this time.

Bloody hell.

"Who's there?"

Silence met his inquiry. Had he stumbled upon a lover's tryst? A thief? A wayward servant or inquisitive guest? He fingered his throbbing shoulder, pressing the pads against the pain.

"Reveal yourself at once."

Silence.

Running his fingers along the settee's back, he located the pedestal sofa table.

Other than shallow breathing, the culprit kept quiet.

Squinting, he made out a light-colored form reclining on the dark blue-and-silver striped cushions. A woman, and by all the stampeding elephants in Africa, he bet his silver buttons, and the two new bruises he surely sported, he knew who lay there.

Like a slowly uncoiling rope, the tension eased from his taut muscles.

He fumbled a bit until he found the engraved silver tinderbox beside the candelabra, and moments later, a wax taper flared to life.

"Hello, Your Grace."

Miss Jemmah Dament, her rosy lips curved upward in a small closed-mouth smile and her face still sleep-softened, blinked groggily.

Hello, indeed. Adorable, sleepy kitten.

He lifted the candle higher, taking in her svelte figure, her delectable backside pressed to the sofa, one hand still cradling her cheek. Surprise and carnal awareness, pleasant and unexpected, tingled a rippling path from one shoulder to the other.

The plain, awkward little mudlark had transformed into a graceful dove. One who rivaled—no, by far exceeded—her sister's allure.

"Well, hello to you as well, Miss Jemmah Dament."

As if it were the most natural thing in the world to be found napping during a ball at her aunt's house, and then awoken by a man crashing into her makeshift bed, she sat up and brushed a wayward curl off her forehead.

Jules set about lighting the other three tapers. Their glow revealed striking pale blue, wide-set almond-shaped eyes, fringed by dark lashes, and tousled hair somewhere between rich caramel and light toffee.

He hadn't seen her up close in...?

How long had it been?

Cocking his head, he searched his mind's archives.

At least since last summer.

Yes, that afternoon in August, in Hyde Park, when she'd walked past wearing a travesty of a walking ensemble. A sort of greenish-gray color somewhere between rotten fish and bread mold.

Yawning delicately behind one slender hand, she smoothed her plain

16

ivory gown with the other.

Except for a yellowish-tan sash below her breasts, the garment lacked any adornment. The ribbon didn't suit her coloring, and although he couldn't claim to be an expert on feminine apparel, the frock seemed rather lackluster for such a grand affair.

Another of Adelinda's cast-offs?

Jules canted his head as he closed the tinder box.

He couldn't recall ever seeing Jemmah wearing anything new. And yet her sister always appeared perfumed and bejeweled, attired in the first stare of fashion. Such blatant favoritism wasn't uncommon amongst the elite, nor did it shock nearly as much as appall.

He, too, was his mother's least-favorite child, but by all the candle nubs in England, *if* he ever had children—in the very distant future— they'd not know the kind of rejection and pain he and Jemmah had experienced because of their parents' partiality.

He'd love and treat his offspring equally as any good and decent parent should.

"Ah, Your Grace, you're surprised to see me, I think."

Rather than coy or seductive, her smile and winged brows indicated genuine amusement. Her vivacious eyes sparkling with secret knowledge, she ran her gaze over him, the full radiance of her smile causing something prickly to take root in his chest and purr through his veins.

"I am, but pleasantly so. Your appearance at these farces is even rarer than my own, Miss Dament."

His by choice, but what about Jemmah?

Did she want to attend and was prohibited?

17

"I'm here at Aunt Theo's insistence. Mama couldn't put her off this time. But I'm afraid even I have too much pride to be seen in a morning gown from three seasons ago. Besides," she lifted a milky-white, sloping shoulder as she fiddled with a pillow's tassel, "I don't know how to dance, and this is a ball after all."

No self-pity or resentment weighted her words, just honest revelation.

Jules had forgotten how refreshingly forthright she was.

Still, how had such an important part of her education been overlooked?

Did Theo know?

Probably, since she'd mentioned trying to intervene on Jemmah's behalf many times. Much to Theo's dismay, Mrs. Dament refused all offers benefiting Jemmah, but when it came to Adelinda...

That was an entirely different matter. For that greedy puss, nothing was spared.

Pity for Jemmah engulfed him.

She unfolded—for there was no other way to describe the smooth, catlike elegance as she angled to her feet—and after sliding her obviously-mended stockinged toes into plain black slippers a trifle too large, and gathering her gloves, dipped a nimble curtsy.

"Please excuse me, Your Grace."

"Wait, Jem." Too forward, that. Addressing her by her given name, but she'd been Jem and he Jules for over a decade before their paths separated.

She hesitated, her pretty blue-eyed gaze probing his.

A swift glance to the mantel confirmed he might spare a minute or two more. He'd told Sabrina he'd be home no later than half past ten. Odd that he should be this happy to see Jemmah. But they were old friends, and as such, once together again, it was as if they'd never been apart.

After all, he'd known her since, as a pixyish imp with eyes too big for her thin face and wild straw-colored hair, she'd tried to hide beneath the same table as he when Lord Lockhart, his godfather had passed.

They'd seen each other intermittently over the years, but seldom traveled in the same social circles. Her father had died—heart attack in his mistress's arms if the dark rumors were true—a year before Jules's elder brother and sister-in-law were killed in the carriage accident that disabled Sabrina.

Jules and Jemmah had much in common.

Both had known grief and loss, endured the disdain of an uncaring mother, and lived in the shadow of an adored older child. But discovering her sequestered here, self-conscious about her unfashionable gown with salty dried tear trails upon her creamy cheeks, roused the same protective instincts he had for his niece.

What you feel for Jemmah isn't the least paternal.

Sensation and sentiments long since dormant—so long in fact, he thought they'd died— slowly, and ever so cautiously raised their bowed heads to peek about.

Jules stepped 'round to the settee's front and offered her a sympathetic smile.

She must've noticed his speculation, because she turned away and swiped at her face, erasing the evidence of her unhappiness.

"I must go. I'll be missed."

No. She wouldn't.

Other than, perhaps, by Theo.

He doubted her mother or sister had given her a single thought the entire evening. Probably forgot she'd accompanied them altogether, so insignificant was she to them.

That weird spasm behind his breastbone pinged again.

Jemmah's pale azure gaze—he couldn't quite find anything to compare the delicate, yet arresting shade to—caught his, and she captured her plump lower lip between her teeth before shifting her focus to the frilly settee pillows.

Her shoulders lifted as she pulled in a substantial breath and notched her pert chin higher, while something akin to defiance emphasized the delicate angles and curves of her face. The earlier light he'd glimpsed in her eyes faded to a resigned melancholy. When she spoke, a kind of weary, beleaguered desperation shadowed her gentle words.

"No one, Your Grace, appreciates being the object of another's pity."

3

At Jemmah's frank pronouncement, Dandridge's deep set amber eyes widened a fraction, immediately followed by a contemplative glint. He probably wasn't accustomed to such candor, but in her limited experience, artifice seldom ended well.

"Say what you mean and mean what you say," Papa had always advocated. "Speak honestly, my precious Jem. But temper your words with kindness and gentleness so they're diamonds, not toads. One is welcomed, even appreciated. The other detested and often feared."

Lord, how she missed her father's jovial smile, perpetually rumpled hair and clothing, and his tender kisses upon her crown. Missed the fairytales he used to tell her as she sat upon his knee. "Toads and Diamonds," "The Sleeping Beauty," "Little Red Riding Hood," and so many more.

Tears stung behind her eyelids, but she resolutely blinked them away. She must continue to be strong. But at times—times like these when humiliation and shame sluiced her—it was so very hard. And she was so very weary and discouraged despite the cheerful mien she presented.

A whisper of a sigh escaped her.

Pshaw.

Enough wallowing in self-pity. Imprudent and pointless.

Perhaps recalling Papa's counsel hadn't been the best example for bolstering her courage, especially since he had died in his lover's bed.

Most mothers would've kept that tawdry detail from their children, but Mama used the ugliness to regularly and viciously besmirch Papa's character to her daughters.

Jemmah in particular.

One didn't have to think overly long and hard to understand why he'd sought another woman's comfort. Not that Jemmah excused his infidelity, but neither could she deny he'd been miserable for most of her life.

So had she, and she longed for the day she might finally, somehow, escape and know joy and peace, not constant ridicule and criticism.

Her emotions once more under control, she returned Dandridge's acute assessment, determined to show her lack of cowardice, and that she wasn't a weak, pathetic creature deserving of his—or anyone else's—pity or sympathy.

Well? Have you nothing to say?

The laurel wreath diamond cravat pin gracing his snowy waterfall of a neckcloth cheekily winked at her, and as if he'd heard her silent challenge, and with an unidentifiable gleam crinkling his eyes' outer corners, the edges of his strong mouth twitched upward.

She'd risked voicing her innermost thoughts, and the handsome knave laughed at her?

Chagrin trotted a spiky path from her chest to her hairline, no doubt

22

leaving a ribbon of ugly, ruddy blotches. No soft flare of flattering, pinkish color accompanied her blushes, but rather ugly splotches mottled her skin, very much resembling an angry sunburn or severe rash.

Papa had attributed the tendency to their Irish heritage.

If that were true, then why didn't Adelinda with her coppery hair suffer the affliction?

Jemmah knew full well why.

Because in that, as was true of everything else, Adelinda took after Mama.

Jemmah's looking glass revealed daily, and objectively, that her light coloring and unremarkable features paled in comparison to her mother's and sister's flamboyant looks with their rich ginger hair and dark exotic eyes. Neither did she possess their high-strung temperaments nor delicate constitutions. All of which Mama contended a lady must possess in order to become a *haut ton* favorite.

As if Jemmah cared a whit about any of that fiddle-faddle.

People mattered far more than titles or positions.

Her rather ordinary appearance, robust health, and kindly nature were more suited for docile cattle or sheep, and as such, frequently served to vex and disappoint her mother.

Indeed, how many times since Papa's death had Mama admonished—her voice arctic and condemning—"You look and behave just like your father, Jemmah. I can scarcely bear to look upon you. You'll disgrace us one day, too. Just you wait and see."

I shall not.

If anyone brought more shame on the Daments, it would be Adelinda.

She'd become so bold in her clandestine rendezvous, someone was sure to come upon her and one of her numerous unsuitable beaux.

Naturally, Mama knew nothing of Adelinda's fast behavior.

After attempting to broach the subject once, Mama had accused Jemmah of envying her sister. She then confined Jemmah to her room with only gruel and broth for two days, and thereafter Jemmah resolved to keep her own counsel on the matter.

Adelinda could suffer the consequences of her rash choices, which likely as rain in England would bring shame and censure down upon all their heads.

Jemmah eyed Jules from beneath her lashes. A partial smile yet curved his mouth.

She knew full well how pathetic she appeared to others. Yet to see fellow feeling engraved on the noble planes of his face and glistening in his warm treacle eyes... Well, by cold, lumpy porridge, the injustice of it burgeoned up her tight throat, choking her.

And her dratted tongue—blast the ignoble organ—saw fit to ignore even a scrap of common sense. Her mouth had opened of its own accord, spewing forth her innermost thoughts. Thoughts she took great care to keep buried in the remotest niches of her mind, even from herself at times.

Still, pity was the last thing Jemmah wanted from anyone, most especially from The Sixth Duke of Dandridge, and for him to also find her an object of amusement, pricked hot and ferocious.

Wealthy and powerful, much sought after, and too absurdly handsome for his own good—*hers too*—made her one-time friend's mockery all the more unbearable.

He slanted his head, the paler hues ribboning his rich honey-blond hair catching the candles' light. Cupping his nape, his gaze traveled from her rumpled hair to her too-large slippers, and she wanted to melt into the floor or crawl beneath the side table and hide as she'd done so often as a child.

"You needn't stare. I'm perfectly aware of my deficiencies, Your Grace."

Hadn't they been drilled into her almost daily for years?

When he didn't answer but continued to regard her with that amused, curious, yet confused expression, her seldom-riled temper chose to snap to attention.

"You, Your Grace, are being rude."

Brow knitted into three distinct furrows, he finally veered his astute gaze away to contemplate the moon through the window and his familiar reserved bearing descended.

The devil take her loose tongue. She'd offended him.

Why, for all the tea in England, had she'd just insulted a duke?

And not just any duke, but Aunt Theo's beloved godson, a man more of a son to her than he was to his own mother. Her aunt, the only person in Jemmah's memory, besides Papa, to show her any compassion or kindness, would not be pleased.

Don't forget how kind Jules—his grace—used to be to you, as well.

Aunt Theo had always admired Jemmah's pleasant disposition, and Jemmah would've been hard pressed to explain why he'd riled her to the point of insolence.

It must've been humiliation-induced anger brought about because

25

he'd felt sorry for her.

Dandridge, the devilishly handsome, wonderful smelling, garbed in the first crack of fashion peer, regarded her with those darkened, hooded eyes and his lips tweaked downward as if she were a pathetic charity case or a poorhouse worker.

He, for whom she'd harbored a secret *tendre* since the first time he'd joined her beneath a lace-edged tablecloth's security almost fifteen years ago, when she'd been a five-year-old imp, and he a brawny, mature lad of ten.

More fool she. But her dreams, no matter how trivial or silly or unattainable, were hers to entertain and treasure, and no one could take them from her. If one didn't have dreams, something to look forward to, then life's everyday tedium and drudgery, Mama's harsh criticisms and fault-finding, might steal all vestiges of her joy.

Jemmah mightn't have much in the way of appearances or possessions, but she had a remnant of pride and a handful of wonderful memories. Still, the realization that Jules pitied her...

Well, her very soul panged with indignation as well as mortification—each as unwelcome as vermin droppings in seedcake or oozing pox sores upon her face.

At least he'd been forced to acknowledge her this time, unlike the half dozen other encounters over the past two years.

In each of those instances, he'd looked straight through her as if she didn't exist or was something as inconspicuous as tree bark, a pewter cloud in an armor-gray sky, or a fingerprint smudged upon a window.

Present, but invisible to all.

An accurate depiction of Jemmah's life, truth to tell.

That rather smarted too, for whenever he entered a room, passed her on the street, trotted his magnificent ebony mount down Rotten Row, she'd noticed him straightaway—discretely observing him through lowered lashes, her countenance carefully bland.

She knew her place. Knew she was beneath his touch.

But to gaze upon his somber handsomeness, and recall how infinitely thoughtful he'd always been to her.

What possible harm was there in that?

They were much like a diamond and a lump of coal.

He the former; she the latter.

The gem's polished radiance and brilliance, its innate and intricate beauty, drew attention without trying, while the grubby fuel was only noticed and needed if a room or stove grew cool.

Speaking of cool, the parlor had grown quite nippy, and Jemmah rubbed her bare arms.

How long had she slept anyway?

She examined the mantel clock.

Only two hours?

Surely it has been longer.

She'd needed the rest after staying awake until a quarter past four this morning finishing Adelinda's gown. But now, she truly must go. Even if Mama and Adelinda hadn't wondered where she'd got off to, Aunt Theo might.

"Please forgive my churlishness, Your Grace. I assure you, it's not typical. I didn't sleep much last night, and I find these sorts of assemblies trying, even under the best of circumstances."

Dressed in castoffs, unqualified to dance with any degree of skill, and aware she sorely lacked her sister's grace and beauty, social events proved excruciating.

Dandridge didn't respond, and to cover the awkward silence, Jemmah bent and tidied the pillows she'd mussed. Satisfied the room appeared as it had when she entered, and that she'd done whatever she could to apologize for her peevish behavior, she swiveled toward the door.

Eager to escape, she hoped to find another cranny to lurk in until Mama deemed it time to depart.

Likely hours from now.

"Would you like to dance?"

His soft request halted her mid-step, and jaw slack, she flung an are-you-serious-or-mocking-me-glance over her shoulder.

He extended his hand, the movement pulling his black tailcoat taut over enticingly broad shoulders and a rounded bicep. The gold signet ring upon his little finger gleamed, as did the jeweled lion's head cuff link at his wrist.

His unbearably tender smile caused Jemmah's blood to sidle through her veins rather like honey-sweetened tea—rich and warm and strong—even as another sensation embedded behind her ribs, slowly burrowing its way deeper—and dangerously deeper, yet.

Dandridge was dangerous for her peace of mind.

Dangerous for the life she'd resigned herself to.

Staring hard into his eyes' unfathomable depths, Jemmah tried to gauge his sincerity and motives.

"One dance, Miss Jemmah. I've never had the honor of partnering you."

More pity directed her way, or a genuinely kind, if somewhat irregular gift?

She might be able to manage an English country dance with reasonable finesse, but a cotillion or quadrille?

Utterly impossible.

"Your Grace, I told you, I don't know how."

More shame scorched her cheeks—probably red as crushed cherries—but she wouldn't break eye contact.

There hadn't been funds for both her and Adelinda to learn. Though Jemmah had begged to be permitted to watch her sister's instruction, Mama refused her even that. She'd taken to peeking through the drawing room window until her mother caught her one day.

Ever after, Jemmah had been confined to her room during dance lessons, rather like in the tale of Cendrillon, except in her situation, there was no evil stepmother.

No fairy godmother to rescue her or a prince to sweep her away, either.

Merely Jemmah's own haughty and proud mother, who hadn't a qualm about voicing her partiality for Adelinda. And why shouldn't she prefer the daughter who was practically a mirror image of herself, rather than the offspring resembling her detested, unfaithful spouse?

"I'll teach you." Dandridge stepped forward and lightly grasped her hand.

She'd forgotten to don her gloves, but he didn't appear to notice her work-worn fingers, and Jemmah refused to be self-conscious about them. Not now anyway. Later she might examine the dry, reddened skin, the roughened cuticles, the overly-short nails, and her face would flame with renewed chagrin.

"I really shouldn't. I'll tromp your toes."

But she would dance, for being in Jules's arms, even for a few stolen minutes was worth Mama's assured disapproval and Adelinda's certain jealousy, as well as the resulting unpleasantness should they find out. The experience, committed to memory, was even worth the risk of scandal.

Never mind all that.

Jemmah melted into his embrace and placed her hand upon his firm shoulder, the muscles rippling beneath her fingertips.

His smile, broad and delighted, exposed straight, white teeth and ignited every plane of his rugged face with joy. Rarely had she seen him smile from sincere happiness, and the transformation in his visage, temporarily robbed Jemmah of her breath.

She managed to restart her lungs and ask, "What will we dance to?"

"Listen." Jules tilted his tawny head, his hair the color of ripe wheat at sunset.

Lilting strains from the string quartet floated from the ballroom. The glorious music, enchanting and irresistible, almost fairy-tale like, nudged her few remaining, crumbling barriers aside.

"It's a waltz." Jules planted a broad palm on her spine—*Oh, crumb cakes, what utter deliciousness*—and cupped her hand in his other.

"Just follow my lead, Jem."

A waltz was most risqué and hardly acceptable in proper circles, which was probably why Aunt Theo permitted the dance. She, too, liked to push acceptability's limitations, one of the things Jemmah adored about her audacious aunt.

Jules proved an adroit partner, and in a few moments, Jemmah had caught on to the simple steps and the one-two-three rhythm.

Much too aware of the broad chest mere inches from her face, she rummaged around for something to say. "I had the privilege of meeting your charming niece, Lady Sabrina, in Green Park last month."

"Out for her daily constitutional with her governess, no doubt. Sabrina likes to sketch the landscape. She's asked to take lessons." His palm pressed into Jemmah's spine, sending her nerves jockeying. "I've been meaning to ask Theo if she could recommend someone."

"I'm fond of drawing myself. Papa taught me."

His thumb brushed the swell of her ribs, and a shiver—at least that was what she thought the melting, buttery feeling was—capered across her hips. Mentally schooling herself, she summoned her composure.

"I'm not gifted by any means, but I am fairly accomplished and would be happy to teach her what I know."

"I think she'd like that."

Jules edged Jemmah closer until his thighs brushed hers, and his hand upon her back induced the most tantalizing frisson down her spinal column—tiny tremors which sent delicious, warm sparks that slowly swirled outward, until her entire body came alive with the tingling sensation.

"I've missed our friendship—missed you—Jemmah. I didn't realize how very much until just now."

31

"I've missed you too."

And she had.

Unbearably.

Particularly since Papa died and she hadn't anyone to act as a buffer between Mama's harshness and Adelinda's cruelty.

Small wonder Jemmah hadn't become bitter or hadn't come to hate and resent her mother and sister. More than anything, their conduct saddened her.

How could they treat anyone, but most especially a family member, so spitefully?

Jules scent, crisp, slightly musky, perhaps even a suggestion of cloves, surrounded her.

She stood so near him, that even in the subdued candlelight, she could see the faintest shadow of his whiskers along his jaw, and when her gaze met his, slightly bewildered, simmering topaz eyes regarded her.

His regard sank to her mouth, and the peculiar stirrings of earlier burgeoned once more.

Only stronger, more insistent.

The faint music faded into the background as he dipped his head lower, then lower still, until his mouth—oh, his lovely, warm, soft, yet firm mouth—brushed hers.

In that instant, Jemmah was lost, utterly, irreversibly, and unreservedly.

She rose up on her toes, entwined her arms around Jules's sturdy neck, and kissed him with the abandon of a desperate woman seizing her one and only chance to kiss the man she'd loved for years.

He groaned deep in his throat, the sound primitive and animalistic, and all the more arousing because of its baseness. Using his tongue, he trailed the seam between her lips, teasing her mouth open, and the headiest of sensations spiraled through every fiber of her being.

Their tongues danced together, mating in an age-old cadence, while thousands of moonbeams ignited behind her eyes.

"Jemmah, my sweet, precious Jem," he murmured against her neck, his voice thick and husky, the sound sending delicious tremors to her toes. "Tell me I may call upon you, tomorrow."

"Dandridge!"

Insistent scratching on the locked door had Jemmah springing away from him.

"I know you're in there," a feminine voice all but hissed. "We must talk. This is no way to treat the next Duchess of Dandridge."

4

The next duchess?

But how could that be?

Jemmah touched her fingertips to her throbbing mouth and backed away from Jules.

She could still taste him on her tongue, feel his powerful arms encircling her, smell his manly scent yet in her nostrils. How glorious his kisses had been. And more fool she, for having allowed it, for now she craved more.

Intuition told her, she'd never, ever have enough of him.

"Dandridge. Answer me."

Scrape. Scrape.

"I saw that Dament chit batting her stubby eyelashes at you. The duchess and your uncles won't approve. I don't know how the Daments are even permitted in respectable circles. They smell of the shop."

The scorching glower Jules hurled at the voice behind the door would've ignited wet wood.

"Insufferable, long-winded baggage," he muttered, hardly above a whisper.

Sacred sausages, Mama would fly into a dudgeon if she ever learned Jules had kissed Jemmah. And she'd kissed him back. And it had been the most wonderful of things. And she'd do it again without compunction or remorse.

And by horse feathers, she *would* let him call on her.

She would.

Well, she'd suggest he meet her here for tea. She daren't risk no more.

But, if he was truly to marry Miss Milbourne...

No, something smelled to high heaven, even if she didn't know exactly what it was, like the time a creature of some sort had died in her attic bedchamber wall.

No man who'd shown such honor, even as a reserved child, grew into an unscrupulous lout. Jules was loyal to his impressive backbone.

She'd bet on it. *If* she had anything of worth to wager.

The least she could do was to hear his explanation, especially since Aunt Theo had happily shared—actually clapped her hands and tittered, and Aunt Theo did not titter—that he had refused the match with Miss Milbourne, despite the furor it caused within his family.

Truly, his availability was the only reason Mama agreed to come tonight, and had kept Jemmah up to the wee hours sewing—to thrust Adelinda beneath Jules's nose in hopes of garnering his attention.

And how could he not notice Adelinda's outward loveliness?

However, her beauty masked an entirely different woman inwardly, and Jemmah ought to know. More often than not, she was the recipient of her sister's calculated unkindness.

Nothing, nevertheless, would deter Mama from assuring Adelinda make a brilliant match before Season's end, and dear Jules had a giant target on his broad back they'd set their conniving sights on.

Jemmah ought to warn him, but surely a man of his station was aware the Marriage Mart considered him prime cattle. A somewhat degrading analogy, but accurate in its crudeness, nonetheless.

With his aristocratic profile yet angled toward the creature scratching at the door, Jemmah permitted herself a leisurely perusal. From his gleaming shoes to his neatly trimmed side whiskers, several shades darker than his hair, he emanated pure masculine beauty.

True, his nose might be slightly too prominent and his forehead and chin a trifle too bold to be considered classically handsome, but his was a strong face—an honorable, trustworthy countenance.

All the more reason she couldn't allow Mama or Adelinda to sink their talons into him.

Jemmah just couldn't.

He deserved someone as kind and thoughtful as he.

Not a selfish, vain girl who cared nothing for him, and who would— Jemmah didn't harbor the slightest doubt—make him wretchedly miserable.

As unpleasant a miss as she was, Miss Milbourne was preferable to Adelinda.

Jemmah's stomach flopped sickeningly, and she swallowed. What a nauseating notion, rather like eating moldy, maggoty pudding.

Adelinda and Miss Milbourne didn't merit him, and somehow,

instinct perhaps, or because Jemmah had loved Jules so long—couldn't remember when she hadn't, truth to tell—she simply knew, neither woman would make him happy.

His Annabel Bright might have, for she seemed gentle and kind the one time Jemmah met her.

That awful, unforgettable day her heart had splintered into pieces like stomped upon eggshells when Jemmah learned Jules was to marry the doll-like in her perfection, dainty, and altogether exquisite young lady.

And when Annabel had died, Jemmah had wept, great gasping sobs into her pillow at night—cried for Jules's devastation and heartache.

She couldn't fathom weeping like that if Miss Milbourne, or even Adelinda had been the one to die, and Jemmah winced inwardly at her uncharacteristic spite.

Thank goodness, to her knowledge, Aunt Theo's invitation to tea didn't include Miss Milbourne, and because Mama barely tolerated her sister-in-law, more often than not, she turned down the invitations as well.

Adelinda seldom rose before noon and had no more interest in taking tea with their aunt than cleaning grates or chamber pots.

Neither of which she'd ever done, unlike Jemmah.

She couldn't help but observe that her aunt's feelings toward Mama seemed quite mutual. In fact, Jemmah had suspected for years, but most especially since Papa's death, that her Aunt Theo's cordial mien and continued hospitable offers were for Jemmah's benefit.

That, and also so Mama wouldn't put an end to Jemmah's visits.

Which was as unlikely as Mama suddenly favoring Jemmah.

She also knew full well that Aunt Theo paid Mama a monthly

allowance intended to assist with the girls' needs.

Jemmah never saw any of it, not a shilling.

In fact, when she'd asked for new stockings for tonight, she'd received a resounding slap for her impertinence. The nubby, mended stockings rubbing against her toes, as well her tender cheek were other reasons she'd sought sanctuary in Aunt Theo's parlor.

For certain, Jemmah's toes would sport blisters by morning.

Some weeks, tea with Aunt Theo's and hearing her aunt's encouragements were all that kept Jemmah from wallowing in self-pity or having a fit of the blue devils.

Treated scarcely better at home than the Daments' maid-of-all work, Mary Pimble, Jemmah treasured the time at Aunt Theo's. They were the only hours free from insults or demands that she perform some chore or task for Mama or Adelinda.

"Dandridge." The voice rose to an irritated screech on the last syllable.

Tap, tap, tappety-tap.

"Open this door!"

TAP

"I must insist."

Miss Milbourne might be admired for her persistence.

If it didn't border on unhinged.

Jemmah dipped her head in the entrance's direction, and her voice, a mere vestige of sound, asked, "*Have* you an arrangement with her?"

No need to ask who *her* was, since Miss Milbourne continued to hiss and scratch like a feral cat sealed in a whisky barrel.

"I most emphatically do not. Miss Milbourne has convinced herself that I shall concede to my mother's and uncles' preference, but she's gravely mistaken." Jules grasped Jemmah's hand, gently yet firmly enough she couldn't pull away without some effort. With the forefinger of his other hand, he traced her jaw. "I mean what I said, dear one. Please allow me to call upon you tomorrow. I've missed you more than I can say."

"Your Grace—"

"Might you address me as Jules, or Dandridge if you prefer, when we are alone? Please?"

He quirked his mouth boyishly, and she couldn't resist an answering bend of her lips.

It had always been so. She was clay, soft and malleable, in his hands.

"Precious, Jemmah, perhaps you'd prefer a ride in Hyde Park tomorrow?"

Heaven and hiccups, no.

It would never do for Jules to pay his address to her at home, and a ride would likely be reported as well. Mama wasn't above locking Jemmah in her chamber to assure Adelinda received his undivided attention.

Good thing he wasn't as besotted as most men by her sister's exquisiteness.

When Adelinda did finally marry—for certain her beauty would snare some unfortunate fellow—how long would it be before her sulks and vile tongue obscured her bewitching beauty and the poor sot regretted his choice?

Still, Jemmah could no more deny Jules's tempting request than she could ignore the impossibility of his calling on her.

The scraping and frenetic whispering at the door had finally ceased, but her alarm increased.

She mustn't be found, here alone with him.

No telling what Mama would do.

Jemmah speared an anxious glance to the other doors.

"It's impossible. Mama won't allow you to call upon me. She had hoped Adelinda would attract your notice, and she'll be furious if you show any interest in me."

"Yes, so I became acutely aware, earlier this evening. However, Adelinda isn't the Dament sister who fascinates me. I've always preferred the one with gold and amber streaks glinting in her hair and eyes so pale blue, I lose myself in their color each time I look into them." He grazed his thumb across her lower lip. "And she has the most tempting mouth, soft, honey sweet, with lips I cannot wait to sample again."

He swept his mouth across hers.

Tender, fleeting, a silent promise.

Joy, and perhaps the minutest amount of triumph that he preferred her—plain and unremarkable Jemmah—over Adelinda's exquisiteness, sang through her veins. A jaunty celebratory tune. And for the first time in the veriest of times, a spark of hope ignited deep in her spirit.

For once, she believed Papa's assurances that she was lovely in her own way, and that someday she'd find the man who gazed at her through love-filled eyes and found her beautiful.

"Do you know what the Dandridge motto is, Jemmah?"

She shook her head. "No."

"In adversity, the faith." Jules's touched his lips to hers again. "I shall find a way, if you want me to."

Her stomach flopped over again, and the air left her lungs on a fluttering breath.

Thundering hogs' hoof beats when he looked at her like that—like she was the most precious of jewels, his gaze reverent, yet also slightly hooded—although logic screeched "No," her desperate heart whispered, "Yes."

Yes. Yes. Yes.

If this was her chance for happiness, no matter how brief or implausible, she damn well—*yes, damn well!*—had every intention of grasping it.

"My aunt invited me for tea tomorrow."

Comprehension dawned on Jules's face, and she entertained another, small victorious smile.

"Ah, I do believe Theo mentioned something of that nature to me as well. I find I am quite available at that hour."

He lifted Jemmah's hand, and rather than brush his lips across her bare knuckles, he turned it over and grazed her wrist.

A jolt shot to her shoulder while her knees, ridiculous, worthless things, decided to turn to mush.

"I shall look forward to it. Now if you'll excuse me," he blew out all but one taper, "I promised Sabrina I'd be home to tuck her in tonight. It's her birthday too. The second since her parents died, but at the first one, we didn't know if she'd recover from the carriage accident. I don't want her to fall asleep without bidding her good-night."

Such a flood of emotion bubbled up in Jemmah's chest that tears blurred her vision as she pulled her gloves on, trying to ignore the frayed spots on the fingertips.

"She's lucky to have such a devoted uncle. Would you wish her happy day for me too?

"I would indeed, and if I may be so bold, might I tell her you'll give her drawing lessons?" He turned her toward the other set of doors. "Naturally, I'll approach your mother and explain I'd like to retain you."

Mama would take any earnings, thinking they were her due, and she'd still expect Jemmah to do all of her regular chores.

"Honestly, Dandridge, I think it would be better if I were to give Sabrina lessons when I come to tea. And please allow it to be my gift to her. I have a standing invitation with Aunt Theo on Mondays and Thursdays. I could use one day for lessons so Mama's suspicions won't be aroused."

His head slightly angled, he considered her. "Very well."

"Aunt Theo usually only sends the carriage 'round for me when the weather is foul, but I'll explain our plan tonight and ask her to send it every tea day. That way, I'll have more time to instruct Lady Sabrina."

"We can discuss those details tomorrow. Until then, my precious Jem." He cupped her shoulders with both hands, and leaning down, kissed her forehead with such reverence, she almost could believe he cared for her as much as she did for him. "Go along. I'll wait a respectable amount of time, and then take another route to the manor's entrance."

She nodded. "All right."

"And Jemmah?"

"Yes?"

A strand of hair had fallen across his brow, and with the warmth radiating from his brandy-colored eyes, he very much resembled the young man she'd fallen in love with.

"Your mother can fuss all she wants, but once I set my mind to something, I am seldom dissuaded. I mean to court you."

5

Incapable of speech, her heart teeming with happiness, Jemmah nodded again and quit the parlor. She could yet taste and feel Jules's mouth on hers, and an odd heat throbbed at her wrist as if branded by his lips.

Glancing down, she half expected to see his mouth's imprint there.

A few moments later, having brought her exuberant smile under control, she edged into the ballroom, as unnoticed as a fly upon the corniced ceiling. No one paid her any mind as she wove between guests, headed toward the empty seat beside the Dowager Lady Lockhart.

Jemmah's silly legs still hadn't returned to their normal strength after Jules's bone-melting kisses, and feeling slightly off-balance, she gratefully claimed the seat.

Her ladyship bestowed a beaming smile on her. "Where've you been, child? I saw you arrive and hoped to have a coze with you. It's been some time since we chatted, and you always brighten this old woman's day with your wit and intelligence."

"How kind of you to say so, my lady. I enjoy your company as well. Aunt tells me you have a cat now."

From the corner of her eye, Jemmah caught site of Miss Milbourne prowling the dance floor's perimeter, a half-pout upon her lips while her miffed gaze roved the ballroom. They narrowed for an instant upon sighting Adelinda dancing with the exceedingly tall, raven-haired Duke of Sutcliffe.

Miss Milbourne wouldn't find what she sought.

He'd already left.

"I do indeed," Lady Lockhart agreed. "A darling little calico I named Callie. I thought the name quite clever."

Miss Milbourne's attention swept over Jemmah without pause, the way one dismissed a potted plant or a piece of furniture.

After all, who'd suspect the nondescript Miss Jemmah Dament had just spent the most wonderful twenty minutes in the embrace of the distinguished and oh, so alluring Duke of Dandridge—the very man the Milbourne beauty wanted for herself?

Unaccustomed confidence squared Jemmah's shoulders and notched her chin higher. She'd never felt more attractive or worthy than she did at this moment, and she had Jules to thank for the new self-assurance.

The dowager gently tapped Jemmah's forearm with her fan. "You're pale as a lily, but your cheeks are berry bright. Are you feeling quite the thing?"

"Yes, my lady. I'm quite well." Very well, indeed. Better than she had been in a great while. "I confess to falling asleep in the parlor, which may contribute to my flushed appearance."

Not nearly as much a duke's ravishing kisses had.

"Your mother has paraded past here thrice searching for you. A ripped hem or some such twaddle. Doesn't she know how to mend a simple tear? Don't know why she or your sister can't see to the task."

Disapproval pinched the dowager's mouth for an instant.

Jemmah was used to urgent summons at all hours of the day and night for whatever trifling needs Mama or Adelinda might have.

Two months ago, she'd walked four miles in the pouring rain to purchase barbel blue embroidery thread for Mama—not azure or cerulean, her mother had insisted, but barbel.

"This is mazurine blue, Jemmah," Mama had scolded when Jemmah returned home sopping wet and shivering. "Fortunate for you, I decided lavender better suited, else you'd turn yourself around and fetch me the color I need."

Never mind the prodigious cold Jemmah contracted as a result of her soggy trek, which left her sneezing and with a reddened nose and eyes for a full week.

On another occasion, she'd been awoken in the wee morning hours when her sister couldn't sleep and deemed a cup of hot chocolate the perfect insomnia cure.

Jemmah had dutifully gone through the time-consuming task of making the beverage only to find Adelinda slumbering soundly when she brought her the required pot and cup.

Snuggled on her window seat, a tattered quilt about her shoulders while she gazed at the stars flickering between moonlit clouds over the rooftops, Jemmah had drunk every last drop herself.

A rare treat indeed.

Oh, and she couldn't possibly forget last month when the family had been invited to the Silverton's soirée.

Jemmah couldn't attend, of course.

After all, since Papa died, they'd been required to economize and naturally there were only funds for one remade gown.

For the eldest daughter.

Always the confounded eldest daughter.

That was the excuse for most everything Jemmah was deprived of.

Nonetheless, she'd dutifully dressed and coiffed Adelinda, even allowing her—Mama's orders to stop being such a selfish sister—to borrow Jemmah's best gloves and the delicate pearl earrings Papa had given her for her sixteenth birthday.

Adelinda had misplaced the gloves and lost an earring.

As Jemmah fought bitter tears, Adelinda had pouted. "You know better than to lend me your things. I always lose them, Germ."

Germ, the hated knick-name Adelinda insisted upon calling Jemmah.

Mama thought it quaint and amusing, a show of sisterly affection.

Balderdash and codswallop. Crafty and mean-spirited better described the moniker.

However, the one time Jemmah dared call Adelinda "Adder"—a fitting moniker since Adelinda meant noble snake, Mama had berated Jemmah for a full thirty minutes before sending her to bed without supper.

Small comfort knowing Jemmah meant precious gem while her sister's name meant a cold, slithery, vile creature.

Mama's given name, Belinda, meant beautiful snake, which was probably why she became so peeved at Jemmah calling Adelinda Adder.

A raspy chuckle filled the air.

"You actually fell asleep, my dear? While all these other young women are trying to snare a husband, you're napping in Theo's parlor. By all the crumpets in Canterbury, I admire you. Indeed, I do."

"No need for admiration, I assure you. I simply didn't find my bed until almost five this morning." Jemmah licked her lower lip and searched for a footman. "Truth to tell I am quite thirsty."

The dowager tutted kindly. "Five, you say? *Hmph.*"

She made a brusque sound of disapproval.

"I'll wager staying up all night wasn't of your own choosing." She opened her mouth then snapped it shut. "I could use a glass of punch myself, my dear. Would you oblige an old woman and fetch me a cup?"

"*Punch?*"

Jemmah tried to hide her shock. Ladies didn't drink the spirit-heavy libation. "Are you sure you wouldn't prefer a ratafia?"

"Too syrupy." Eyes flashing with mischief, the dowager shook her head, and the ostrich feathers tucked into her stylish coif bobbed in agreement.

"Lemonade? Or perhaps an iced champagne?" Jemmah offered hopefully. Rather frantically, truth be told.

"I think not. Too insipid. Like men, I prefer something with a bit— actually, a great deal—more vigor and potency."

Not quite believing her ears, and trying to subdue the heat crawling up her cheeks, Jemmah tried one last time.

"Tea? Wine?"

Lord, she couldn't just stride up to the table and snatch a glass of punch. Tongues would flap faster than flags in a hurricane.

Cocking her head, humor sparring with patience in her gaze, the dowager chuckled. "My dear Miss Dament, do you truly believe none of the ladies present tonight ever imbibes in alcohol?"

Not publically.

"Look there, beside Lord Beetle Brows." With her cane, the Dowager Lady Lockhart gestured at a proud dame.

Lord Dunston does have rather grizzled eyebrows.

"See Lady Clutterbuck?"

How could I miss her in that primrose gown?

"She trundles her thick backside off regularly and takes a nip from the flask she has hidden in her reticule."

Jemmah bit the inside of her cheek to keep from giggling.

"Over there," the dowager swung her cane toward a regal dame, epitomizing *haut ton* elegance. "Lady Dreary—

"I believe that's Lady Drury—"

"*Hmph.* She's as dreary and cold as frozen fog on a grave. But that was beside the point. Her ladyship is most clever—keeps whisky stashed in her vinaigrette instead of ammonia or smelling salts."

How, for all the salt in the sea could Jemmah have forgotten the ... erm ... *unique* labels the clever dowager attributed to others? Sometimes she explained a name's genuine meaning, but others, as she'd just demonstrated, a droll play on words.

A speculative glint entered her ladyship's watered-down-topaz-colored eyes. "Even Lady Wimpleton, whom I admire very much indeed, is wont to take a nip on occasion."

Jemmah laughed and threw her hands up in defeat. "You win, my lady. I shall return shortly. Pray my mother doesn't espy me."

Though how she would manage the task without Mama hearing of it or some other nosy dame deciding it was her duty to chastise Jemmah, she hadn't yet conceived.

"I can deal with Belinda well enough, my dear. You're kind to humor an old woman's idiosyncrasies."

As Jemmah neared the table, a footman loading a tray with filled punch glasses smiled a polite greeting. "Good evening, Miss Jemmah. Mary said you were attending your aunt's ball."

"Frazer Pimble, isn't it?"

Here was Jemmah's answer to her dilemma. Most providential to come upon her maid's brother.

"Aye." He nodded once, a kindly smile emphasizing the swath of freckles across his nose and cheeks.

"May I impose upon you?" When he nodded, Jemmah angled toward the ballroom's west side. "See that lovely lady in the gold and black, with the spray of black ostrich feathers in her hair. The one holding a cane and peering in our direction?"

"I do, miss."

"She desires a glass of punch, and I don't dare take it to her." Jemmah bent a tiny bit nearer and murmured, "Can you imagine the gossip? Would you be so kind as to put a serving in a teacup for her?"

Frazer gave a quick glance around. "Leave it to me, miss. Do you need a beverage as well? If I may be so bold, you look a bit flushed."

"I would love lemonade, if it wouldn't be too much trouble."

He nodded and gave a small wink. "Return to your seat, and I shall be along straightaway."

Jemmah resumed her seat and had just turned to explain the plan to the dowager when, true to his word, Frazer approached, carrying a tray with a glass of lemonade in addition to a teacup and saucer.

He presented the china cup to the elderly dame, and Lady Lockhart's eyebrows crept up the creases of her forehead to hang there suspended.

"Tea?" fussed the dowager, giving Jemmah the gimlet eye. "I most definitely declined tea."

"Oh, but this is a *very special* brew, my lady. I'm sure you'll quite like it." Frazer inclined his head, and the dowager's eyes rounded.

She took a dainty sip, then smiled in pure delight. "Indeed. An exceptionally fine brew. Thank you."

Frazer left them, and her ladyship turned an approving eye on Jemmah.

"That was well done of you, Miss Dament. Clever too." Her watery gaze bored into Jemmah for a long moment before she nodded slowly, as if coming to a conclusion. "I've been of a mind to sponsor a worthy young woman this Season, someone to act as my companion too. I would be honored if you'd consider the proposition."

Jemmah choked on her lemonade.

Eyes watering and swallowing against the burning at the back of her throat, she gaped.

Smack her with a cod.

A way out?

A way to escape Mama and Adelinda?

She wiggled her toes and gave a tiny glee-filled bounce upon her seat.

Aunt Theo had tried for years to persuade Mama to let Jemmah live with her, but truth be told, Mama was reluctant to lose Jemmah as a servant.

But turn down the dowager's sponsorship?

That Mama wouldn't do.

The only thing she valued more than Adelinda was money, something the Daments were perpetually short of.

Jemmah laid her hand atop the dowager's. "I would consider it the greatest honor to be your companion, your ladyship, and there's no need to sponsor me. I'm not meant for routs and balls and such."

"Oh, posh. What rot. Of course you are, my dear," Lady Lockhart assured Jemmah. "But if it makes you more comfortable, you may begin as my companion straightaway. We'll take the Season sponsorship a jot slower."

"Companion...?" Mama sidled up to them, a ribbon-thin, forced smile tweaking her mouth's corners. "If anyone is granted a sponsorship and the privilege of being her ladyship's companion, it must, quite naturally, be Adelinda. I'm sure you understand, my lady. She's the elder daughter, after all."

All hail the elder daughter.

Bah!

"Are you entirely daft, Mama?" Adelinda hissed near Mama's ear, her usual artificial smile making her seem the mild-tempered innocent to the casual onlooker. The fury in her coffee-colored eyes told an entirely different tale.

Lady Lockhart slid Jemmah an I-knew-she'd-pitch-a-tantrum look.

Adelinda grumbled on, a pout upon her rouged mouth.

"You expect *me* to wait upon another? An *old* woman? At her beck and call?" She huffed her outrage, flinging a hand toward the dowager while thrusting her dainty chin upward in haughty arrogance. "*I* am not companion material. Most especially not to a deaf, demented, aged crone."

Her chin descended an inch as if granting a royal favor. "Jemmah may act as the companion, and as the eldest, I shall accept the sponsorship."

La de dah.

The last she uttered with the austerity and entitled expectation of a crown princess.

Jemmah lifted her cup whilst eyeing the dowager.

Lady Lockhart planted both gnarled hands upon her cane's floral handle and cut Adelinda a glare of such scathing incredulity, only the dame's irises remained visible.

This ought to be very entertaining.

Her ladyship was precisely the person to knock Adelinda and her pretentious superiority off her self-appointed pedestal and onto her well-rounded arse.

"An old crone, most certainly, but not at all deaf, Miss Dament."

Jemmah bit the inside of her cheek.

Most diverting, indeed.

The dowager's gaze raked over Adelinda who didn't have the refinement to look abashed, but rather contentious.

"I'd have to be demented to consider *you* for the position. But since it's already been filled by your utterly charming sister, we needn't worry on that account, need we?" She graced Jemmah with a wide—yes, distinctly smug—closed-mouth smile. "Oh, and the two go hand in hand—the sponsorship and the position, lest there be any confusion."

Adelinda's smile slipped a fraction and displeasure pursed her mouth. However, accomplished in artifice, she quickly masked her true feelings and pressed her point.

"My lady, surely you cannot mean to waste expense and time on my plain, wholly unexceptional sister, when both would be so much better spent on the more attractive of the pair of us. The little toad is hardly worth the effort, and I fear you'll find the outcome most unsatisfactory."

Adelinda tilted her head and summoned her syrupiest, most beguiling fake-as-a-purple-wig-on-donkey expression. The calculated one that inevitably ensured she acquired whatever the pampered darling coveted at the moment.

"Thank you for your kind words, *sister.*" Jemmah couldn't attribute the acidic taste on her tongue to the lemonade she'd just choked on.

How could Adelinda be such a cruel, insensitive bacon-brain?

Adelinda laughed, the often practiced before her looking glass tinkle ringing hollow and shrill rather than light and musical. Snapping her fan open, she fiddled with the spines, expectation still arcing her winged brows.

Dense as black bread.

"*Hmph.*"

A sound very much like a stifled snort or oath escaped Lady Lockhart. She fumbled in her reticule for a moment then glanced up in triumph as she withdrew a pair of wire-rimmed spectacles. "Aha, here they are."

She extended them to Adelinda.

"I believe you are in more need of these than I am, if you think your sister is inferior to you in any way, but most especially in comeliness."

In a soundless challenge, the dowager's eyebrows crept upward as well.

They glared at each other, brows elevated and eyes shooting daggers in a silent battle.

At the imagery of Lady Lockhart's and Adelinda's eyebrows jousting, Jemmah muffled a giggle.

"I simply cannot believe this treachery." Adelinda averted her gaze first, and in her typical harrying fashion, turned an accusatory scowl on Jemmah. "How long have you been scheming behind my back, Germ? Worming your way into her ladyship's good graces so you could steal this opportunity from me?"

"You know as well as I, Adelinda, that I rarely am permitted to attend these functions, and I haven't had the pleasure of Lady Lockhart's company in months. And—"

"One year, two months, and ... ah ..." Lady Lockhart scrunched her eyes as she examined the ceiling, her mouth working silently. "...twelve days. Valentine's Day last year, it was."

She veered her knowing gaze at Jemmah. "You spent most of the afternoon hiding in the library."

How on earth had she remembered that?

Mama seemed to rouse herself from her gawking stupor and touched Adelinda's forearm. "We'll discuss this later, darling."

After taking a long pull from her teacup, God knew she needed it after a confrontation with Adelinda and Mama, the dowager bestowed a satisfied smile on Jemmah. "After tea tomorrow, we'll need to see to acquiring you a wardrobe suitable for a young woman of your new station."

"But... but..." Jealousy contorting her face, and seemingly oblivious to the small crowd that had gathered, hanging onto each recklessly-spoken word, Adelinda planted her hands on her hips and confronted their mother.

"Mama, tell Germ she can't. You won't allow it."

Jemmah straightened.

No. No. No.

They would not steal this opportunity from her.

Mama opened her mouth, but before she could affirm Adelinda, Aunt Theo's voice cut the air, firm and unrelenting.

"Oh, she'll allow it, all right."

They swung their attention to Aunt Theo, her approach having gone unnoticed due to Adelinda's unbecoming show of temper and the semi-circle of intrigued spectators blocking their view.

Smiling at her guests, Aunt Theo angled her head before suggesting, "I'm sure you'll allow me a moment for a private family conversation."

As Aunt Theo cordially looped her arms in Mama's and Adelinda's elbows, the onlookers scattered like roaches in sunlight. Drawing her mother and sister nearer, Aunt Theo dipped her head, her face granite hard.

"You've overstepped the bounds, Theodora. I shall determine which of my daughters is most suited for the position." Mama slid Adelinda a smug, sideway glance.

"As I said, Belinda, you will allow Jemmah this honor. Because if you refuse," Aunt Theo directed her wrath squarely at Adelinda, "this selfish, spoiled bratling will feel the full effects of my displeasure, and I assure you, after I'm done, a haberdasher won't consider Adelinda for his wife."

6

Sighing, feeling more content than he had in—well, in months, perhaps years—Jules untied his cravat, and after tossing it atop the French baroque table behind the sofa, sank onto the charcoal damask-covered cushions.

He'd bid a sleepy-eyed Sabrina goodnight, then retreated to his study to contemplate the evening's remarkable events.

One specific incident, that was.

Stumbling upon Miss Jemmah Dament, and in an instant his life had changed.

He touched two fingertips to his lips, not surprised to find a cock-eyed smile bending his mouth. In the last two hours, he'd smiled more than in the past two years, and his providential encounter with Jemmah had set him on a new course.

By all the chirping crickets playing a grand symphony beyond the study's French window, a path he eagerly anticipated.

He'd found his diamond in the rough.

Perhaps not so rough, except for her humble attire.

Jemmah would polish up brilliantly, and then those who'd ignored her, overlooked her loveliness, would grind their teeth in vexation.

She'd blossomed into a remarkable and sensuous young woman. Tall, lithe, and boasting delightful, rounded womanly curves, two of which had taunted him unmercifully above her bodice, her features and form had embedded themselves in his memory.

A self-depreciatory, yet joy-filled chuckle, burgeoned in his chest then rumbled forth, filling the silent, fire-lit room.

Mere hours ago, he'd avowed himself indifferent to marriage, and now, he calculated just how soon he might take the charming, witty, a trifle shy and awkward, but wholly delectable and precious Jemmah Dament to wife.

If someone asked him how he could be so absolutely positive he should do so, he couldn't have answered them with logic and reason, for neither had anything whatsoever to do with the giddiness—yes, by all the cigars at Whites's, *giddiness*—humming through him.

He just knew.

Simple as that.

Not a damned lucid thing about it.

Like wild creatures recognize their offspring, a river discerns what course its waters must flow, wildfowls' instincts urge them to fly south for the winter, or even the sun understanding that it must rise every morning and then slowly descend each eve—

He knew.

Drowsy, content, and resolute, Jules shut his eyes and daydreamed about when he'd see his precious, sky-eyed Jemmah again.

Was tomorrow too soon to propose?

"Miss Jemmah. You needs wake up. Now. The mistress wants you to run an errand."

At the frantic whisper and Mary Pimble's small hand insistently shaking her shoulder, Jemmah cracked an eye open. A bit of drool leaking from her mouth's corner and her head resting on her forearms, she surveyed the assortment of papers, pens, and drawings scattered mere inches before her line of vision.

She must've fallen asleep over her sketches while trying to decide which to take with her to show Jules at tea today.

After wiping her mouth, she yawned and blinked sleepily.

By all the brandy in Britain, no one could fault her for her for dozing off.

After all, the clock had struck two before she'd managed to undress Mama and Adelinda, see their sheets warmed, and their chamber fires stoked, the whole while subjected to their rancorous litanies of why Adelinda ought to have reaped the dowager's favor, not Jemmah.

Their mutual fury over Aunt Theo's blunt threat to cease all monetary support had nearly sent Mama into apoplexy, and for the first time ever, Adelinda's face had mottled bright red as she sobbed and ranted into her abused pillow.

Jemmah arched her stiff back and stretched her arms overhead, almost touching the slanting ceiling's rough boards with her fingertips.

"A missive arrived for you, too. I hid it in my pocket." Her eyes wide and curious, Pimble whispered, "It's from a *duke*."

A thrill fluttered Jemmah's tummy.

Pimble fished the hunter green-beribboned rectangle from her apron and pitched a worried gaze toward the door as Jemmah stood and stretched again while glancing to the busy street.

Bless Pimble.

It wouldn't be the first time Mama or Adelinda intercepted a missive meant for Jemmah.

"Thank you, Pimble."

Jemmah accepted the note, stamped with Dandridge's seal.

Mama definitely would've confiscated the letter. She had Dandridge earmarked for Adelinda.

Jemmah flipped it over to examine the bold, slashing strokes across the face.

Too bad the duke had other plans.

The smile quirking Jemmah's mouth as she traced his writing with her fingertip might've been a teeny bit jubilant.

Or a lot.

For someone who seldom prevailed, this triumph was far more profound. Something to be cherished and kept private, away from prying eyes. Formerly servants' quarters, perched three stories above the street, her tiny bedchamber allowed her that luxury.

Mama and Adelinda loathed climbing the stairs, especially the last narrow, steep risers, and the room was generally either arctic frigid or blistering hot. But the chamber had served as Jemmah's private haven for over a decade, and she was content here even if it lacked creature comforts.

She cracked the seal and using the window for light, perused the unfamiliar writing.

My Dearest Miss Dament,

I eagerly look forward to renewing our friendship and would consider it the greatest privilege if you would permit me to escort you to the theater tonight.

Theo is attending as well, so we'll be well chaperoned.

I anticipate the hours until I next see you today,

Dandridge

Pleasure, secretive and acute, bent Jemmah's mouth again as she refolded the letter.

Amazing, how in less than twenty-four hours, her prospects had changed so dramatically. Attending the theater was out of the question, of course. She quite literally hadn't a single gown appropriate for such a lavish affair; not that she was complaining.

Last night, she'd had scant to look forward to, and today...

Well, for one thing, Jules would be at tea and perhaps Lady Sabrina also. So, too, would her soon-to-be employer, the Dowager Lady Lockhart.

God love that dear, feisty woman.

Last night, unperturbed and fully aware of her position and power, she'd regally looked directly at Mama.

"You best teach that one to retract her claws." The dowager bounced her gray head toward Adelinda, the ostrich feathers atop the dowager's head pummeling one another with the motion. "Envy turns even the comeliest of young ladies into ugly, spiteful creatures no one wants about. Not at all becoming, I assure you. And if you both wish to continue to be welcome in Society, as Theo has implied, you'll behave as is expected of someone awarded the privilege."

Jemmah had barely refrained from clapping.

She would've permitted a triumphant smile, except, blast her worn-out slippers, she'd felt pity for Mama and Adelinda. More so that neither had showed the least chagrin or remorse, and the censure leveled at them from those eavesdropping on their conversation had Jemmah's face flaming in embarrassment for her family.

It had always been so.

She might think uncharitable thoughts and on occasion grumble beneath her breath, and for good reason too. But in the end, a deep-rooted hope that Mama and Adelinda would change —or perhaps it was naught more than fanciful wishing—stirred the remnants of her compassion.

A moment later, Aunt Theo's carriage trundled to a stop before their humble cottage, earning curious stares from passersby. Only this time, Jemmah's anticipation of leaving for a few hours meant even more than it usually did.

Today might be the last she'd return to this house as a resident.

Hereafter, she'd only be a visitor; if Mama deemed to invite her, that was.

Jemmah had best not hold her breath waiting for that invitation any time soon.

Unlike Jemmah, Mama did not possess a forgiving nature.

"Good news, miss?"

Pimble puttered about, not doing much of anything, but every moment the maid spent here was far more pleasant than returning below.

"Of a sorts, yes."

Better not to divulge too much to Pimble, yet. Jemmah slipped the letter into her reticule, afraid to leave it in her room.

"Mama's up earlier than I expected."

The servant offered a lopsided, apologetic smile. "And if I may be so bold, in as a foul a mood this morning as I've ever seen her."

A wonder Mama had roused herself before noon; a guarantee she'd be crotchety the rest of the day. Far worse for poor Pimble when Mama or Adelinda felt peevish. Both were as prickly and hard to handle as an infuriated hedgehog.

"Jemmah, are you going to dawdle the day away?"

Breathing heavily, her skirts swishing about her ankles, Mama trudged into Jemmah's chamber. Her pretty, plump, slightly rosy face puckered in displeasure when her gaze lit on the many sketches pinned to the rafters, depicting drawings from new fashions to birds perched upon flowering tree branches.

"I sent Pimble to fetch you a full half hour ago. Whatever is keeping you both?"

Jemmah brushed the wrinkles from her simple Pomona green day gown, or at least tried to, before going to stand before the small, slightly blurry, rectangular looking glass hanging from a support beam.

She smoothed her hair and repinned a few loose strands as she watched her mother in the reflection.

Pimble ducked from the chamber, making good her escape.

Smart girl.

If only Jemmah might do the same.

"It's only been ten minutes, Mama, and I'm afraid the errand will have to wait until after I call upon Aunt Theo and the dowager takes me shopping this afternoon." She flicked her fingers toward the arched, four-paned window, the lower right divided by a long crack. "The carriage already awaits outside."

Scrutinizing her reflection, she frowned.

Dark circles ringed her eyes, and the dress, a brilliant shade on Adelinda, made Jemmah's skin appear sallow. She did quite look forward to acquiring a gown or two in hues which flattered her coloring, rather than wearing more castoffs from Adelinda, as Jemmah had for as long as she could recall.

Did that make her shallow, or simply a typical woman who enjoyed looking her best?

Especially now that she had a reason to care about her appearance?

Drat, if only she had a fichu to drape about her neck to diminish the gown's ill effects on her appearance. Perhaps she could leave her redingote on?

"Tell me what it is that you need, Mama, and I shall be happy to take care of it before I return home. Or perhaps, if the matter is terribly urgent, Pimble or Adelinda might attend to it for you."

Not the least mollified, her mother angled away from the table where she'd been poking about, occasionally scowling or grimacing at something she saw.

"Don't get impertinent with me, young lady. You know full well Pimble has more than enough to do, and whilst you reside here, you're expected to do your share."

As Adelinda does?

"You're not Lady Lockhart's pampered pet just yet," Mama snapped, as she tossed the drawings she'd been examining onto the scarred, uneven table top.

By King Solomon's treasure, if Adelinda's wasn't still fast asleep— *snoring*—Jemmah would skip her breakfast. Her gaze fell to the unappetizing glob plopped in the wooden bowl atop her desk.

Oh, that was right. She'd eschewed her plain porridge breakfast earlier.

Mama cut Jemmah a disdainful look and crossed her arms. "You know full well, as the eldest, it ought to have been your sister receiving Lady Lockhart's benevolence."

Ah, here came the true reason Mama dared the strenuous climb.

"A dutiful daughter and affectionate sister would've insisted upon it. I cannot quite conceive your selfishness, Jemmah. I truly cannot. Excepting," she notched her chin higher and gave a contemptuous sniff, "you are your father's daughter."

A jab to Jemmah's ribs with a short sword would've hurt less.

She pivoted, incredulity and injustice spiking her temper to a heretofore new height.

From their hook on the post's other side she snatched her unadorned straw hat and seven-year-old faded blue redingote, more appropriate for an adolescent than a woman grown.

"I've never been deliberately selfish, nor treated you or Adelinda with a margin of the unkindness you've both regularly bestowed upon me." She blinked away the stinging tears blurring her vision and fastened the garment's frogs at her throat. "I have an opportunity to leave this household. And by truffle-hunting pigs, I'm seizing it!"

"Just like that." Mama snapped her fingers, anger crackling in her slit-eyed gaze and strident voice. "You'd desert your family with no care of how we'll manage?"

"If you'd shown me even a jot of kindness or consideration. Ever asked what I desired. Ever set aside your self-centeredness, and your..." Jemmah inhaled a raggedy, tear-logged breath, "...*hatred* of me, I might've urged her ladyship to consider Adelinda too."

Eagerness, or perhaps desperation, gave the planes of Mama's face a softer, more vulnerable mien.

Almost like the mother of long ago, before she'd found everything about Jemmah objectionable and ridicule worthy.

Mama wrung her hands and licked her lips. "Think of your sister. And me. We're not as accustomed to hardship and want as you are."

Holy hypocrisy. Did Mama hear herself?

Jemmah jerked her head up and clamped her jaw against the hot retorts tickling her tongue. Hell's teeth, even now Mama attempted to use guilt to sway her. Not out of concern or thoughtfulness.

Oh, no.

Always—*always, dammit!*—to benefit her and Adelinda.

Not this time.

She must have seen the denial in Jemmah's rigid form and compressed lips, because Mama rushed across the room, and clutching at Jemmah's arm stuttered, "I'll ... I'll permit you to attend more functions. And ... and even order material so you can stitch yourself a couple of new gowns. If funds permit, of course. However, surely you must know, I can't possible manage the house without your help."

She procured what was no doubt meant to be a heartening smile. But the calculated glint in her eye and the rigidity of her barely-upturned lips revealed her true sentiment.

Jemmah was far past politesse.

Years of injustice and ill-treatment had taken their toll, and she feared—dreaded—becoming rancorous like her mother. So full of hatred and resentment, her presence was toxic to everyone who encountered her.

"Tell me, Mama. Will Adelinda attend fewer functions then? And start contributing to the upkeep of our home rather than act the spoiled puss and lie abed till afternoon while I wait upon her?"

Mama blinked at Jemmah as if she'd asked her to waltz naked covered in peacock feathers through Hyde Park.

"I thought not."

Jemmah jerked on her gloves, putting her forefinger through the threadbare tip of the right one.

Hounds' teeth!

Something very near a growl bubbled up the back of her throat. "The carriage awaits. I must go."

Before she vented every wounded, ugly, and pent-up thought now careening about in her head.

"It's not too late, Jemmah," Mama pleaded. "You still can refuse the position. Insist that Adelinda have it instead. I'm certain Theodora and the dowager will yield to your wishes if you stand firm and tell them that's what you want."

"But it's not what I want. It's what *you* want. And as always, it's what benefits you and my sister without a care of how I'll be affected."

Jemmah bit her tongue to stop the rest of her infuriated thoughts from spewing forth. After stuffing her hat on her head and tying the ribbon, she grabbed her reticule and the stack of sketches she'd set aside for today, then marched to the doorway.

"I'm going now, lest I say something I'll regret."

"Well, I most assuredly have no such misgivings." Mama stabbed a finger toward Jemmah, all the malice and animosity she'd held partially in check until now, etched onto her harsh features. Undeniable, glaring, and meant to draw blood.

To wound.

"I regret the day you were born, Jemmah Violet Emeline. I shall be well rid of you, and the constant reminder of your blackguard of a father staring at me through your countenance. Go, and do not return. You are no longer welcome beneath this roof!"

Jules whistled as he strode the several blocks to Theo's house, his boots clacking in a comfortable rhythm upon the damp pavement.

Given the cannon-gray clouds suspended across the horizon, perhaps not the wisest choice. A more sensible man might've ridden or taken his curricle, but not only did he enjoy the exercise, he had an ulterior motive for choosing to walk.

Theo had sent her carriage for Jemmah, which meant she'd return home the same way.

His conscience chastised him.

Conniving wretch.

Righto, indeed, I am, Jules agreed cheerily.

He intended to accompany her and ask her mother for permission to pay his addresses. The idea had taken root last night, and by this morning was firmly entrenched.

Most likely, in fact, he'd wager on it, Mrs. Dament would initially object. However, no caring parent would deny their daughter a duchy, for that was Jules's eventual intent. And that he believed, was fairly certain, truth be told, he was halfway—*all the way?*— to being in love with Jemmah already, well ... that was just a tremendous bonus.

On the ride, he might very well hold Jemmah's hand or even pinch another savory kiss or two. Or a dozen.

At the provocative notion, his nether regions twitched. Again.

Worse than a frog on August-heated pavement, by Jove.

Since last night, he'd been hard as the cast iron statues gracing the corner pillars of Theo's grand house too. He hadn't slept more than fifteen uninterrupted minutes without his aroused, disgruntled body pulling him from slumber, demanding release.

Touching his hat's brim, he acknowledged acquaintances he encountered along the route, earning him several wide-eyed, stupefied expressions.

London was unaccustomed to the Duke of Dandridge sporting a Cheshire's broad smile or tipping his hat in a cordial manner. The spring in his step and the idiotic grin carved on his face took even him by surprise.

Jemmah had done this.

In a twinkling, his childhood friend, now turned into a gloriously lovely woman, had unlocked his dormant heart. Had him casting off his melancholic shroud and regarding the world with a newfound, optimistic view.

Seeing her again last night...

Everything had become as clear to him as newly-polished crystal.

Jemmah was what he desired. She always had been.

That was why he'd been so drawn to Annabel. Blonde and blue-eyed, she'd resembled Jemmah, even boasting a similar temperament.

His spirit, his intuition, whatever part of him that acknowledged Jemmah had been branded upon his soul, had tried to tell him that very thing.

Only he'd been stupidly deaf and blind to the promptings—hadn't recognized them, hadn't even known what he craved until she'd drowsily smiled up at him, the full radiance of her smile tilting his world topsy-turvy.

Then as if the narrow crack in the doorway he'd been peering through with one eye suddenly sprang wide open, he could see everything, down to each perfect, minute detail.

And yes, by God, he savored the implausibility, relished the paradox, laughed out loud at the glorious coincidence that drove him to slip into the very room she slept within.

"You're looking especially chipper today, Dandridge," drawled a familiar bored voice. "Did you enjoy the ball after all?"

Pennington, blast his bunions.

Jules met Pennington's and Sutcliffe's amused gazes.

"I'm surprised to see either of you about. Thought you were off to the gaming hells after leaving Lady Lockhart's last night."

"We did." Sutcliffe cocked his head, regarding Jules for a lengthy moment. "Pennington, did my eyes deceive me or was Dandridge smiling? You know that queer thing where his mouth twitches upward occasionally?"

He veered Pennington a falsely-confused glance. "The phenomenon occurs so rarely, I cannot be sure."

"No, Sutcliffe, I saw it too. Thought I might be still feeling the effects of our late night." Pennington made a pretense of examining Jules's face with his quizzing glass.

"You're both utter twiddlepoops."

Jules stepped around them and continued on his way. He wasn't ready to explain his happiness, nor was he prepared to endure their sarcasm and mockery. Not when it came to his feelings regarding Jemmah.

"Twiddlepoops? *Twiddlepoops*?" Sutcliffe repeated, affronted. "Damn. Dandridge, are you getting soft? Dandies, fops, and moon-eyed bucks are twiddlepoops." He thumped his chest. "Pennington and I are knaves, scoundrels, jackanapes, blackguards, rakehells, reprobates. But never anything as tepid and asinine as a twiddlepoop."

"I should say not," Pennington agreed with a sharp jerk of his head. "I'm truly offended."

Sutcliffe fell in step beside Jules, his expression contemplative.

Pennington came alongside Jules as well, and eyes narrowed, rubbed his chin. "Does this have anything to do with the chit you kissed at Lady Lockhart's last night?"

Jules stalled mid-stride.

"You saw?"

How, in bloody hell?

"Old chap, the draperies were wide open." Pennington slapped Jules on the shoulder. "Not to worry. Sutcliffe and I were having a smoke. No one else ventured to the house's rear. Only we witnessed the pathetic peck you gave the pretty thing before she tore from the room. You really need to work on that, old boy. I was almost embarrassed for you."

Ah, so they'd only seen the last kiss.

"Who is she?" This from Sutcliffe, wearing a sly grin.

"None of your business."

Jules resumed his walk and lengthened his stride.

He couldn't compromise Jemmah.

"Devil it," Pennington said as he replaced his quizzing glass. "He's protecting her. Must be serious then. I didn't recognize the gel. Did you?"

He leaned around Jules to poke Sutcliffe's shoulder.

Sutcliffe shook his dark head. "No. But she did look familiar. We could ask Lady Lockhart, I suppose."

"Oh, for God's sake. She's someone I knew a long time ago. Someone I shall do anything to protect from gossip and speculation."

Hands on his hips, Jules glared back and forth, prepared to wipe the smirks off their faces.

Instead, both regarded him with calm, keen interest, but not a hint of ridicule.

Pennington grinned, his one green eye and one blue eye twinkling with suppressed mirth. "Are we to wish you happy?"

Jules sighed and shook his head. "Not yet. But I intend to change that as soon as possible. And you," he jabbed a finger at each of them in turn, "are to keep my confidence in this matter. I'll have your words, gentlemen."

"Of course," they murmured in unison, a trifle too quickly and subdued for Jules's comfort.

Sutcliffe nodded at an acquaintance, and after he'd passed, extended his hand. "We leave you here, but please accept my heartiest best wishes that you are successful. Just be careful, my friend. Such behavior is totally out of character for you, and that's why I'm inclined to believe you actually love Miss Dament."

Thundering hippopotamus's hooves.

How the hell had they learned Jemmah's name?

"Damn it, Sutcliffe. We agreed not to reveal we knew who she was." Pennington scowled darkly. "You never could keep a secret."

"True, but look at him." Pennington gestured toward Jules. "I cannot bring myself to taunt someone so obviously smitten. Can you? 'Twould be cruel, and we do profess to being his closest chums."

"I'm standing right here, and can hear every word." They wouldn't talk. That Jules knew beyond a doubt. "You're sure no one else saw her with me?"

"You can rest easy on that account, Dandridge," Pennington said.

"Well, keep your ears open, just in case. I must be off. I'll be late for tea at Lady Lockhart's." With a wave, Jules continued on his way, ignoring their chorus of guffaws.

Damn them.

They knew he didn't attend tea.

Not until Jemmah turned up in his life again.

He truly wasn't given to rash, impulsive behavior.

Quite the opposite, in fact.

Which was one of the reasons he knew, beyond whimsy or doubt, Jemmah must be his.

Oh, his mother and uncles would pitch conniption fits equal to the Regent's, but in the end, they'd concede.

What choice had they?

He was the Duke of Dandridge.

He controlled the purse strings.

His word was law, and it was far past time they acknowledged his position rather than treating him like a feckless, incompetent booby in need of their constant guidance.

His gratified chuckle earned him a curious glance from a pair of plump matrons dressed in the finest stare of fashion.

How wonderfully free and unencumbered he felt.

But how to persuade Jemmah that he was serious in his intentions after years of scant contact with her?

Such impulsiveness on Jules's part would've send a buzz through the *ton*'s elite parlors if he were a rakehell or knave, but his reputation as a grave, severe sort made the notion preposterous to all but Theo, Sutcliffe, and Pennington, and he anticipated a full-blown cacophony when word leaked out.

And it would.

All it took was two or three visits to the same address, and the upper ten thousand would eagerly check their post daily for a wedding invitation.

How could he expect Jemmah to take him earnestly when what he proposed flew in the face of common sense and contradicted his typical behavior?

True, she'd kissed him like a long-starved woman, but he suspected she had been deprived of affection for years.

Had she responded because she desperately craved acceptance and love, or because she felt something for Jules?

Male pride demanded the latter, but prudence suggested the former.

Mightn't Jemmah's reaction be attributed to both?

Yes.

That seemed most logical.

He stepped to the side, permitting a nurse and her three rambunctious charges to pass.

Jules would use every advantage to win Jemmah and her mother over. He began making a mental list of tactics he intended to use.

A few minutes later, he rounded the corner onto Mayfair, just as Theo's carriage rumbled to a stop before her mansion. He quickened his pace, his pulse keeping time with his hurried stride.

Jemmah alit, wearing a simple blue coat, a trifle too short, and a plain straw bonnet. She reached inside the conveyance, and after withdrawing a battered valise, faced the grand house.

Did her shoulders slump the slightest? The regal column of her neck bend as if she bore a weighty burden?

"Miss Dament."

His regard never left her as his legs ate up the distance between them.

Never had he beheld anything half as lovely as when she turned, and upon spying him, joy blossomed across her face. All these years of being a sensible, logical sort, and now he felt as giddy as a lad in short pants or a foxed-to-his-gills tippler at being gifted a wondrous smile.

"Your Grace."

She dipped into a smooth curtsy as he bowed, but not before he saw her red-rimmed eyes, framed by spiky lashes.

And the telltale salty trail across her cheeks once more.

An ink-stained fingertip poked from the gloved hand clutching the valise. Perhaps the drawings she'd promised were tucked within the dilapidated piece of luggage that was older than she, if it was a day.

She'd known deprivation, and a dull ache settled in his gut at the awareness.

Much had happened to his Jemmah in the years since they'd parted ways, most of it not good.

As the carriage rattled away, he took her valise and her elbow, but rather than escorting her up the front steps, Jules directed her 'round back, toward the mews.

Confusion knitting her brow, she cast a glance behind her.

"Where are we going?"

"Where I can have a word with you in private."

Once hidden from the street, he placed his forefinger beneath her chin and raised her face.

"What has happened, dear one?"

The light faded from her lovely eyes, and the tears pooled there slowly leaked from the corners.

Such anguish of spirit reflected in her soul that he gathered her in his arms.

To hell with decorum and propriety.

She needed comfort.

Simple as that.

Sagging into his chest, she wept softly, brokenheartedly.

Her scent, that light clean smell of soap and lavender and perhaps the tiniest hint of rose water wafted upward as her shoulders shook with her grief.

"My dear, Jemmah. Please tell me. What has caused you such distress?"

Her hat's tattered edge scraped his chin as she struggled to compose herself.

"Mama has turned me out, and I've nowhere to go but to impose upon Aunt Theo's hospitality."

"Why would she do such a thing?"

He veered a swift glance around.

Good.

No one ventured near or detected their presence behind the neatly-trimmed seven-foot shrubs bordering Theo's house.

In a few concise, shuddery sentences, Jemmah explained what happened after he left the ball last night.

"So, because I refused to cede the opportunity to Adelinda, as I have almost everything of import my entire life, my mother put me from our house. I was only permitted to take what I could fit in one bag."

Jules stroked her slender spine, desperate to comfort her. "Well, I can think of two ladies who will be euphoric at this turn of events. Three, if you count Sabrina. She was over the moon with excitement when I told her you'd generously offered to teach her drawing."

He wasn't exactly distressed either.

Her change in circumstances played quite nicely into his intent to woo her.

Jemmah sniffled and dashed her fingers across her face. "May I impose upon you to borrow your handkerchief?"

Great galloping giraffes.

The poor darling didn't even own a scrap of cloth with which to dab her impossibly expressive eyes.

Jules passed her the starched and neatly-folded monogrammed square and waited while she dried her face, then blew her nose. Once she regained her self-control, he collected her bag and tucked her hand into the crook of his elbow.

Gazing down at her, he smiled tenderly. "I'd be a liar if I pretended I'm not thrilled I shall be able to call upon you here now."

An adorable flush swept her face, accompanied by a winsome upward tilt of her mouth.

"Yes, there is that to look forward to. If Aunt Theo agrees to me staying with her."

"She will, of course. And do you look forward to me paying my addresses?"

He hadn't meant to go that far just yet, but the opportunity had presented itself, and he had impulsively told her he meant to court her.

Rather than using the front entrance, he steered her to the open French windows outside the ballroom.

Servants drifted in and out of the room, clearing up the remaining vestiges of last night's celebration.

Theo's poodle, Caesar, trotted through the empty ballroom, ebony nose and tail in the air, his nails clicking on the parquet floor.

Instead of answering straightaway, Jemmah tilted her head and regarded him through those thick, tear-damp lashes, her speculative gaze penetrating, yet reflective.

"The dowager has offered me an opportunity someone in my position isn't likely to have replicated."

"So have I, my precious Jem."

Drawing her to the side of the house, Jules pulled her near. A damp breeze fluttered the cherry blossoms, sending a pink petal shower onto the sandstone pavers they stood upon.

"Why now, when you've scarcely paid me any notice for years?" She fiddled with her reticule strap. "I know I acted... Well, I was awfully glad to see you last night, and I did enjoy the dance. And after too. Very much, in fact. But that was... is a fairytale. I'm not a simpleton. Women like me don't have the Duke of Dandridge paying them court when there are far lovelier, more suitable, and wealthier prospects."

"Then don't think of me as the duke, but as your friend of many, many years. One who has never held another as dear, and one who with all of his heart, wants to be more." He trailed his finger along her jaw. "Much more, if you'll let me."

Jules settled his lips onto hers, tasting once again the sweetness of her mouth. He poured all of his yearning, his love into the kiss, communicating what he so desperately needed to tell her.

Without prompting, Jemmah opened her mouth, and using the skills he'd taught her last night, proceeded to send any vestige of logical thought he retained, spiraling out of control.

Holding her face between his palms, he angled her head to kiss her deeper still, savoring her velvety tongue sparring with his.

A muffled *woof,* followed by snuffling near his ankles reined in his passion.

What was Jules thinking, kissing her in broad daylight?

Evidently, even a pragmatic somber fellow such as himself, once besotted, didn't think at all clearly.

What a splendid realization.

Still, he'd already been seen kissing her once, and even if his intentions were honorable, he'd not bring censure upon Jemmah.

Theo stepped halfway out the door and pulled her bold-colored Norwich shawl more snugly around her shoulders.

"My footman said he heard voices out here. Whatever are the two of you doing?"

"I'm trying to persuade Miss Dament to permit me to court her."

Jules didn't care who knew, and he needed Theo as an ally.

"And I haven't agreed, as yet." The warmth radiating from Jemmah's eyes encouraged him.

She would agree. She must.

A smile wreathed Theo's face, so exuberant, her ruby earbobs trembled.

"Well, if that isn't the most splendid news I've heard in a great while." With a swift glimpse about the courtyard, she beckoned them. "Come inside and tell me all."

Her focus alit on the portmanteau near Jemmah's foot, and her questioning gaze vacillated between Jules and Jemmah.

"Are you eloping?"

Jemmah gave a small, water-logged laugh and shook her head. "Nothing so romantic, I'm afraid, Aunt Theo." She summoned a brave smile. "I'm in need of a place to stay. Indefinitely."

"Ah." Theo looped her arm through Jemmah's leaving Jules to collect the beaten-about-the-edges valise. "You are welcome for as long as you want, my dear. I'm quite thrilled, actually."

"I'm ever so grateful, Auntie." Jemmah hugged her aunt's arm.

Theo tossed a saucy glance over her shoulder.

"Now, tell me, what's this business about Dandridge courting you?"

Three glorious weeks later.

Jemmah angled first one way, and then the other before the floor length oval looking glass.

The black-edged cerulean-blue walking ensemble was quite the loveliest thing she'd ever seen. But then again, that was what she thought with each new gown dear Aunt Theo or the Dowager Lady Lockhart bestowed upon her.

And each time, she'd insisted they'd gifted her quite enough and forbade them to purchase her a single thing more.

They'd laughed and pooh-poohed her.

One would think it should be easy to become accustomed to the gorgeous gowns, fallalls, fripperies... scented soaps and lotions... enough sleep for the first time in years. But it wasn't easy, and Jemmah still couldn't as yet reconcile herself to this new way of life.

Each time she approached the dowager about beginning her companionship duties, the dame dismissed her concerns, insisting there was time enough to worry about that later. She wouldn't even permit Jemmah to attend her on their evenings out, claiming Aunt Theo more than capable of the task.

Aunt Theo would then take Lady Lockhart's arm, leaving Jules to offer Jemmah his elbow. She suspected the two of match-making. How could she fault the dears when she desired the same thing?

After supper tonight, they were off to the theater again.

Oh, that first time had been so magical.

In a hastily-altered, borrowed gown of Aunt Theo's, Jemmah had entered on Jules's arm, for once appearing in public confident and proud.

Tucked in Auntie's gallery box, Jemmah had tried to watch the ballet performance, but his hand holding hers, his lips mere inches away as he whispered in her ear, the timbre of his melodic baritone causing delicious little tremors...

Why, she couldn't even recall the name of the ballet they'd watched.

Dabbing a bit of lily of the valley perfume behind each ear and upon each wrist, she grinned at Caesar sprawled before her balcony doors, muzzle on his black forepaws, and his big soulful eyes watching her every move.

He'd taken to her, almost as if he sensed she needed unconditional love, and Aunt Theo didn't seem to mind. Or if she did, she kept the knowledge to herself. But Jemmah's aunt also loved her without restriction, and even that would take time to become accustomed to.

She would, though.

She had every reason to, and he'd be here shortly.

Jemmah's stomach tumbled in that wonderful wobbly way it did whenever her thoughts gravitated toward Jules. A wonder she could hold her food down with all the cavorting taking place in her middle these days.

"Miss Jemmah, that color becomes you. You look like a real lady, you do." Mary's mouth tipped into a cheeky grin as she fluffed the bed's pillows. "Forgive my impertinence, but your sister would gnash her teeth if she saw you now."

Undoubtedly.

"I'm so glad you're here, Mary."

Within a week of Jemmah's leaving, Frazer Pimble had approached Jemmah and revealed Mama had dismissed Mary without reference. And since Aunt Theo insisted Jemmah needed a lady's maid—to do what, for pity's sake?—quite naturally, Jemmah had been determined to see Mary have the position.

Having two Pimbles in the household caused a bit of a conundrum at first, but Aunt Theo, always one to throw convention into the gutters, advised everyone to simply call the maid by her given name.

After tying her bonnet's ribbons, Jemmah gathered her reticule and parasol.

Everywhere one looked, signs of an early spring were evident. Including the bright vivid green fern fronds, sunny jonquils, cheery primroses, and the shining orb in the sky splaying its golden fingers across the heavens.

Her heart glowed with warmth every bit as permeating and pleasurable.

These had been the happiest weeks of her life, and sometimes when she awoke in the middle of the night and the familiar despondency cloaked her, she had to remind herself she'd left her oppressive life behind.

Goodness, so much had changed in such a short while.

Not the least of which was Jules's actively courting her—

Without permission.

Mama had refused to receive him each time he'd approached her on the matter.

He vowed he wouldn't give up, that she'd eventually come around.

He didn't know Mama.

She held a grudge and was about as malleable as dried mortar.

Sighing, Jemmah booted her unhappy musings aside.

As Jules had done every day since Jemmah had come to live with Aunt Theo, he'd be here momentarily for their daily outing. They'd explored all of the major parks and Covent Garden, visited Astley's Amphitheatre, eaten ices at Gunter's, and shopped along Bond Street several times.

Today's plans included an excursion to Vauxhall Gardens.

She intended to return in the evening sometime too, but for this initial visit, she wanted to see the famed gardens in the daylight.

A soft knock rapped at her bedchamber door.

"Come."

Jemmah drew on one soft kid glove.

"His Grace, the Duke of Dandridge, awaits you in the gold parlor, miss." Pimble winked at his sister. "Let me know if Mary gets sassy. I'll straighten her out, right quick, I shall."

Mary stuck out her tongue and laughing, chucked a pillow at her brother's head.

Observing their antics, Jemmah twisted her mouth into a wistful smile.

She didn't remember ever playing like that with Adelinda.

"Never fear. Your sister attends her duties with conscience and efficiency. Mary, collect your cloak. I don't want to keep the duke waiting."

Ten minutes later saw Jemmah comfortably seated in Dandridge's landau as his driver expertly tooled the conveyance along the busy lane. Mary dutifully sat in the rear groom's seat to allow Jemmah and Jules privacy while still acting the part of chaperone.

As he was wont to do, despite the slight impropriety, Jules promptly tucked Jemmah's gloved hand into his buff-clad one. He bent his head near, his breath tickling her ear.

"I called upon your mother again yesterday."

"And?"

Jemmah searched his face, reading the answer in his compassionate gaze.

Drat Mama's obstinance and pride.

"She refused me once more."

The sun bounced off the diamond in his cravat, and the hunter green of his jacket reflected in the jade flecks in his irises.

Such kind, gentle eyes, yet also intelligent, alert, and assessing.

"I'm not surprised. In her bitterness, Mama blames everyone else for her circumstances. She sees herself as the victim, and that prevents her from hearing reason."

Jemmah returned the mild, reassuring squeeze he gave her fingers.

The comfortable *clip-clopping* of the horses' hooves on the cobblestones, the sun's caressing rays, as well as the vehicle's plush seat had her blinking sleepily and fighting a yawn.

"I'm sure it's been quite difficult for her and Adelinda, now that Mary's left and Aunt Theo has withdrawn her financial support."

Jules made a confirming sound in the back of his throat, causing his Adam's apple to bob. "I've no doubt, but once we are wed, I fully intend to provide her with an allowance as long as she agrees—"

Jemmah clutched his hand, and jaw sagging, she stared in stunned incredulity.

Confusion yanked his brows together, and he patted her hand twice.

"Why do you look at me like that? Don't you want me to give your mother any funds? I thought you'd be pleased, but if not—"

Shaking her head, Jemmah's mouth quivered.

"No, no. It's not that at all. I think it very generous of you, and most forgiving too."

More forgiving than she was capable of so soon.

Mama didn't deserve Jules's magnanimity.

He bent nearer, and brazenly brushed his lip across the top of Jemmah's ear.

"Then what is it?"

Jemmah slid Mary a covert glance.

Completely absorbed in the passing scenery, the maid hadn't heard Jules.

Jemmah scooted a little nearer, brushing her thigh against his in a most provocative way.

Keeping her voice low, so neither the driver nor Mary might overhear, she murmured, "You said... Well, at least I thought you said, 'When we wed.'"

She raised hopeful eyes to Jules's.

How pathetic she must look. How mortified she'd be if she'd misunderstood.

They'd never discussed marriage, but his courting and repeated visits to Mama must mean he'd contemplated the matter at some length. And when the time was right, he'd broach the subject with Jemmah.

Although, as long as Mama refused to let him officially address Jemmah, they'd little choice but to wait for her to come of age or elope to Gretna Green.

Not an entirely awful notion by half.

Actually, a rather grand one. Mayhap she should mention it to him.

If he proposed.

And if he didn't? If she'd misheard?

Well then, when the dowager returned to the country, Jemmah would accompany her.

Thank goodness she had the promised position to fall back upon. The knowledge brought her a great deal of comfort.

Tenderness bent Jules's mouth and pleated the angles of his face, deepening his fascinating eyes to a simmering cognac.

"Indeed, I did say that very thing, my precious Jem. I thought you understood that's always my intention, my sweet, since I found you cozily slumbering in Theo's parlor. To make you my duchess, the keeper of my heart."

She couldn't quite subdue her tiny elated gasp.

Sudden wariness filtered across his face, and he straightened a bit. "Did I assume wrongly? Misjudge your affections?"

"No, not at all, Your Grace."

"Jules," he reminded her.

Jemmah's eyes misted and giving him a tremulous smile, she dragged her handkerchief from her reticule. Chin tucked to her chest, she angled her parasol and discreetly dabbed her eyes. "I didn't dare dream something so wholly marvelous would happen to me."

"Dare I hope your answer is yes? It's not too soon?"

Jemmah gave a jerky nod, afraid she'd weep for joy if she spoke.

The carriage gave an abrupt shudder as the rear wheel sank into a hole, jostling them against each other.

Jules beaver hat smacked her parasol, skewing it to the side.

As he straightened it, he sought her eyes.

"Yes, it's too soon, or your answer is yes?"

"Yes, I'll marry you, darling man," she whispered, perhaps not as quietly as she might since she didn't care who knew this wonderful news.

They'd still Mama to convince, of course, but Jemmah refused to let that obstacle steal a single speck of her elation.

Jules released a long, shuddering breath.

"Thank God. I almost swallowed my heart. I think it's still lodged somewhere in my throat." After patting his neck, he winked and tucked her scandalously closer. "We can discuss the details while we wander Vauxhall, and I promise to propose properly. Too many ears, right now."

He waggled his eyebrows toward Mary.

"But, I must tell you," his voice dropped to a low purr, causing the most remarkable of sensations to sprout in unmentionable areas. "I adore you, Jemmah, love."

A plump tear did escape then. One of pure, unadulterated joy.

"And I love you too, Jules."

Had for years, but she wasn't ready to share that just yet. Not until they were alone, and she could show him just how ecstatic she was.

Knuckle bent, he caught the wayward droplet. "I only want to see tears of happiness in your beautiful blue eyes from now on."

"They will be."

Sparing a glance overhead, Jules closed his eyes. "Doesn't the sun feel glorious?"

"Yes." Though he was far more spectacular.

Trailing her gaze over his refined profile, she put her other hand to her middle to still the odd spasm that always occurred when she gazed upon him thusly. She didn't remember a time she hadn't loved him, and that he felt the same...

Galloping turtles, such glee made her lightheaded.

Gone was the stiff, stern, unapproachable peer others had mocked for his severity. Jules now let the rest of the world see the man she'd always known existed beneath his prickly, protective exterior.

A contented sigh passed between her lips.

A half an hour later saw Mary settled beneath a tree with a book and several gossip rags, while Jemmah and Jules strolled the gardens. She'd lived in London her entire life and had never been inside Vauxhall.

Father's pockets had always been in dun territory, made worse by the funds he frittered away on his mistresses.

"Have I told you how beautiful you are today, Jemmah?" Jules deep voice rumbled low in his broad chest.

A pleasure-born blush bathed her that he would think her so. "No, but I know a taradiddle when I hear it. But it does my womanly pride wonders to hear the nonsense, nevertheless. You forget, I have a looking glass."

He tweaked her nose. "And you, my dear, are blind to your own loveliness."

"Well, isn't this a coincidence. I was just speaking of you, Jemmah."

Upon hearing Adelinda's spiteful voice, Jemmah spun around.

Boils and bunions.

Attired in a lovely emerald green and peach gown—new and expensive if she wasn't mistaken—Adelinda hung on the arm of an attractive man Jemmah didn't recognize.

Where had Adelinda come by monies to purchase a gown of such high quality?

And who was this newest admirer? Another of Adelinda's unsuitable swains, no doubt.

He might be handsome, but something unnerving, dark and oily, shadowed his soulless eyes.

From the languid way his gaze slid over Jemmah before something more than polite interest sharpened his features, she'd bet all the buttons in France he wasn't a respectable sort. In fact, he made her want to race home, dive beneath the bedcovering, and pull them over her head to block his leering gaze.

Adelinda's perusal of Jemmah was no less thorough, but the look in her eye could never be described as appreciative or cordial.

"Miss Dament. Perkins." Jules still possessively cradled Jemmah's elbow, and he gave the new arrivals a distinctly cool and the briefest possible greeting.

Not friends, then.

"Dandridge." Perkins's equally frosty acknowledgement confirmed her suspicion. The smile Perkins then bestowed on Adelinda didn't quite reach his shrewd eyes. "Aren't you going to introduce me?"

Mouth pinched in displeasure, Adelinda raised an annoyed brow.

"My sister, Jemmah. Jemmah, Mr. Samuel Perkins. He owns a club on Kings Street," she said all smug superiority.

The last was declared as if he maintained a private suite at Buckingham Palace.

"So, Adelinda, this is the younger sister you've told me so much about."

I'll wager she has.

Perkins's lascivious chuckle sent Jemmah's skin scuttling, and unnerved by the predatory glint in his eye, she edged nearer to Jules.

His palm tightened on her arm the merest bit before he looped her hand through his elbow, the movement drawing her closer.

"You misled me, my dear Adelinda," Perkins said with another slippery upward twist of his mouth. "Your sister's a diamond of the first water if I ever saw one."

He dares address Adelinda by her given name?

Appearing like she'd been served amphibians or reptiles for supper,

94

Adelinda managed a sickly smile.

"I've nearly convinced Mama to permit you to return home, Jemmah. If you put off your grand airs. After all, you cannot expect to take advantage of Aunt Theo's benevolence indefinitely."

Still the same spiteful Adelinda, though granted, a trio of weeks was hardly time enough to change one's character.

It was long enough to fall more profoundly, marvelously in love with Jules.

"I won't be returning, Adelinda. Of that you may rest assured."

Jemmah sent Jules a secretive glance, but her sister saw it.

Adelinda stepped closer, her perceptive gaze narrowed. "If you think—"

"Dandridge, darling. I thought I saw you from across the way."

Oh, for all the kippers in Kensington.

Two misses determined to trap Jules in their webs, and this one with the audacity to call him darling in public?

Momentary uncertainty skipped about the tattered edges of Jemmah's composure.

Inhaling a bracing breath, she swung 'round to see Miss Milbourne, accompanied by two men she didn't recognize, but whose unusual topaz eyes and honeyed hair decreed them Jules's relatives.

Jules's forearm stiffened beneath Jemmah's fingers.

"Miss Milbourne. Uncles."

Ah, the famed Charmont uncles who believed Jules incapable of making his own decisions.

Tension thicker than custard settled onto the uncomfortable group, everyone eyeing the other with speculation and suspicion.

Miss Milbourne minced closer, absolute perfection in an exquisite ivory and plum confection, all frothy, feminine lace. And she smelled positively divine.

Drat and dash it all.

Why couldn't she have a flaw or two or three?

Buck teeth?

A hairy mole upon her nose?

Crossed eyes? *Fangs*?

"I've missed you." She ran her white-gloved fingers down Jules's chest, and blinked coyly at him from beneath her preposterously thick eyelashes.

Brazen as an alley cat twitching her tail for a mate.

"I've been otherwise engaged." The steely look he impaled his uncles with had them shuffling their feet and raptly examining the foliage.

Cowards.

Acutely aware of the elegantly coiffed, perfumed, and hostile woman standing but inches away, taking her measure, Jemmah arched a starchy brow. She was newly-betrothed to the Duke of Dandridge, and for all of Miss Milbourne's posturing and attempts to intimidate, the woman was, quite frankly, and most gratifyingly... the loser.

Her condescending gaze flicked to Jemmah, and Miss Milbourne's pupils contracted to pinpricks as she oh-so casually twirled her parasol.

"So I see," she drawled. "I'd heard rumors you were doing the pretty and escorting your godmother's dowdy ward about town. I must say, I never took you, of all men, for a nursemaid, Dandridge. Most decent of you, inconveniencing yourself to oblige Lady Lockhart's unreasonable requests."

Adelinda's giggle, earned her an exasperated glower from Perkins.

"Yes, quite right, Miss Milbourne. No man has ever willingly directed his attention at my frumpy sister."

At her sister's barbed insult, Jemmah stiffened and set her jaw against the oath bucking to escape the narrow barrier of her lips.

A duchess doesn't tell ladies to go bugger themselves.

Miss Milbourne and Adelinda exchanged a gloating glance.

Enough of these two vixens trying to draw her blood with their jealousy. "You can both—"

"Rest assured, ladies, I'm never coerced into doing anything I don't want to." In an intimate, comforting gesture, Jules laid his other hand atop Jemmah's. "And you're woefully incorrect if you presume there is any woman on earth I'd rather spend time with than my betrothed."

"**B**etrothed?" sputtered Miss Milbourne and Miss Dament in horrified unison.

Each appeared to have swallowed wriggling spiders whole.

Jules quashed his laugh, but couldn't contain the slow, satisfied upsweep of his mouth.

He bent his neck and murmured in Jemmah's ear.

"I beg your pardon for announcing it this way."

The Uncles stood slack-jawed and dazed, too.

Zounds, their expressions were priceless.

Jemmah dimpled and lifted a shoulder, whispering back, "I rather enjoyed the results."

Jules did laugh then, a mirth-filled explosion from his middle, which drew the attention of two lads chasing a pug with a ball in its mouth.

God, he loved her unique perspective on things.

But so much for the romantic proposal he'd intended within the arched arbor facing yonder pond. Inside his coat pocket an emerald-cut, rare blue diamond, a shade darker than Jemmah's eyes, lay nestled in its ivory velvet box.

He'd arranged a picnic luncheon complete with champagne in the quaint retreat. Damn his eyes, he'd even hired musicians to play in the background and a boatman to make sure the pond's many swans paddled by in a timely fashion.

His precious Jem warranted such regal treatment.

"You can't marry the duke, Jemmah." The elder Miss Dament pointed a shaky finger at her sister, her voice wavering every bit as much as the wobbly digit extended toward her sister. "You must have Mama's consent. And, she'll never give it. Never."

"Then I'll wait until I'm of age. Or we'll elope." Jemmah's quiet, confident reply sent her sister into high dudgeon.

Face puckered and turning the most spectacular shade of puce, Miss Adelinda fisted her hands and growled. Actually growled, before giving them her back and stomping across the green.

Perkins followed, but not before daring one last lewd appraisal of Jemmah.

He'd bamboozled Adelinda, the imprudent chit.

The club Perkins owned was nothing more than a low-end gaming hell and whorehouse. If the girl had taken up with the likes of him, she was thoroughly ruined. If she wasn't careful, she'd be spreading her legs for his paying customers.

Jules couldn't even buy her respectability now, which only made his case for winning Jemmah stronger. Mrs. Dament couldn't count on her eldest daughter making a suitable match and directing funds her mother's way.

He could, however, pay them a substantial sum to retire to the country.

Permanently.

If they agreed to never bother Jemmah again.

Yes, that was just what he'd do. As soon as he returned home. Mrs. Dament would have no choice but to agree now.

"Elope? Preposterous," blustered Uncle Darius, finally finding his tongue, while Uncle Leopold waggled his head up and down like a marionette on a string.

"Utterly absurd. What would people say?" Leopold managed at last.

"Then I suggest you put your support behind Miss Dament and me, Uncles. And convince Mother to do the same. For I shall have *no* other, and all attempts to dissuade me will be met with swift recourse. Do I make myself clear?"

They nodded, albeit grudgingly. And then, mumbling something about needing to count cigars or some such rot, they departed, their tawny heads bent near. Every few steps, they tossed a befuddled and disgruntled glance at Jules.

He didn't give a fig whether they approved or not.

He smiled down into Jemmah's upturned, amazingly composed face. Lambasted thrice in ten minutes and here she stood, the epitome of grace and poise, beaming with love for him—*for him!*

His heart had chosen well.

Statue still, her countenance pale as the scalloped lace edging her fashionable spencer, Miss Milbourne peered around.

Blinking slowly, as if someone had whacked her upon the head with her frilly parasol, she murmured, "Excuse me. I see an acquaintance I must speak with."

Head held high, she spun about and glided toward the pond, where nothing but a few ducks napped in the sun.

Taken to chatting with ducks, had she?

"Ho, what have we here?" Sutcliffe gave them a jaunty wave from across the green, and ambled their way accompanied by Pennington. Brow furrowed, he turned and watched Miss Milbourne's progress.

Jules shook his head and rolled his eyes toward the greenery overhead.

"My God. Did someone extend invitations unbeknownst to me?"

"Invitations? Is there a special occasion I'm unaware of?" Sutcliffe's attention veered to the departing uncles, Miss Milbourne, and lastly Jules. His grin threatened to split his face in two upon greeting Jemmah.

"Miss Dament." He bent into an exaggerated courtier's bow. "May I say how delighted I am to see you taking the air with Dandridge?"

"As am I." Pennington clasped a hand to his waist and bent low, too.

Jemmah canted her head, and eyes sparkling, offered them a bright smile. "Thank you, your graces. You're exuberance is... refreshing."

"*Is* there any special reason you're visiting the pleasure gardens today?" One hand on his hip, Sutcliffe, as subtle as a nubby toad on a pastry, attempted a nonchalant expression.

"I intended to propose, if you must know, you two interfering tabbies. But they," Jules jabbed his thumb in the direction of his uncles' and Miss Milbourne's departing figures, "ruined the occasion."

"By Jove, that's the best news I've heard in ages!" Pennington pumped Jules hand while Sutcliffe bent over Jemmah's. "Not that they ruined the occasion, but that you've at last declared yourself."

"I wish you the greatest happiness, Miss Dament," Sutcliffe said. "Now, we'll take our leave and let our friend be about this most important business."

Rubbing his thumb across the back of Jemmah's hand, Jules remained silent as the pair strode away. Everything he'd planned to make the day romantic and memorable had been quashed.

"Jules?"

He met Jemmah's slightly disconcerted eyes. "Yes, my dear?"

"Why is everyone staring in our direction?"

Jules raised his head and took a casual glance around.

She was right, though several people hastily looked away, finding either the sky or the ground profoundly fascinating.

Damn, the news of his intentions had travelled faster than the wind in sails, thanks to Jemmah's bitter sister.

Hmm, perhaps not a bad thing at all. With a few dozen witnesses...

He withdrew the ring box from his pocket.

"Jules?" This time Jemmah's voice went all soft and melty, as did her eyes. "Here?"

"Indeed."

Raising the lid, he folded to one knee.

His valet would scold him soundly for getting grass stains on his pantaloons. But this was right in its simple, unpretentiousness.

Just like his precious Jemmah.

With the sun shining upon them, bees busy gathering nectar, a frog or two croaking in the ponds' underbrush, while various birds called to one another, he would ask her to be his duchess.

"Jemmah, you are the jewel I've carried in my heart since I was a wee lad of ten. No one else makes me smile like you do. You consume my thoughts, and I cannot imagine any greater joy than spending the rest of my life with you." He smiled into her shining eyes. "Will you marry me?"

Jemmah squatted and extended her left hand.

Leave it to her to do something wholly unexpected.

"I shall, Jules. I've loved you for so long, I don't remember what life was before I did." She gave a little self-conscious laugh, as he slipped the ring on her finger.

"As a little girl, I imagined myself a princess, wearing a sapphire and diamond tiara, and locked in a tower. And you were the handsome prince who rescued me. On a white steed, of course, and carried me off to his castle to live happily ever after."

"Well, the duchy has a castle, and I believe several tiaras too. I own a white horse or two as well," he said assisting her upright. "And I shall strive every day to make you happy."

"I need nothing but to be with you to be deliriously so."

Then, in typical Jemmah fashion, she levered onto her toes, and kissed him.

On the mouth.

In public.

And it was perfect.

Epilogue

Chalchester Castle, Essex, England
July 1810

"**D**arling, Teodora giggled again."

Grinning in her excitement, Jemmah, holding her three-month-old daughter, gingerly picked her way between the smooth stones to Chalchester Lake's edge. The afternoon sun's rays reflected off the water as if a thousand brilliant diamonds had been cast across its surface.

She'd believed she couldn't be happier when she married Jules just over a year ago; after Mama had finally agreed to the match, because Adelinda found herself scandalously pregnant.

But Jemmah had been wrong.

Each day as Jules's wife brought her a new measure of joy and contentment she'd only dreamed of.

Oh, there'd been worries in the beginning, but not between her and Jules.

He'd kept his word and settled Mama and Adelinda in a charming cottage in Sussex, with a generous monthly allowance. But after Adelinda lost her babe and ran off with a traveling performer, Mama had fallen gravely ill, dying shortly thereafter.

The rancor and bitterness she'd harbored for so long, combined with a broken heart killed her, the doctor said.

On her death bed, Mama had pleaded for Jemmah's forgiveness, and she'd given it. She refused to harbor malice, for eventually, it would corrupt her soul as it had Mama's and Adelinda's.

Jemmah had no idea where her sister was now, but truly hoped she'd found even a small degree of the peace and joy Jemmah had.

Her bonnet's lavender ribbons stirring in the faint breeze, and the gravel crunching beneath her half-boots, she made her way to her husband.

Jules, standing knee deep in the gently-flowing current, and holding a fishing line, glanced behind him.

Teodora cooed and waved her little fists.

"She's a happy darling. Like her mother."

"Like her father too, although you do your best to convince people otherwise."

"Well, how else can I maintain my dour reputation?"

He chuckled as he stepped from the river, and after laying his pole beside the blanket spread upon the shore, extended his arms.

Jemmah laid Teodora within his sturdy, secure embrace.

The baby promptly smiled at her father, her almond-shaped eyes the same unusual topaz as his, and seized his forefinger in her tiny grasp.

She yawned and blinked sleepily.

Jules adjusted the infant then draped his other arm across Jemmah's shoulders. "We are happy, aren't we?"

Blissfully so.

Her head resting against his brawny shoulder, Jemmah nodded. "I'm so glad we decided to live here after marrying, rather than in London. I never realized how much I didn't like the hubbub. I enjoy visiting once in a while, especially since Aunt Theo won't venture to the country, but honestly, I never want to live in the city again."

"Did you really love me all that time we were apart?" Jules gazed down at her with such adoration, her heart stuttered a bit. "When you never spoke to me or even saw me?"

Jemmah poked his rib. "I've told you so dozens of times. I think it puffs your head to think so."

"It puffs other things too." He looked meaningfully at the bulge in his trousers.

"Well, husband, I believe I might have just the cure for what ails you." Jemmah took their sleeping daughter from him and once she'd tucked Teodora into her basket beneath a tree, extended her hand. Asleep in the shade, their daughter would be safe. Besides, they were but a few steps away. "There's a lovely little grove yonder."

"Duchess, do you mean to have your way with me in broad daylight?"

The seductive twinkle in Jules's eyes and tugging at his delicious mouth told her he liked the notion every bit as much as she.

Following an animal trail through the grass, she arched him an invitation over her shoulder as she began to disrobe.

"I do, indeed, Your Grace."

Only a Duke Would Dare

1

Colchester, Essex England
Late June 1809

Twilight's gloom lengthened the shadows in the old cemetery as Theadosia—humming *Robin Adair*, a Scottish love song certain to vex her father—wended her way through the grave markers and the occasional gangly rose bush or shrubbery in need of pruning.

Having lived at the rectory her entire life, she found the graveyard neither frightening nor eerie. Those lying in eternal rest included a brother who'd died in infancy, several townspeople she'd known, and even a few gentry and nobles for whom Father had performed funerals. As children, she and her sisters and brother had frolicked amongst the stones and statuary, playing hide and seek and other games.

Situated on the east side of All Saints Church to catch the rising sun each morning, the churchyard provided a convenient, often-used shortcut to the parsonage's back entrance.

"Why?"

A deep, anguished whisper drifted across the expanse.

Though she didn't believe in ghosts and despite her velvet spencer, an icy prickle zipped down her spine, causing the hairs on her arms to stand at attention.

Lifting her robin's egg blue chintz gown with one hand, she paused and glanced around but saw nothing out of the ordinary. A plump, greyish-brown rabbit, enjoying a snack before finding its way home for the evening, watched her with wary, black-button eyes. After another moment of studying the familiar landscape, Theadosia continued on her way.

She must've imagined the voice.

The wind had whipped up in the last few minutes. Sometimes, the two ancient oaks acting as sentinels at the cemetery entrance groaned in such a way that the swaying branches sounded as if they were moaning in protest.

Perhaps Jessica's chickens had made an odd noise, Theadosia reassured herself as the wind lashed her skirts around her ankles. Situated on the other side of the parish where the vegetable and flower gardens were, the chickens often made odd sounding cackles and clucks.

The empty basket that had held the chicken soup and bread she'd delivered to the sick Ulrich family this afternoon banged against her thigh as she resumed her humming, even daring to sing a line from the song since she'd inspected the area and her parents weren't present to chastise her.

"Yet him I lov'd so well—"

"Why'd you do it?"

The same tormented baritone rasped through the burial ground once more.

That, by Jehoshaphat, she had *not* imagined.

She stopped again and turned in a slow circle, trying to peer around the greeneries and headstones. Many were large and ornate, and she couldn't see past the nearby stone markers.

"I jus' want to know why."

The rabbit froze for a second before darting into the hedgerow.

A shiver tiptoed across Theadosia's shoulders, and she swallowed against a flicker of fear.

Come now, Theadosia Josephine Clarice Brentwood. You are made of sterner stuff.

Besides, ghosts didn't slur their words. At least, she didn't think so.

Gathering her resolve, she pulled herself to her full five-feet-nine inches and called, "Who's there?"

She squinted into the dusk. The voice had come from the graveyard's far side. The side reserved for aristocrats and nobles.

Another wind gust whistled through the dogwoods and flowering cherry trees bordering the cemetery's north side and tugged at the brim of her new straw bonnet. She held it tightly to keep it in place.

Once more, a mumbled phrase—or perhaps a sob this time—followed on the tails of the crisp breeze.

What distraught soul had ventured into the graveyard at this hour?

Visitors usually came 'round in the morning or afternoon. On occasion, they even picnicked amongst those who'd gone before them. Superstitions and unwarranted fears usually kept mourners away as darkness descended, however.

Whoever the person was, they were in distress for certain, and Theadosia's compassionate nature demanded she offer to help. Slipping the basket over her forearm, she strode in the direction she thought she'd heard the voice coming from. As she rounded a weeping angel tombstone, so old and discolored the writing could scarce be read anymore, she skidded to a halt.

A man—a very startlingly attractive man—lay amongst the dead.

Rather, surrounded by a low, pointed iron fence, he lounged atop what must be his greatcoat, his back against a six-foot marble marker. Even in death, the dukes and duchesses of Sutcliffe, as well as their immediate kin, kept themselves separated from the commoners—those they deemed beneath their illustrious blue-blooded touch.

That was what the locals claimed, in any event.

She'd never found the Sutcliffes uppity or unfriendly. A mite stuffy and formal, for certain, as nobility often were, but never unkind. Not that she'd spent a great deal of time in any of their company.

Preposterously long legs crossed at the ankles and his raven hair disheveled as if he been running his fingers through it, the gentleman took a lengthy swig from a green bottle.

Whisky.

Father would kick up a fierce dust if he found out.

The tanned column of the man's throat, a startling contrast to the snowfall of a neckcloth beneath his chin, worked as he swallowed again.

Something had him overwrought.

As he lowered his arm, she widened her eyes.

He's home!

Theadosia's heartbeat stuttered a trifle as she raked her gaze over Victor, the Duke of Sutcliffe. Though she hadn't seen him in three and one-half years, she easily recognized his grace.

A wave of sympathy swept her.

She also knew what tormented him.

His father's suicide.

'Twas his father's grave he sat upon.

Eyes closed, his sable lashes fans against his sculpted cheekbones, the duke lifted the bottle once more.

"You didn't even leave a note telling us why."

Theadosia wasn't supposed to know the reason the seventh duke had hanged himself. Such things were never discussed except behind closed doors. Her Father, the rector of All Saint's Church, frowned upon gossip or tattle of any sort.

What she thought surely must be a tear leaked from the corner of his grace's eye. His obvious grief tore at her soft heart.

She shouldn't.

Her parents wouldn't approve. In fact, Father absolutely forbade it.

Biting her lower lip, Theadosia closed her eyes for an instant.

She really, *really* should not.

But she would.

She couldn't bear to see the duke's suffering.

Reservations resolutely, if somewhat unwisely, tamped down, she passed through the gaping gate.

"Your father had stomach cancer. I overheard Papa telling Mama one day after your father . . . That is, after he died. Papa felt guilty for not telling you and your mother, but the duke swore him to secrecy, and of course he had no idea your father would . . ." Why people choose to keep such serious matters from their families boggled the mind.

Eyelids flying open, his grace jerked upright.

His hypnotic gaze snared hers, and yes, moisture glinted there.

Her heart gave a queer leap.

She remembered his vibrant eyes, the shade somewhere between silver and pewter with the merest hint of ocean blue around the irises. Not cold eyes, despite their cool colors. No, his eyes brimmed with intelligence and usually kindness, and they crinkled at the corners when he laughed. He'd laughed often as a young man; her brother James had been one of his constant companions whenever his grace was in residence at Ridgewood Court.

"Cancer?" His eyelids drifted shut again, and he nodded. "*Ahhh.*"

That single word revealed he understood.

Mayhap he'd find a degree of peace now.

"Thank you for telling me," he said.

"I've always thought you should know."

He should have been told years ago.

Bracing himself on his father's headstone, the duke maneuvered to his feet. With the whisky bottle dangling from one hand, he squinted as if trying to focus his bleary-eyed gaze.

"Theadosia?" Uncertainty raised his deep voice higher on the last syllable as he looked her up and down, an appreciative gleam in his eye.

"Thea, is that truly you?"

Only her siblings and dearest friends called her Thea.

His surprise was warranted. Mama said Theadosia had been a late bloomer. She'd almost despaired of developing proper womanly curves.

She bobbed a half curtsy and grinned.

"It is indeed, Your Grace. I'm all grown up now." At sixteen—embarrassingly infatuated with him and possessing a figure a broomstick might envy—she'd believed herself a woman full grown. Time had taught her otherwise.

The duke's extended absence had caused a great deal of conjecture and speculation, and many, including her, wondered if he'd ever return to Colchester.

She so yearned to ask why he'd come back after all this time, but etiquette prohibited any such thing.

He hitched his mouth into a sideways smile as his gaze roved over her.

"I'll say you are. And you've blossomed into quite a beauty too. Always knew you would."

He'd noticed the thin, gawky girl with the blotchy complexion? She'd barely been able to cobble two words together in his presence.

A delicious sensation, sweet and warm, similar to fresh pulled taffy, budded behind her breastbone. She shouldn't be flattered at his drunken ravings. In fact, she ought to reproach him for his brazen compliment. After all, he was a known rapscallion, a man about town, "a philandering rake," Papa avowed. Nevertheless, it wasn't every day a devilishly handsome duke called her beautiful.

Actually, rarely did anyone remark on her features.

Her father frowned on the praise of outward appearances, which explained why the gentlemen he'd encouraged her to turn her attention to couldn't be said to be pleasing to the eye.

The Lord tells us not to consider appearance or height, but to look at a man's heart, he admonished Thea and her sister regularly.

Easier to do if the man didn't boast buck teeth, a hooked nose to rival a parrot's beak, or a propensity to sweat like a race horse: the last three curates, respectively.

His grace, on the other hand, was most pleasing to the eye. Oh, indeed he most assuredly was.

Deliciously tall—perfect for a woman of her height—and classically handsome, his face all aristocratic planes and angles. Even the severe blade of his nose and the lashing of his black brows spoke of generations of refined breeding.

Papa, a plain featured, thick man himself, had married a Scottish beauty. It truly wasn't fair he demanded otherwise of his offspring.

Why couldn't he find a good-hearted *and* somewhat attractive man to woo his middle daughter?

Was that too much to ask?

But she knew why.

Because a handsome face *had* turned his eldest daughter Althea's head, and she'd run off with a performer from the Summer Faire. For the past two and a half years, Papa had forbidden anyone to utter her name.

Theadosia's heart ached anew. How she longed for word from her beloved sister, but if Althea had ever sent a letter, Papa hadn't mentioned it. His blasted pride wouldn't permit it.

Even Mama, more tolerant and good-natured than Papa, didn't dare remind him what the Good Book said about pride and forgiveness.

Sighing, Theadosia ran her gaze over the duke again.

James would be delighted when he came up from London next.

"A pleasure to see you again, Miss Thea."

A charming smile flashed across his grace's noble countenance as he bent into a wobbly gallant's bow—dropping the whisky bottle and nearly falling onto his face for his efforts. He chuckled at his own clumsiness.

She dropped the basket and rushed forward to brace him with one hand on his broad—*very broad*—shoulder and the other on his solid chest. Being a prudent miss, she dismissed the electric jolt sluicing up both arms. This was not the time for missish shyness or false pretenses of demureness.

Imagine the scandal if his grace were found insensate, reeking of whisky, atop his father's grave? This was *not* the homecoming she'd imagined for him over the years.

"Do have a care, sir, or you will crack your skull." Supporting his great weight, for his form wasn't that of simpering dandy, but a man accustomed to physical exertion, she slanted him a sideways glance. "I believe you've over-indulged."

A great deal, truth to tell.

"How ever will you manage your way home to Ridgewood Court?"

"The same way I came to be here in this dreary place." Giving her a boyish sideways grin, he waggled his fingers in the general direction of the lane. "I shall walk, fair maiden."

"I think not. 'Tis a good mile, and you're in no condition to make the hike."

"Do you fret for me, Thea?" His rich voice had gone all low and raspy.

He lowered his head and pressed his nose into her neck as he wrapped his arms around her and pulled her flush with his body.

Shouldn't she be offended or afraid?

Yet she wasn't either.

"*Mmm*, you smell good. Like sunshine and honeysuckle."

He smelled of strong spirits, horse, and sandalwood. And something else she couldn't quite identify. She couldn't very well lean in and sniff to determine what the scent was, as he'd boldly ventured to do.

His grace inhaled a deep breath, another unnerving sound she couldn't identify reverberating in his throat. "Intoxicating," he rumbled against her neck, his lips tickling the sensitive flesh.

Trying—*unsuccessfully*—to ignore the heady pleasure of being near him, Theadosia tilted her head away whilst bracing her hands against the wall that was his chest.

"You are the one who's intoxicated and don't know what you're saying."

Why must she sound breathless?

The exertion of holding him upright. That must be it.

"Your Grace." She gave that unyielding wall a shove. "You must release me before someone sees us."

Not much chance of that with evening's mantle descending, but it was foolish to tempt Providence.

"I'm not so foxed that I don't know what to do with a beautiful woman in my arms."

There was the rogue Papa had warned her and Jessica about.

The sharp retort meant to remind him of his place was replaced by a sigh as his lips brushed hers.

Once.

Twice.

And again, with more urgency.

Did she resist as a proper, moral cleric's daughter ought to? Summon outrage or indignation? Even the merest bit?

Lord help her, no.

Was she as wanton as Althea?

Did such wickedness run in families?

She stood there, ensconced in his arms, and let him kiss her. She may have even kissed him back, but her mind was such a muddle of delicious sensations, akin to floating on a fluffy cloud, she couldn't be certain.

His soft yet firm lips tasted of whisky and something more.

Passion, perhaps?

"And here, Mr. Leadford, are the church burial grounds."

"We have graves dating over two hundred years ago, prior to the erection of All Saint Church's current buildings."

Her father's voice, drifting to her from several rows away, succeeded in yanking Theadosia back to earth and apparently sobered his grace as well. At once she disengaged herself from his embrace.

She risked much if she were caught. Everything, in fact. Papa had expressly prohibited his remaining daughters to be unchaperoned in the company of males over the age of twelve.

"I'm confident you'll feel as blessed as I do as you assist in the shepherding of my flock." Pride resonated in Papa's deep voice, quite useful for his booming Sunday morning sermons. "I confess, I've been a trifle lax in my paperwork the past few months. The last curate was a Godsend when it came to organization, record keeping, and correspondences. Such matters are not amongst my strengths."

"Fret not, for those are my fortes as well, Mr. Brentwood," a pleasant but unfamiliar voice replied."

"I'm well pleased to hear it," her father replied.

Another new curate?

That made four in as many years. A quartet of unattached males seeking a modest woman of respectable birth to take to wife. Thus far, she and her younger sister, Jessica, had been spared.

Fortunately, each of the former curates had selected a docile— *ambitious*—parishioner from the congregation to wed before moving on to their own parish.

Unfortunately, All Saint's Church had few unassuming, unattached misses of marriageable age left.

"Thea . . .?"

The duke reached for her again.

"*Shh!*"

She pressed her gloved fingers against his lips, and he promptly gripped her hand and pressed a kiss to her wrist.

"Stop that," she whispered, tugging her hand away whilst silently ordering the fluttering in her tummy to cease.

"My father's near. I *cannot* be found in a compromising position with you. He'll be livid. *Please.* Let go, sir."

She'd be disowned on the spot. Cast out and shunned. Her name never uttered by her family again. She'd never see them again either. Ever.

Imagining Papa's infuriated reaction sent a tremor down her spine.

Even in his stupor, the duke must've sensed her fright and urgency, for he released her at once and put a respectable distance between them.

"I'd prefer you call me Sutcliffe or Victor."

What did she owe that honor to?

Sutcliffe she might consider, but she could not use his given name, except in her mind. Only the closest of relatives and friends might address him by anything other than his title.

As Theadosia stepped even farther away and righted her bonnet, her foot struck the whisky bottle. Her gaze fell on the forgotten basket outside the fence. *Bother and rot.* She could only pray her father's tour didn't include this portion of the grounds.

An exclamation, followed by a flurry of whispers, made her whirl toward the lane paralleling the churchyard.

The elderly Nabity sisters, bony arms entwined and heads bent near, stood on the pathway.

What had they seen?

Theadosia closed her eyes.

Pray God, only her conversing with the duke, a respectable distance between them, and nothing more.

His grace turned to where she peered so intently. Wearing a silly, boyish grin, he bowed once more, this time with more control, though he swayed on his feet in imitation of a sapling battered by a winter tempest.

"Good afternoon, dear ladies. I do hope I'll have the pleasure of speaking with you after services Sunday. I've missed your keen wit and your delicious seed cake these many years."

In unison, their sagging chins dropped nearly to their flat-as-a-washboard chests, before they bobbed their heads in affirmation and, tittering in the irksome manner of green schoolgirls, toddled off. Probably to make their famed confection.

"I think you said that just so they'd make you seed cake." The rascal.

"You've found me out."

An unabashed grin quirked his mouth, and she pressed her lips together, remembering the heady sensation of his mouth on hers.

"Theadosia? What the devil goes on here?"

2

*P*apa.

Stifling the unladylike oath she wasn't even supposed to know, let alone think or say, Theadosia shot the duke a now-look-what-you've-done glance. Papa would be horrified to know what naughtiness she'd learned from her closest friends over the years.

Where they came by the knowledge she had no idea, nor did she want to know.

His grace had the good sense to arrange his face into a solemn mien, though she swore mischief danced in his half-closed eyes. Hard to tell with the fading light, however.

Affecting nonchalance despite her runaway pulse and the fear of discovery tightening her tummy, she summoned a sunny smile and edged forward until her gown covered the forgotten bottle of "devil's drink", as her father called whisky.

"Papa. Look who's returned to Colchester."

She swept her hand toward the duke.

Papa's expression remained severe as he took the duke's measure.

Not good.

Perchance if she distracted her father by mentioning his latest fundraising venture to improve All Saints, he wouldn't become angry at what he was sure to deem her most indecorous behavior.

"His grace was telling me how eager he is to hear you preach this Sunday, and he said he'd be honored to contribute the balance needed for the new chamber organ. You'll be able to order it now. Isn't that marvelous? Imagine how lovely the music echoing in the sanctuary will be every Sunday and at Christmastide."

One of Papa's stern brows twitched in interest.

Perfect. He'd taken the bait.

Now to gently reel him in.

Contriving her most grateful smile, she caught the duke's eye.

Distinct amusement and a mite of 'what-are-you-about-now?' danced along the edges of his face.

"And his grace suggested it only fitting that the choir have new cassocks and surplices. He insists upon covering their cost as well. Isn't it a blessing?"

Would God judge her for fibbing?

He well should.

Even if the lies were well intended?

Or contrived out of dread?

More on point and of greater worry now, would the duke deny her declarations?

The chamber organ's cost was most dear. For over two years the congregation had fund-raised, but Papa said they still hadn't collected half the necessary monies. To volunteer the duke's purse was beyond the pale, but she truly must divert Papa from jumping to the wrong—*actually accurate*—conclusion.

Why had she been so impulsive?

She should've alerted her father that someone was in distress in the cemetery, and not taken it upon herself to intervene.

But then she wouldn't have been kissed until she forgot she was a reverend's daughter.

"Naturally, if there is to be a new organ, the choir is deserving of new robes," the Duke of Sutcliffe murmured in a droll tone.

Was that a wink, the brazen bounder?

Had Papa seen?

Her father's speculative gaze flicked between her and the duke, then the ostentatious marker behind his grace before his features relaxed, and he offered his version of a sanctimonious smile: mouth closed, lips tilted up a fraction, his expression benign.

Placing his palms together in a prayer-like pose, he dipped his gray-streaked head the merest bit.

"Your benevolence is much appreciated, Your Grace. I'm sure our Lord is as delighted as I that you've chosen to follow your parents' practices of regular church attendance and generous patronage to the parish."

"As you say, Mr. Brentwood."

His grace inclined his head, all traces of his earlier boyishness and inebriation now concealed. Either the duke was practiced at artifice or he was a superb actor. Or mayhap he hadn't been as tippled as she believed.

Thank goodness he hadn't disputed her grand declaration about his generous donation.

Later she'd have to apologize and beg his forgiveness for her duplicity.

"Permit me to introduce our newest curate, Your Grace." Papa indicated the amiable clergyman who hadn't stopped smiling since he'd rounded the tombstone. "Mr. Leadford, this is His Grace, Victor, Duke of Sutcliffe, and my daughter, Theadosia. Sir, Theadosia, this is Mr. Hector Leadford."

Possessing piercing blue eyes in an unremarkable, but kind face, Mr. Leadford bowed.

Something about him raised her nape hairs, but she couldn't put her finger on what.

"Your Grace. Miss Brentwood. It is a pleasure to make both of your acquaintances."

His gaze lingered a mite longer than entirely professional, or necessary, on Theadosia, and distinct appreciation glinted in his striking eyes.

Mayhap his interest is what she's sensed.

"I hope you enjoy our township, Mr. Leadford, and that you'll feel at home here very soon."

Theadosia returned his smile, mindful to keep hers polite but slightly distant lest she encourage his regard. Exactly as she and Jessica had been taught to do. In Papa's view, encouraging male attention was akin to running naked through Colchester banging on a drum.

The only man's esteem she desired—had ever desired—stood but a few feet from her. A man far beyond her reach, she knew full well. A man she measured all others against, which was truly unfair, for it was impossible for anyone else to compete with the duke. In her mind, at least.

A man whose elevated station required Papa's deference, but also a man of whom her father would never approve. The Duke of Sutcliffe was precisely the kind of man Papa disdained—one who lived for pleasure alone, or so her father claimed. Honestly, she didn't think he admired anyone other than clergymen, and none other would do for his daughters.

The wind whistled between the tombstones, and the duke leaned down to retrieve his coat and hat. Dusk was fully upon them now, and the candlelight shining from the windows of the parsonage lent a welcoming glow to the graveyard.

Theadosia sent him a short, speaking glance before lowering her attention to her feet in what Papa would assume was diffident behavior, but was, in fact, the only hint she could give the Duke of Sutcliffe.

She couldn't move lest the bottle be revealed.

If Papa discovered his grace had been imbibing hard spirits whilst on Church grounds, he'd have an apoplexy. It wouldn't do for her father to ban the most powerful man in the county from All Saints Church. Nor would it do for Papa to offend the newly returned duke. And it most assuredly would not do for her to be caught hiding the bottle.

Papa's wrath, though rare, was terrifying.

Sutcliffe draped his coat over his forearm and, holding his beaver hat between his forefinger and thumb, pondered his father's grave.

"I beg your indulgence, though the hour grows late. I would appreciate a few more moments' privacy."

Papa pressed his lips together in sympathetic understanding and nodded.

"Yes, of course. Mr. Leadford, let's enjoy a glass of port in the salon before supper, shall we? I do believe I smelled chicken fricassee and cherry pie earlier." He waved the other clergyman before him and paused to glance over his shoulder. "I look forward to seeing you and your mother Sunday morning."

"It was a pleasure to make your acquaintance," Mr. Leadford repeated as he bent to retrieve the discarded basket. He'd clearly discerned who it belonged to, and it appeared he intended to be the gallant.

Beaming his approval, Papa didn't even ask why she'd abandoned the basket.

Praise the Almighty for small favors.

As soon as her father faced away, Mr. Leadford's attention sank to her bosoms, then lower still, and her stomach clenched.

Now her nape hairs stood straight up and wiggled about, and she resisted the urge to retreat from his frank perusal.

Pray to God Mr. Leadford wasn't Papa's choice of a husband for her.

At twenty, Theadosia couldn't hope to continue to claim she was too young to wed, and that Papa intended to select a man of his own ilk for his younger two daughters became more apparent every day.

It was her own fault she wanted more than spiritual companionship.

No, her friend, Nicolette, was partially to blame for sneaking Theadosia romance novels to read. They lay tucked beneath a floorboard under the bed she and Jessica shared. Nicolette had promised to lend her latest books when Theadosia saw her next.

God help her if Papa ever learned of them. He wasn't a harsh or unreasonable man; he simply had a very strict moral code he vehemently enforced. More so since Althea had eloped.

Sutcliffe inclined his head before turning his attention to Theadosia and bidding her farewell with a nod and a penetrating look.

"Miss Brentwood."

"Your Grace." She curtsied but didn't move.

Papa was too close.

Without a doubt, though evening was upon them, he'd see the bright green bottle.

"Theadosia, why are you standing there?" Giving her the gimlet eye, her father pressed his mouth into a stern line. "His grace requested privacy. Hurry inside. Your mother and sister need your assistance with supper. Come along now."

Speaking low to Mr. Leadford, Papa angled in the direction of the Church, and the duke seized the opportunity to drop his hat—right at her feet.

"I beg your pardon."

His mouth twitched with concealed amusement.

She neatly stepped aside as he squatted and retrieved the hat whilst tucking the bottle beneath the folds of his coat with his other hand.

"Oh, well done, you," she whispered, quite enjoying their colluding.

"Thank you for saving me much embarrassment." His confidential tone heated her to her toes. "And for telling me about my father's illness."

"Theadosia Josephine Clarice!" More than impatience tinged Papa's voice. "Stop dawdling."

Had he discerned her interest in the duke?

"I'm coming, Papa."

"Mr. Brentwood?"

His grace stared past her head.

Papa turned, one grizzled brow cocked in inquiry.

"Yes?"

"I can see that my father's grave has been well tended, and I thank you."

Theadosia had taken on the duty, though she'd be hard put to give an excuse as to why. She'd convinced herself it was for the Duchess of Sutcliffe's sake. Still grieving, the woman visited her husband's grave for an hour every Sunday after services. When the weather permitted, she took lunch there too, her servants setting a table as fine as if she were dining at Windsor Castle with the king.

Poor lady.

Papa's keen gaze slid to Theadosia again, but he merely dipped his head and didn't reveal her secret. Curious that. It was of no matter if the duke learned of it.

"I'd deem it an honor if you and your family, and Mr. Leadford, of course,"—that last seemed an afterthought on the duke's part—"would join us for dinner at Ridgewood Friday next."

Fingers crossed, she held her breath. She'd have time to finish her new gown by then. A couple of months ago, Papa had permitted Mama, Jessica, and Theadosia each four new gowns, as well as a new bonnet, gloves, and slippers. They'd never been afforded such luxuries before, and now that his grace had returned, she was even more grateful she'd not have to attend supper in one of her remade garments.

An intimate dinner with the Sutcliffes.

Oh, the marvel of it.

Her dearest friends, Nicolette Twistleton, twins Ophelia and Gabriella Breckensole, and their widowed cousin Everleigh Chatterton would demand all the details about the dinner when she and Jessica next met them for tea.

Please let Papa say yes. He must. *He must.*

She made her way to her father's side, but her dratted feet refused to budge an inch farther before she heard his reply.

"It would be our pleasure, Your Grace. I shall inform Marianne."

Papa's attention gravitated to the grand marble marker again.

Victor—that was, Sutcliffe—had found his father that awful night. He'd cut his body loose, and carried his sire into the house. Such was his anguish, afterward, he'd hacked the willow down and burned every last branch, even setting fire to the stump.

In the days following the duke's suicide, that topic had been on everyone's tongue except the Brentwoods'.

"If I may be of assistance in any way, do let me know. I am always available to counsel parishioners." Papa's offer was genuine. He truly cared for his flock and those that were suffering.

"There is one thing, if I may?" A wry smile bent the duke's mouth up on one side as he placed his hat atop his dark head. "I should very much appreciate you performing my wedding ceremony in August."

Theadosia flushed hot. Then cold. Then hot again.

Moisture flooded her eyes, blurring the grass she stared at.

He's betrothed.

That was why he'd returned. Of course he'd want to get married here. Why hadn't she considered such a thing? His homecoming wasn't because he'd missed Colchester at all. He'd probably leave straightaway after he exchanged vows too.

Swallowing gut-wrenching disappointment, she forced her feet to move. Stupid to have entertained fanciful hope all these years: a child's ridiculous fantasy. Daughters of rectors couldn't—shouldn't—yearn for passion and adventure. That was the drivel of romance novels. No, they married men of equal station. Staid, religious fellows with nice eyes and kind faces.

But not men who leered at bosoms.

"Indeed. Congratulations." Sincere excitement lit her father's voice. Except for Christmastide services, he adored nothing more than performing wedding ceremonies. "Do we know your future duchess?"

Did they?

Please God, not one of my friends.

No, the girls would've mentioned something as monumental, and there'd not been as much as a whisper about the Duke of Sutcliffe's upcoming nuptials.

An outsider then.

Likely some elegant, blue-blooded debutant with unblemished alabaster skin, petite feet, and a dowry so immense a team of dray horses couldn't pull the treasure.

Theadosia's dowry wouldn't fill a teapot. Or a teacup, for that matter.

She couldn't resist a last glance over her shoulder, and her gaze collided with Sutcliffe's.

"Perhaps." Another smile, this one humorless, hitched his grace's mouth up a notch. He seemed to speak directly at her.

"I confess, I don't know who she'll be yet."

3

The next afternoon, after suffering through a wretched head-pounding, stomach-churning morning thanks to his over-indulgence, Victor made his way to the sunroom.

The same gilded-framed portraits and paintings lined the walls, the same Aubusson rugs adorned the floors, and the same valuable trinkets and knickknacks topped the rosewood tables as he strode the wide corridor to the west wing.

Everything remained as it had been when he left, and yet nothing would ever be the same. He'd seen the very worst in himself as he tried to bury his grief and anger. Drinking, womanizing, and gaming—engaging in all the vices his sire had abstained from and denounced.

Rubbing his left brow with two finger pads, he closed his eyes for a moment. A niggling ache had settled there. Past experience had taught him the pain would remain with him for several hours. How many more hangovers must he endure before he forswore drunkenness?

How heartily disappointed Father would be. Mother too.

With justification, for until yesterday, Victor had intended to find the dowdiest, most biddable mousey miss to take to wife. And when he returned to London to resume his philandering lifestyle, he'd leave her at Ridgewood to keep Mama company. That plan hadn't altered, but knowing Father had taken his life instead of letting cancer steal it from him had made a difference in how he felt about his sire.

Not enough of a difference to make him want to stay at Ridgewood, though the knowledge stripped him of the excuse to carouse to excess anymore.

Partially.

Now a new fear taunted him. Grandfather had also died of cancer, as had an uncle. Was Victor the disease's next victim? Did that horror lurk in his future?

A smirk of self-reproach tipped his lips as he knocked softly on the doorframe of the sunroom's open door.

"Do you have a moment, Mother?"

Pulling her spectacles from her nose and laying aside the volume she'd been reading, she smiled a warm greeting and patted the settee.

"Victor, darling. Of course I do. What is it you need, dearest?"

Two years past her fifth decade, with only a few silvery strands amongst her ebony hair, his mother was a lovely woman. He'd inherited her hair and mouth, but it was his father's eyes that peered back at him in the mirror each morning.

His stomach tumbled.

Would he ever get the image of those bulging sightless orbs out of his mind?

He kissed her upturned cheek, the lightly powdered flesh soft and unlined. Nudging her raggedy cat, Primrose, out of the way, he settled onto the ruby brocade cushion beside his mother. Now his dark maroon jacket would be covered with orange and white cat hair.

Primrose cracked open her one citrine eye and yawned, baring her needle-sharp fangs before lazily stretching and hopping onto the floor. In the most immodest display, she proceeded to groom herself.

Why ever had he thought to have the mangy beast delivered to Mother when he'd found it lying injured beside a barrel on London's wharf?

Because he knew his mother was lonely.

Her blue eyes brimming with happiness, she patted his cheek as she had when he was a small lad.

"I'm glad you're home, Victor."

She'd never complained about his neglect, which served to increase his guilt all the more.

Naturally, he'd written at least weekly and sent gifts too. His two sisters had visited regularly, their husbands and offspring in tow. Mother told him as much in her letters. But other than the dozen staff members who kept Ridgewood Court operating without a hitch, and her spoiled beyond redemption one-eyed cat, no one else resided in the house.

Thrice he'd directed the coach to be readied for the journey from London to Colchester. In the end, the grotesque image of his father's dangling body slowly spiraling 'round and 'round sent him in search of strong drink instead.

Damn him for a selfish arse; if it weren't for the stipulation in his father's will that he marry by his seven-and-twentieth birthday, or everything unentailed, including Ridgewood Court, transferred to his cousin, Victor mightn't have returned even now.

He'd never know why Father added that addendum only a few months before he died. At the reading of the will, Mother had been equally startled about the extra provision.

But she loved Ridgewood Court. It was here she'd come as a giddy new bride and here she'd given birth to her three children. And it was here that her husband, the man she'd adored for eight-and-twenty years, had taken his own life.

Did Mother know Father had cancer?

She would suffer no more loss or pain if Victor could prevent it. For certain she would not lose her home, which meant he had just over a month to locate a suitable bride. He'd chosen to return to Colchester, to his boyhood home, hoping there or somewhere in Essex, he could find a woman content to remain at Ridgewood while he resumed his life in London.

Small likelihood of that if he wanted an heir. But did he after all, given the cancer that ran in the family line? Even less possibility he'd be anywhere near as happy as his parents had been, for theirs had been a love match.

In fact, if he stood any chance of meeting his father's deadline, he would have to enlist Mother's help. He shouldn't have waited this long to come back to Ridgewood, but every time he considered returning home, the vision of his father's lifeless body stopped him.

Even now the image tormented him.

The corpse had been warm when Victor found him.

If only he'd been a few moments sooner he might have saved his father's life. But he hadn't known about the cancer either. Would watching his father die a slow, agonizingly painful death truly have been better?

Mother clasped Victor's hand and gave his fingers a tiny squeeze.

"Victor? What is it? You look troubled, and it's only your first day home."

"Mother, there's something about Father's death you might not know."

Her blank expression revealed what he suspected. She hadn't known either.

"He didn't just—" He paused and covered her hand with his. "Father had stomach cancer."

She gasped, pressing a palm to her throat as tears welled. Struggling for control, she withdrew a lacy scrap from her sleeve and dabbed at her eyes. At last, she collected herself and raised grief-ravaged eyes to his.

"I suspected he was ill, but when I questioned him, he said it was nothing to fret about. When and how did you find out?"

"Yesterday, at All Saint's Church. Theadosia Brentwood told me. She overheard her father some time ago and feared speaking of it. I'm glad she did. It was the not knowing why that ate away at me."

"Trust me, darling, I well understand that." She gave a tremulous, fragile smile. Sniffing, she touched the handkerchief to the corner of her eye again. "Cancer." She nodded, lips pressed tight. "Yes, he wouldn't have wanted to die that way, the way his uncle did. It was awful."

Hanging himself was so much better?

Victor shook off his morbid mental musings and forced a cheerful smile.

"I hope it's not an imposition, but while visiting Father's grave yesterday, I invited the Brentwoods and the new curate to dine with us next Friday."

Best not tell Mama he'd been a maudlin drunk when Thea came upon him.

Thea.

He'd nearly been struck dumb upon seeing her. Her soft brown eyes, the color of lightly burnt sugar—as sweet and warm too—had lit up in delight when she recognized him. An answering joy had peeled inside his soul as well.

By God, she'd grown into a beauty.

Even soused as he had been, he noticed the glow of her ivory skin, her finely arched brows, that pert pink rosebud mouth, and those jaunty reddish-blonde curls framing her oval face.

No timid mouse there.

She most definitely did not fit into his well thought out scheme of marrying and abandoning his bride.

Now where had that thought come from? It was ridiculous, surely.

"We've plenty of time to prepare. It's not an imposition at all. In fact, with your permission, I'd like to have a house party in a couple of weeks or so." Mama's eyes glittered, and she clapped her hands twice in excitement. "Oh, let's do have a ball too, Victor. That is if you're agreeable. It's been a long while since music and gaiety filled Ridgewood. Your sisters could come stay as well."

How could he deny her?

Relaxing against the back of the settee while hooking his ankle across his knee, he nodded.

"Yes, I think that's a grand idea. Do invite the Brentwoods, won't you?"

"All right darling, but I doubt they'll attend."

He stopped toying with the tapestry pillow. "Why?"

"I don't think you're aware, but the eldest Brentwood girl eloped a couple of years ago. With a traveling musician or acrobat or some such unpromising person." She waved her hand casually. "It caused quite a stir. You should be aware the reverend won't speak of her at all, nor will he permit others to. His daughters are rarely permitted social functions that aren't church related. He may not allow them to attend the house party or ball."

"That's awfully harsh, don't you think?"

It explained why Thea had been worried about being caught with him yesterday. It also dashed his excuse to hold her in his arms again while he waltzed her 'round the ballroom or terrace.

Mother rolled a shoulder. "He's a man of rigid beliefs, and while I do not approve of his daughter's scandalous behavior, I think it wiser to be merciful and slow to judge. We don't always know what motivates someone to take extreme action."

Sorrow turned her mouth down.

Now she spoke of Father.

Even after all this time, she grieved for him. They'd been soulmates, and when Father died, a part of Mother had too. Little chance she'd marry again. Still . . . Mayhap he'd add a name or two to the guest list. Available gentlemen of a certain age of whom *he* approved. No rogues or rakes, no men of *his* ilk, for his Mother.

He hesitated a moment. Might as well crack on and ask for her help in acquiring a bride. It might help distract her. "I'm certain you recall I must wed in August, or the unentailed property transfers to Jeffery."

Jeffery was a decent chap, and yet it grated to think he'd inherit simply because Victor had dawdled too long in finding a duchess.

"I know, dear." A soft, understanding smile curved her mouth. "And I knew when you were ready, you'd come home and face that dragon. I honestly cannot fathom what possessed your father to add that stipulation."

Neither could Victor, unless it was to guarantee the duchy an heir. "We'll never know, but I hope you will be able to advise me in my search for a bride. You know more than I who the eligible young ladies are in the area, and you know what I require in a duchess."

He'd no doubt that whomever he selected, the chosen lady would eagerly agree to the match. What sensible woman would turn down becoming a duchess?

Expression contemplative, her attention focused on the gardens beyond the mullioned windows, she held her chin between her thumb and bent forefinger.

"What about love, my dear? I'd much rather you waited until you found someone you love."

Victor sighed and rubbed his fingertips across his forehead.

"I shan't have you lose your home because of my selfishness." He pressed his lips together. He'd cause her no more unhappiness. "I know you love Ridgewood."

"Darling, I can live anywhere as long as my children visit. Your sisters invited me to live with them numerous times, but I've stayed at Ridgewood for you." Patting his hand, she offered a gentle smile. "To give you a reason to return and face your demons."

She'd stayed here alone when she could've been with one of her daughters and grandchildren? All the more reason he could not disappoint.

"And it's because of your generosity, Mother, that I cannot ignore the codicil."

"Victor, even the best of marriages endures many challenges, and I worry that without love . . ."

"I've considered that, but the most I can strive for at this late juncture is to find someone compatible. Father robbed me of the chance for love."

Just as well.

Not one to deceive himself, he knew there was scant risk of a shattered heart in a marriage of convenience. Mother was a far stronger person than he, because he wouldn't take the chance of loving someone with all his being as his parents had. He'd seen what that kind of affection had done to his mother. Seen her utter devastation. No, better to not have emotions involved, most particularly since he was rushing into the *blessed* event, and he too might perish from cancer.

Fine lines of concern fanning the corners of her loving eyes as she searched his face, his mother seemed to come to a decision. She inhaled deeply and clasped her hands.

"All right. Let's start with a guest list that includes all the eligible young women in Essex."

"All of them?" Precisely how many were there? "I was thinking of a half dozen of the most quiet and acquiescent—"

Her delighted laughter rang out.

"Oh, darling, no, no." Another trill of laughter filled the room. "You'd be utterly miserable with a biddable wife. Oh, my goodness no! You're too intense to tolerate a compliant, submissive duchess for long. She'd bore you within months, and I fear your eye would stray. That would be unfair to her, since I know too well you are a man who will demand fidelity from your duchess. No, I think a spirited girl who gives as good as she gets is a far better choice for you."

Hell and damnation.

She'd just thrown a huge hurdle in his plan, even if she was bloody right.

"To avoid hurt feelings, however, I shall invite all the unmarried ladies in Essex. Even the Nabity spinsters. Does that satisfy you?"

Her mouth trembled, and he grinned. Her good humor was contagious.

"Perhaps you ought to select those of childbearing age, unless you don't want more grandchildren?"

Could he really subject his children to the same sort of pain he'd endured if this new fear of cancer became a reality? And what if his children were susceptible to the demon disease?

What choice had he?

Let Jeffery inherit the duchy too? What good would that do? They shared a grandfather and their paternal grand uncle had died from cancer.

"I may not produce any offspring, you know."

"*La*, Victor Nathanial Horatio, don't say such a wicked thing! The Sutcliffes have never forfeited in that department." She swatted his arm, and as she rose from the settee, she chuckled. "You must admit hosting a ball and inviting all the eligible women in the area so you might find a duchess is similar to the fairytale, Cendrillon, is it not?"

Victor also stood. He draped his arm around her shoulders and kissed the crown of her head.

"Except I'm no prince, and there won't be a magical happily-ever-after."

"Don't be too sure. I knew the moment I saw Sutcliffe I'd marry him, and he swore he fell in love with me during our first dance." Lost in her long-ago memory, a sad, fragile smile tipped her mouth. After a moment, she collected herself and patted his shoulder. "If you've anyone else you'd like to invite to the house party and ball besides the friends you already wrote to ask if they might visit, you can tell me their names later."

Yes, as well as the middling-aged banker *Jerome* DuBoise and the widower Major Rupert Marston. One gentleman or the other might possibly be the solution to Mother's loneliness.

"It's times like this I do wish I had a secretary. Primrose is going to help me, aren't you sweetums?" She bent and scooped the tabby into her arms. "Now you run along, dear. Get some fresh air. I have to speak with Cook about next week's menu, and I have a guest list to compile."

She did indeed know Victor well. Understood this talk of weddings and brides and balls exacted a toll he couldn't keep hidden.

"Thank you, Mother. I think I'll go for a walk before my ride. There's another dragon I need to face."

This one a massive, angry, fire-breathing demon he must conquer before it destroyed him.

If he was going to marry and stay at Ridgewood Court for any length of time, he must face the image tormenting him. After giving her another hug and scratching Primrose behind her scruffy ears, he strode to the door.

"Oh, Victor. We need to set a date for the ball. There's a full moon in three weeks. Is that too soon?" Mother had followed him to the doorway. "That way you have time left if you don't find your bride before then or on that night."

Her forced cheerfulness didn't fool him. She didn't approve, but because she loved him, she'd support his rash decision.

"Three weeks is fine." Feeling decidedly wicked, he winked. "In fact, why don't you put *Duke seeks Duchess* on the invitation. No better yet, *A dance will decide the Duke of Sutcliffe's duchess.*"

"You inherited your father's droll sense of humor, darling, but I think you may be onto something. Let me ponder on it." She waved her hand at him, indicating he should proceed her out the door. "Now shoo."

One lodestone's weight lifted from his shoulders, Victor left the house after asking Grover, the butler, to send word to the stables to have Acheron saddled.

Mother would indeed see that every eligible miss in all of Essex was invited to the ball. All he had to do was pick one to be his duchess. But how to determine the right one? Or rather, not the worst one?

What did he really want in a wife?

Biddable and bashful, or boisterous and bold?

A vixen or an angel?

Why couldn't she be a bit of both?

Thea's impish smile flashed to mind.

He'd tasted that sweet mouth yesterday. Sampled enough to make him want more. Crave more than settling for a marriage of convenience. *A marriage of necessity.*

But time was against him, and he'd been selfish long enough, and no force on God's Earth would prevent him from marrying in order for Mother to remain at Ridgewood.

Somehow, he didn't think Theadosia Brentwood was the type of woman to marry for station or convenience, more was the pity. He sighed. Else he'd end his search for a duchess before it began. It didn't matter that she was a commoner. He couldn't care less that she'd never left Colchester in her entire life and knew nothing of *haut ton* customs.

Or that the minx had lied most adeptly yesterday.

He'd seen the apology in her soft gaze, had noticed her silently pleading for him not to betray her.

Surely, if he offered for her, she'd be content to remain here, near her family, and yet enjoy the privileges a duchess warranted while he returned to London. She didn't seem the demanding sort. But neither was she a timid, agreeable dowd. Not by a long way.

Even though he'd been in his cups, she'd piqued more than his interest. Theadosia Brentwood wasn't the type of woman a man left behind and forgot about while he caroused in London.

He hadn't missed Mr. Brentwood's hawkish regard either. The man was no simpleton, and Victor would vow the reverend guessed something more had transpired between Thea and him, but had chosen to keep quiet about the matter.

The fact that Thea had volunteered a sizable purse to pay for the chamber organ and new choir robes probably had a lot to do with the rector's silence. She'd looked so contrite after telling her tarradiddle. Victor would never humiliate her by disputing her claim; she'd made it to protect them both.

He couldn't remember the last time he'd anticipated anything as much as seeing Thea again. Friday next couldn't arrive soon enough for him. Then, hopefully Pennington, Bainbridge, Westfall, and Sheffield— four of his closest cohorts—would attend the house party and ball. Dandridge and his bride too.

Almost like old times when the chaps had come up from university.

Almost . . .

He forced his feet to take the meandering path that led past the stables toward the dovecote. A trio of giant willows graced the meadow near the lake, their wispy branches rustling softly. No trace remained of the tree Victor had cut down and burned.

As nature does, she'd reclaimed the charred ground. Now lush grass covered the area, the verdant carpet scattered with the pinks and yellows of ragged robin, buttercups, red campion blossoms, and birds-foot trefoil.

The tightness in his chest lessened with each step until he stood where the willow had once towered. Closing his eyes, he filled his lungs to capacity then blew out a long breath of air. For the first time in over three years, he understood why his father had taken his life.

He'd wanted to be in charge of his own destiny, not at the whim of a ruthless disease.

Now Victor could let go of his pain and confusion. His anger too.

"I forgive you, Father," he murmured softly. "I cannot judge or blame you any longer. I never should've."

For if he faced the same circumstances, might he not do the same?

No. He wouldn't.

He'd choose to fight death until his last breath.

Peace engulfed Victor, and an even greater weight fell away, this time from his soul.

A turtledove cooed nearby. It probably sat on a nest in one of the willows.

He opened his eyes and smiled, for the first time truly glad to be home.

Through the ash copse beyond the field, a flash of color caught his attention. A group of women ambled along the lane leading to Colchester, and one wore a familiar straw bonnet bedecked with blue roses.

Thea.

In a trice, he dashed to the stables and mounted Acheron. Like an infatuated buck, he galloped the gelding around the lake to intercept the ladies where the woods paralleled the track before a sharp bend in the road.

As he emerged from the shadow of the trees, the women stopped chatting and glanced upward.

Reaching to doff his hat, he realized he'd been so consumed with thoughts of his father, he'd forgotten it. His gloves too. He bent slightly at the waist instead.

"Good afternoon, ladies."

He intended the greeting for them all, but his attention centered on the tallest woman dressed in a fetching cream and cerulean gown. The colors made her lips appear rosier and her eyes more chocolaty brown today. They also complemented her strawberry-blonde locks to perfection.

"Good afternoon, Your Grace." Surely Thea's smile was a trifle more exuberant and warm than politesse required. "I trust you enjoyed your walk home yester eve?"

Minx. She was taunting him.

"It was most . . . sobering."

Her eyes widened the merest bit, and he swore her mouth twitched at his jest.

Whisky wasn't addling his senses today, and he looked his fill.

She was even more impossibly exquisite. The sun filtering through the leaves overhead revealed a smattering of freckles across her nose and cheeks that he'd missed yesterday.

Too adorably perfect.

Absolutely the wrong sort of female to be his duchess. He'd not be able to leave a woman like her behind, only to visit her a couple of times a year. So why did he not go on his way?

"I'm sure you remember my friends and my sister." Thea saved him chagrin by rattling off their names in case he didn't. She lifted a gloved hand and indicated each young woman in turn. "Miss Jessica Brentwood, Miss Nicolette Twistleton, and Miss Ophelia and Miss Gabriella Breckensole."

As one, the other ladies dipped into graceful curtsies.

"It's a pleasure to see you again, ladies."

He vaguely remembered the Breckensoles and Miss Twistleton, and Jessica Brentwood, naturally. She greatly resembled her sister, though her hair was blonder and her eyes bluish-green instead of rich, warm cocoa he could drown in.

Perhaps one of these very women might be his duchess in a few short weeks. He already had a strong inclination as to which one he favored. But she wasn't the wisest choice if he intended to stick to his well thought out scheme to find the perfect duchess: amendable, compliant, undemanding, polite, and easy to get on with.

Boring.

Blast him for a fool, but Mother was right.

Thea approached Acheron, a look of wonder upon her face. "Oh, he's beautiful. His coat has a silvery glint. I've never seen the color before."

Acheron flared his nostrils, taking in her scent. Then the shameless beast nudged her chest.

She patted his neck and giggled, a musical gurgle that wasn't the least grating or squeaky, as feminine laughter often was.

"Aren't you the lovely one?" Thea edged to Acheron's other side. Her tone confidential, and low enough that only he could hear, she said, "Thank you for not exposing me yesterday. Please forgive my lies. I assure you, it's not a normal habit."

He bent to pat the horse's neck and whispered from the side of his mouth, "Anything for a damsel in distress."

Her eyes widened in pleased wonderment.

On impulse, he touched her cheek and whispered, "Permit me to call upon you tomorrow."

A shadow flitted across her radiant features, and she shook her head, casting an anxious glance in the direction of her sister and friends. "No. That's impossible. Papa doesn't permit me callers. It's too soon after your arrival home, in any event."

No callers? Did the reverend intend to make his daughters spinsters? Was this because of the elder sister dashing off with an unbefitting fellow?

Victor wasn't giving up that easily. Theadosia Brentwood intrigued him as no woman ever had.

"Then walk with me. Meet me at the east end of Fielding's orchard, by Bower Pool at ten o'clock tomorrow morning?"

"All right." A pleased smile slanted her mouth, and her cheeks pinkened becomingly as she dropped her gaze, her focus once more on his horse.

Only with supreme effort did he subdue the ridiculous smile that threatened to split his face.

The other women remained unnaturally quiet. Any time his sisters had been in their friends' company, the chatting and tittering seldom ceased, and certainly never for more than a second or two.

Drawing his attention away from Thea petting and cooing to his horse whilst cramming down a wave of jealousy that the animal was permitted what he was not, Victor raised his head.

The foursome stared at him.

Their regard, curious and speculative, perhaps even sympathy-tinged, gave him pause.

Thea had told them about his upcoming nuptials.

151

She must've also told them he didn't have a bride yet.

He could see it in their inquisitive gazes.

Except Jessica Brentwood. Her expression didn't reveal her thoughts. He'd be bound the Brentwood misses had become adept at hiding their feelings with a father as severe as the reverend.

The news that the Duke of Sutcliffe sought a bride by August would spread faster than a fire in dried hay. Maybe inviting all the available females of a marriageable age to a ball wasn't the wisest decision.

Blast, of course it wasn't, but he didn't have much choice now, did he?

He'd dilly-dallied too long to go about courting, wooing, and paying his addresses, and with time running short, this strategy was the best he could think of.

A derisive snort almost escaped him.

Only a duke would dare *this* idiocy.

He considered Thea's bent head again.

Why look any further?

Wheels rattling and hooves *clopping* alerted him to a conveyance's approach.

He felt Thea's gaze on his face as surely as if she ran her long fingers over his features. He met her pretty sable-lashed eyes, and in their depths, he spied pity too.

That was too much.

Pity most certainly was not what he wanted from Theadosia Brentwood. Feeling very much the callow youth, he tipped his head.

"I look forward to dinner next Friday, Misses Brentwood. Ladies it was a pleasure to see you again."

He'd held his tongue about the house-party and ball. They'd learn about it soon enough in any event. Given Mother's efficiency, invitations would be posted by Monday. At least she had something to look forward to, something to occupy her time.

Forcing himself to ride on and not look back to see if *she* watched his retreat took rugged self-control. He'd be unwise to show partiality to anyone yet. Particularly given the good reverend's reputation for propriety.

What would Mr. Brentwood do if he knew Thea had agreed to walk with Victor unchaperoned?

Tar and feather him? Lock him in irons? Excommunicate him?

As he veered Acheron toward Ridgewood's drive, he looked over his shoulder, unable to resist one last glimpse of Thea.

Instead, he encountered the reverend's formidable glower.

4

Four days later, Theadosia cast a casual but hurried glance behind her as she turned down the path leading to Bower Pool.

Good. No one was in sight, and she relaxed a trifle.

It had taken some doing to manage an hour's absence each day, but her parents encouraged benevolent visits and assumed she was about charitable tasks. Taking her basket along aided in the pretext. There was always an ill parishioner to take soup to, a lonely elderly widow to share a cup with, or errands to run in Colchester.

Jessica had lifted her fair brows the past couple of days, but said nothing.

Theadosia might have to take her sister into her confidence but was reluctant to do so since Jessica would also suffer Papa's anger if he found out about her clandestine meetings.

Theadosia gave a small, wry shake of her head.

Look what she'd been reduced to.

Sneaking about to meet a man, much the same way Althea had.

Theadosia willingly risked Papa's wrath, for every minute with Victor became a cherished memory. Their friendship, her greatest treasure. To hope for more wasn't wise, and so she didn't allow herself that luxury. She took every moment she was gifted and refused to look too far into the future, because looming on the horizon was the knowledge he'd come home to wed.

Just as he had the two previous days they'd met, Victor waited for her, tossing rocks into the calm pool while lounging against a stone as tall as he.

She stopped to observe him for a few moments, tracing every plane of his handsome face, simply soaking in his masculine beauty. She could look at him forever. The high slash of his cheekbones, the noble length of his nose, his granite jaw, and his jet-black hair glistening in the morning sun.

He seemed eager to meet her each day too.

Could the illustrious Duke of Sutcliffe truly esteem a humble parson's daughter?

Did he enjoy their friendship as much as she?

Joy bubbled in her chest, and a soft happy noise escaped her.

A mama duck quacked a warning, and her brood of eight peeping ducklings followed her into deeper waters.

Victor turned as Theadosia approached, a ready, welcoming smile tipping his strong mouth. However, it was his seductive hooded eyes that never failed to make her stomach quiver, her blood quicken in her veins, and her breath to throttle up her throat.

My, but he was a splendid specimen of manhood.

Some woman was going to be very lucky.

If she hadn't already been half in love with him before he'd returned, she'd had fallen completely sugar bowl over bum for him now. It probably would only lead to heartache, but each time he asked her to meet him again, she'd agreed.

Though they dared spend but an hour together each day, they talked about most everything. Parting became more difficult each time she had to say farewell.

After church last Sunday, he'd lingered outside; she was certain he did so in order to speak with her, but Papa had sent her and Jessica directly home, in Mr. Leadford's company, no less.

The annoying man had blathered nonstop about his previous position, his hope to have his own parish soon, and then—the queerest thing, truly—said he'd intended to wed shortly.

He'd wasted no time in that regard.

Scarcely in Colchester a week and he had designs on some young woman?

Which poor maid had he chosen for that dubious honor?

Or mayhap he was enamored with a woman he'd left behind. Did the poor dear know of his roving eye? Despite his genial smiles and pleasant countenance, something about Mr. Leadford reminded Theadosia of a serpent.

Straightening to his impressive height, Victor plucked a salmon-colored rose off the rock beside him. Lifting the bud to his nose, he ambled her way, all sinewy grace.

Could any other man sniff a flower and still appear so wholly masculine?

"Ridgewood's rose gardens are in full bloom, Thea. I wish you'd permit me to give you a tour before their blossoms fade."

From habit, she scanned the area, searching for anyone else. After confirming they were alone and offering an apologetic smile, she relaxed a touch more.

"You know I cannot unless Mama or Jessica accompanies me. Even then, we'd have to have a legitimate charitable excuse to call. Papa wouldn't approve of me visiting just so that you could show me your gardens."

"Then let me call at All Saints, and I'll speak to him—convince him I've only honorable intentions."

And exactly what were his intentions?

She longed to ask but also feared his answer. He'd never given the slightest hint he might consider her for his bride. Why would he, when at least a score of women of noble birth lived within an hour's drive of Ridgewood?

Naturally, he was expected to pick someone of his own station, to keep that patrician lineage pure.

Wasn't that the way of the world?

"It's too soon, Victor."

She doubted Papa would ever permit him to call. He disapproved of everything about the duke. She'd bite off her tongue before she told him that, however. "Since Althea eloped, he's become most protective."

He held the rose out. "Here. I picked this for you. It's my favorite color of rose. It makes me think of your hair."

"Thank you. It's lovely." She accepted the lush blossom and couldn't

157

resist inhaling the sweet fragrance. "We only have pink and white wild roses at All Saint's, and they don't smell half so wonderful as this."

As had become their habit, they began walking the pond's edge. Clouds littered the sky, but the temperature had warmed these past couple of days, so she only wore her spencer. She tucked the rose into the vee of the jacket, where she'd remember to remove it and hide it in the basket before she reached home.

The sweet aroma wafted upward, and, every now and again, her chin brushed the silky petals. She'd press it between the folds of a heavy book for safekeeping, to take out and look at when the blue devils overcame her.

By deliberate design on her part, perhaps on his as well, they never discussed his upcoming marriage. He also never touched her, except to help her over a stone, and then he released her the moment she regained her balance.

Theadosia found herself wishing he wasn't such a gentleman.

Papa was wrong about Victor. So wrong.

He was the most chivalrous, considerate man she'd ever met.

"You've received the invitation to the ball?"

His question was casual, but the tenor of his voice held a more serious note.

"Yes, but Papa hasn't said whether we are permitted to attend."

Mama, at Theadosia's and Jessica's behest, promised to do her utmost to see that they were allowed to go.

She edged the basket higher.

"I brought lemonade and seedcake." She gave him a coy look. "It's the Nabity sisters' recipe. They brought a cake by yesterday."

His eyes lit up, and he motioned to a large moss-covered root beneath a trio of giant beech trees.

"Let me remove my coat, and we can sit on it."

A few moments later, they relaxed atop the fine fabric, nibbling the delicious cake and sipping lemonade straight from the bottle. Theadosia couldn't help but notice the biceps and other muscles straining at the fabric of his fine lawn shirt.

She also couldn't help but observe the strong column of his throat or his lips when he put the bottle to his mouth and drank the sweet beverage.

Closing her eyes, she tilted her face upward, enjoying the sunlight filtering through the gently rustling leaves.

This was bliss.

"Thea?"

How she loved hearing her pet name on his lips. The way he said it, the low burr rolling off his tongue sounded like an endearment.

"*Hmm?*"

"Why did you agree to meet me, and continue to do so when you know your father will disapprove and you risk punishment?"

His voice came from nearby. Very near, his breath warming her ear and sending the most delicious tremors from her neck to her belly.

Slowly, as if waking from a deep slumber, she opened her lids, her gaze tangling with his molten stare. He was so close, she could see the silver shards in his eyes and smell his clean, woodsy scent.

"Because you asked me to."

It was much more than that, but even as brash as she'd been to defy

Papa, she wasn't about to confess her most private secrets to Victor.

He was a man of the world, she an inexperienced parson's daughter.

His lazy smile washed over her like warm, fragrant oil.

"And would you do anything I asked you to?"

He gave her a raffish wink and waggled his eyebrows.

She giggled, then notched her chin upward.

"Certainly not, sir. I'm a reverend's daughter, the model of modesty and decorum."

"If I weren't a selfish man, I'd not keep asking you to meet me." He flicked a bit of something off her shoulder. "You risk much, and it's wrong of me to put you in that position. If only I might go about things the proper way . . ."

"I know what I'm doing, Victor. There is truth in what you say, and when I think it's grown too risky, we'll have to stop. But for now, let's enjoy each other's company."

He'd marry soon, and no new bride—marriage of convenience or not—wanted her groom meeting with another woman.

He took her hand and turned it over, running his fingertips across the inside of her wrist.

"Do you know what I'm most afraid of?"

This strong, commanding man was afraid of something?

"No. Tell me."

Giving in to the urge to touch him, she leaned into his shoulder, enjoying his firmness pressed against her.

Staring across the pond, he drew in a lengthy breath. "Cancer. My father was the third person in his lineage to succumb to it. How can I be sure that I or my offspring won't be cursed with the disease too? Is it even fair for me to have children and subject them to that possibility?"

Angling her head, she searched his dear face.

"Victor, we are never sure of anything in this life, nor can we know why good people become ill and die while others who are wicked through-and-through live charmed lives." She rolled a shoulder as she slipped her fingers between his thick ones. "We either live our lives to the fullest while we can, or we allow fear to steal any chance of joy or happiness from us."

His eyes deepened to charcoal as he tipped her chin upward with a crooked finger.

"Thea, would you ever—?"

At that moment, two bony-legged boys, following a pair of spaniels, charged from the cover of the trees. When they spied Victor and her, the children skidded to a stop and gawked.

Drat and double drat.

She didn't know the lads, but that didn't mean they hadn't recognized her or the duke.

After elbowing each other and whispering back and forth, they bent into awkward bows.

"Yer Graces," the older fellow said.

Theadosia shook her head. "Oh, I'm not—"

Barking and yipping, their dogs shot off after a rabbit, and after a hasty salute, the boys followed suit.

One little chap's excited voice echoed back to her.

"Wait 'til Mum hears we saw the duke and duchess close enough to spit upon."

5

Smoothing a hand over the periwinkle satin covering her lap, Theadosia curled her toes into her new beaded slippers. Unfamiliar rebellion tickled her tongue, and it took supreme effort to school her countenance into a compliant expression.

Papa was simply being impossible.

Mulish and pig-headed.

And unfair. *So dashed unfair.*

On the opposite carriage seat, legs crossed, his hands folded and resting on his paunch belly, he gave Theadosia and Jessica his sternest look. The darkling scowl he leveled at the worst sort of sinners. A glare neither of them deserved.

Well, maybe Theadosia merited it, but Papa didn't know about the duke's kiss or the secret walks with him, nor would he ever, so he had no call to be severe and cross.

"You represent our household and All Saints Church tonight, my dears. I expect modest and decorous behavior from you both. You will only answer direct questions from his grace, and as briefly as possible."

Sternness scored deep lines in his face and pleated the corners of his eyes. "Do I make myself clear, daughters?"

"Yes, Papa, but won't the duke think that discourteous of us?"

Theadosia dared challenge him, while Jessica nodded her head and gave her sister a puzzled sideways glance. It wasn't often that a Brentwood offspring argued with their sire.

Since coming upon them walking home that afternoon last week, he'd lectured them multiple times regarding the matter. He clearly did not approve of the duke, yet he couldn't afford to affront All Saint's most generous benefactor either.

He was being unfair to Victor. Not once had he attempted to kiss her again or even hold her hand. She'd been the one to hold his.

She felt far safer with him than the ponce at her side just now.

Mr. Leadford, staring out the window and seated on Thea's other side, no doubt by deliberate design, tipped his mouth upward at the exchange, as if privy to some great secret.

This past week, he'd been a constant, annoying presence. Pulling out her chair for meals—*every blasted meal*, offering to carry whatever she happened to be holding, and continually appearing when she was alone in the house or gardens.

Surely Papa wouldn't approve any more than he'd approve of her secret outings with Victor.

Three days ago, her father had entered the drawing room as she played the pianoforte and seen Mr. Leadford leaning far too close whilst pretending to study the music. Her skin had practically peeled itself from her flesh and scuttled under the bookshelf to hide.

Oddly, instead of objecting, Papa offered a peculiar smile and left the room.

Worse though than that uncomfortable moment, was Mr. Leadford's touching her the past few days.

Far beyond the pale.

First a slight brushing of hands, then boldly skimming her waist or back. Yesterday, he'd *unintentionally* walked into her and bumped her behind with his groin.

If that had been an accident, she was a nun.

She'd nearly gone straight to Mama and complained.

Except he was wily, always pretending not to notice the contact or begging her forgiveness for his clumsiness. Every instance could be excused as inadvertent. He didn't fool her though. The more time she spent with him, the more she became convinced Mr. Leadford's pious façade hid a lecher's heart.

She'd even warned Jessica to avoid him and to never be alone with the curate.

If Papa thought to play matchmaker, he'd best rethink that notion. Day old porridge—make that moldy, maggoty gruel—ignited more enthusiasm in her than the curate.

Besides, another had captivated her heart, and she prayed his repeated invitations to walk together meant he found her equally as fascinating, though he'd said nothing of the sort.

Mama, sitting between James and Papa, gave Theadosia an understanding smile.

"Oscar, the girls have always been models of propriety."

As had Althea before her *descent into sin* as Papa called it.

"There's no reason to expect they will fall short tonight, and I do believe Theadosia is correct. If they aren't cordial, our hosts may take offense. Then All Saint's Church might suffer from the Sutcliffes displeasure." Her soft brogue and reassuring words lessened the tension within the vehicle a trifle.

Nonetheless, Theadosia couldn't dispel a peculiar sense of foreboding.

"There will be multiple chaperones present." Mama tucked her arm into the crook of Papa's elbow and gave him a cajoling smile. "I don't think we need to worry about impropriety on anyone's part."

Exactly. Victor had been the epitome of gallant behavior. So much so that she'd wanted to box his ears and demand he kiss her again.

Guilt plagued Theadosia for deceiving her parents, but the emotion paled in comparison to the love simmering in her heart. If she had to be creative and less than forthright in order to see Victor, so be it.

Just as Althea had her beau.

Except Victor wasn't Theadosia's suitor.

A small frown pulled her mouth downward before she caught herself and arranged her face into a neutral expression.

It shouldn't be like this.

Theadosia longed to be straightforward with her parents, but Papa especially made that impossible, and she wouldn't give up those precious times with Victor.

She wouldn't. Not yet, in any event. That time would come far too soon.

"His grace was perfectly respectable when he came upon us the other day," Jessica ventured before giving Theadosia a secretive sideways look.

And every day they'd met too.

Theadosia wanted to applaud her shy sister's boldness.

"So was the serpent in the Garden of Eden," Papa snapped. "Yet Eve gave into temptation, and look where that landed mankind."

Why was he in such ill humor these past few days?

Surely the chance encounter he'd come upon with them and the Duke of Sutcliffe hadn't caused this foul temper.

Gads, imagine how riled he'd be if he knew of her walks?

Theadosia had been excited to dine at Ridgewood Court, and now, Papa had all but ruined the event.

Must he always be so stuffy and severe?

Must he continuously anticipate the worst when it came to his children?

"Come now, why all the fuss?" James's ready grin flashed as he nudged Theadosia's slipper. He possessed Papa's sandy blond hair and square jaw, but also had Mama's eyes, which the ladies quite admired.

As she'd anticipated, when James had arrived, he'd been delighted to learn the duke was in residence.

"Pon my rep, Sutcliffe is the greatest of gentlemen. Don't listen to the gossip. I assure you it's embellished."

Mr. Leadford made a sound suspiciously like a snort, earning him an acerbic look from James.

"Father, you've no need to fret for my dear sisters, I assure you."

Theadosia bumped his foot back in thanks. The habit had started as young children when they disagreed with something their father said and wanted the other to know they stood with them, but didn't dare voice their thoughts.

In the Brentwood house, Papa's word was absolute, uncompromising law.

Papa made a disbelieving noise in the back of his throat. "The duke is in the market for a wife. By August, no less. Told me so himself." His thickening chin edged upward in self-importance. "He's asked me to perform the ceremony."

That truth dampened her spirits no small amount.

James's eyebrows shot to his thick hairline. "Zounds? Truly?"

"Yes, James, I was there when he said it."

Seeing Theadosia's confirming nod, her brother drummed his fingertips on his thigh.

"That's news to me. The *le beau monde* too." He chuckled and rubbed his chin. "I can well imagine the teeth-gnashing by the many damsels that missed their opportunity to become the next Duchess of Sutcliffe. Did he mention how he intends to acquire his bride, since he disdained to pick from those in London for the Season?"

Why, James was enjoying this, the scamp.

"No, he did not, and it's of no import to us." Papa very clearly did not find the situation amusing. "Your sisters are not amongst those under consideration."

Theadosia squelched her cry of protest.

Why not?

"And pray tell me why not?" Bless James for his boldness. "Thea and

Jess are accomplished and beautiful, kind and intelligent. I daresay Sutcliffe should be ever so lucky as to marry one of them. I'd quite like to call him my brother-in-law."

James gave Theadosia a secret, naughty half-wink, and her heart skipped a beat.

He couldn't possibly know of her infatuation or the secret rendezvous.

She'd been so careful and had told no one.

Not even Jessica.

In fact, she never spoke of Victor to ensure no one suspected her *tendre*. A girlish fascination she ought to have outgrown, particularly since she'd neither seen nor heard from the duke those three plus years when he'd been gone.

Oh, she'd written to him a score of times, but the letters were never posted. In fact, she'd always burned them upon completion, never having the nerve to actually send them off.

Nevertheless, similar to an ember laying dormant, the moment she saw him again, the feeling sparked anew. She'd almost burst into flames when he'd kissed her, and the fire burned hotly still. It grew in intensity each time they met.

In fact, she could yet feel his firm mouth on hers if she closed her eyes.

A proper young woman would've been appalled when Victor kissed her. Would've promptly left and reported the offense. Perhaps even slapped his face. But she'd wanted that scrumptious kiss, wanted more of them even now.

Papa settled farther into the corner of the carriage.

"Theadosia and Jessica are simple country lasses, James—*he means unsophisticated and ignorant*—destined to marry men of the cloth."

And there it was.

What Theadosia had suspected for some time now. Unaccustomed anger toward him and Althea welled up within her.

Jessica slipped her hand into Theadosia's and gave her fingers a squeeze.

A silent rebellion.

She'd no more interest in marrying a man of the cloth than Theadosia did. No more than Althea had, but had her actions condemned her sisters to lives neither wanted?

Was Theadosia to have no say at all about whom she married?

Jessica either?

Mr. Leadford perked up upon hearing Papa's declaration and drew his attention from the passing scenery to strip Theadosia bare with his oily gaze again.

Why did no one notice, save she?

He met Papa's eyes for a second before glancing at Theadosia and giving her an eerie half-smile. "Fancy clothes and titles can turn a young woman's head, but the Good Book says God is not a respecter of persons, and neither should we be."

"And it also says to give honor to whom honor is due," Theadosia said.

Pompous twit.

Who did he think he was, lecturing her? If she didn't know otherwise, she'd think his look possessive.

Yes, something went on here.

She scooted closer to Jessica, not that the cramped carriage allowed her to put much distance between herself and Mr. Leadford.

Every time the vehicle hit a bump, he pressed his thigh into hers.

At first Theadosia believed it unintended, but after the third time, given his previous lewd behavior, she changed her mind. The unscrupulous man took advantage of the jostling to touch her, the *roué*.

His accommodations might be on the other side of the parish, but she'd begun putting a chair beneath her bedchamber door handle before retiring.

"Your sisters are not accustomed to suave rakehells' charms, James," Papa said.

Good Lord, why wouldn't Papa let the matter go?

"James, I expect you and your mother to keep a sharp eye on the girls tonight. I covet your help as well, Hector."

Hector? Not Mr. Leadford?

Papa had *never* addressed the other curates by their given names.

Mama rolled her eyes, her impatience with the subject at an end.

The queer flopping in Theadosia's belly had as much to do with her growing suspicion as Mr. Leadford's sly touches.

"As you wish, sir." Mr. Leadford gave a deferential nod, his submissiveness as phony as Dowager Downing's ill-fitting false teeth.

Toady. Cur. Debauchee.

Straightening his cuff, Papa nodded his satisfaction. "One cannot be too cautious when dealing with aristocrats."

For heaven's sake, he made the Duke of Sutcliffe sound like Satan's offspring, and yet he remained oblivious to the evil sitting a few feet away.

Victor had never regarded her in the lascivious manner Mr. Leadford did.

The carriage lurched once more, and Theadosia almost yelped when his fingers brushed her waist.

Eyes narrowed, she clamped her jaw.

So help her, if Mr. Leadford touched her one more time, curate or not, she'd scream and pinch his roving hand.

James shook his head, concern replacing his earlier humor. "You don't know Sutcliffe as I do. There's no need to worry. He's a decent chap through and through."

Dear James exaggerated, but his loyalty to the duke was sweet.

Even in Colchester one heard tattle of the Duke's exploits. She supposed he was no different than any other young blood in London. Privilege, position, wealth, and power were taken for granted by those who possessed them, and one didn't have to be terribly astute to know the *haut ton* had a separate set of rules for the behavior of those welcomed into their elite ranks.

And still, knowing full well his reputation, she'd freely agreed to see him. Had eagerly done so—would continue to.

James bumped her foot again and waggled his eyebrows as if to say, "Don't worry."

Lucky James.

He could leave after Sunday service and likely wouldn't find his way home for another month. There'd be no one to champion her and Jessica. His position as a barrister saved him from Papa's interference in his life. He had greeted James's choice to refuse to enter the ministry with his usual bluster. But in the end, her brother had prevailed and was permitted to pursue his dream.

Theadosia wouldn't be allowed the same license.

Women rarely were.

A few minutes later saw them ushered into Ridgewood Court's formal drawing room. Once before, after the former duke died, the Brentwoods had sat upon these sage and gold brocade chairs and settees. They'd called to pay their respects and for Papa to confer with her grace about the funeral arrangements.

Confident in her second-best new gown of palest blue-lavender, Theadosia covertly searched the room for Victor.

He wasn't there.

The two days since she'd seen him had crawled along, inch by endless inch, and worry he might not join them after-all stole her earlier joy.

Wearing a stunning wine-colored gown edged in gold and black with matching rubies at her throat and ears, the duchess stopped petting a bedraggled, one-eyed cat and greeted them with a warm smile.

"I'm so delighted you accepted Sutcliffe's invitation. Now that he's home, we intend to entertain more often. I'm sure you've received the invitation to the house party and ball by now."

"Indeed, Your Grace," Mama affirmed. "It arrived two days ago."

Theadosia exchanged glances with Jessica. Had Mama convinced

Papa to permit them to attend?

"You must all promise to come. It's to be a very special occasion. Why, there's never been anything quite like it in all of Essex. I shan't take no for an answer." The duchess looked directly at Theadosia and smiled again.

She'd forgotten how tall the duchess was. It made her feel less conspicuous and awkward.

"Of course we shall." Mama agreed before Papa had an opportunity to contrive an excuse not to. "I, for one, cannot wait. A fairytale masquerade ball sounds so fascinating."

On occasion, Mama's Scottish temper flared as red as her hair. The determined set of her chin brooked no argument. They would attend the house party and ball, except, unlike the other guests, they'd return home to sleep, their journey lit by the full moon. Unless the weather continued to be exceptionally cool, as the summer had been so far, and clouds filled the sky.

The butler entered bearing a tray with a sherry decanter and glasses.

"Shall I pour, Your Grace?"

"Yes, please, Grover." Her smile brightened even more as she glanced toward the entrance. "Ah, there you are, Sutcliffe."

Theadosia slowly turned, bracing herself for the onslaught of emotion and sensation that beset her each time she saw Victor. Her breath stalled nonetheless. Formal togs suited him well. The truth was, he could wear rags, and she'd react the same.

He directed one of his dazzling smiles at her; the one that made her pulse dance and her stomach tumble, and, uncaring who witnessed the exchange, she smiled back, letting the upward arc of her mouth reveal how delighted she was to see him.

In short order, Theadosia found herself seated on a settee between him and Mr. Leadford, each holding a glass of sherry. Rather, she'd unwisely sat upon the settee to pet the bedraggled cat, and Mr. Leadford had promptly plopped down on the other cushion.

Much like a large raptor hunting its prey, he'd swooped in to claim his quarry.

She'd nearly fallen off her seat when Sutcliffe lifted the cat, and after setting the miffed feline on the floor, took its place.

He'd sport orange and white hairs on his behind when he stood.

Theadosia eyed him from the corner of her eye. She didn't quite know what to think.

He almost acted . . . jealous.

Preposterous notion. Delicious, wonderfully absurd idea.

Jessica and James stood beside the fireplace, entirely too amused expressions on their faces as they looked on. She gave them a narrowed-eyed, stop-being-great-loobies-look.

Her parents chatted with the duchess, but Papa's frequent unsettling glances in Theadosia's direction had her shoulders cramping with tension.

Something was off.

She didn't know what, but every instinct she possessed screeched a warning.

Ever since Mr. Leadford's arrival, Papa hadn't been himself. Always serious and not ever inclined to silliness, he'd become short-tempered, impatient, and critical as well.

Even Mama had raised her brow askance several times.

Mr. Leadford, his countenance all congenial interest, rested his forearm on the arm of the settee and cocked his head.

"How does your search for a bride go, Your Grace?"

6

His question bordered on impertinent, but for the life of her, Theadosia couldn't prevent herself from glancing at Sutcliffe.

How *did* his search go?

Bloody, horridly awful, she hoped.

They'd not discussed that subject during their walks. She hadn't wanted to know if he'd chosen a bride yet. Not likely, since he'd only been home a short while, but not impossible either.

She deciphered nothing from his closed expression. So very different than the man in the cemetery with his easy smile and twinkling eyes, or the relaxed companion who'd strolled beside her by the lake.

Sutcliffe shifted his attention to her for a moment, and something fascinating flashed in those cool grey depths. Just as quickly, the gleam vanished, and he took a sip of sherry.

"It *goes*."

He crossed his legs, and, resting a long arm across the settee's carved back, dismissed Mr. Leadford.

"Miss Brentwood, do you and your sister ride? Our horseflesh isn't getting enough exercise, and I am hopeful you might be willing to take a horse out a couple of times a week."

As it had in the cemetery and that day they'd shared seedcake, the world shrank until it was just the two of them.

What was it about this man that stirred her very soul?

His mouth ticked up on one side. "Do you ride?"

What had he asked her?

Oh, yes, did she ride?

"I do, but not terribly well. I'd appreciate the opportunity to practice."

If Papa could be persuaded to agree.

About as much of a chance of that as the Regent serving them dinner wearing a pink wig. No wonder Althea had revolted under their father's firm hand or that James had escaped to London rather than follow in their father's footsteps. Mutinous stirrings plagued Theadosia also, and if Papa continued down this track of oppressiveness, Jessica might well rebel too.

"Surely your stable hands are capable of exercising your cattle." Mr. Leadford did not ride. In fact, from what she'd observed, horses frightened him. "Miss Brentwood admits she doesn't ride well. I'm sure she's only being polite by agreeing. A gentleman wouldn't impose—"

"No, Mr. Leadford, I am not simply being polite." The infuriating man. How dare he? "Please do not speak on my behalf. Unlike you, I quite like horses, and it is no imposition to take a horse out now and again. In fact, I would consider it a refreshing change of pace."

Enough was enough.

She'd risk Papa's ire by speaking her mind. He must be apprised of Mr. Leadford's behavior: his galling forwardness and impudence. He, too, was a representative of All Saint's Church and, since Sutcliffe's entrance this evening, had been nothing but insolent.

Leveling Mr. Leadford a scathing scowl that would have wilted a man with any degree of common sense, Victor shrugged. With an offhand flick of his fingers he answered the curate.

"I am short-staffed at present, and we've not had many visitors of late to take advantage of our stables. Guests will be arriving for our house party in a fortnight, but the horses need to stretch their legs before then."

"I cannot imagine why you must marry so soon, especially since you haven't even selected a bride. A bit of a conundrum and no small degree of awkwardness, I should say."

Is he an utterly ill-bred buffoon?

His abrupt change in subject earned him a cocked brow from Sutcliffe.

No doubt the smile Leadford bestowed upon her was meant to flatter, but all it did was turn her stomach.

"*I* could only wed a woman who'd captured my regard." His calculating gaze trailed over her, and she barely resisted the urge to fold her arms over her breasts. "Then *I* would court her for a respectable period before our wedding, to prevent gossip or speculation."

The bounder mocked Victor whilst attempting to stake claim to her.

If they'd been alone, she'd have unleashed her temper and tongue.

"Some of us aren't allowed such luxury." Sutcliffe's dry as chalk response only served to confuse Mr. Leadford.

"Since when is love a luxury?" Mr. Leadford asked.

"When you hold a title, circumstances compel decisions, not

emotions." Even to Theadosia's ears Victor's clipped response resonated with aloofness.

Inexplicable disappointment dampened her mood.

Again, Sutcliffe's gaze found hers. This time, his held a trifle longer, and something invisible passed between them, almost as if he sent her a silent message.

Why must he marry in such haste? He'd never told her.

There must be a compelling motive. He didn't seem a man of impetuous whims.

"I'm sure the Duke has his reasons, and in truth, they aren't any of our business, are they?" Theadosia arched a condemning brow at Mr. Leadford as she lifted her glass and took a drink.

A man of God should be more discreet and considerate.

The butler entered, thankfully interrupting the stilted silence on the settee. "Dinner is served, Your Grace."

"Excellent. Shall we pass through?" The duchess accepted Father's extended elbow.

Victor rose and, since Mama was the highest-ranking female, offered her his arm. The look he slid Theadosia suggested he'd rather have escorted her, and her heart leapt at the secret glance that passed between them.

"Mrs. Brentwood, I wonder if I might persuade you to make that delicious marmalade I remember so well?" Victor said. "I've not had the like in years. I even brought oranges home, hoping you'd indulge me."

A flush of pleasure tinted Mama's cheeks. "I would deem it an honor, but I must confess Theadosia's surpasses mine these days."

179

He looked over his shoulder, and pleasant warmth swathed Theadosia again. "Then might I persuade you, Miss Brentwood?"

Oh, he could persuade her to do a whole lot more with those sultry glances.

"Of course. Just have the fruit delivered to the parsonage. I can make it next week." Did she sound too eager? "I'd planned on making preserves anyway."

There, that made her willingness a little less obvious.

James's mouth hitched upward an inch before he schooled his features.

Drat and blast.

He knew. Or at least he suspected.

Mr. Leadford, the uncouth boor, offered her his elbow. Did the man know nothing of protocol? As the eldest daughter, she was to have gone in with her brother. James outranked him, but unless she wanted to appear intolerably rude, she must accept the curate's proffered arm.

A slight grimace pulled her generally jovial brother's brows together as he escorted Jessica past. She rose up on her toes and whispered something in his ear, and he nodded, then shrugged.

Theadosia barely rested the tips of her fingers atop Mr. Leadford's arm as he brought up the rear. She'd prefer touching a dead rat. Her revulsion would definitely be less.

Mama and Papa had taken seats to the right and left of Victor, and a footman was in the process of refilling Papa's wine glass. He'd also indulged in two sherries before dinner. Most unusual behavior. He rarely drank more than one glass of spirits during an entire meal.

James had claimed his rightful position beside Mama, and Jessica sat opposite him.

Which meant Theadosia was spared Mr. Leadford's presence next to her for the meal, for only two chairs remained.

On opposite sides of the table.

Praise God and hallelujah.

His ignorance proved her saving grace. Otherwise, she'd be sitting where Jessica sat, and have to endure his intolerable presence with a forced smile whilst trying to keep down her meal.

Mouth turned down, his annoyance as obvious as the red pimply thing on the end of his chin, his attention wavered between the empty chairs. He paused before sluggishly dragging Theadosia's chair out.

"I beg your pardon, Miss Jessica. I believe I've committed a *faux pas* and usurped your brother's right to escort your sister to the table. Please sit here, and Miss Brentwood can take her rightful place."

Beside him.

The smile he gave Jessica might've won over another, but she wasn't having any of it.

She might be timid, but her insight and intelligence were razor sharp. As regally as if she were the grand hostess this evening, she unfolded her serviette.

"I do thank you, but since we are already seated, and I should not like the soup to grow cold, let's remain as we are. What say you, Your Grace?"

She looked to the duchess for confirmation.

Another bravo for Jessica tonight. Two times in one evening she'd voiced her opinion. Perhaps she was outgrowing her bashfulness.

"Indeed, Miss Jessica. I do so loathe cold white soup."

The duchess lifted her spoon, and pointedly looked to the other vacant chair.

"Of course, Ma'am," Leadford mumbled, the tips of his ears tinted red as he held the chair out for Theadosia.

To Theadosia's credit, she suppressed her jubilant smile as she slid onto the seat but couldn't resist a secret wink in Jessica's direction.

Victor saw it and lifted his wine glass an inch in a silent salute.

"Spared by a hair, sister dearest," James whispered in her ear.

The meal proceeded pleasantly for several minutes. Theadosia's attention seemed to have developed a mind of its own and kept straying to the head of the table. More than once she caught Victor's eye, and something glowed there that fanned the fire burning within her ever hotter.

She'd better take care lest Papa notice too.

He'd emptied his wine glass twice already, and this was only the third course.

Mama had noticed too, and a little furrow wrinkled her forehead.

"Miss Brentwood," her grace touched the back of Theadosia's hand. "I've never thanked you for attending my late husband's grave."

Theadosia swung her focus to the duchess.

How did she know?

The duchess must've seen the question in Theadosia's expression.

"I mentioned it to Mrs. Brentwood after church one Sunday. She told me it was you who saw to the grave's care."

Cutting her mother a swift glance, Theadosia nodded, offering a closed mouth smile and lifting a shoulder.

"It was no bother. Truly."

She far preferred tending the graves and gardens than the myriad of indoor chores that always needed doing.

"I'd like to thank you by inviting you to tea next Wednesday. Just you and me." The duchess took a sip of wine, her regard on Victor. "Perhaps you would consider helping me with the final plans for the ball as well? I truly could use an assistant. There are so many details to oversee, and Sutcliffe is quite useless when it comes to these sorts of things. He suggested I ask you."

He had?

Theadosia didn't need a mirror to tell her bright color tinted her cheeks. Had she been so obvious that even his mother noticed her frequent glances toward her son?

"I would deem it an honor, ma'am."

If Papa permitted it.

Theadosia would appeal to Mama. If anyone could make Papa agree, it was her mother.

Mr. Leadford narrowed his eyes, and he stabbed a piece of pheasant quite viciously. "Is the ball to be a celebration of the duke's upcoming nuptials?"

As sometimes happens during social gatherings, all conversations paused at the same moment and his question rang out loudly.

Silence, awkward and heavy, filled the room.

Her grace turned a frigid stare on him, whilst delivering a polite set down. "The ball is a celebration of my son returning home after an extended absence."

Swallowing mortification for Victor, Theadosia kicked Mr. Leadford under the table.

Hard.

Twice.

He grunted, harsh lines scoring his face and his eyes accusing her.

"I beg your pardon. Muscle spasms." She forked a carrot and blinked in exaggerated innocence. "I've had them since childhood. Just one of my *many* embarrassing faults."

Not entirely an untruth. She'd had a few instances of her leg muscles jerking before her eighth birthday but not one since. As for her faults, until recently when she'd taken up telling tarradiddles, Papa had seen to it she'd make the ideal parson's wife.

All the more reason to start engaging in further mischief.

Her grace's mouth trembled, and Theadosia thought perhaps approval sparkled in her pretty eyes.

With a flick of his long fingers, Victor indicated he wanted more wine. Once the glass had been filled, he lifted it and looked 'round the table, almost in a challenge.

His focus returned to her for a fleeting second before he leveled Mr. Leadford a bored stare.

"Truth to tell, if all goes well, I intend to select my duchess at the ball."

He did?

Without knowing the woman in advance?

Why would he do such a thing? He'd not mentioned anything of the sort to her.

This was real life, not a fanciful fairytale where happily-ever-afters were guaranteed.

She'd no right to feel vexed or deceived, and yet she did.

Was marriage truly so unimportant to him, just a duty he had to fulfill? His response to Mr. Leadford earlier hinted at that very thing, but she'd not have believed Victor so callous and uncaring. Then again, he'd left his mother alone for years.

True, but he'd also wept over his father's grave.

Did his fear of cancer have anything to do with his cold-hearted decision?

Tears burned behind her lids, and Theadosia sank her gaze to her plate.

How could she attend the ball and stand by silently, watching him select his duchess?

She willed the wetness to cease. By George, she would not cry and give herself away. Later, when she was alone, she could sob into her pillow and berate herself for a nincompoop. But for now, she marshaled her composure and put on a brave face.

Nonetheless, she couldn't possibly help his mother plan the dance. Now wasn't the time to cry off, however. A note tomorrow would suffice.

"Tut, Sutcliffe, you jest. I've said so often, but it's true. You have your father's dry humor." His mother shook her intricately coiffed head, her earrings swaying with the motion. "The ball is merely to help you become reacquainted with everyone since you've been away for so long."

"We're to celebrate a union soon as well," Papa said.

Mouth parted in astonishment for the second time in as many minutes, Theadosia abruptly turned her head in his direction. His speech wasn't slurred, but his lopsided smile bespoke drunkenness, a trait he railed against from the pulpit on a regular basis.

He wouldn't meet her eyes, but instead drained his glass once more. Something in his countenance sent an alarm streaking down her spine.

No. He wouldn't. Not like this.

Not without telling her first. Not without asking if she was agreeable to the match.

"Brentwood, you are betrothed?" Victor's mouth curved into a congratulatory grin and he raised his glass to James. "I wish you happy."

A mixture of concern and bewilderment puckering his usual jovial features, James shook his head.

"No, Sutcliffe, I am not. And to my knowledge, neither are my sisters."

He gave their father a hard, relentless stare.

A perplexed scowl pulled Victor's ebony brows together low over the bridge of his nose.

Mama, her posture as stiff as the table their food sat upon, very carefully laid down her fork and narrowed her eyes to mere slits. Sparks fairly flew from her accusing gaze.

"Whatever are you talking about, Oscar? Have you made an arrangement without speaking to me first? When we agreed you'd never do any such thing again?"

"I am her father." Papa seized his glass once more, blinking in puzzlement when he realized it was empty. He held it up, tipping it back and forth to indicate he wanted it refilled. "It is my right."

Her parents didn't squabble in public, and a blush of mortification heated Theadosia from neck to hairline. Jessica's flushed face revealed she was likewise as discomfited.

Never had Theadosia been so embarrassed.

Never so utterly terrified. Or angry.

A footman dutifully refilled Papa's glass after receiving the slightest nod from Victor.

"We'll discuss this at home." Mama's tightened mouth revealed her displeasure, but she wouldn't argue in front of the Sutcliffes. Once they were home, however, she'd ring her husband a proper peal.

He swallowed, and after casting Mr. Leadford a harried glance, wiped his mouth with his serviette. He lifted his glass high.

"Please join me in a toast to celebrate Theadosia's upcoming betrothal to Mr. Leadford."

"No! Papa, no. You cannot do this to her. You cannot be so uncaring."

Theadosia barely heard Jessica's cries, for the room spun 'round and 'round.

"No . . ."

She struggled to her feet, knocking her glass of wine over in the process.

The crimson spread across the white tablecloth.

Like my lacerated heart.

She couldn't look at Victor. Couldn't bear to see the pity or accusation in his glance.

"I . . . I need . . ."

I shall not marry that vile toad. I shan't. I shan't.

She touched her forehead, surprised to find the skin cool and clammy. The spinning increased, faster and faster. She stumbled again, banging into the table.

"She's going to swoon." The duchess jumped up and wrapped an arm around Theadosia's shoulder. "Sutcliffe!"

Theadosia couldn't hear through the whooshing in her ears. Everything became muffled, and everyone moved sluggishly. She tried to find Victor, but her vision had gone black.

"I shan't marry him." Hands extended before her, she shook her head, trying to clear her vision and hearing. "I shan't. I sha—"

"Thea!" Familiar arms, strong and sturdy, encircled her an instant before oblivion descended.

Torn between anger and frustration, and after having stayed up the entire night, Victor approached the parish's front gate. Though not quite nine o'clock, too early for a social call, he would wait no longer to approach Reverend Brentwood with a unique proposition.

He intended to ask for Thea's hand in marriage, and dower Jessica too.

Only a cod's head would pass up such a generous offer. If that didn't prove incentive enough, he'd keep enhancing his proposition until Brentwood agreed.

No official betrothal announcement had been made yet, no banns read, so Leadford couldn't claim breach of promise. Even if he tried, Victor would pay him off. He'd do anything to remove the wretch from Colchester and from Thea's life.

From her traumatic reaction last evening, she clearly had no notion her father had arranged a match with the curate.

Such anger had engulfed Victor toward the reverend for her public humiliation. What kind of father sprang something of that importance on his daughter during a dinner party? Given the smug satisfaction on Leadford's face, he'd known in advance and had enjoyed Theadosia's mortification.

Whilst sitting beside her on the settee last night, Victor hadn't missed her shudders of repulsion when Leadford pressed near. She couldn't stand the man.

Under no circumstances could she be forced to marry and bed that maggot.

Glancing around, Victor shifted the crate of oranges and gave the door a sharp rap.

The promised marmalade provided him the perfect excuse to call. Not that he really needed one. His position afforded him many privileges, and in this instance, he didn't hesitate to take advantage. He should have done so earlier, but out of consideration for Theadosia and her worry about his reception, he'd yielded to her wishes.

A quaint white arched gate covered in untamed white and pink roses stood ajar at the side of the house. Beyond the flagstone footpath visible through the opening, neat vegetable and flowerbeds basked in the morning sunlight. Chickens clucked, and a rooster crowed somewhere beyond the old, weathered, dry stone wall surrounding the grounds.

A flash of pink and green chintz appeared momentarily on a stone bench only partially visible from where he stood.

Thea?

He knocked again, hoping to avoid seeing her until he'd spoken to her father. Victor wanted to tell her himself of the change in plans for her future. Surely, if she must submit to an arranged marriage, she'd be more amendable to wedding a duke instead of Leadford.

After all, she at least knew Victor, and from that stirring kiss they'd shared, she wasn't unaffected by him. Perhaps sexual attraction wasn't the best foundation to build a marriage upon, but it was better than him proposing to a stranger or her marrying a lecherous rotter.

Victor had seen Leadford's kind before. London teemed with that sort of vermin.

A man whose public façade hid an evil side. He hadn't missed Leadford's attempted peeks down Thea's bodice or the cawker's brushing against her. It had been all Victor could do not to pick the degenerate up by the scruff of his neck and shake him until his nice teeth rattled.

From his turned down mouth, James had noticed too.

Where was he, anyway?

Still abed? Not typical of him. More likely, he'd gone out for a ride as Victor and James had done as young men home from university.

Victor could use an ally in his quest, and given James's disapproval last night, Victor felt confident his long-time friend would support his suit.

He'd raised his hand to knock for the third time when Miss Jessica opened the door.

"Good morning, Your Grace. To what do we owe this honor?" Her gaze dropped to the oranges. "Oh, that's right. Thea is to make you marmalade."

A shadow darkened her pretty features, and lips pressed into a thin ribbon, she looked behind him. "She's in the garden."

"How is she?" he asked. "I know she suffered quite a shock last evening."

He'd been the one to carry Thea to the parlor, and he'd paced behind the settee while smelling salts were fetched. When her lashes fluttered open, it was his eyes she first met, and the despair glinting in those velvety depths bludgeoned him like a mule kick to the gut.

She'd silently pleaded with him, mouthing, "Help me."

In that instant, he was determined to do whatever was necessary to save her from Leadford.

"She's . . . adjusting to the news." After another glance toward the garden, Jessica shut the door. "Shall I fetch her for you?"

"Later. I'd like to speak to the reverend first. Is he home?"

Victor set the oranges down before passing her his hat and gloves.

Expression shuttered, she nodded as she set them on the entry table.

"Please have a seat, and I'll let Papa know you're here."

Rarely had Victor been inside the parsonage, even when he and James had spent a great deal of time together as youths. It remained much the same as he remembered.

Uncustomary nerves caused his palms to sweat and his stomach to clench.

He wouldn't have believed asking for a woman's hand would unsettle him this much. Wasn't that what he'd intended to do anyway? The only difference was, he was doing so before the ball rather than after.

Yes, but Thea wasn't just any woman, and the outcome of his conversation with Reverend Brentwood mattered far more than it ought to. As much for Victor as Thea.

"Sir? Papa will see you in his study." Jessica's countenance revealed nothing. "I'll let Thea know you are here as well."

"Thank you."

Victor followed her down the parish's time-worn corridor. If memory served, the building was nearly two hundred years old. Everywhere he glanced, evidence of decades of wear met his perusal.

Jessica stopped outside a slightly off kilter open door.

"Papa, the Duke of Sutcliffe."

Once inside the smallish, rather stuffy room, Victor took it upon himself to close the door.

"Thank you for seeing me without prior notice."

Mr. Brentwood cut an unreadable look at the closed door before waving his hand to one of two cracked leather chairs angled before his desk. Elbows resting atop the ink-stained surface, the rector cupped one hand over the other.

Was it Victor's imagination, or was Mr. Brentwood's calm demeanor meant to conceal the edginess his shifting gaze, taut jaw, and stiff shoulders couldn't hide?

Through the window behind the reverend, Victor glimpsed Jessica speaking to Thea. Both women turned toward the house, and even from where he sat, Victor could see the dark circles beneath Thea's red-rimmed eyes.

Shoulders squared, she held her head high, brave and unflinching.

Such admiration welled within his chest, he couldn't breathe for a moment.

By God, he'd save her from the fate her father planned for her, even if he had to abduct her.

Victor sank onto the chair, and the old leather crackled in protest.

"What can I do for you, Your Grace?" Mr. Brentwood's voice held the same chill his gaze did.

Might as well get straight to it.

Taking a bracing breath, Victor tore his glance from the vision of loveliness staring at the parsonage.

"I'm here to ask for Miss Theadosia's hand in marriage. I have a special license and would like the ceremony to take place immediately."

The rector acted neither surprised nor shocked. Instead he leaned back in his equally worn chair and pursed his lips.

"A special license? With the bride's name blank? How did you manage that?"

Definite censure there, though he must know a greased palm often made impossible things possible.

Victor scratched his neck as he nodded.

"Yes. I must wed before the sixteenth of August, and I wasn't certain how long it would take me to find a bride. In the event there wasn't enough time to have the banns read, I had a special license prepared, just in case. Now I'd like to use it to join with Miss Brentwood in marriage."

"Then I regret to tell you that you've come in vain." Mr. Brentwood repeatedly rubbed his fingers across his thumb, definitely not as collected as he would have Victor believe. "I've promised her to Mr. Leadford, and my . . . *um* . . . honor requires I keep my word."

His honor or something else?

"With all due respect, Mr. Brentwood, I'm offering Theadosia multiple titles, a life of comfort and privilege, and the means to assist her family. I am also prepared to bestow a five-thousand-pound dowry and a house in Bath upon Miss Jessica."

A noise echoed outside the door, and Victor angled his ear toward the panel.

Was someone listening at the keyhole?

After a moment, the reverend drew his gaze from the door. Not a doubt he'd heard the commotion as well.

"I appreciate your generosity, but Jessica, like Theadosia, will marry a man of the cloth, and therefore, has no need for a large dowry."

Moisture beaded Mr. Brentwood's upper lip, and he wouldn't meet Victor's eyes as he switched from fidgeting with his fingers to brushing his thumb against the pages of the open Bible he must've been reading when Victor interrupted.

Was this only about his daughters marrying clergymen?

Then why the uneasiness?

Victor rested his elbows on the arms of the chair and hooked an ankle over his knee.

He would poke the lion and see what he stirred.

"I'll also pay for a complete upgrade and refurbishing of the parsonage, Church, and grounds."

Extreme perhaps, but since its inception, the duchy had supported the church. There'd been no major improvements in decades, and in truth, a renovation was past due.

That offer gave the reverend pause.

An enthusiastic sparkle entered his eyes as he swept a swift glance about the fusty office and then the Church, visible through tall, narrow windows. He drew in a deep breath and pressed his fingers to his temple, his expression contemplative.

Only a self-centered cull would deny his family and parishioners what Victor proposed.

Only a selfish cull bartered for a bride as if she were a piece of property sold to the highest bidder.

True, but this was for Thea's own good.

Releasing a resigned sigh, his shoulders slumping the merest bit, Reverend Brentwood shook his head once. A guarded look returned to his squarish features.

"Again, I must refuse your magnanimous offer, Your Grace."

Of its own accord, one of Victor's brows flew high on his forehead.

Was the man dicked in the nob?

It was one thing to be zealous about one's beliefs—that, Victor could respect and even admire—but it was another entirely to force a daughter to marry a man she clearly loathed. Especially when the match would not improve her position or benefit anyone except the reprobate marrying her.

"You would deny your daughters the opportunity to improve their stations?"

The words had no sooner left his mouth than Victor realized how arrogant they sounded and that he'd made a grave mistake.

"What I mean is—"

Mr. Brentwood slammed his hand down, rattling the ink pot, and shot straight upward. Bracing his hands upon the desk, he glowered down at Victor, his contempt palpable.

"I know precisely what you meant. That a mere member of the clergy, a humble man, a poor man, is inferior to your blue-blooded peerage and heavy purse. You've wasted your time and mine, sir. Theadosia will marry Mr. Leadford as soon as the banns are read."

Victor laced his fingers and considered the cleric.

"She doesn't love him, and in fact, is afraid of him. Terrified, I'd say."

That truth had been as glaringly apparent as the god-awful blemish on Leadford's chin last night.

"And do *you* profess love for her, Your Grace?"

A sneer curled the reverend's upper lip as he regarded Victor with the revulsion he might a pimp siskin.

"Perhaps not love—*yet*—but I have immense regard for her and want to provide for her and protect her."

"And you think Leadford does not? *He,* at least, professes affection."

"Leadford might be a man of the cloth," Victor said, "but he is not the more honorable between us, as I believe you are already aware."

"Honor?" Casting his mocking gaze heavenward, Mr. Brentwood choked on a scoff.

"God above, *he s*peaks of honor.

"Even in Colchester, Duke, your sinful *exploits* are known. You're a womanizer and a drunkard. Did you really think I didn't see the whisky bottle Theadosia tried to hide? You dared to blaspheme holy ground with the devil's drink, and persuaded her to aid you in your irreverence."

And yet, the good reverend had kept his silence these past days.

Why?

Because Victor was paying for the new organ and choir robes. That said much about the man of *God's* character and his priorities.

The nostrils of Brentwood's wide nose flared, revealing an abundance of unattractive hair. "I also know you kissed her. Treated my Theadosia like a common strumpet."

Another muffled bump echoed through the study door.

Whoever eavesdropped had ceased being covert.

"The Nabity sisters told me so the other day." The reverend shook his head and slammed his fist atop his open Bible, crinkling the page. "I vow, I shan't have another daughter sullied by a handsome face."

Victor refused to discuss the kiss and have it reduced to a tawdry episode.

It had been a taste of pure heaven, and despite the impropriety, he didn't regret it. Theadosia had enjoyed it too, and he clamped his jaw to refrain from telling the rector to bugger himself for daring to use Thea's name and strumpet in the same sentence.

Victor neither frequented brothels nor dallied with harlots. The risk of disease was too great. Besides, now he had a killer disease in his bloodline to fret about.

"All the more reason Theadosia and I should wed at once to prevent any tainting of her reputation—as well as yours and the parish's." That latter might be a trifle overdone, but he wasn't leaving anything to chance.

Cutting his hand sharply through the air, Brentwood shook his head in disdain. "She's Miss Brentwood to you, and she's not one of your whores to be tossed aside when you grow bored with her. I don't doubt for a moment you'd resume your lascivious lifestyle within weeks of marrying her."

Damnation. That was exactly what Victor had planned to do, but that was before he'd decided to make Thea his wife.

"Your accusations and concerns are just. I've not lived a monk's life, but I give you my word upon my father's grave and the dukedom, that I would be faithful to her. I hold Theadosia in the highest esteem and would never deliberately cause her sorrow."

But do I love her?

How could he so soon?

For certain, he felt something compelling, and it wasn't just lust. He was quite familiar with *that* carnal urge. But was it love?

It mattered naught.

He'd do what he must to keep her safe from Leadford. And if, after they'd married, she wanted a divorce, he'd grant her one.

If she'd have him and agreed to, Victor would elope with her today. They could be across the border and wed within hours.

God, to see Leadford's face when they returned. Victor could savor that satisfaction for a great while.

"I cannot believe you, as a loving father, would force Thea to wed against her will." He wasn't ready to toss in his cards just yet. If Brentwood insisted on this ridiculousness, he'd do so knowing others were well aware of what he was making Thea to do.

"It's no concern of yours." Face a mottled red, Mr. Brentwood ran a finger between his cravat and neck, then wiped his brow and upper lip with his handkerchief. Did he always sweat buckets or only when under fire?

"Now I shall bid you good day," Brentwood said, scarcely this side of civil. "I have a sermon to finish preparing."

Victor rose and after pulling his jacket into place, cocked his head.

The reverend fidgeted with his Bible, looking everywhere but at him.

"Doesn't your honor and paternal affection demand you consider your daughter's happiness? Would you subject her to a lifetime of misery? Surely you know, or at least suspect, what type of wretch Leadford is. He'll abuse her for certain. Can you live with that knowledge?"

Jaw slack, Brentwood paled to a ghastly shade before summoning his bluster once more.

"Do not presume to impugn my integrity. I know what is best for my daughter. You are no longer welcome in this house, and I forbid you to see or speak to Theadosia. I cannot in good conscience ban you from attending church services, lest your immortal soul suffer, but you shall not approach her."

Something suspicious was going on here. The reverend was far too overwrought. Far too defensive and irrational. Like a man concealing a dark secret. Something that might ruin him and his way of life if it became known.

James might be just the person to prod around a bit in that area. Horse's hooves had echoed in the drive a few moments ago. Hopefully it was James returning home, and before departing, Victor intended to have a word.

"I've known you to be a reasonable man my entire life, Reverend. Always fair and just, if a trifle hard and unyielding at times. This community and your parish respect you, as much for your dedication to them and your position as for your commitment to your family. The Reverend Brentwood I know would never force his daughter into a loveless marriage, much less with a man who gropes her whenever you aren't looking."

Mr. Brentwood's head jerked up, and his gaze clashed with Victor's. Within the clergyman's gaze, anguish warred with indecision and . . . *fear?*

Did Leadford have something on him?

He must.

What the hell would cause Mr. Brentwood to sacrifice a daughter to a man of Leadford's character?

Victor extended a hand, palm upward. "Mr. Brentwood, I can help you, but only if you tell me what is going on."

Self-righteous outrage snuffed out the other conflicting emotions from the reverend's countenance.

Pride would be the cleric's downfall. He'd do anything to save face. Even subject Thea to a debaucher.

"Once more you cross the mark, Your Grace." His hand unsteady, Mr. Brentwood pointed to the door. "Please leave before I forget I'm a man of God and lose my temper entirely. My daughter is none of your concern."

We'll see about that.

Victor strode to the exit. His earlier anxiety had dissipated, and he had one focus now.

Protect Theadosia at all costs.

Was whoever who'd been listening still outside?

Making a pretense of grasping the handle and wiggling it, he gave whoever it was time to flee. If he had to guess, he'd vow Miss Jessica couldn't contain her curiosity. Hopefully, she'd repeat everything to Thea.

This wasn't over.

No, indeed.

Never before had Victor's ability to keenly read people been as important. It was what gave him such an advantage at cards and other gaming, and was one of the reasons he'd been able to amass his fortune.

In the past fifteen minutes he'd learned something interesting.

He opened the door, and after checking to be sure the corridor was empty, faced Mr. Brentwood.

"Leadford's blackmailing you, isn't he?"

8

Why had Victor sought an audience with Papa?

Fighting back stinging tears for the umpteenth time since last night, Theadosia marched through the Fielding's apple and pear orchard, her basket rhythmically thumping against her hip as she trudged along. She refused to succumb to the moisture prickling behind her eyelids. She wasn't a blasted watering pot.

When Jessica had rushed into the garden and told her Victor had called, asking to speak to their father, Theadosia's heart had dared accelerate in hope. For what, she wasn't certain, but Victor had seen her desperation last night.

He'd given the slightest nod when she'd mouthed, "Help me."

It was much too brazen of her. She'd no right to ask it of him, but from the moment he'd re-entered her life, she'd trusted him more than any other person. Although they'd only spent a few days together, she believed he would aid her.

Then, first thing this morning, he appeared at the parsonage door. Surely that must mean he'd found a way out of her horrible dilemma.

She could not—would not—marry Mr. Leadford.

How could Papa expect such a thing?

If she refused, would he disown her as he had Althea?

Her situation wasn't the same at all. Her sister had eloped with a man she adored, but Theadosia was being forced to marry a sod she loathed. Nonetheless, her father expected blind obedience from his daughters, especially after Althea's betrayal.

He might very well chastise Mama for allowing Theadosia to leave the house on this errand. When she'd swooned last night—a first for her—he'd been livid that she'd humiliated him thusly. Oh, he hadn't permitted the duke and duchess to see his ire, but the instant they'd settled into the carriage, he'd threatened to lock her in her room until the wedding.

Mama, angrier than Theadosia had ever seen her, had called him an unreasonable tyrant and presented him the back of her head. This morning, she still wasn't speaking to him.

That was also a first.

Mama must've known Theadosia needed to escape the house, especially after she'd seen Victor sitting in Papa's study. Her mother had defied Papa and sent Theadosia to deliver a cold meal to the Fieldings. Plump, cheerful, and obviously adored by her equally jolly and rotund husband, Mrs. Fielding had delivered her fifth child yesterday.

Theadosia loved children, especially babies, but she'd rather become a dried up, shriveled prune-of-a-spinster than allow Mr. Leadford to bed her.

A forceful shudder rippled down her spine at the disgusting notion, and she hunched deeper into her spencer.

She'd brought a shawl today as well, but in her haste to leave the parish, had forgotten her bonnet. This summer was proving to be one of the coolest she could ever remember. However, revulsion rather than the disagreeable weather caused the chill juddering her spine.

Drawing in a deep breath, she ordered her careening thoughts to order. Responding like a ninny wasn't going to help the situation.

A plan. That was what she needed. A logical plan.

And she needed one speedily.

On the ride home last evening, her father had declared he intended to read the banns for the first time this Sunday. If Victor hadn't persuaded him otherwise during his visit, that was.

How she'd wanted to slap Mr. Leadford's smug face as he leaned against the squabs, all self-satisfied arrogance. She'd bet her boot buttons he'd orchestrated this, but how, in such a short time?

Another wave of frustration engulfed her.

How could Papa be so callous? So hard-hearted?

How could he completely disregard her feelings and wishes? What possible reason could there be for rushing the nuptials? She scarce knew Mr. Leadford.

She might argue the same about Victor, but that was much different. She enjoyed his company and anticipated seeing him. When she wasn't with Victor, her thoughts continually drifted toward him. Upon first awakening, he infiltrated her mind, and as she drifted off to sleep, he hovered on the perimeters of her consciousness.

Now she understood why Althea had fled with Antione Nasan, a French artist who'd been sketching likenesses with a traveling troupe.

He'd approached Papa and asked for her hand in marriage. Papa had all but thrown him out of the house, and he *had* locked Althea in her room. Two nights later, she'd picked the lock and fled with her lover.

Jessica and Theadosia had kept watch to make sure Papa didn't catch her. He had no idea they'd conspired together. Theadosia suspected Mama knew the truth, but she'd never hinted at any such thing.

Theadosia inhaled deeply again, savoring the earthy aroma beneath the gnarled trees where a few wax cap mushrooms had sprung up. Mere weeks ago, these same trees had dripped with fragrant pinkish-white blossoms, promising an abundance of fruit this autumn. Unless Papa changed his mind about her marrying Mr. Leadford, she wouldn't be here for the harvest.

If she must, she'd run away.

To Althea in France.

Just this morning, in a hushed whisper, her mother had confessed she'd secretly been writing to Althea and receiving letters in return. Althea had two little boys, and her husband had become a successful portrait painter. For months, she'd been begging Mama to visit and bring Jessica and Theadosia.

Her mother hadn't dared.

Risking Papa's fury, James had helped Mama and Althea correspond.

He'd help Theadosia escape too. She didn't doubt it.

But to never see her mother or Jessica again? That risk was very real. A probability, unless Papa died.

Pain stabbed Theadosia to her core, and she slapped a hand to her middle, gasping at the agony of that awful truth.

There must be another way.

How could Althea bear it?

Because she had a man who loved her and whom she loved in return.

Tears threatened again, but Theadosia swiped them away.

As she climbed the gentle slope toward the lane leading to the Fielding's house, she caught a movement from the corner of her eye.

Alarm skittered across her shoulders, and she whirled to face her stalker.

"Why are you following me, Mr. Leadford?"

He emerged from behind one of the gnarled old apple trees and offered a repentant smile.

"I was looking for an opportunity to speak with you but feared I'd startle you." He thrust a handful of blossoms toward her. "Here, I picked you flowers."

Likely filched from the Church's gardens.

Sliding the basket onto her other arm, she made a pretense of adjusting the cloth covering the food and grasped the bottle of lemonade. She'd not hesitate to crack him over the nog with it if he attempted to accost her.

"So, you skulk about like a thief? Couldn't you have waited until I returned home?"

Skewing a brow, she leveled him a dubious look, but made no effort to take the fast-wilting blooms.

She didn't like being alone with him one jot, and the Fielding's house was still a quarter of a mile away. He'd already proved he was no gentleman.

If only she had told Mama about his harassment. She would've sent Jessica too. Except Theadosia had really wanted to be alone to sort out her thoughts.

Angling away, she dismissed him. "I must go. The Fieldings expected me some time ago, and my mother awaits my return. We've preserves to make."

Not exactly the truth, but he needn't know that.

"Permit me to accompany you." He hurried to reach her side, his gaze straying to her breasts.

He tried to lay the flowers in the basket, frowning when she drew it away.

"I don't like my betrothed walking about unescorted."

"As to that, we are not officially betrothed, and I intend to do everything in my power to see that we never are." She tightened her grip on the bottle. Though not nearly as large as the duke, Mr. Leadford wasn't a simpering fop either. He could easily overpower her. "I'd prefer to walk alone, if you don't mind" *And even if you do.* "I've done so dozens of times without fear of harm."

"But I do mind." He grasped her elbow, none too gently, and yanked her to his chest. Triumph glittered in his frosty blue eyes.

His reptilian smile sent a ripple of stark fear through her.

"You *will* marry me, Theadosia. I have the means to force you to."

"I don't think so."

They whirled to see a hatless and gloveless Duke of Sutcliffe sauntering up the hill.

Despite his leisurely approach, his chest rose and fell quickly as if he'd been hurrying. Everything about him shouted masculine animal grace, but primal danger exuded from him too. His gaze took in the hand gripping Theadosia's arm, and the murderous look he leveled Mr. Leadford caused another hair-raising shiver to scuttle across her shoulders.

He wasn't a man to cross, and she was glad his ire was directed at Mr. Leadford.

"Release her, Leadford."

In three more long-legged strides Victor was upon them.

Mr. Leadford drew himself up, retaining his harsh grip upon her arm.

He shook the flowers at Victor. "I'm her betrothed, and it's my right—"

"I told you to release her."

Victor stepped nearer, and Mr. Leadford's bravado slipped a jot. He didn't back away or relinquish his hold, but his Adam's apple bobbed up and down like a frightened mouse caught on a shelf, and his shifty gaze skittered about as if determining the quickest escape route.

In a deadly calm but unyielding voice, Victor said, "You are not formally betrothed, and as she objects to your touch, you are accosting her." He glanced at Theadosia for confirmation, and she gave a vehement nod. "Perhaps the magistrate should be informed. Doubtful you'd retain your position afterward."

That did it.

Mr. Leadford retreated a step but wasn't ready to quit the field just yet, it seemed.

"I do not appreciate your interference, Sutcliffe. We are betrothed. Her father verbally contracted with me, and the rest is just formalities."

Again, he waggled the poor abused blossoms.

Theadosia released her vice-like grip on the bottle while edging closer to Victor.

He promptly tucked her hand into the crook of his elbow and held it to his side. Something a long-time married couple might do.

At once, her fear dissipated, to be replaced by the familiar sensation of coming home she experienced each time he touched her.

"It's Your Grace to you, and *I* don't appreciate *you* waylaying Miss Brentwood with your unwanted attention."

His glare murderous, Leadford jerked his chin up, an unfortunate decision, since it drew attention to the impossibly large boil there.

"That's because you want her for yourself." Again, Theadosia longed to slap the smug half-smile from his face. "I heard you offer for her, but Brentwood turned you down flat."

Something hot and gratifying blazed behind her breastbone. Theadosia searched Victor's striking features, afraid to believe what she'd just heard.

"Listening at the keyhole, were you?" He flicked Leadford a contemptuous glance. "Why am I not surprised?"

"You truly asked for my hand?" That dream had finally become a reality, if for all the wrong reasons, and her father had squelched it without regard to her desires.

Victor spared her a brief glance and a fond smile. "Yes, I did."

That was how he'd intended to help her?

Leadford's gloating laugh disturbed the orchard's tranquility.

"You couldn't even buy her hand for all of your illustrious titles and riches. You were so pathetic, all but begging, offering to dower her sister and refurbish the parsonage and Church. And Brentwood still said no."

Mr. Leadford laughed again, this one more maniacal than humorous.

He's mad. Dear God, Papa has promised me to a madman.

Theadosia shrank into Victor's side, and he wrapped his arm about her waist.

At Victor's boldness, Leadford balled his fists, crushing the flower's stems. His face glowing crimson, his chest rising and falling with his heavy breathing.

"He also forbade you to see her, and you can be sure I'll tell him you ignored him."

Victor didn't flinch under Mr. Leadford's verbal assault. In fact, his cool control was a stark contrast to the curate's flushed-faced agitation.

"I'm counting on it. And you can tell him I'll continue to do so until *she* tells me to stop."

"Which I never will." That truth might as well be known.

The delighted smile Victor bestowed upon her did all sorts of peculiar things to her insides.

"You heard her. Do be a good fellow and be gone." Victor jerked his head in the direction he'd just come. "My patience wears thin."

A robin red breast swooped from an apple tree and began poking about the soil a few feet away.

Leadford tossed the flowers to the ground, and the panicked bird took to the air with an outraged chirrup.

"She is mine, Sutcliffe, do you hear me? Theadosia is mine. In a matter of weeks, she will be in *my* bed, pleasuring *me*. Won't that gnaw at you? Me, the lowly clergyman, rogering her day and night, anywhere and any time I desire. Getting her with child, over and over."

"Never," Theadosia and Victor said simultaneously.

Victor splayed his fingers across her ribs, the movement thrilling and soothing at the same time. "I shall make Thea my wife, Leadford. You'd best prepare yourself for that eventuality."

She nodded her head, finally allowing her revulsion for Leadford to show. "I would never marry you. Never."

A self-satisfied smile replaced Leadford's fury. All smug superiority, he bent one knee and rested a hand on his hip.

"Not even to keep your precious Papa from prison?"

Theadosia stiffened, her heart diving to her belly. She cut Victor a swift worried glance before wetting her lower lip. She didn't want to ask, dreading the answer, but she must know.

"Just what are you implying?"

"It's quite simple, my dear. If you don't marry me, I'll reveal what I know, and your father will go to prison for a very, *very* long time." He clutched his throat theatrically. "Why, he might even . . . *hang*."

Theadosia jerked as if skewered.

"I don't believe you. Papa would never do anything immoral or illegal."

Except . . . these past few days he *had* been out of sorts. Like a man carrying a tremendous burden. Oh God, was there truth to Leadford's despicable accusation?

"All men are capable of treachery if circumstances decree it. Could you live with yourself, Theadosia? Knowing you could have prevented your father's fate? Knowing your mother and sister will be cast out of their home, disgraced and impoverished? And to think, you might've alleviated their hardships by being unselfish and wedding me."

What he said couldn't be true.

Her father valued honesty and integrity above all else.

Leadford brushed his hands down the front of his simple black coat, ridding the fabric of a couple of stray petals. "If I weren't a moral man, I wouldn't bother marrying you. Your father would've still agreed to give you to me, though. You should know that."

"No," she breathed.

Even as she denied his claim, she knew he probably spoke the truth.

"One more word, Leadford, and I'll lay you out flat."

Voice gravelly with barely suppressed fury, Victor lunged forward a pace.

"*Tsk*, Your Grace. Such a violent temper. I'll pray for that vice along with *all* of your others. Now I'll leave you to say your farewells. You won't be seeing each other again. I'll see to that. I'm off to inform the reverend of your clandestine meeting. I shouldn't be the least surprised if he locks you in your room and sends me to acquire a special license straightaway, *my dear*."

"You are vile through and through." On the cusp of completely losing her composure, Theadosia averted her face.

"Just think, *sweetheart*, we might be wed within a day." Leering, he leaned forward into her line of vision. "Oh, by the by, I expect a virgin in my bed, else I'll have to tell the authorities what I know about the Honorable Oscar Brentwood. Such a shame if we're wed and dear Papa finds himself imprisoned anyway."

After another gloating grin, he gave a jaunty wave and made his way down the hillside.

Unmoving, unable to rip her focus away, she watched, unblinking until he disappeared from sight. She inhaled a wobbly breath and pressed her fingertips to her forehead.

"That's why my father insists I marry him," she managed through her tear-clogged throat. "Papa has committed some sort of crime."

9

S hutting her eyes, Theadosia battled despair.

How could she send her father to prison? Or worse?

"I don't know what to do, Victor. I cannot allow Papa to be imprisoned or risk him hanging. Nor can I see Mama and Jessica turned out into the street, destitute, though I'm confident James would help. But life with that wretched excuse of humanity would be utterly unbearable. It makes me positively ill to think of . . ."

Her flesh shrank in repulsion when Leadford gazed at her. How could she ever tolerate his touch?

A tear leaked from her eye, and Victor brushed it away with his thumb. He gathered her into his arms and kissed the hair near her temple.

"Don't under-estimate my power and connections, darling. Leadford is blackmailing your father. I deduced that much this morning. We have to find out what for, and toward that end, I've enlisted your brother's help. Leadford won't stop after forcing you to marry him. He'll continue with the extortion. Your father must be made to see the only way out of this cesspool is for him to come clean and confess whatever it is that he's done."

Eyes still closed, she relished the comfort of his embrace.

"Why is he so determined to have me? We've only known each other a short while, but I saw something in his eyes that first day. He's obsessed, and it's terrifying. I don't know what he's capable of." She shuddered and burrowed deeper into Victor's chest.

She'd only been reacquainted with him for the same amount of time, and yet she was more comfortable with him than any other person, including Jessica.

"I suspect, my sweet, he's after the rectorship, the Church, all of it. All Saint's is a wealthy parish." Victor kissed her temple again whilst running his hand up and down her ribs. "I also believe he's unhinged. I sent a letter to a friend of mine, the Duke of Westfall, a few days ago. You'll meet him at the ball."

"*If* I go—" She started to protest.

He shushed her with a fingertip to her lips. "You *will* attend."

His confidence did him credit, but he didn't know her father as she did.

"As I was saying," Victor said, "Westfall enjoys dabbling in amateur investigative work, and I've asked him to poke around and see what he can uncover about Leadford. Something stinks to high heaven regarding that churl."

"Victor, I didn't expect you to ask for my hand when I asked you for help."

Theadosia spoke into his delicious, manly smelling, oh-so-firm chest. She could stand like this for hours. For a lifetime.

"Believe me, I wanted to, and I wouldn't have done so if I hadn't. I've been entertaining the idea since I first kissed you." He tilted her chin upward, his penetrating gaze probing hers. His held a tantalizing promise. "Which I intend to do again. Now."

"Oh, yes. Please."

She raised her mouth to his, sighing when his lips met hers. This kiss was different than the first, more reverent, but simmering with restrained passion nonetheless.

With a guttural groan, Victor crushed her to his chest and plundered her mouth. His tongue swept hers, and she instinctively met each thrust.

Only the clanking of the basket's contents drew her reluctant attention away from his blistering kisses. Giving a shaky laugh, she jostled the container. "I almost dropped this, and poor Mrs. Fielding needs all the respite she can get with five little ones now."

Victor framed her face between his hands, his expression so earnest Theadosia's heart cramped.

"Thea, elope with me to Gretna Green. Today. I can have a carriage readied within the hour."

"Your chivalry is touching and appreciated, Victor, but what kind of a woman would I be if I allowed you to make such a sacrifice for me? You were to pick your bride at the ball, remember? I'm hardly duchess material."

"Trust me, darling, it's no sacrifice. I adore you and want to marry you. I intended to ask you at the ball. I've not been able to get you out of my thoughts since we met in the cemetery. When I try to sleep, you invade my dreams. When I'm looking through account ledgers, I lose track of where I am, because I keep remembering our kiss. If we eloped, you'd be safe from Leadford for now and always."

Feeling like she might fragment, she forced her mouth into a smile and laid her palm against his cheek. Even through her glove she felt the bristly, dark stubble shadowing his lean jaw. Was he a man who had to shave more than once a day?

As he had in the churchyard, he gripped her hand and bent his shiny midnight head to kiss the inside of her wrist.

"I cannot, Victor. Not until I know what Leadford is using to blackmail Papa. I shan't be the cause of my father's imprisonment." She couldn't even contemplate him hanging. "Nor can I face being shunned by my family. You don't know Papa. He's uncompromising. We're not even allowed to say Althea's name. If you and I wed and he doesn't go to prison, I mightn't ever see my mother or sister again."

How could she choose between the man she loved and her mother and sister?

Could James be persuaded to arrange clandestine meetings?

Would Mama flout Papa in that matter too?

Victor's feature's tightened.

"You are not the cause of your father's dilemma. The reverend's done something, likely criminal, and Leadford knows what it is." Condemnation tightened his features, and his voice took on the harsh note she'd come to recognize as a sign of controlled ire. "Your father has only himself to blame, and it's cruel to keep you from seeing Althea. Where's the forgiveness he preaches from his pulpit?"

"Everything you say is true, but he's still my father, Victor, and I love him despite his faults. Surely you can understand that after your father—."

"I know, and I do understand." He kissed her forehead and breathed out a deep sigh. "Fine. We don't elope, but will you marry me, Thea? And trust me to help your father?"

"I want to say yes, Victor. I truly do." She dropped her gaze as a blush heated her cheeks. "I've dreamed of becoming your wife for a very long time."

There, she'd said it.

Given him a hint as to her feelings. A union between them might be a marriage of convenience for him, but for her it would be a love match.

"You have? Truly?"

The hot, hungry gleam in his steel grey eyes nearly unhinged her knees. He captured her mouth in another sizzling kiss, and several blissful moments passed before he reluctantly lifted his lips.

"I cannot tell you how happy it makes me to know you've thought about becoming my wife. I didn't want a cold, affectionless union, but feared I'd have to settle for one. I know we can be very happy together."

For the first time, she allowed the love she'd kept hidden to show in the adoring gaze she lifted to him. He hadn't said he loved her, but his joy at her declaration surely meant he also had feelings for her, didn't it?

"Then yes, I shall marry you."

He cupped the back of her head with his strong hand, tenderness softening his features. "We must wed by August sixteenth or all of my unentailed properties and monies are awarded to my cousin. My mother would have to vacate Ridgewood Court, and I shan't let that happen."

Victor had to marry to keep from being disinherited?

Her earlier euphoria melted away.

There was nothing chivalrous or gallant about that.

She'd known from the beginning that he must wed swiftly. He was a far better choice than Mr. Leadford, and she'd be an idealistic ninnyhammer to reject his offer—even if she was simply a means to an end for him.

"August sixteenth? But . . . that's only a few weeks away."

"It is, and I *shall* be married by then."

A moment ago, Theadosia's heart had been so full she almost wept, and now she wanted to sob from heartbreak. She leaned away from his forceful embrace, dreading his answer, but she must have the truth.

"Are you saying if this business with my father isn't settled in a month, and I cannot marry you yet, you'll wed another?"

His expression grim, Victor nodded.

"I don't wish that, but I am honor-bound to protect my mother even as you must protect your father." Even to his own ears, it sounded weak and unconvincing.

She edged away, her heart fracturing more with each retreating step.

"You're marrying to retain wealth and property and to keep your mother in her opulent mansion. I'm being forced to wed a reprobate to keep my father out of prison and to prevent my mother and sister from becoming homeless."

She shook her head, a tear trailing down her cheek.

"They are not the same things at all, Victor. I was a naive fool to think I was anything other than a convenient means to an end for you."

Her heart heavier than it had been when she left the parsonage that morning, Theadosia sighed as she pushed open the kitchen door. The scent of fresh-baked bread, and what smelled like a beef roast filled the warm room. She hadn't eaten today, and normally the scrumptious smells would have sent her in search of a biscuit or two.

Not after her heartbreaking departure from Victor.

He hadn't denied her accusation. He'd just stood there, his handsome face hard and uncompromising, as she walked away, each step rendering another crack in her heart.

Though he professed to want to marry her, he'd marry another to keep his money and property and to protect his mother.

The duchess didn't face imprisonment or hanging. She might have to live in a different mansion. So blasted what? She'd still live a pampered, privileged life.

Reason whispered the hard, inescapable truth.

Victor couldn't be expected to wait and sacrifice his inheritance or his mother's home on the chance Theadosia escaped the fate her father had orchestrated for her.

He'd vowed he'd do everything within his power to uncover the truth.

But how long would that take?

Weeks?

Months?

She didn't have the latter.

To lose Victor before he was even hers ripped her heart ragged about the edges.

After setting the basket atop the worktable, she pushed the loose curls off her forehead and headed toward the bedchamber she shared with Jessica.

She wanted to think, and she urgently needed to speak with James. He must be told what had happened.

Had Mr. Leadford already tattled to her father as he'd threatened?

Would Papa truly lock her in her room?

Yes. He had Althea.

Theadosia's situation was impossible. No matter what she decided, she'd hurt someone she loved. She'd have to choose the lesser of two evils, and either would leave scars and a broken heart.

Protect my mother even as you must protect your father.

Victor's words played through her mind once more, all but ripping her aching heart from her chest.

As she neared the staircase, Mama's angry voice carried down the corridor.

"You've gone too far this time, Oscar. I didn't agree when you banished Althea, and I surely shan't stand by and watch you force Theadosia into a marriage with a despicable man I cannot abide."

Theadosia crept down the corridor on tip-toes, mindful to avoid the squeaky floorboards. As she reached the drawing room, Jessica edged from the adjacent doorway, a finger to her lips.

She silently urged Theadosia inside the study.

"They've been arguing almost since you left," Jessica whispered in her ear.

"Has Mr. Leadford returned?"

Jessica shook her head, the blond curls framing her face bouncing.

"No, but that's the reason I'm hiding in here. If he comes back, I want to make sure he doesn't eavesdrop." Color swept up her cheeks. "I know I am guilty of the doing same, but I'm doing so because I want to help. He'd only use whatever he hears for his own gain."

No small truth there.

Tears filled Jessica's eyes. "Lord, I cannot abide the man, and I cannot bear the idea that you might have to wed him. He's a disgusting pig."

Wrapping an arm around her sister's waist, Theadosia gave her a hug. "I'm going into the drawing room. Mama and Papa are discussing my future. Yours too. I cannot stand idly by and not voice my opinion. Besides, I saw Leadford a bit ago, and he threatened me and Papa."

Jessica's pretty eyes widened, and her jaw sagged. "I knew he was evil."

"You have no idea just how much so." Theadosia shuddered in remembrance.

Best not to mention Victor had also been there or his proposal. Theadosia knew what her sweet sister would say about that.

A horrible thought struck her, stealing her breath.

If she married Victor, might Leadford turn his vulgar attention to Jessica?

Another reason she could not marry Victor straightaway.

"I'm taking our daughters, and we're going to live with James until you come to your senses." Mama's voice broke. "Wasn't losing one daughter enough, Oscar? I cannot lose another."

Didn't Mama know James let lodgings at the Albany? He didn't have room for them, and Theadosia didn't think women were permitted to reside there either.

"I'm coming with you," Jessica said, with a determined tilt of her small chin.

Theadosia grasped her hand, and mouth flattened into a firm line, entered the room.

"You cannot leave with Theadosia, Marianne. It's impossible."

Father sank into a chair, and raising a shaking hand to his ashen face, knuckled away a tear.

"Why not, Papa? Why have you promised me to Mr. Leadford when you know I detest him?"

Theadosia, holding Jessica's hand, hovered at the entrance.

Startled, he glanced up for an instant, then dropped his gaze to his lap and said nothing.

When had he become a coward?

Face taut, Mama also looked toward the doorway. She motioned to the faded settee before the window. "You might as well come in since this involves you both."

Though Theadosia felt a degree of compassion for her father, he'd put her in a horrible predicament. He must own his wrongdoing and acknowledge his selfishness.

After taking a seat, she met his doleful gaze straight on. "Mr. Leadford says if I don't marry him, you will go to prison. You might even hang."

"God above, Oscar, what have you done?" Mama, asked, her voice breaking again. Pale as her lace fichu, she stiffly lowered herself to a chair. Pressing an unsteady palm to her chest, she swallowed.

Jessica squeezed Theadosia's fingers as Papa stared out the window, his face creased and haggard.

"I thought that if I provided Theadosia and Jessica with some of the luxuries young women like, they mightn't be tempted to sin as Althea was." He slid them a repentant look.

Hence the new gowns and fripperies.

"I understand it's hard being a rector's wife and children," he murmured, his voice so low, Theadosia had to strain to hear him. "I also know that I give our food and other belongings, even money, to the poor to such an extent that we must economize. We must go without and live a simple, frugal life. But I also realize women want pretty things, and the girls were getting of an age, I feared they'd look for the wrong type of young man, as Althea did."

Her father's generosity had been out of character, but Theadosia hadn't questioned where he'd acquired the funds for their new garments, bonnets, and shoes these past few months. She'd assumed he'd received an increase in wages.

"We mightn't wear the first stare of fashion or eat delicacies, but we've always had enough. So what exactly are you saying, Oscar?"

Mama wasn't letting him transfer the blame to them.

Head lowered, he covered his eyes with his fingertips.

"I've been borrowing from the tithes and organ fund, and also keeping monies I said were sent to the Diocese," he admitted, still not meeting their gazes. "It's been six months since Benedict left, and I didn't think Leadford would notice the small discrepancies in the account ledgers. I swear I meant to pay back every penny."

So livid, her red hair almost crackled with her ire, Mama narrowed her eyes. "You've been gambling again too, haven't you? Just like before we moved here."

Papa's chin sank to his chest, and his shoulders slumped. "Yes."

Mama's lips trembled, and she shook her head. "You swore to me, Oscar. On the Bible. You vowed you'd *never* touch dice again."

Theadosia exchanged a dumbfounded glance with Jessica. Papa a gambler?

"How much, Oscar?" Mama demanded. "How much have you stolen?"

"Leadford says it's almost five hundred pounds."

Five hundred? It might as well be five thousand.

Jessica gasped, and Mama collapsed against her chair.

"I don't remember taking that much." Papa had never been very good at bookkeeping or figures, something he readily admitted to. "I have repaid a little from my wages."

James strode into the drawing room, his expression fierce.

"Did I hear correctly? You've been embezzling Church funds and gambling? To the tune of five hundred pounds?" He made a disgusted noise in the back of his throat and whirled away from Papa. Plowing a hand through his hair, he spun back to face him again.

"My God, Father. Do you have any idea how harsh the courts are on men of the cloth?" James threw his hands in the air. "Men who preach righteousness and honesty and then betray the Church's and their parish's trust?"

Theadosia rubbed her temple. This was much more awful than she'd imagined.

"You realize Leadford won't stop at marrying me, don't you? You'll be under his thumb, groveling about whenever he decides he wants something more. You've ruined us, Papa. How will we ever be free of him?"

Her father raised his eyes, his harrowed expression fraught with shame. He glanced first at Mama's stricken face, then at Jessica, and lastly at Theadosia.

"Forgive me, my dears." Moisture shimmered in his eyes. "It's even worse than that, I'm afraid."

"How could it possibly be worse?" Disbelief strangling his voice, James plopped onto the settee's arm.

"Leadford claims since the women used the stolen monies to buy gowns and fallalls, they are accessories to the crime." Entreaty in his gaze, Papa shrank into his chair. "If we don't do exactly as he demands, he vows to send your mother and sisters to prison too."

10

Two mornings later, after a pair of sleepless nights reliving Thea's last heart-wrenching words, Victor once again rapped on the doorframe outside the solarium's open door.

"Mother, a word if you've a moment."

She set aside her correspondence and, removing her spectacles, smiled warmly.

"Dearest, forgive me for saying so, but you look exhausted. Didn't you sleep well again last night?" She picked up the bell atop her petite writing desk. "Shall I ring Grover for coffee?"

"No, I've already had three cups, thick and black enough to tar a roof." He bent and kissed her upturned cheek. "I spent the night pacing my bedchamber, and I've come to a most difficult decision."

"Have a seat and tell me what has you so disgruntled. Has it to do with Theadosia?"

He gave her a sharp look.

How did she know?

"Don't look so taken aback, darling." She gave him one of her motherly smiles; the one that said she knew something he didn't think she did. "I saw how you gazed at her the other night. But there were also other hints as to your feelings."

"What hints? I've been most inconspicuous." Had even lied to himself about his motives and actions.

She held up her hand, fingers extended and ticked them off one by one.

"You impulsively invited the Brentwoods to dinner—you are never impulsive, dear." Thumb. "You asked that I be sure to invite them to the ball." Forefinger. "You asked me to make certain they would attend too. You also suggested I ask Theadosia to help me with the planning. You disappeared almost every day at the same time and were seen with her near Bower Pool."

Middle finger, ring finger, and little finger, one right after the other.

She elevated a fine eyebrow. "The Walter boys' mother is sister to our larder maid."

Ah, the rascals had tattled to their mother.

His mother touched her other thumb with her pointer finger. "And from God knows where, you procured a case of oranges for marmalade."

She wiggled the beringed digits in front of his face. "You are clearly besotted, and I couldn't be happier for you. Especially since Theadosia obviously returns your affection."

He shook his head and chuckled. Did nothing escape his mother?

"I love her. I think I loved her before I left three years ago but didn't recognize that's what I felt."

"So why the glum face? You have your bride." She gave him a

229

brilliant smile. "Should we make an announcement at the ball?"

"It's not that simple." He took a seat beside her, and as succinctly as possible, explained all.

"I knew there was something unsavory about that troll of a man." Lips pursed, she wrinkled her nose. "And to think he sat at my table. I shall instruct Grover to throw out the serviette he used."

How the butler was to tell the difference between that particular serviette and the other twenty or thirty, Victor couldn't imagine.

"I shall find a way to deal with Leadford," he said, "but I'm concerned about what this means for you."

She took his hand between hers.

"Victor, listen to me. I can make my home anywhere, as long as my children and grandchildren visit me often. Ridgewood is only a building. Yes, there are lots of wonderful memories here, but you love Theadosia. You must do everything to make her your duchess. If that means your birthday comes and goes and you are not wed, then so what? Jeffery will gain a fortune and several holdings. He'll be ecstatic. I never held with that addendum to the will anyway."

Was there ever a more wonderful mother?

"There will likely be a scandal, Mother. Scads of gossip and tattle-mongering when everything comes out. Rest assured, there will be those who say I've married beneath myself."

"Oh, pish posh. That always makes the romance more exciting. Why, I called off my betrothal to a Russian prince to marry your father. Cousin Cora was only too happy to take my place."

"Do tell. A Russian prince? I might've been a prince rather than a mere duke?"

"Constantine never stood a chance. He didn't hold a candle to your father's wicked good looks." She leaned forward and kissed Victor's cheek. "Now go be a hero. Women adore men coming to their rescue, but do let her think she helped too." She winked. "Now go, do whatever you must to save our dear Thea."

Two hours later, Victor handed Acheron's reins to a groom at the Blue Rose Inn at Essex Crossings. James had sent a missive 'round that morning saying he urgently needed to speak with his old friend.

Victor nodded to the patrons as he made his way to a table in the far corner.

James, his expression as morose as Victor had ever seen, stared into a tankard.

"I presume you don't have good news?"

James spared him a caustic glance before taking a long pull of ale. "No."

"What's happened?"

By the time James had finished speaking, Victor was hard put not to jump up and go in search of Leadford and rearrange his face. Instead, he quaffed back the rest of his ale.

"Is there any merit to what Leadford claims? Can the women be tried and convicted as accomplices?"

James slowly shook his head, his expression thoughtful.

"They can be tried, but Father has written a statement that he alone was responsible. As far as I know, Mama and the girls didn't have access to the books, though that might be hard to prove. The scandal would be horrendous, but I don't think they'd be convicted. Father would, however."

Victor hooked his arm over the back of his chair.

"What if I repay the funds and your father resigns effective immediately? I would even be willing to restore and refurbish the parsonage and Church. Do you think the Church would consider clemency then?"

That fell just short of bribery in Victor's estimation, but experience had taught him incentives went a long way. Even with those who claimed a Godly calling.

Folding his arms, James tilted his chair back. "Not as long as Leadford is around to stir things up." He sighed and scrubbed a hand across his eyes. "I'm not saying my father shouldn't take responsibility for what he's done, nor should he escape punishment. But we both know if he was a peer, he'd never see the inside of a cell."

Signaling the barkeep for another tankard, he looked toward Victor to see if he desired another as well.

Victor angled his head in affirmation.

"What if he was related to a peer? And if he agreed to do some sort of penance?"

"Maybe." Shrugging, James accepted the foamy tankard. The mug at his mouth, he paused and a teasing grin tipped his lips

"Wait. Related to a peer? You and Thea?"

"I already proposed. She said yes if this business with Leadford is settled. Your father, on the other hand, very vehemently said no." Victor stretched his legs out before him, one hand resting on the table. "I think he might be persuaded to change his mind if he weren't being coerced by Leadford."

James's smile widened, and he slapped his knee.

"I knew it. Thea couldn't keep her eyes off you, and you weren't any better. I must say, I couldn't have chosen anyone finer for her."

"Then you approve?" It was nice to have one Brentwood in his corner.

James still wore a silly smile. "Heartily."

"May I look at the accounts?" Victor asked.

"Of course. I did last evening. Honestly, they're such a scribbled mess, I cannot make heads or tails of them." James tossed a coin onto the table and rose. "There's still the matter of Leadford's blackmail."

Victor followed him to the door. "I've been thinking about that. What do you suppose the Church's views are on blackmail and extortion? I heard him threaten Thea too."

James paused in putting on his hat. A slow, pleased smile turned his mouth upward.

"Why, I should say, every bit as unfavorable as embezzlement."

His smile victorious, Victor held the door open. "I think it's time we paid Leadford a visit."

Victor sat in the parsonage's cozy, outdated parlor sipping tea with Mrs. Brentwood and James. He'd taken a cursory glance at the Church's ledgers earlier. They were a muddle, but even so, he identified several instances of altered amounts, two as recent as this past week. He couldn't be sure, of course, but to his eye, it appeared more than one person had changed the entries dating back at least two years.

Someone might argue one or more of the women in the household had abetted the reverend, but more likely it was the curate in charge of bookkeeping.

If all went as Victor had planned, it wouldn't matter.

James thought Victor's scheme feasible as well.

"Your daughters aren't at home?" Victor asked, even as he sought Thea. Like a ray of sunshine, she always brightened any room she was in and filled him with a peace he found nowhere else. "I should like them to be present as well."

"Theadosia is inquiring if our recent purchases might be returned." Faint color lined Mrs. Brentwood's cheekbones as she brushed a crumb off her lap, her hand unsteady. "When I saw you ride up, I sent Jessica out the back entrance to retrieve her sister."

The poor woman looked like she hadn't slept either. How could she when her husband faced disgrace, scandal, and imprisonment, and a blackmailing rotter had demanded her daughter marry him?

"I expect my husband and Mr. Leadford home for the midday meal at any moment," she said. "Mr. Cox suffered a broken leg when he was thrown from his horse yesterday. Oscar does so enjoy bringing a bit of encouragement to those convalescing."

Sugar tongs in hand, she wrinkled her forehead. "Did I already add sugar to my tea?"

She spoke to herself, and Victor met James's concerned gaze over her bent head.

With a little shrug, she added a fifth lump of sugar, and stirring her very sweet tea, gave them a fatigued smile.

"Oscar truly loves his parishioners, but I expect you're here to discuss that other unpleasantness, aren't you?"

"When everyone is present since it concerns them as well." Victor forced himself to drink the tea, but after the coffee this morning and two tankards of ale, his stomach protested against any more liquids.

"He'll have to resign, won't he?" Mrs. Brentwood looked first to her son and then to Victor. Her bravado slipped, and she gave a defeated little nod. "Yes. Of course he will. I presumed as much."

She touched a bent knuckle to the corner of her eye.

"He has no choice, Mama." James leaned forward, his elbows on his knees. "If Father's to be granted any grace, he must show true humility and remorse. He can never be trusted with a parish again. You must know he'll be defrocked."

The column of her throat worked, and she blinked several times.

"Yes. I thought so. I'm not sure what we'll do, but Oscar will think of something."

If he wasn't rotting in a prison cell.

Victor stared into his cooling brew. He'd been mulling over that very detail. Everything depended on whether Brentwood was brought up on charges. And that depended on whether Leadford could be convinced to keep quiet.

He permitted a satisfied upturn of his mouth. He believed he had just the means to ensure Leadford did.

A ruckus in the entry and a door *clunking* shut announced someone had returned.

"Have you decided yet, Oscar?" Leadford asked. "I really do think it best if I procure a special license and the ceremony takes place at once."

"That worm cannot marry my Thea, James," Mrs. Brentwood whispered fiercely. A mother's protectiveness rendered her voice and expression fierce. "He simply can *not*."

"Mrs. Brentwood, he shan't," Victor said. "I need you to trust me in this."

Features tight, her worried brown eyes so like Thea's, she gave a quick nod.

"I'm not discussing that right now, Hector." Disdain riddled the reverend's hushed voice. "Besides, it appears we have callers."

Mrs. Brentwood rose and sailed to the entrance.

"Oscar, the Duke of Sutcliffe is here, as is James. I've sent Jessica for Theadosia. His Grace wishes to speak to all of us."

"I'll just bet he does," Leadford all but sniggered. A moment later, he swaggered into the parlor, greeting Victor and James with a surly, "Gentlemen."

He helped himself to a handful of biscuits before flopping into an armchair. No doubt he thought he controlled the situation. Was he in for a nasty surprise.

Jubilation thrummed through Victor, blaring triumph's fanfare in his blood.

Mrs. Brentwood sent Leadford a censuring frown as she returned to her seat and lifted the pot.

"Tea, Oscar?"

"No, thank you." Mr. Brentwood gave Victor the briefest tilt of his chin in greeting. Mortification fairly radiated off of his stiff form. "James, what goes on here?"

James stopped drumming his fingertips on the arm of the settee. "The Duke and I—"

More commotion in the entry announced the girls' return.

Thea glided in, her arms laden with packages wrapped in brown paper and tied with strings. She stalled at the entrance when she saw everyone.

Mrs. Brentwood took in the bundle Thea laid atop the table near the door. Her welcoming smile dissolved. "No luck, dearest?"

Again, Thea's gaze swept the room's occupants, her delicate nose flaring as she encountered Leadford's bold regard.

She sliced him a frigid look.

"I'm afraid not, Mama."

"Oh, I hope the tea is hot." Jessica, her cheeks whipped rosy by the wind, looped her hand through Thea's elbow and guided her to the settee that Victor sat upon.

"I'm quite chilled," she said, perching on the arm of her mother's seat instead of taking the only remaining chair beside Leadford.

Even as she accepted her steaming cup of tea, the tumultuous clouds outside released their generous contents.

"Was there ever such a cool summer?" Mrs. Brentwood idly remarked to no one in particular.

With a graceful swish of skirts, Thea sank onto the cushion beside Victor. After balancing her umbrella against the seat, she declined tea with a small shake of her head as she removed her bonnet. Not the cheerful one with the blue roses, but a frumpy straw affair with but a single green ribbon frayed at the edges.

"What was so urgent Jessica had to drag me home before I finished my errands?"

Everyone looked to Victor. He hooked his ankle over his knee and examined the fingernails on his left hand. "We are all aware that Leadford's blackmailing Mr. Brentwood, are we not?"

Everyone gave a cautious nod.

The reverend's face reddened, but Leadford didn't even have the decency to look abashed.

He lifted a shoulder, his manner cockily confident.

"Don't make me out to be the villain. I'm simply taking advantage of an opportunity to better my situation." He flicked his biscuit-crumb covered fingers toward Mr. Brentwood. "He has only himself to blame for stealing Church monies."

Thea grasped the handle of her umbrella.

Was she contemplating thwacking Leadford?

Victor would quite like to see that.

Lips pressed together, the reverend remained silent, his focus on his folded hands. Even Victor felt a dash of empathy for the chagrined man.

"When was the last time you altered the books, Mr. Brentwood?" he asked.

Surprised, the cleric blinked. His thick, silver-peppered brows furrowed in thought, he scratched his chin. "At least four months ago. I've been saving what I took and slowly doling it out so it wouldn't be obvious to Marianne."

"Four months ago, you say? Then why do the ledgers clearly show at least two adjustments last week?" Victor slash Leadford a what-do-you-have-to-say-about-that glare.

Straightening his spine in indignation, Mr. Brentwood turned his contemptuous regard upon Leadford. "You accuse me, threaten to ruin my life, blackmail me and coerce me to agreeing to let my precious daughter marry you, and then you commit the same sin?"

For the first time, Leadford looked uncomfortable. He wet his lower lip and shifted his feet. "No, no, I haven't." He pointed at Brentwood. "You're the only one who's guilty of that crime."

Victor suspected the previous curate might've had sticky fingers too, for Brentwood clearly had no idea how to keep books properly. A wonder there hadn't been consequences before now.

It didn't matter. Victor intended to repay every penny.

"I have a proposition. One that I think will work to everyone's benefit." He gave Theadosia a reassuring smile.

A tiny glimmer of something shimmered in her eyes for a moment, then faded.

A tendril had come lose when she removed her hat, and the wavy strand teased her ear. Was her hair half as soft as it looked? He longed to find out, to see the mass unbound and draped about her shoulders and back.

If all went well, he would.

"Do you trust me, Thea?"

Her pretty eyes went soft around the edges. "Of course I do."

"I think you're forgetting who has the upper hand here." Leadford made a rude noise, his bluster returning. "There's nothing you can do or say—"

Victor raised his hand. "Hear me out."

"Yes, do hush, Mr. Leadford," Mrs. Brentwood said. "I've had quite enough of you. In fact," she slid her husband a sideways glance, then squared her shoulders. "In fact, you need to be gone from All Saint's within the hour. We'll take our chances with the courts and the Church."

Leadford's mocking laugh rang out. "You'd subject your daughters to prison? Do you know what they do to pretty young women there? Shall I tell you?"

He'd probably enjoy the telling, the depraved sot.

"Enough. It won't come to that." Victor stood and, hands clasped behind his back, paced away. "I'll repay all of the missing funds. I don't care who took them, but I shall assure the books are balanced down to the last groat."

Jessica gripped her mother's hand, and hope lit Mrs. Brentwood's wan features.

"As generous as that is, Your Grace," Mr. Brentwood said, "it doesn't excuse the fact that I committed a crime and I've a gambling addiction."

"Exactly." Leadford pounced, claws barred. "If the Diocese were aware, you'd be defrocked, and you'd face a prison sentence or hanging."

James jerked his head in Leadford's direction. "Men do not hang for theft, you dolt."

"He'd still go to prison. Probably die there. Then what of his wife and daughters?" Leadford's left eye twitched. A dead giveaway he was nervous as hell.

Victor laughed and splayed a hand on his nape. "You really didn't think this through, did you? James would care for his family, naturally."

Leadford pushed to his feet. "I'm going to write an overdue letter. We'll just see who's laughing then."

"You might want to rethink that, Leadford," James said, before yawning behind his hand. "Do you honestly think the courts or the Church will look kindlier on an extortioner? I'm a barrister. I should know. Particularly since it can be argued you also stole from the Church."

Victor patted his coat pocket. "I have a letter here from my friend, the Duke of Westfall. He did a little snooping around for me. I was actually surprised to hear from him so soon. Seems you were a rather unsavory chap in your last two positions. The Church didn't want a scandal so they moved you on each time. Theadosia is not the first young woman to spurn your attentions, is she?"

"Oh, well done you, Your Grace." A fragile smile curved Theadosia's mouth, and her face glowed with optimism.

"Well, well, what an interesting turn of events." James leaned back and folded his arms. "The self-righteous buggar has a history *he'd* rather not be made known."

"Nothing was ever proven." Leadford plucked at his collar, his face a rather peculiar shade of greyish-green.

"Here's what's going to happen, Leadford." Victor rested his hands on the back of the settee, Thea's satiny neck mere inches away. He gripped the wood tighter.

"I'm going to give you a large purse, and you're going to disappear.

And that means you'll never accept a clergyman's position again. If I ever see you or even hear your name whispered again, friends of mine with questionable connections might be encouraged to abduct you and maroon you on a remote—a very, *very* remote—tropical island."

Leadford's jaw sagged to his chin, and he deflated like an impaled hot air balloon. He looked from person to person, then wet his lips.

"Fine. I'll go. But only because you threatened me."

Victor hitched a shoulder. "Just as you threatened Theadosia and her family."

"When do I get my money?" Leadford asked.

Greedy sod.

"Be at the Blue Rose Inn at Essex Crossings at . . ." Victor withdrew his timepiece. "Four o'clock."

After a glare all around, Leadford stomped from the room.

Mr. Brentwood sighed then pushed to his feet. "I'm grateful you've rid us of that vermin, Your Grace. And I'm indebted to you for your offer to repay the funds I borrowed."

Still couldn't admit he'd stolen the money, could he?

"You didn't borrow them, Papa. You stole them and used Mama, Jessica, and I as an excuse to do so." Theadosia's quiet but resolved voice pinned him to the floor.

"You're right, Theadosia." His shoulders drooped, and he seemed to shrink into himself at her censure. "Nonetheless, I humbly accept your offer, Your Grace. I've no wish to spend the remainder of my life in prison, even though it's what I deserve for betraying my flock and my family. If you'll excuse me, I need to write a letter of resignation."

"Mr. Brentwood, *all* of the offers I made previously still stand, if you are willing to accept them." Victor re-pocketed his watch. "If I may be so bold, perhaps you might suggest in your letter that you persuaded me to restore the Church and parsonage as part of your recompense. And I, too, shall be writing a letter on your behalf."

"Thank you. Your generosity and kindness do you credit, and I do accept *all* of your proposals." The reverend's attention shifted to Theadosia. "Please forgive me, my dear. I've been unforgivably hard-hearted, selfish, and obstinate." He closed his eyes, anguish contorting his face. "And prideful. So blasted prideful."

In a flash, she was in his arms, hugging her father.

"Of course I forgive you, Papa. Does this mean we can see Althea again?" she asked swiping tears from her cheeks.

"Yes, if she can forgive a stubborn, foolish old man." Mr. Brentwood shuffled from the room, a broken man.

"Please excuse me, Your Grace. My husband needs me." After a brief curtsy, his wife swiftly followed him.

Victor turned to James and withdrew a sizable envelope from his pocket. "This is for Leadford. Will you meet him on my behalf? I also want an agreement in writing. I'm taking no chances with that wretch. Can you deal with that as well?"

"I'd be happy to, just to see the look on his face when I make him sign it." James rose and stretched. "I must say, I thoroughly enjoyed you taking that rotter down a few pegs." He reached for Jessica's hand. "Come, pet. I'm ravenous. Let's see what we can rummage up in the kitchen, shall we?"

Jessica smiled at Thea. "We can keep our new gowns after all. We won't have to attend the ball in our old frocks."

She accepted James's help, and then with a bounce in her step, they departed.

Thea canted her head, giving him a joyous smile.

"You're our hero, Victor. Yesterday, I believed there was no hope and today, you've set everything to rights."

Once again, his mother had been correct. Women adored heroes.

Her exquisite face radiated with love for him. It humbled and exhilarated at the same time.

How he'd resented coming back to Colchester, resented the stipulation in Father's will. As it turned out, Father had known what was best, even when Victor didn't.

Cupping her shoulders, he bent and kissed her petal-soft lips.

"Not everything, my love."

"What else is there?"

An endearing perplexed frown creased her forehead.

"There's the matter of a proper proposal after your father just agreed that I might." He fingered her tempting lock of reddish blond hair.

"He did no such thing."

"Oh, but he did. I said *all* of my offers still stood, and he said he accepted *all* of them."

She angled her head.

"Do you love me, Victor?"

"I do." He tweaked her nose. "I love you so much I cannot find adequate words. I told my mother this morning that I realized I did before

I left three years ago. I also told her that I would marry no other save you and that if that meant I wasn't wed by my birthday, dear Cousin Jeffery would suddenly become a wealthy chap."

Tears sparkled in her eyes, and she grasped his lapels.

"Did you truly?" She leaned away, her expression wary. "Was the duchess upset about possibly losing her home?"

"On the contrary, my love. She ordered me to do whatever I must to save you." He kissed her nose. "I think she's already rather fond of you."

"Poor Jeffery. He'll be so very disappointed."

Thea twined her arms about Victor's neck.

He cocked a brow. "And why is that?"

"Because we'll be married by your birthday, silly man." She raised up on her toes, drawing his head downward. "Now kiss me, my dearest love."

"With pleasure, Duchess."

Victor grasped her waist and lifted her, sealing their troth with a kiss that branded both their souls.

Epilogue

Ridgewood Court, Masquerade Fairy-tale Ball
21 July, 1809

Searching for her husband of almost ten hours, Theadosia ran her fingers along the gold satin ribbon-covered handle of her masquerade mask. Several gentlemen whose names she couldn't recall in the flurry of introductions—except for the Dukes of Dandridge, Pennington, Westfall, and Bainbridge—had hustled him off toward the terrace after the first set.

Grinning, something he'd done most of the day, his hands palm upward and extended in resignation, Victor had winked and allowed his mischievous friends to tow him away.

"I'll be back as soon as I can escape these rakes, Duchess."

Probably sampling a bottle of spirits whilst toasting—*or reproving*—his stupidity for jumping headlong into the parson's mousetrap less than a month after he'd returned to Colchester.

She and Victor hadn't had a moment alone the entire day. After the ceremony this morning, there'd been an extravagant breakfast, and the rest of the time had been filled with activities for the house party as well as guest after guest wishing them happy. And to think they had nearly a week more of this chaos before leaving for their wedding trip.

A smile tugged her lips upward.

Truth to tell, she didn't mind, for her dearest friends and Jessica were gathered around her, each resplendent in fanciful gowns of silk and satin. Her own fairy-tale confection, a purple and gold creation so divine she'd almost been afraid to wear it, shimmered with thousands of tiny seed pearls.

Victor had secretly commissioned it and surprised her with the gown this afternoon, along with a pair of golden slippers covered with hundreds of glass beads.

"For my very own Cendrillon," he'd said, gathering her into his arms for a spine-tingling kiss. "Have I told you how happy I am, my darling?"

"No more than I, Victor." She kissed the corner of his mouth. "It still feels like a dream, and I'm afraid I'm going to wake up."

"As long as you wake up beside me every day for the rest of my life." He gazed longingly at the enormous four-poster bed dominating her bedchamber. "If I wasn't determined to not rush our first joining, Duchess . . ."

His voice had gone low and husky, his eyes hooded with desire, and answering passion had warmed her blood.

She grabbed his hand, tugging him toward the bed. "We've hours before—"

After a short rap on her door, the bubbly lady's maid assigned to Theadosia barged in. The servant's eyes rounded in surprise, and a blush scooted up her already ruddy cheeks.

"Beg your pardon, Your Grace." She curtsied, her focus glued to the floor. "I didn't know you were here."

Sighing, he'd kissed Theadosia on the nose.

"I've just given my wife a new ball gown. Please see that the wrinkles are removed before tonight, and I want her hair worn down, please."

The extraordinary amethyst and diamond parure set Theadosia wore, complete with a tiara fit for a princess, had been another gift from him, delivered as she dressed for the ball. She did feel like royalty, and today had been nothing short of magical.

She'd been the one to suggest that they wed today to save her mother-in-law additional work preparing for a grand wedding. It also spared Theadosia's parents a great deal of awkwardness.

Papa had performed the ceremony, but neither he nor her mother were attending the ball. He'd vowed he didn't deserve the privilege, but more probably, humiliation kept him away, as well as a renewed oath to avoid gaming of any sort, including cards. The news of his resignation and the reason behind his hasty notice had traveled swiftly through Colchester and the surrounding area.

Next week her parents would sail to Australia, accompanying a shipload of convicts and soldiers. The Church had magnanimously offered her father a position there as vicar; no one else showed the least interest in such a remote, primitive post. He'd been so grateful not to be defrocked, he'd eagerly accepted, but only after asking if Jessica might live with Theadosia and Victor. He would not risk towing his unmarried daughter halfway across the world, exposing her to dangers unknown.

Althea and her family were expected in two days. Mama had wanted to see her daughter and grandchildren before sailing to Australia. Especially since she and Papa would be gone for three years; time enough for the gossip to settle.

Craning her neck, Theadosia searched the ballroom for Victor once more. Silly to miss him so much. Only a few minutes had passed.

"Thea, I think it was terribly rude of the Duke of Bainbridge to commandeer Sutcliffe the way he did. Surely he knows a groom's place is at his bride's side on their wedding day." Jessica slipped her hand into the crook of Thea's arm. Wide-eyed and excited, she too scrutinized the ballroom, no doubt hopeful her dance card would be filled before evening's end.

"Don't fret, Jessica. It's just the way of men. They only think of themselves. He meant no offense. They never do." A tinge of bitterness crept into Nicolette's voice.

Her betrothed had tossed her over for an heiress two seasons ago. Ever since, she'd become a consummate flirt, gaining a reputation for crushing any man foolish enough to try to pay his addresses.

Nicolette brushed her gloved hands down the front of her embroidered white satin gown. The royal blue velvet half coat perfectly matched her eyes, which sparkled with mischief at the moment. "I don't recall ever being in the company of so many seductive scoundrels, do you, Gabriella and Ophelia? What great fun we'll have this week."

Wearing identical gowns, except for the color, the twins shook their heads.

"No, not to mention so many devilish dukes," Ophelia said, a skeptical brow arched.

Mirroring her twin's action, Gabriella lifted a matching eloquent eyebrow. "Sutcliffe certainly travels in exclusive circles, Thea."

Like Theadosia, the twins had never left Colchester. They lived with their aged grandparents and rarely attended anything more exciting than a tea or church. To liven things up, they were known to switch identities every now and again. Few people, except their family and dearest friends, could tell them apart.

"Ah, there you all are at last. I almost despaired of finding you in this infernal crush. I suppose that means the ball is a smashing success." Everleigh Chatterton glided toward them, her silvery gown, trimmed in black satin, accenting her white blonde hair. She'd been widowed almost two years ago but still wore half-mourning colors right down to her jet and diamond locket and earrings, as well as her ebony silk gloves.

Theadosia suspected Everleigh's extended mourning period had far more to do with discouraging the attention of besotted men attracted to the stunning beauty like bees to blossoms, rather than any lingering grief she felt for the loss of her much, *much* older and despised husband.

Jemmah, the Duchess of Dandridge and Rayne Wellbrook, Everleigh's step-niece, accompanied her. They smiled in greeting whilst vigorously waving their fans.

"Lord, but it's stifling," the Duchess of Dandridge said. Hers had been a fairy-tale match too.

Thea glanced from friend to friend, and finally to Jessica. If only they might have their happily-ever-afters as well someday.

She would pray they did.

The Duchess of Dandridge had the right of it, nonetheless. The ballroom had grown beastly hot in a short period. If only Thea might slip outdoors for a breath of fresh air, perhaps even run her hands through the fountain bubbling in the garden.

"Is that tall, dark man still behind me?" Everleigh murmured as she also flicked her horn *brisé* fan open. Behind her silver mask, her jade green eyes sparked with annoyance.

An exotic looking gentleman followed her, accompanied by the Dowager Duchess of Sutcliffe and the banker *Jerome* DuBoise, her nearly constant companion since his arrival four days ago.

"Yes." Theadosia nodded, searching for an excuse to whisk her friend away. "Why don't we get some ratafia? I'm quite parched."

"Theadosia my dear, where's Sutcliffe off to? I thought for certain he'd stick to your side the entire evening." The dowager duchess fairly glowed under Mr. DuBois's obvious admiration.

"A few of his friends wanted to wish him happy." Thea returned her smile. Her mother-in-law already treated her like a beloved daughter. "I think it was really an excuse to indulge in a tot."

The dowager chuckled while gesturing to the tall man. "Do let me introduce Griffin, Duke of Sheffield. He's nephew to Mr. DuBois and quite the world traveler."

She efficiently finished the introductions, and after the women curtsied, Everleigh half-turned away, just short of snubbing the duke. Her marriage truly had been an awful affair and had left hidden wounds she refused to speak about. Even though she was only three and twenty, she'd sworn off men and marriage.

251

"Another duke?" Ophelia whispered soto voce to her twin. "How many does that make? Five or six?"

The Duke of Sheffield flashed a dazzling smile, his teeth white against his tanned face.

"Actually, there are ten of us. Myself, Dandridge, Sutcliffe, Pennington, Bainbridge, Westfall, Kincade, Asherford, San Sebastian, and Heatherston. The last three aren't here, however, and Kincade and Heatherston are Scots. We met at *Bon Chance* several years ago, and have been the greatest of friends since."

Bon Chance?

Wasn't that the scandalous gaming hell run by Madam Fordyce?

"Oh my, ten you say?" Ophelia appeared suitably awed, while her unimpressed twin hunched a shoulder.

"They're just men, Ophelia," Gabriella said.

"I imagine you've a great many interesting stories you could tell." Nicolette batted her eyelashes. She appeared such a coquette, but any man foolish enough to take the bait soon found himself verbally skewered.

"There's Sutcliffe now." A proud smile illuming her face, the dowager pointed her closed fan.

Theadosia's gaze tangled with Victor's across the room, deliciously irresistible in his formal togs, as he strode toward her. Several other gentlemen, including the other dukes, each with varying degrees of disinterest or boredom etched on their aristocratic features, also ambled toward the cluster of women.

She wasn't the least surprised the male guests flocked to her exquisite friends. They were in for a surprise though, for none of the women gave a rat's wiry tail about impressing peers, social position, or how many titles a man held. A rarity to be sure, but that was one of the reasons the women were such close friends.

After bowing, Victor pulled Theadosia to his side. "I beg your indulgence, but I'm abducting my bride for a waltz on the terrace. You ladies should also dance."

He sent a swift, stern look to the other males standing there. "Gentlemen, behave."

He didn't even wait for a response, but whisked Theadosia out a side door. No sooner had they left the ballroom's noise and heat than he swept her into a secluded corner and into his arms, crushing her to his chest and kissing her like a man long-starved.

She opened her mouth, welcoming him in. Her hunger grew, desire sluicing through every pore. Pulling her mouth free, she panted against his neck.

"Darling, do we dare forego the rest of the ball?"

The temperature inside the ballroom was nothing compared to the scorching need blazing within her.

"I'm a duke. I would dare anything for you, Duchess." Victor released a raspy chuckle. "Come. There's a back entrance."

Like naughty children, they clasped hands and ran to the other side of Ridgewood. Less than ten minutes later, after a few stops to indulge in blood sizzling kissing, Victor opened her bedchamber door.

Theadosia gasped, slowly spinning in a circle.

Dozens of candles lit the chamber, the glow casting romantic shadows to the farthest corners. A cheery fire burned in the hearth, and on the table near the window, a bottle of champagne chilled in a bucket between plates of sweetmeats and dainties. But it was the bed that commanded her attention. The bedding had been pulled to the foot, and coral and peach rose petals covered the ivory satin sheets.

"Oh, Victor. Did you arrange this? It's so romantic."

She lifted up on her toes and pressed a kiss to the corner of his firm mouth.

"I did." He pivoted her to unlace her gown. "And I told your maid she wouldn't be needed."

He made short work of divesting Theadosia of her clothing, but when he reached to pull her chemise over her head, she crossed her arms and backed away.

"No, you undress now. I want to see you."

A lazy grin curled his mouth.

"Your every wish is my command."

She watched him in the looking glass as she removed the tiara and earrings, and was about to unclasp the necklace when he closed his hand over hers.

"Leave it on. I want you wearing it when I make love to you."

He lifted her hair, pressing hot kisses to her neck, and a low moan escaped her.

Meeting his searing gaze in the mirror, Theadosia swallowed.

Wearing only his trousers, he radiated masculine beauty. Hair black as midnight covered his sculpted chest, the fine mat disappearing into the vee at his waist.

This glorious man was her husband.

She turned, offering him a siren's smile. Gazes still locked, she untied the ribbons at her shoulders, allowing her chemise to settle at her feet.

Victor froze for an instant before he scooped her into his arms and strode to the bed. Reverently, as if she were as fragile as the petals he lay her on, he lowered her to the mattress.

He shucked his trousers and slid onto the bed. "Let me take you to paradise, darling."

"Oh yes, Victor." She eagerly curled into his side, and sometime later when the heavens burst behind her eyelids and her body quaked with bliss, she cried, "I love you."

"And I love you, Thea," he groaned, finding his own release.

When their breathing had returned to normal, Victor raised Theadosia's hand to his lips and kissed her fingertips.

"For as long as I have breath in my body, Theadosia, I shall love you. You are branded on my spirit. My soul is finally whole."

"As is mine." She traced a finger along his jaw. "I suppose we have Leadford to thank."

Victor skewed a brow in astonishment. "And precisely how do you figure that devil is in any way worthy of our thanks?"

"Because, husband dearest, he forced your hand." She nuzzled his chest, then giggled when he tickled her ribs.

"Vixen."

"Enough talk." She climbed atop him, relishing the sensation of his firm, sinewy body beneath hers. "Take me to heaven again."

A December with a Duke

1

09 December, 1809
Ridgewood Court, Essex England

A chorus of laughter spilled from the drawing room, the gaiety echoing down the gleaming marble-floored corridor. The jollity neither enticed Everleigh nor piqued her interest. A hand resting on the banister and her foot poised on the bottom riser, she slanted her head, listening.

That did not sound like the small, intimate gathering Theadosia, Duchess of Sutcliffe, had promised for the nearly month-long house party.

Only close friends and family had been invited, Thea had assured her when she cajoled Everleigh into staying at Ridgewood Court rather than going home to Fittledale Park each evening. Probably because she knew full well Everleigh wasn't likely to return every day, if at all.

Thea had vowed there wouldn't be a soul who would make Everleigh feel the least uncomfortable, nor any rapscallions inclined to pursue widowed heiresses almost four-and-twenty years of age.

Only eleven people had gathered for tea this afternoon. Afterward, the men—the Duke of Sutcliffe, three other peers of the realm (all dukes as well) and James Brentwood, Thea's brother—had gone riding.

Not Everleigh's definition of a cozy assembly. Two or three at most fit that description.

Nonetheless, the number was sufferable, for a few days at least. Especially since the other females included her cousins Ophelia and Gabriella Breckensole, as well as her step-niece Rayne Westbrook and Theadosia's sister, Jessica. The other women planning to attend the house party would join them for dinner.

Who else had arrived while Everleigh napped the afternoon and early evening away in an attempt to ease the megrim still niggling around her temples?

Too much excitement—make that tension caused by her dread of gatherings—inevitably brought a headache on. A dose of powders and a lie-down in a darkened chamber with a cool, damp cloth across her eyes had reduced this one to a dull annoyance. Still, the minor throbbing provided a perfect excuse to retire early should the need arise.

Another burst of laughter erupted, this one mostly masculine chortles.

That boisterous din couldn't be merely the five men from tea. Precisely how many upper crust chaps had been invited? The same number as females to balance the dinner table?

If so, that likely meant four more strutting peacocks. No doubt pampered and privileged gentlemen with nothing better or more meaningful to do with their time than fritter it away at a house party. Or, as experience had taught her, indulge in a dalliance or two *or three* for the party's endurance.

How many times had she witnessed that very thing during the two miserable years she'd been wife to Arnold Chatterton? How many times had her depraved husband carried on with one shameless gillflurt or another whilst Everleigh barricaded herself in her bedchamber to escape the vile intentions of the other debauchees in attendance?

A shiver juddered across her shoulders, and she firmed her mouth and gave a little shake of her head.

Chatterton was dead.

He had been for almost two years.

He couldn't hurt her anymore.

Neither could his son.

In any event, Theadosia, the daughter of a reverend, wouldn't tolerate those sorts of shenanigans beneath her roof. But how was Thea to know who prowled about in the middle of the night, or what fiend might waylay and force themselves on an unsuspecting lady?

Would all the guests remain until Christmastide?

Boxing Day?

Twelfth Night?

If so, Everleigh assuredly would not.

She enjoyed her solitude too much, hence her turreted bedchamber at Ridgewood, specifically selected for its privacy and isolation from the rest of the guests. Only two other bedchambers and the nursery lay in that wing—all blessedly unoccupied. At least they had been when she'd made her way to her room this afternoon.

She'd heard nothing on her way down to dinner to suggest otherwise.

Descending the last stair, she wrapped her lace shawl closer around her shoulders and weighed her options. She could return to her chamber and request a carriage to take her home. She didn't much care that doing so would certainly advance her reputation for icy aloofness. But it would also hurt Theadosia's feelings, and that Everleigh did care about.

A great deal, truth to tell.

Theadosia was one of the few people who hadn't judged her, who had remained a true friend.

On the other hand, Everleigh could muster her courage and see who'd arrived and then decide whether to escape. Waylaying a footman and asking him to reel off the names of the guests probably wasn't a good idea, though of the choices, it held the most appeal.

Confound Thea, *the compassionate, meddling wretch,* for her tender heart and her ongoing efforts to entice Everleigh into Society again. Drat Thea's determination to help Everleigh overcome her fears and heal. And above all, a pox on her hints that Everleigh should consider allowing suitors to call upon her.

Even—*God forbid*!—contemplate marriage once more.

Didn't she want children? Thea had asked kindly.

With all my heart.

But marry? Be leg-shackled again? Under a man's thumb, and her every movement dictated?

No. *No!*

Never. *Ever.* Again.

She refused to subject herself to *le beau monde's* marriage mart or consider matrimony. Her experiences in those areas had proved intolerable, and she'd no wish to repeat them.

Some things one never recovered from, but unless a person had lived through that awfulness, they simply couldn't understand, so Theadosia couldn't be faulted for her efforts. Everleigh's wounds mightn't have been physical, but the scars on her soul had all but crippled her ability to feel.

Theadosia and Sutcliffe's union was a love match. How could Thea possibly appreciate Everleigh's aversion to marriage?

To men?

Or her immense dislike of December?

How she loathed the month.

She'd first met the aging banker, Arnold Chatterton, and his son Frederick, at a Christmastide ball four years ago. After following her about and generally making a nuisance of himself the better part of the evening, Frederick had come upon her unawares when she'd naively stepped outside for a breath of fresh air. He'd dragged her into the hothouse and forced himself upon her.

Then the sod had bragged to his father about his conquest, destroying any hope she had of salvaging her reputation by keeping silent about the despoiling. Seems deflowering innocents was a perverse game with them.

Arnold, the old reprobate, seized his chance to gain a young wife, and offered her marriage and a settlement to keep the tale quiet. She'd refused at first, but in February, she'd wed him. Seven months later, she gave birth to a darling baby girl, only to lose precious Meredith a fortnight before Christmas that same year.

Arnold still insisted she host all manner of reprobates and degenerates for the Yuletide holiday then and the year afterward as well. In all that time, she didn't see her cousins or friends for fear they'd meet the same fate she had at either Arnold or Frederick's hands.

But after Meredith died, Everleigh wrote her mother and confessed all. She'd written Ophelia, Gabriella, and Theadosia too, bribing a sympathetic milliner with a pair of kid gloves to post the letters for her.

That January, Arnold and Frederick, two drunken sots on their way home from whatever foul company they'd kept that evening, had been robbed and shot multiple times. They'd both died.

She hadn't cried a single tear.

Nor did she smile when the will was read, and as Chatterton's closest living kin, she was left his entire fortune. She'd give it all up, every last penny, if Meredith had lived.

Mama too. She'd died from consumption in March of that awful year.

"Mrs. Chatterton, are you lost? May I direct you to the drawing room?"

She started and clutched a hand to the base of her throat, her pulse jumping against her fingertips. A familiar surge of fear-induced adrenaline zipped through her veins. She'd been so lost in her reverie she hadn't heard the blond Adonis masquerading as a footman approach.

He smiled, male appreciation gleaming in his eyes.

That look she knew well. She didn't recognize him from her other visits. He must be new to his profession, else he'd have learned to conceal his inclinations better.

"I am Hampton." He splayed a snowy while glove against his puffed-out chest. "May I be of service?"

The way he lowered his voice when he said service, suggested he offered her something other than directions.

"No."

She shook her head, skewing her lips downward slightly at her subdued cream gown, trimmed in black and pansy. Perhaps she should've worn the violet bombazine. That frock boasted a higher bodice and didn't flatter her coloring as much as this one did.

"I was just erecting my ramparts and fortifying my buttresses before entering the fray."

"You're wrecking . . . what?"

His handsome face contorted in puzzlement.

Hampton might possess a god's physique and sculpted facial features, but the gorgeous chap was dumb as mud.

"Never mind." She gathered her skirts whilst pointing down the passageway. "It's along there. Third door. Right?"

"No, the drawing room is on the left, Mrs. Chatterton."

Because there aren't any doorways on the right side, featherbrain.

She was hard put not to gape at his obtuseness.

"I would be *happy* to escort you." Another rakish smile lit his features.

On second thought, mud might shine brighter than this fellow.

Exasperated by his forwardness, she arched a starchy brow.

"There's no need. I've been here before, and I'm certain you've duties to attend to. I shan't keep you from them."

There. She'd just reminded him of his position, and if he wanted to keep it, he'd best stop playing the flirt. Next time, she'd report him to Theadosia. Unlike Everleigh's deceased husband and his philandering cohorts, she didn't dally with servants.

Looking somewhat like a rambunctious puppy who been scolded for nipping too hard, Hampton inclined his head, and she swept past him.

Bolstering her lagging courage, and with shoulders as rigid as the marble her black silk slippers swished upon with each step she took, she marched toward the drawing room. She'd rather know now whether she'd need to give her regrets to Theadosia and depart for home.

At the doorway, she pressed a palm to her roiling stomach, shut her eyes, and drew in a long, steadying breath.

Compose yourself, Everleigh Lucy Katherine Chatterton.

She swallowed, forced her eyelids open, and formed her mouth into a self-possessed smile, assuming the cool, standoffish mien that had served her well as a buffer these past four years.

Damn Arnold Chatterton and his evil spawn for turning her into this creature, hiding her fear behind Arctic reserve.

A few steps into the room, she halted, and the smile curving her lips became brittle.

Thirty or more people attired in evening finery occupied the chairs and settees, as well as every nook and corner. Panic clawed its way up her throat, stealing her breath, and restricting her lungs.

This was a mistake.

She shouldn't have come. Not just to dinner, but to Ridgewood Court.

How could she have failed to consider the guests living within a reasonable carriage journey?

Buffleheaded nincompoop.

Too late to turn tail and run now.

Or was it?

Long ago, she'd ceased caring what people thought of her; when she'd been accused of marrying Arnold Chatterton for his immense wealth. Ridiculed for doing so, given his reputation for whore-mongering and other more abhorrent habits. Scorned and shunned because of the vulgar company he kept. Yet those same elitist hypocrites skulked into his bank for loans on a regular basis.

She'd held her head high and never let on how the whispers, cutting looks, and judgments wore away at what little self-respect she had left.

They didn't know the truth of it.

Most people still didn't, and it would remain that way.

She scanned the room again, noting a few more friends, acquaintances, and neighbors. Not all strangers then. This might be bearable. While married, she'd managed larger, much more raucous crowds many times with no lasting ill effects.

Save her nerves wrought ragged for a week afterward.

Which was one reason she avoided large assemblies.

Her attention snared on a dark-eyed man towering above the others, and his well-formed mouth slid upward a fraction as he acknowledged her regard.

Bother and blast.

The disturbing Duke of Sheffield.

Expression bland, she forced her gaze away even as her stomach toppled over itself in the unnerving manner it did when she sensed a man desired her. Other women might be flattered, possibly encourage the beau's interest.

Not she, by juniper.

On a night not so very different than this, just such a man had ruined her. Destroyed her life. Stolen her future.

Oh, she could feign politesse when necessary, but for the most part, she avoided men, trusting few other than James Brentwood and Victor, the Duke of Sutcliffe.

Mouth firmed, she took in the others present, aware that Sheffield's keen focus never left her. With a little start, she realized her skin didn't crawl with the knowledge. She hadn't considered he'd be here. She ought to have. After all, he'd been at Theadosia and Sutcliffe's wedding ball.

She dared a covert peek at him.

Eyes hooded, he still stared, but not menacingly.

No, if anything, she'd say he appeared intrigued.

Hadn't she made it clear that night she'd no interest in him?

Or any man for that matter.

Which is exactly what she'd said to him when he'd asked her to dance for a third time at the ball. Surely, he must've known doing so was outside the bounds.

Or, perchance, he was as dense as mud too. Must be an inherent characteristic of immensely good-looking men. Beauty and brawn but a distinct shortage of brains.

Ironic that beautiful women were often accused of being flighty and lacking in intelligence, when she'd met an equal number of men who fit that description.

A moment later, her cousins, Theadosia, and Rayne glided up to her, their troubled gazes a contrast to the welcoming smiles framing their mouths. They formed a protective semi-circle around her, their bearing guarded.

Her nape hair raised.

Her protectors were in full defensive mode.

Why?

"Everleigh, don't tell me you're still in half-mourning? It's been almost two years since Father Chatterton and Frederick died. Your . . . devotion is *touching*."

Caroline's high-pitched sarcastic drawl rose above the quiet murmuring, succeeding in doing what Frederick's widow intended: drawing every eye to Everleigh.

Mortification fixed her to the Aubusson carpet.

How many of those staring knew her secret shame?

Humiliation burgeoned from her middle, sweeping up her chest and neck, and infused her face with heat.

Swathed in a shockingly immodest carmine-colored gown, Caroline's abundant bosoms were on full display. She lifted a sherry glass to her rouged, smirking lips as she stepped from the shadows where spiders and centipedes and other unpleasant creepy crawlies were wont to loiter.

Some nerve she had pretending any affection for Arnold. Father Chatterton, indeed. Not once had she addressed her father-in-law half so kindly.

Features stern and expression steely, the Duke of Sheffield folded his arms, and leaning one broad shoulder against the doorframe leading to the music room, regarded Caroline with the same distaste as one might warm elephant dung between one's toes.

Theadosia jutted her chin toward Caroline the merest bit.

At once, her sister Jessica and brother James shifted to block Caroline's view. The Dowager Duchess of Sutcliffe followed their lead, and with the distinguished banker, Jerome DuBoise, in tow, she also took to the field like a general leading the troops and commandeered Caroline's attention.

Known for flaunting Society's rules, even Caroline didn't dare insult her host's powerful mother and continue targeting Everleigh.

Childless and older than Everleigh by fourteen years, Caroline most certainly wasn't grieving. No, she'd tossed off mourning weeds a mere six months after her husband's ill-timed death. The only person who'd loathed Frederick Chatterton more than Everleigh stood across the room enjoying the drama she'd stirred.

"Ignore that witch." Ophelia's overly bright smile belied her clipped words. "She's still furious you inherited everything."

That wasn't the only reason Caroline despised Everleigh. Few knew why save those standing around her now and Nicolette Twistleton who speared Caroline a lethal glance as Nicolette wended her way toward them.

Frederick had delighted in boasting to his wife that he'd sired a child with Everleigh whilst Caroline remained barren after sixteen years of marriage. His cruelty inflamed her hatred of Everleigh, and she made a point to bare her needle-sharp claws and draw blood at every opportunity. Given they'd lived in the same house until Chatterton died, life had been hellish day in and day out.

Only Rayne's presence had made living at Keighsdon Hall bearable.

"Why is Caroline here?"

With an expert flick of her wrist, Everleigh splayed her hand-painted lace fan. She cut Theadosia a side-long look. Had she known in advance, her friend would've told her—warned her. Of that, Everleigh had no doubt.

"Surely you understand I cannot stay if she remains, Thea," Everleigh said.

Theadosia presented her back to the drawing room's occupants.

"She arrived with the Moffettes," Thea said, with an apologetic grimace. "I'd forgotten they're distant relations to her, on her mother's side, I believe. They're mortified she imposed upon us. Mr. Moffette admitted he considered trussing her like a goose and stuffing her in the larder when they left, and Mrs. Moffette all but told Caroline she wasn't welcome, but the daft woman paid her no mind."

Probably because she'd anticipated seeing Everleigh and couldn't resist inflicting more wounds.

Known for her pleasant temperament, Theadosia pinched her lips together and a slight scowl wrinkled her forehead. "Given her reputation for histrionics, I feared she might say things better left unsaid and cause an ugly scene if I insisted she leave at once."

"Since Uncle Frederick died, she's been hopping from relation to relation, like a starving flea looking for an ever-fatter dog." Rayne made a rude noise and wrinkled her nose. "She wears her welcome out in a hurry."

Arnold's ward, and a welcome ally against the Chattertons, Rayne had soon become like a sister to Everleigh. After his death, it was only

270

natural the two continue to live together, but at Fittledale Park, the pleasant estate Everleigh purchased outside Colchester. That *other* house, where she'd experienced nothing but misery, was sold and the monies donated to a children's home.

Caroline had nearly had an apoplectic fit when Everleigh turned her out. Not penniless, as she deserved—and claimed to all who would listen—however. She'd blown through the five thousand pounds in short order, sold the modest but comfortable house in Kent Everleigh had gifted her, and, henceforth, relied upon the goodwill and generosity of her numerous kind-hearted relatives.

"Thank goodness the Moffettes are off to their daughter's to spend the holiday with their first grandchild." Gabriella's hazel eyes rounded in distress, and she sliced a glance over her shoulder. "*She* won't stay on when they leave, will she?"

"Only an utterly gauche bacon-brain would do so." Ophelia—an exact replica of her sister tonight, except she wore the palest blue gown and Gabriella the softest green—also slid Caroline a covert peek.

Nicolette edged nearer, murmuring, "That sounds precisely like something Caroline Chatterton would do. I'm not above shoving her in the lake and hoping she catches lung fever."

Everleigh laid her hand on Theadosia's forearm. "Forgive me, but I'm afraid I'm off as soon as my carriage is readied. I shan't subject myself to that woman's animosity. Two years of her enmity was more than enough."

"No. Please don't go." Theadosia shook her head, her strawberry blonde hair glinting gold in the candlelight. "You are one of my dearest friends, and I so want you to celebrate Christmastide and Twelfth Night with us."

"And your birthday too," Gabriella said, slipping an arm around Everleigh's waist.

Everleigh had hoped thirty-one December might pass without marking her four-and-twentieth birthday.

"Besides, do you have any idea how hard it was to convince Grandfather and Grandmother to allow us stay at Ridgewood for weeks?" Eyes wide, Gabriella bobbled her head in a silly fashion and grinned at her twin. "When we live but four miles away?"

Ophelia chuckled as she adjusted her glove on her arm. "That did indeed take a great deal of finagling, and they only permitted it if you act as our chaperone. Else we'll have to go home and miss part of the festivities. Grandmama and Grandpapa are ever so stuffy. Why, they snuff the candles at precisely nine o'clock every night."

Poor darlings.

They'd lived with their paternal grandparents since their parents had died of typhoid when they were five. A widow, Everleigh's mother didn't think she could provide for them, nor was their room in their modest cottage. Still, the girls had visited one another often.

"Everleigh, you deserve some joy and happiness," Nicolette said, and the others agreed with overly bright, encouraging smiles and nods.

"I shall make it clear to Caroline she is not invited for the duration. I don't care if that's unchristian or impolite. She's just mean-spirited and will put a damper on the house party." Theadosia regally inclined her head toward the butler.

Grover acknowledged the sign with an equally noble dip of his chin before leaving the room.

Everleigh must've been the last to arrive downstairs. Now dinner could be served.

Theadosia touched Everleigh's elbow. "I understand if you'd rather a tray were brought to your room tonight, but please don't leave. I have ever so many wonderful things planned for the yuletide. I don't want you to spend it alone again and . . ."

She glanced round the circle of women, then took Everleigh's hand in both of hers. "And . . . we know what day tomorrow is, dearest."

The day Meredith had died.

Tears blurred Everleigh's vision, and she dropped her gaze to her hand clutching the fan.

"I shouldn't have come. I'll only dampen everyone's spirits with my doldrums."

"Nonsense, darling." Nicolette hugged Everleigh. "We only all agreed to inundate Thea and Sutcliffe for weeks because we care so much for you."

Despite her shameful past, her friends loved her. "Thank you, but I'm just not—"

"Papa?"

A child's frightened voice called out.

Everleigh, along with her friends, swung their heads toward the doorway.

"Papa?" Sobbing echoed in the corridor.

"I want my Pa-pa!"

2

At once, Griffin straightened, bent on preventing one of Sarah's shrieking tantrums.

Why wasn't she asleep?

Another nightmare?

What was she doing out of the nursery?

And how the devil had she managed the stairs and not become lost?

He'd barely found his way to the drawing room this evening. But then again, though he'd been friends with Sutcliffe for years, Griffin had only stayed here once prior at Sutcliffe's wedding ball.

That was also the first time he'd laid eyes on the Ice Queen, Everleigh Chatterton.

Even her unique name appealed in a way that made no logical sense.

By all that was holy, she was exquisite tonight.

From her intricately styled gardenia-white hair to her eyes, the arresting green of the Scottish Highlands in spring, and her soft raspberry pink mouth, pressed into a severe line at the moment. Her milky gown, trimmed in muted black lace and purple velvet, emphasized her bountiful breasts without revealing their lushness. She was, in short, a brilliant white diamond amongst vivid gemstones.

He'd no business noting those particulars about her.

Sutcliffe, Pennington, and Bainbridge had made it brutally clear; Mrs. Everleigh Chatterton was not on the market. Would never be if her avowals could be believed.

Griffin, however, *was* on the marriage auction block.

Sarah needed a mother. But not just any mother. She must be a warm, tender-hearted woman who'd accept and love the child as her own. One who didn't care a whit about Sarah's origins. That had proved much harder to achieve than he'd anticipated.

That was why he'd attended dozens of balls, soirées, and musicales, the theater and opera, and house party after house party these past months, seeking the perfect duchess.

He couldn't drag Sarah about with him forever, but until he had a duchess to look after her, he wouldn't leave her when he traveled, sometimes being absent for months. He had no plans to cease his explorations and voyages until well into his dotage, so a wife had become essential. His hosts knew in advance if they wanted him present, she and Nurse must accompany him. Sarah had suffered enough trauma in her young life.

"Papa?"

Attired in her nightclothes, cute pink toes peeking from beneath her gown and her riot of untamed sable curls falling over her shoulders, the ebony-eyed child toddled into the drawing room, clutching a one-eyed, almost bald raggedy excuse for a doll. A pathetic memento from her former life.

"Papa?"

He maneuvered around a settee, but the expression of utter delight blooming across Everleigh Chatterton's face hitched his step.

Squatting to Sarah's level, she gave a gentle closed-mouth smile and held out her arms.

"Who is your papa, darling? I shall help you find him."

Not so frigid after all.

Or was it just him she disliked?

Griffin braced himself for Sarah's wail of outrage upon having a stranger speak to her, let alone attempt to touch her. In the year the almost three-year-old had lived with him, he still hadn't quite grown accustomed to her spine-scraping vocal outbursts.

Thank God they'd become less frequent. Those first few weeks, his ears rang even in his sleep, such was the force of Sarah's screams.

Instead of screeching at the top of her lungs, Sarah tottered into Mrs. Chatterton's arms.

His jaw came unhinged for an instant, and something behind his ribs wobbled.

Sarah touched the shimmering platinum curls framing Mrs. Chatterton's face.

Rather than get annoyed at having her coiffeur mussed, wonderment widened Everleigh Chatterton's pretty smile.

"Are you an angel?"

Starry-eyed and breathless with awe, Sarah gently fingered an iridescent snowy curl.

After being introduced to Everleigh Chatterton last summer, Griffin had asked his Uncle Jerome DuBoise about the entrancing widow who wouldn't set foot in London and barely spoke to men. Chatterton had been one of Uncle's competitors, and there'd been no love lost between them, yet Uncle had been remarkably guarded in what he revealed about the widow.

Head canted, a crooked finger against his mouth, Griffin observed her interacting with Sarah.

Had Everleigh Chatterton married her elderly banker husband for his money, then had an affair with his son as the tattle-mongers whispered? Had the Chatterton men's shootings truly been a robbery gone wrong or actually assassinations as a few still dared to conjecture?

"Nurse says angels have white hair." A fragile, sad smile tilted Sarah's little mouth. "My mamma lives in heaven. Her name is Meera. Have you seen her?"

"Hardly an angel." Caroline Chatterton's nasty muffled laugh lanced through the air. "More like a soiled dove."

How dare *that* immoral hellcat cast dispersions on Everleigh?

Uncle had also shared some unsavory tidbits about the other Mrs. Chatterton. Of course, Griffin had no way of knowing she'd be here tonight or that he'd have the misfortune of meeting her. That was an unlucky coincidence.

In two strides he was beside her.

"That's beyond enough, Mrs. Chatterton. I'll remind you an innocent child is present."

"So I see, though why some nitwit presumed it appropriate to bring what is obviously some sort of half-breed by-blow to an exclusive *ton* gathering does boggle the mind, does it not?"

Caroline Chatterton arched her back, thrusting her barely clad breasts ceilingward as she cast her sultry glance around the room.

If that was for his benefit, she'd wasted her time. He preferred women who didn't feel the need to blatantly display their wares.

Expression coy, she ran her finger around the rim of her glass. "Whose brat do you suppose she is?"

"Mine."

Her jaw sagged. The rouge on her cheeks standing out like candy stripes against her ashen face, her chagrinned gaze darted here and there.

Her bigotry inflamed Griffin's fury. Rage tunneled hotly through his veins, but he casually adjusted a cuff link.

"Which means, Mrs. Chatterton, that half-breed urchin brat outranks *you*."

Caroline's mouth snapped shut, and after she speared him a murderous glare, she stalked off.

James Brentwood chuckled and spoke quietly into Griffin's ear.

"God save the King, hail Mary, and hallelujah, someone has finally rendered the sluttish shrew mute. Now if you could please find a way to encourage her departure . . .?"

"Good riddance," the Dowager Duchess said with a satisfied nod. "The only nitwit present tonight just flounced away."

"Hear, hear," Uncle Jerome agreed. "Not a pleasant sort at all. None of the Chatterton's were. Except that one." He slanted his head toward Everleigh. "There's more to being a lady than breeding, and Everleigh

Chatterton is quality through and through."

Everleigh stood straight, then rested Sarah on her hip. Her black lace shawl slipped off, exposing a gently sloping ivory shoulder. She shifted Sarah to one arm, and gathering the folds of the shawl, tugged if off.

The Duchess of Sutcliffe stepped forward and accepted it from her.

The ladies who'd swooped in to protect Everleigh Chatterton when she'd arrived exchanged covert glances, their expressions a mixture of compassion and concern.

Sarah promptly laid her cheek against Mrs. Chatterton's bosom, stuffed her thumb in her mouth, and began twirling a strand of hair with her other hand.

Now it was Griffin's turn to gawk like a country bumpkin come to Town for the first time.

Sarah was not a docile child.

What spell had the Ice Queen cast over the minx?

Everleigh's clear bottle-green gaze roved over the guests, no doubt searching for the child's father.

Face flushed, Nurse scurried into the room a few moments later. "I beg your pardon, Your Grace."

Ten noble heads swiveled toward the door.

"Oh, dear me. So many dukes." She choked on a giggle as she fanned her face with her hand. "I meant the Duke of Sheffield, if you please."

Even more flustered, she twisted her apron, her rounded cheeks candy-apple red.

"Ten dukes under the same roof for weeks." The dowager chuckled as she slowly scrutinized the guests. "I suggest when we're gathered, we address their graces by their titles to avoid further confusion."

A few others murmured their agreement.

Uncle Jerome tucked her hand into his elbow, beaming down at her as if she'd solved world poverty. "Excellent idea."

She colored prettily under his praise.

If Griffin wasn't mistaken, his uncle would propose to the dowager before year's end. They were well-matched, and he expected she'd accept.

Would that Everleigh Chatterton was similarly minded, but *le bon ton* knew the Ice Queen viewed marriage with the same favor as simultaneously acquiring the pox and the clap.

Griffin made his way to where she held a drowsy Sarah.

Mrs. Chatterton's winged brows arched high, and her pretty eyes fringed with gold tipped lashes rounded when she realized whose child she held.

"I'm sorry, Your Grace." Her face rosy from exertion and chagrin, Nurse gave Sarah a fond look, as she dipped into a clumsy curtsy.

"Little Miss was having trouble going to sleep. I brought her below, and we had a cup of warm, honey-sweetened milk in the breakfast room. With all the extra people in the house, I didn't want the staff to put themselves out on our behalf. She must've heard the adults and come in search of you when I returned the cups to the kitchen."

More likely Mrs. Schmidt had dozed off again, and Sarah had escaped the kindly woman. He'd need to see to hiring a governess sooner than anticipated. Sarah wasn't an easy child to mind, and Mrs. Schmidt was simply too advanced in age to keep up with her.

"Come, cherub. I'll see you to bed now." He reached for Sarah, but instead of launching herself into his arms as was her habit, she burrowed deeper into Mrs. Chatterton's pleasantly rounded chest and wrapped a thin arm around her neck.

"No, Papa." She shook her head against Mrs. Chatterton. "I want Angel Lady to tuck me in."

He smoothed a hand over her dark, silky head, vainly trying to tame the curls.

"Darling, we cannot inconvenience Mrs. Chatterton."

"I don't mind." Everleigh's face softened in the way only a mother's does, and she touched a cheek to Sarah's crown. "Truly."

The Duchess of Sutcliffe's gaze swung between him and Everleigh. "I'll ask Grover to delay serving dinner."

"No, please go ahead, Thea. I'm sure we'll just be a few minutes," Everleigh said.

She met Griffin's eyes, hers almost shy, and in the deepest depths of those pools he saw an unspoken need.

"Not more than ten," he assured her. It would likely take that long for everyone to be seated. "Mrs. Schmidt, please make sure the nursery is readied. I don't want to delay Mrs. Chatterton's return any longer than necessary."

With another little bob, Mrs. Schmidt scurried from the drawing room.

"Are you sure you don't want me to carry her?"

Griffin spoke quietly into Everleigh's ear as they entered the corridor.

She gave a slight shake of her head as she gazed at the sleepy child nestled against her.

"I don't think she'd approve." A tender smile curved her mouth. "I'm rather shocked she's taken to me so."

So, by thunder, was he.

A short while later, after pulling a crocheted coverlet over Sarah and tucking it around her shoulder, Everleigh brushed the back of her fingers against the girl's cheek.

"She's so precious. You are very blessed."

Had her voice caught?

Here was the kind of woman he desired for Sarah's mother. A woman who recognized children were gifts to be treasured, no matter their birth.

"I am indeed."

Forefinger bent, he caressed the sleeping child's satiny cheek too, and he accidentally bumped Everleigh's hand.

An electrical jolt shot to his shoulder and across his chest so strong, it froze him in place for an instant.

Everleigh stiffened and moved away the merest bit, almost fearfully.

"She's adorable when she sleeps, but has a stubborn streak a mile wide when she's awake." He removed her pathetic stuffed doll with few remaining strings of dirty black yarn for hair from her clasp. "She doesn't like to be told no."

"I wonder which parent she gets that from?"

The merest hint of sarcasm shaded Everleigh's murmur, and she slid him a teasing sideways glance.

Wonder of wonders.

All it took for the Ice-Queen to thaw was a child.

"Surely you don't mean me?"

Affecting a wounded expression, he held his hand with the doll to his chest.

She rolled a shoulder and stepped away, gazing 'round the quaintly furnished nursery. She appeared wistful. Sad.

"Mrs. Schmidt, Maya's eye is loose again." He handed the nurse the shoddy doll. "Please sew it on tighter. I'm afraid Sarah might choke on it if it were to come lose."

Mrs. Schmidt *tsked* and *tutted.*

"Of course, sir. I do wish the little mite would take to one of the other dolls you've given her. I'm afraid Maya hasn't many days left in her, and then what will we do?"

"A pox on you for suggesting such an unthinkable thing." His wink belied his words. On a more serious note he added, "Let's hope she doesn't need Maya as much when the time comes."

With a hearty sigh, Mrs. Schmidt sank heavily into an armchair, then examined Maya's frayed seams.

Griffin extended his elbow to Everleigh. "We'd best get ourselves to dinner, Mrs. Chatterton. I wouldn't want to incur the new Duchess of Sutcliffe's wrath for being overly tardy."

After the slightest hesitation, she touched her fingertips to his forearm, and another tremor of awareness coursed through him.

"Theadosia doesn't get angry about things like that. She's one of the kindest people I know. She won't mind that we are late." With a last melancholy glance around the nursery, Everleigh allowed Griffin to escort her from the room.

"How many children do you have, Mrs. Chatterton?"

A look of utter devastation swept her features, before she lowered her eyes and withdrew her fingers from his arm.

"None."

"But I thought . . ."

He clamped his teeth together, wracking his brain. How many years had she been married? Hadn't Uncle Jerome mentioned a pregnancy when he spoke of her? Griffin couldn't recall now, but he'd be asking at first opportunity.

"Forgive me if I caused offense. I assumed you did because of how naturally you took to Sarah and she to you. You have a mother's instincts." Oddly bereft after she withdrew her hand, he tucked his thumb inside his coat's lapel. "She doesn't often let anyone but Nurse and me touch her."

Everleigh tilted her head, her keen gaze roving his face.

"Then I am honored she permitted me to carry her." A ghost of a smile touched her soft mouth. "I always thought I'd have made a good mother."

"You're not too old to have children."

She couldn't be more than five and twenty, and if Sarah was an example, Everleigh clearly adored children.

A noise very much like a derisive snort escaped her.

"True, but I've no intention of bringing illegitimate offspring into this world and submitting them to that sort of ridicule, and nothing short of Jesus Christ himself appearing with an acceptable man in tow would induce me to ever marry again."

Jerome had mentioned her marriage was a misalliance of monumental proportions. If she had married for money, did she regret her choice? If she hadn't . . .

What other reason could there be for marrying a degenerate nearly old enough to be her grandfather?

Love? Could she have loved the elderly reprobate after all?

"Tell me about your Sarah," Everleigh said. "How old is she?"

They'd made the landing, and Griffin took her elbow as they began the descent. "She's almost three. In fact, her birthday is the thirty-first of this month."

"So is mine!"

When Everleigh smiled with genuine happiness, joy bloomed across her face, making her even more impossibly lovely. She touched a finger to the onyx and pearl locket resting just below the juncture of her throat and collar bone.

Damn him for a fool.

She wore a mourning locket.

Maybe she really had loved the ancient sod she'd been married to and was able to overlook his indiscretions and other deplorable vices. Some swore love covered a multitude of sins.

Grief settled over her as tangible and dense as woolen cloak. "Had she lived, Meredith would've been three last September."

Was he supposed to know who she was?

"Meredith?"

3

For the second time that night, Everleigh stopped on the last riser.

He truly didn't know?

"Yes, my daughter, Meredith."

She touched the locket again. A lock of wispy, thistle-down soft white hair lay tucked inside. Struggling to wrestle her grief into submission, she focused on the long case clock's pendulum swinging back and forth.

She paced her breathing with the slow *tick-tock* for a handful of rhythmic beats.

Did a parent ever recover from the loss of a child?

No. Life just took on a new reality.

"Tomorrow is the three-year anniversary of her death."

Why had she shared that?

The Duke of Sheffield did the most startling, the most perfect thing in all the world.

He drew her into his arms and held her. He didn't offer condolences or advice. He didn't try to change the subject or pretend he hadn't heard her at all.

He simply offered her comfort, and it felt so utterly splendid, just allowing someone to hold her. Someone who permitted her to show her grief for a child conceived in the worst sort of violation and violence, but who had been adored nevertheless.

For this brief interlude, Everleigh didn't have to be strong. Didn't have to maintain her frigid façade, and it was wonderful to be herself. That almost brought her to tears as well.

What was more astonishing was she wasn't afraid of his touch.

How long had it been since she didn't flinch when a man touched her?

They stood chest to chest and thigh to thigh in intimate silence for several moments until the clocked chimed the quarter hour and interrupted the tranquility. They really must join the others for dinner, or God only knew what sort of unsavory tattle might arise.

"Thank you for your kindness, Your Grace."

She disengaged herself, more aware of him as a man than she'd any business being.

He simply nodded, though the amber starburst in his eyes glowed with a warmth she couldn't identify.

At the bottom of the stairs, he once again placed her hand on his forearm, and steered her toward the dining room. Evidently, he didn't feel the need to fill the stillness with inane chatter.

She liked that about him. It was fine to speak when something needed to be said, but it was equally acceptable to let silence fill the comfortable void when it didn't. At home, she'd sit with her eyes closed and listen to the quiet, especially in the early morning when the countryside began to wake.

A few minutes later, they entered the dining room. Several people noted their entrance, including Caroline, who raised a superior brow, then murmured something to Major McHugh on her right. The major's wiry grey eyebrows scampered up his broad, furrowed forehead, and skepticism and disapproval jockeyed back and forth for dominance in his acute regard of Everleigh.

Whether by chance or Thea's maneuvering, the two remaining vacant chairs were at opposites ends of the table. Everleigh wasn't certain if she should feel vexed or grateful, but her estimation of the Duke of Sheffield had increased a few degrees this past half hour. Not enough to garner further interest, but she no longer considered him a licentious rake to be avoided at every turn.

An hour and a half later, as the ladies made their way to the drawing room for tea and to play whist while the gentlemen enjoyed their port, she made her excuses to Thea. She'd chew hot coals before enduring Caroline's unpleasant company any longer.

"I'm going to retire early," Everleigh said. "I fear my headache from this afternoon never completely went away."

That was the truth.

Thea took her elbow and drew her aside as the other ladies filed into the drawing room. Ophelia, Rayne, and Gabriella stopped strategically just beyond Theadosia and Everleigh, blocking the view of any curious eavesdroppers.

Everleigh's heart swelled with gratitude. She truly did have the most marvelous friends.

"You will stay on, won't you, Everleigh?" Thea looked past the trio quietly chatting a few feet away to Caroline seated on a settee and directing a haughty glare toward them. "I promise, she'll be gone before you come down to breakfast if I have to bundle her, tied hand and foot, into the carriage myself."

Pretty doe-like eyes flashed to mind, followed by a black coffee pair set beneath straight brows the same rich shade.

"If Caroline is gone, I'll stay a couple more days. That's all I can promise for now."

Grinning, Thea hugged her.

"Excellent. Tomorrow we'll attend church, of course. It is also Stir-up Day. I want all the guests to stir the Christmas pudding and make a wish. I've charades planned for the evening, along with mulled cider from Ridgewood's very own apples." Theadosia's eyes twinkled with excitement. "The women are going to make kissing boughs—mistletoe has been drying for a fortnight, and the gentleman will go stalking. Cook absolutely insists on fresh venison for the Christmas feast. That's just to start the festivities. I've much, much more planned."

Theadosia had always adored Christmas.

"It sounds like a great good"—*exhausting*—"time," Everleigh managed to say without seeming overwhelmed.

It truly did for someone who enjoyed large assemblies and holiday traditions. She preferred a quiet gathering: family, close friends, a Yule log crackling in the hearth, steaming spiced cider, a mistletoe sprig, and perhaps Twelfth Night Cake.

Another swift perusal of the drawing room revealed Caroline no longer sat on the settee. Maybe she'd crawled back into her hole or rejoined her coven.

One could only hope.

Everleigh bussed Thea's cheek and wiggled her fingers farewell to the others.

"I'll see you in the morning."

Instead of going directly to her chamber, she stopped at the library. Better to keep her mind occupied than let her musings have free rein. Besides, reading always made her drowsy. Tomorrow would prove difficult enough without a sleepless night.

As she perused the shelves, she removed her gloves.

What should she read?

Something entertaining?

Educational?

Or a boring tome?

Once she'd selected one of each type, she continued on her way, shawl over her forearm, and her gloves draped over the books. Laughter filtered down the passageway, and she bent her mouth into the merest semblance of a smile. Tonight had been much more pleasant than she'd expected.

Except for Caroline's presence, of course.

Just as she reached her bedchamber and grasped the door handle, her nemesis emerged from the shadows near the floor-to-ceiling window alcove. She seemed to have a habit of slithering out of dark corners. Caroline held a glass half full of what looked to be brandy, a favorite and common indulgence.

Been raiding Suttcliffe's liquor cabinet, had she?

"It wasn't enough you seduced my husband and persuaded Arnold to wed you to hide the bastard swelling your belly, Everleigh. You managed to manipulate him into changing his will, then turned me out onto the street to starve."

Caroline had merely alluded to those things before. Either drink or fury had emboldened her to speak them outright tonight. Thank God she'd not done so in front of the others.

"Not a single word of that is true, as you well know."

One eye on the nursery three doors down, Everleigh opened her chamber.

Caroline took a long pull from her glass, then, eyes narrowed until they were almost closed, advanced toward Everleigh. She pointed the forefinger of the hand holding the nearly empty glass and fairly hissed, "If it's the last thing I do, I'll make you pay, you cold, unfeeling bitch."

"You're drunk, Caroline." Also a frequent occurrence. "Go to bed before you embarrass yourself."

Again.

Caroline stalked nearer, her once pretty face contorted with hatred and showing the ravages of too much drink and other unhealthy indulgences.

"I've heard ugly rumors, Everleigh. Murmurs that someone hired rum pads to kill Arnold and Frederick and make it look like a robbery."

That was the first Everleigh had ever heard any such thing, and the accusation gave her pause as well as sent chilly prickles across her shoulders.

Could such a thing possibly be true?

Wouldn't there have been an inquiry long before this?

Were people, perhaps even those at this gathering, speculating about whether she'd been behind her husband's death?

Everleigh glanced toward the nursery again as she crossed the threshold. "Keep your voice down. Sarah is sleeping a bit farther along the passage."

Even as she spoke, a child's muffled cries echoed.

"Do you think I give a whit about that merry-begotten?" Caroline finished the rest of her brandy and leaned indolently against the wall, the glass dangling from her fingers. "Who, besides you, hated Arnold and Frederick enough to want them dead?"

Any of a dozen people Everleigh could name, including the foxed woman standing before her.

"I've done nothing wrong, and I'll not listen to your vile accusations." No doubt conjured by jealousy and hatred. "I had no knowledge of the attack on Arnold and Frederick until the sheriff delivered the news."

She laid her belongings on the table beside the door, undecided if she should knock at the nursery. It wasn't her place to offer to help with Sarah, but she was partially responsible for the child's sleep being disturbed.

She spared Caroline a brusque glance.

"If the authorities had reason to believe something afoul of the law occurred, they would have investigated already," the Duke of Sheffield said.

Everleigh and Caroline swung their attention to him ambling toward them, all masculine prowess and power. His black evening attire accented the broad span of his shoulders, and the corridor seemed to shrink with his virile presence.

Everleigh forced her gaze away.

Just because she'd noticed his manliness, it didn't mean anything. She was, after all, still a young woman.

"Unless, Mrs. Chatterton, you know something no one else does?" He cocked his head at a considering angle then rubbed the scar dissecting his slightly bent nose with his forefinger. "But then, you'd have to explain to the authorities why you've withheld information all this time. I believe that's a criminal offense too."

Arching her back, the calculated movement thrusting her voluptuous breasts out and upward, Caroline stretched like a contented cat. More like an eager-to-be-bred tabby twitching her tail before a tom. She gave him a secretive smile as she glided past and tapped his chest with her empty glass.

"We'll just have to wait and see, won't we?"

She sent a sly look behind her, flicking Everleigh a glance that clearly said she found her wanting.

"I do hope you have an alibi, Everleigh."

Mouth pinched, Everleigh stared at Caroline's retreating back.

Was she serious?

Did she truly intend to make a claim that Everleigh had something to do with the robbery and murders? Surely no one would believe such an assertion at this late date. Nevertheless, her stomach twisted with anxiety.

"Are you all right?" Sheffield also watched Caroline flouncing away.

"Did she upset you? You've gone quite pale."

Everleigh sighed and pressed her fingertips to her right temple where the pain had taken on a renewed vigor.

"Caroline delights in upsetting me, but yes, I'm fine."

"Are you sure?" He touched her cheek with a bent knuckle. "The light behind your eyes is gone."

Light behind her eyes?

What nonsensical drivel.

She wouldn't have thought he was the sort to bandy platitudes about.

"Ridiculous. I've but a pesky headache."

Her response was starchier than she'd intended.

He chuckled and swept a strand of hair off his forehead. "No need to get prickly, and I regret you're not feeling well."

"I cannot believe she'd resort to such fabrications just to hurt me." Everleigh absently rubbed her hairline near her ear.

Judging from the strain of the fabric, he rested what surely must be a well-muscled shoulder against the wall.

"Envy and jealousy can turn even the most decent men into fiends, but when someone is already despicable, there's no telling what they're capable of." He spared a thoughtful glance toward the stairs. "The Duchess tells me Mrs. Chatterton will be gone in the morning. We're well rid of her, but I think you still must be on your guard against her."

Everleigh touched her locket, running her fingers across the diamond floweret atop the jet. "Believe me, I have been for four years."

"Do you have an alibi? Someone who can vouch for you?"

He seemed genuinely concerned, not just prying.

She sighed and stretched her neck from side to side, hoping to lessen the knots of tension that had taken up residence there.

"My husband kept me a virtual prisoner. I hadn't access to funds to hire someone to commit the foul deed, and even my jewelry was kept locked in a safe so I couldn't use it to bribe a servant. I rarely left the house, and when I did, two of my husband's henchmen accompanied me to prevent any escape attempt."

Not that she would've tried, for fear Arnold would harm her family as he'd threatened.

"He really was a bloody blighter, wasn't he?"

Disgust and anger riddled the duke's clipped speech.

"He was."

She clasped her hands behind her back, then leaned against the doorjamb.

"The former staff can vouch that I was never permitted personal visitors, and the only guests we entertained were the miscreants and other dregs of society my husband invited. The night he and Frederick were slain, I was . . ."

She paused, lost in the dreadful memory.

"You were . . .?" his grace prompted with an encouraging closed-mouth smile.

She'd not told anyone about the thrashings.

"Let's just say I was incapable of leaving my bed, and the sheriff can testify to that."

The duke's intense gaze probed hers, and she didn't doubt his mind flipped through numerous scenarios to explain why she would've been abed.

His eyes turned stone hard, as did the sharp angles of his face.

He'd hit upon the truth. Rather more swiftly than she'd have thought.

"Chatterton beat you?" he said, his voice fury-roughened.

Whenever Arnold had tried to copulate and couldn't get his limp member to cooperate. He'd never once been able to bed her; her one small victory. That she wasn't about to tell the duke. Instead she gave a curt nod.

"That damn bastard." Posture rigid, Sheffield dropped his balled hands to his sides. "No wonder you're so afraid."

Sarah's fussing continued to carry through the closed nursery door.

Uncomfortable at having shared something so intimate, she scrambled to change the subject.

"I apologize for waking your daughter."

He cupped his nape, giving her a guarded look from beneath hooded lids.

"Actually, Sarah is not my daughter."

4

Early the next morning, a thick velvet-lined mantle over her black and white striped woolen walking dress and redingote, Everleigh rapped on the nursery door.

She dismissed her misgivings.

Surely the duke couldn't object to Sarah taking a walk, particularly if Nurse accompanied them.

Quiet murmurings beyond the thick panel assured her Nurse and Sarah were awake as well. The door edged open, and a surprised but pleased smile crinkled Nurse's face.

"Mrs. Chatterton. I thought Young Miss and I were the only ones awake at this hour."

Everleigh looked beyond the plump servant to where Sarah sat fully dressed with an oversized pink bow in her hair, playing with her shabby doll.

"I'm an early riser myself. I thought perhaps Sarah would like to take a walk with me. The frost has made lovely patterns in the gardens, and I saw a rabbit and deer from my chamber windows."

At once upon hearing Everleigh, Sarah scampered to the nursery door and pulled on Nurse's skirts.

"May I? Please? Maya too?"

Sarah held up the dilapidated rag doll.

"I'm not sure Miss Sarah ought to be outside. She's still not quite accustomed to England's cold weather." Indecision crimped the nurse's mouth.

Other than saying Sarah was orphaned and born in Southern India, the duke hadn't revealed much more about the child he'd taken in. Everleigh hoped to learn more about the fascinating little girl today.

Sheffield had edged up another notch in her estimation too. She'd best be careful or she might find herself actually admiring him, and that wouldn't do at all. Admiration could lead to other sentiments. Dangerous sentiments for a widow committed to keeping her independence.

"If I promise not to keep her too long? You can tell me when you think she's had enough and we'll come in straightaway. I'm certain Sarah would benefit from the fresh air and exercise."

Perhaps it was because Meredith had died on this day, or maybe Sarah had stirred dormant maternal instincts, but in any event, Everleigh couldn't stay away from the child.

Nurse conceded with a nod and a smile. "You've convinced me. It would do the tike good to run about."

Excellent. Mrs. Schmidt wasn't the type of nurse who thought children should march along like miniature soldiers or sit perfectly still for hours on end.

She leaned in and whispered to Everleigh, "Maybe the little mite wil take her lie-down without a fuss if she capers about outside a bit."

Hope tinged the tired servant's voice. She was a trifle too advanced in years to be chasing after such an energetic child.

A few minutes later, Everleigh held Sarah's hand as they stood on the edge of Ridgewood's neat-as-a-pin gardens and watched a doe nibble the green's, succulent frost-tipped grasses. A smaller deer, likely her fawn, sampled a nearby shrubbery.

"Is that her baby?" Sarah asked whilst rubbing her cold-reddened nose with her bare hand.

Where had her mitten gone?

Everleigh nodded as she searched the ground for the lost mitten. "I think so."

Mrs. Schmidt, her chins tucked deep into the folds of her cloak, looked on with less enthusiasm.

Heavy pewter clouds covered the sky, hiding all evidence of the sun and hinting at a brewing storm. A brisk breeze toyed with the ribbons of Everleigh's and Sarah's bonnets. It was chilly, but not unbearably so. More importantly, no one else had ventured outdoors yet and the solitude was sheer bliss.

Likely, most of the guests were either eating or getting ready to attend church services in Colchester. It was expected, and that meant a quiet house for a few hours more.

There was a day when she'd have joined them, but Arnold—spawn of Satan—hadn't allowed her to go, and Everleigh had never started attending after he'd died.

"What goes on here?"

At the sound of the Duke of Sheffield's voice, Sarah whipped around and then, giggling, her little arms wide, ran to him

"Papa!"

His midnight-blue caped greatcoat gave his black hair, visible beneath his hat, a bluish tint. The unrelenting breeze taunted the cape's edges as well as the hem of Everleigh's cloak.

"Papa, Mrs. Chatterton showed me deers. When we gets inside, she promised me hot choc'late and clodded cream," Sarah finished in a breathless rush.

"Is that so?" He scooped her into his arms, then whirled her in a circle.

Her delighted screeches frightened the deer away.

He stopped and slung one sturdy arm beneath her thighs. "Did you break your fast already, my pet?"

"Yes, Your Grace." Nurse's kind eyes pleated around the edges in approval. "Little miss had a good appetite this morn. She ate everything but the pickled herring."

"Cannot say that I blame her," Everleigh muttered, then chagrined she'd spoken her thoughts aloud, blushed.

But really?

Pickled fish for breakfast?

She had never been able to appreciate that particular food, let alone breaking one's fast with the smelly little blighters. Almost as revolting as blood sausage; a favorite of Arnold's.

"Well then that certainly deserves hot chocolate." Amusement sparkling in the duke's eyes, he nuzzled Sarah's cheek, and she giggled again.

"With clodded cream," she reminded him.

"With clotted cream," he agreed solemnly, his gaze seeking Everleigh's over the top of Sarah's head.

His leisurely perusal and the equally unhurried smile bending his mouth upward sent her stomach to fluttering. Surely in hunger, for she hadn't eaten yet.

What compelled a man to take an orphan in and treat her as if she were his own? Such a person must be intrinsically decent, mustn't he?

"I hope I didn't overstep." Everleigh drew near and straightened Sarah's rumpled gown and claret toned coat, then handed her Maya. "I saw the deer from my chamber and thought she'd enjoy seeing them too. I'm afraid they've run off now. We had a lovely walk through the gardens as well."

Sarah nodded, bumping her head on his chin.

"Ow." She clapped a little dimpled hand to her injury.

Everleigh waited for the howl of displeasure, but instead, Sarah took the duke's face between her little palms and insisted he look at her.

"Papa, we sawed a frozen spider web. It looks like Nurse's crotch dollies."

"Oh my." Merriment rounded Mrs. Schmidt's eyes, and shoulder's shaking, she coughed into glove.

"Crocheted," he gently corrected, his mouth twitching in an effort to contain his mirth. "Nurse crochets doilies."

Everleigh met his eyes, and she almost erupted into giggles.

"I've always enjoyed an early walk myself, but the breeze grows stiff." He lowered Sarah to the ground. "You go with Nurse now, and Mrs. Chatterton and I shall be along directly. We can all enjoy a cup of chocolate together in the nursery. How does that sound?"

"I want biscuits with my hot choc'late. An' a story too." Sarah scowled at Nurse's outstretched hand.

"Sarah, we ask politely. Please may I have biscuit and a story with my chocolate?" the duke gently corrected her.

"Yes, Papa." Sarah turned those big eyes to Everleigh. "Please, biscuits an' a story?"

"I'm sure something can be arranged," Everleigh said, keeping her smile under control. It wouldn't do to unravel the duke's effort to teach Sarah manners. "I'll stop by the kitchen and ask. I think I heard the Duchess of Sutcliffe mention gingerbread last night."

"Ginger . . . *bread*?" Her nose crinkling in confusion, Sarah looked between the duke and Everleigh. "I wan' biscuits. Not bread."

"Gingerbread is a kind of biscuit made with . . ." The pleading glance he sent Everleigh silently asking for help warmed her cold toes.

"Molasses, cinnamon, and ginger, and they are shaped like stocky little men." She used to make them with her mother to celebrate the Christmas season. "I like to bite the head off first."

"I wonder why?" The merriment lighting his face revealed he teased her.

"Go along now." He urged Sarah toward Nurse. "And make sure you are agreeable to Mrs. Schmidt, lest I have to deny you your treat."

"I be good, Papa. I promise." Skipping along, her dilapidated doll dragging the ground, Sarah began singing a nonsensical song about chocolate and biscuits and deer.

"She's an absolute darling." Everleigh accepted his extended elbow.

He smiled as he watched her romp away.

"You didn't answer me when I said I hoped I hadn't overstepped, so I presume I did. I should have asked first. Please forgive my forwardness, Your Grace. I've little experience with children."

Only a few weeks with an infant born healthy, but who'd sickened rapidly, and died just as swiftly.

He turned back to her and picked a piece of black fuzz from his bent arm.

"You mistake my silence as censure, Mrs. Chatterton. I simply didn't want to speak in front of Sarah. I have no objection to you taking her for an outing. What I do have a concern about is her growing too attached to you. As I told you last night, she lost her mother under difficult circumstances."

Everleigh swallowed her disappointment and stared at the swaying trees.

He was right, of course.

There was also the danger that she'd grow too attached to Sarah.

"I understand. Please forgive me for not considering that. I was going to ask if we might walk every morning, but I think that might not be wise. In fact, I hadn't decided if I was going to stay for the duration of the party, but given Sarah's reaction to me, I believe it best if I leave directly."

Startling, the depths of her distress, when yesterday she'd been on the verge of leaving anyway.

Releasing his elbow, she drew her cloak closer as she erected her cool, protective mien. She'd let her guard down, and look where it had landed her?

Tilting her face upward, she inspected the heavens again.

Yes, a storm brewed. Hopefully the clouds didn't portend snow or Cook mightn't have her stag. Just as well as far as Everleigh was concerned. A fat goose sufficed for Christmas dinner. Let the noble deer live another season.

Snow also meant she'd have a more difficult time getting home. Best to leave straightaway then.

"If you'll excuse me. I need to pack and write Theadosia a note."

She swiveled toward the house, but he touched her shoulder.

"Please don't leave, Everleigh."

His tone compelled her to meet his gaze, and she couldn't look away. The way he'd murmured her name, almost reverently, took her aback. Made her want what could never be. What she'd chosen to forsake for her peace of mind and physical wellbeing.

It—he—wasn't worth the risk.

And yet she still didn't look away from his captivating gaze, the deep russet of his eyes willing her not to break whatever bond linked them at this magical moment.

Foolish, Everleigh!

Haven't you had enough pain for a lifetime?

She toyed with fire, and with a man of his caliber, experienced and devilishly charming, she'd get burned. Charred to cinders.

"What goes on in that beautiful head of yours?" He touched her cheek again, then spread his fingers until they framed her jaw.

304

Given the temperature, the black leather should've been cool to the touch, yet heat seared her face.

"I see wariness and confusion," he said. "But mostly, dread of being hurt again."

At last she dropped her gaze to the buttons on his greatcoat. Mouth dry as parchment, she swallowed.

"Why should I stay, Your Grace?"

"Because I'm inclined to take the risk and grant your request. Sometimes it's necessary to take a chance. Particularly if we seek something worthwhile."

She gave him a hard look.

Was he still talking about Sarah?

Withdrawing his hand, he swept the house a casual glance.

"I've not seen Sarah this animated or cooperative since . . . Well, ever. As I said last night, she hadn't reached her second birthday when I sailed from India with her, and she's had a hard time adjusting. Her reaction to you is nothing short of miraculous."

"She likes my hair." Everleigh raised a hand to her temple. "She says it's angel hair."

"Hair your shade is rare, even in England. She's never seen the like." He gathered her hand and placed it in the crook of his elbow once more.

"You aren't interested in becoming a duchess, are you?"

At once she stiffened and opened her mouth to ring him a peal, but his jovial wink sucked all the ire from her.

He but teased.

"No. Not a duchess or wife to any man of any station ever again."

She couldn't speak plainer. Best to nip any wayward notions he might have in the bud. Only a fool didn't learn from past experience.

Rather than taking offense, a sympathetic smile to tipped his mouth, and compassion simmered in his dark gaze.

"I admire your pluck. And your strength. You are a remarkable woman, Everleigh Chatterton."

If he'd said he worshipped her beauty or some other flattering hogwash she'd heard before, she'd have been able to dismiss his compliment. Instead, foreign warmth seeped into her bones.

He steered her around an ornate marble fountain topped with a trio of cherubs and four crouching horses beneath. No water flowed today, probably a precaution against the freezing weather.

"Have you eaten yet?" he asked.

"No, I intended to after my walk."

"You don't attend Sunday services in Colchester?"

"No." She shook her head before glancing over her shoulder. A caravan of vehicles rattled and squeaked their way down the drive. "I know it's expected, but I've not been able to since . . ."

She touched a gloved finger to the oval locket, barely detectable beneath her cloak and redingote.

Would he judge her as so many others had?

She glanced upward, searching his expression for any sign of censure.

"I cannot stop being angry with God for letting Meredith die."

She hadn't been angry with Him after being ruined or forced to wed Andrew. At least not this lingering inability to let go of her hurt. But when she lost her baby too? Well, that had pushed the limits of her faith, and her beliefs had shattered under the weight of her anguish.

Sympathy softened his features. He covered her hand with his and squeezed. "You have my sincerest condolences. I cannot fathom the depth of your grief at such a tremendous loss."

"Thank you." She drew in a deep breath, filling her lungs to capacity, willing herself not to cry in front of him. After a second, she released the air in a whoosh.

"Why don't you attend church, Your Grace?"

He looked thoughtful for a moment.

"I didn't want to leave Sarah only a day after arriving. True, she mightn't even know I'm gone, but I don't want to put Mrs. Schmidt in that position." He glanced overhead for a long moment. "At one time I too struggled with anger toward God. When my parents died, but especially after Sarah's mother died, and she was left an orphan. Time has helped ease that disappointment, and a realization that the matter was out of my hands. What I did afterward is what counts."

"You must've loved Sarah's mother very much."

An odd twinge pinched her lungs.

He looked so taken aback, she almost chuckled.

"Meera was a friend, nothing more. Her husband Rajiv saved my life five years ago. I was set upon by thieves. They beat me severely. That's how I got this."

He pointed to his scarred nose.

"But Rajiv chased them off then took me to his house. People would call it a hovel here, but he and Meera had made it into a comfortable home. Though they were poor, they somehow paid for a physician to treat me, and they nursed me back to health until I was well enough to tell them who I was. Rajiv refused to let me repay him, though I know he could've used the money."

He stopped and leaned against a Grecian statue.

"Every time I went to India, I visited them. Rajiv wouldn't accept money but allowed me to bring gifts. Sarah's doll is one of the them. The time before last, when I arrived, Meera told me Rajiv had died. A bull elephant went berserk and trampled him."

Everleigh sucked in a sharp breath. "That's awful."

A muscle in his jaw flexed.

"Meera and Sarah were on the verge of starving. I made arrangements to send them funds and supplies monthly, since she refused to leave India and come to England. It was the least I could do."

He grew silent for a moment, his bent forefinger pressed to his lips as if he struggled to control his emotions.

There was more to this man than she'd ever have guessed.

"The last time I was there, I learned that Meera had died. A sickness of some sort. I never did find out what exactly. Another family occupied their house, and Sarah was living in a crate behind it. I don't know why they didn't take her in, or if she had any other family, but I knew at once I must take her from there. If I'd been even a week later, she'd have starved to death."

They resumed walking, the frozen gravel crunching beneath their feet.

"The poor little dear."

Tears blurred Everleigh's vision, and she bit the corner of her lower lip against a sob.

Voice husky, she managed, "You are a truly decent man, Your Grace."

He chuckled. "Not everyone would agree with you. I'm no saint, and I don't pretend to be, but common decency demanded I help the child of the man who saved my life."

He mightn't be a saint, but plenty of people wouldn't have thought Sarah their responsibility.

They'd made the house, and he opened the door for her.

"What say you, we have our breakfast in the nursery?" he asked as she stepped inside.

Everleigh grinned for the first time in a long while. "That sounds delightful."

"There you are."

Everleigh went rigid as Caroline's strident voice shattered the pleasant mood.

5

G riffin gnashed his teeth to keep from telling Caroline Chatterton to bugger off.

"I thought you were leaving," he said crisply as he closed the door.

Attired in a dusky green traveling gown, she turned her seductive gaze on him, trailing his form in a manner that made him want to take a bath.

Her rouged mouth twisted slightly to the side.

"I am, just as soon as I've had a word with Everleigh. The carriage awaits me even now. My cousins in Kent are anxious I spend the holiday with them."

Balderdash. Her cousins probably didn't know she was about to show up on their doorstep and ruin their holiday.

"We don't have anything to say to one another. Please excuse me." Everleigh made to move past her.

"I have a proposition." Caroline played with the fingers of the gloves she held, her arrogance slipping a notch. "I think it would be beneficial to us both, most especially you."

Everleigh sighed but faced her. "What is it?"

"Can we speak privately?" Caroline slid Griffin a pointed glance.

"I'll wait for you in the nursery." He didn't bother lifting his hat in farewell to Caroline.

"I'll be along shortly," Everleigh said. "Don't wait for me to break your fast."

"How positively domesticated you two sound." Jealousy made Caroline's voice strident.

"Should we expect a joyful announcement soon?" She made an exaggerated 'O' with her mouth and pressed two fingers to her lips, feigning surprise. "But I thought you'd sworn off ever marrying again." Her vapid gaze dropped to Everleigh's middle. "Unless . . . you're breeding another bastard?"

"Watch your tongue, Mrs. Chatterton." Griffin unbuttoned his overcoat. Made for the bitter cold, it was much too heavy for indoors. "You not only disparage Everleigh, but you besmirch me with your innuendos, and I assure you, I don't take kindly to insults or to my honor being sullied."

What a malicious harpy. It was a wonder Chatterton the younger didn't do himself in, married to a shrew like her.

Except for the minutest flinch, Everleigh maintained her poise.

"On second thought, Your Grace, I should like a witness to my conversation with Caroline. A man of standing whose word is respected and who can vouch for what is said."

Irritation crimped Caroline's mouth. "That's really not necessary—"

"Oh, but it is. If you want me to stay and listen to this *proposition*."

Everleigh folded her arms. "You see, I've learned to protect myself, and I have you and the other Chattertons to thank for making me so cautious."

Caroline's fuming gaze waffled between Griffin and Everleigh. Lips pursed and looking like she'd sucked moldy bread, she gave a condescending sigh. "I truly don't understand why you must always be so difficult."

"I'm hungry and cold, Caroline. Get on with it before I change my mind."

Everleigh removed her bonnet as she spoke.

"Oh, very well." Caroline leveled Griffin a peeved glare, but he merely cocked a brow in response.

"I believe I can help you with the unpleasant tattle I've heard of late. I shall squash any murmurings I hear about your involvement in Arnold's and Frederick's deaths in exchange for ten thousand pounds." Caroline declared it as if granting a royal pardon.

Griffin barely stifled an incredulous snort. She had ballocks; he'd give her that. Not a jot of common decency however.

Her gaze skittered away from his reproachful stare.

A hint of color highlighting her cheekbones, she tilted her pointed chin to a haughty angle. "I also promise not to ask for any more funds from you."

How magnanimous.

"Let me make sure I understand you clearly." Everleigh waggled her bonnet toward the other woman. "If I concede to your blackmail—for that's what this is—you'll squelch the rumors *you* started? Do you think me an imbecile? You'll squander any monies I give you just as you did those I already paid you, and then you'll demand more."

Everleigh was absolutely right. Mrs. Chatterton was a parasite who'd keep coming back as long as she believed her extortion would work.

"I wouldn't be too anxious to turn down my offer. I can destroy you." Caroline advanced toward Everleigh, all semblance of civility having flown. "You'd best be careful an accident doesn't befall you as well."

"Have you forgotten I'm standing here, Mrs. Chatterton?" Griffin said, squaring his shoulders. "For that sounded very much like a threat to me. You'd best hope nothing does happen to Everleigh, because yours is the first name I'll give the authorities, along with a sworn statement that I heard you threaten her."

Stepping forward, he blocked her path to Everleigh. "I think you should leave now."

"I'm leaving, but rest assured, Everleigh, you haven't seen or heard the last from me." Caroline jerked on one of her gloves as she stomped away.

"By the by, Caroline. . .?" Everleigh pulled at that tips of one gloved hand.

Caroline glared over her shoulder as she crammed her hand into the other unfortunate glove.

"If anything *should* happen to me, Rayne and my cousins have been named my heirs." Everleigh had unclasped her cloak and, after shrugging if from her shoulders, lay it across an arm. Tone as frosty as the ground outside, she said, "You won't get a six-pence, even in a Christmas pudding. However, if you are willing to sign a contract with very specific terms, I may consider advancing you funds one *final* time."

Caroline let loose an oath Griffin had only heard seasoned doxies use before as she flounced down the corridor.

"I do believe that was a no."

His jest earned him a slight smile as they made their way toward the stairs.

"Everleigh, you don't owe her anything."

"I know, but I also know how utterly terrifying it is to be a woman without anything in a man's world. If she agrees in writing to never bother me again, it would be worth it. I'll consult with my solicitor after the first of the year and see what he suggests."

Something pleasant tumbled against his ribs.

"Does that mean you're staying for the duration of the house party then?"

Why did her answer matter so much?

He was wasting time with her: a woman who might be a splendid mother to Sarah, but who had no interest in marrying. What he ought to be doing was determining if any of the other female guests would make a suitable mother. And if he found one that would, could he abide being married to her, let alone faithful, for the decades to come?

That shouldn't be too terribly hard to tolerate, since he still intended to travel extensively—at least six months out of the year. He'd already postponed a trip to Greece and another to Rome since bringing Sarah to England.

Could he bear being away from Sarah that long? He'd grown quiet attached to the little minx and she to him.

Everleigh remained silent as they ascended the first flight of stairs.

One of her hair pins had come loose and was in danger of slipping from her hair.

He drew her to a halt before the stairway to their floor.

She cast him a questioning look.

"Just a moment. Your hairpin is coming out."

He pushed the pearl capped pin into her hair, taking a moment to brush a finger across the soft strands. Her hair really was extraordinary, as fair as milk. No wonder Sarah had asked if she was an angel.

Everleigh's perfume—light, faintly tinted with vanilla and perhaps lilies—wafted upward, the scent as addictive as any opioid.

Neck bent, she remained absolutely motionless.

A gut-wrenching thought pummeled him.

Was she afraid of him?

Or did she grieve for her daughter?

Insensitive clod. He'd nearly forgotten the significance of the day.

"Everleigh?"

Very slowly and just as gently, he placed a bent finger beneath her chin and edged it upward.

"Are you afraid of me?"

Her brilliant green eyes rounded before her gold-tipped lashes fluttered downward, fanning her high cheekbones. Color blossomed beneath the dark fringe. No Ice-Queen here. In fact, other than that brief interlude when she said she was going to leave, she'd been almost cordial to him.

He brushed his thumb across her chin, just below her peach-tinted lower lip. Each time he touched her skin the satiny smoothness awed him.

315

Was she that flawless all over?

"Are you?"

She shook her head. "No. At least I don't think I am, but you do make me uneasy in a queer way."

His chest expanded in profound relief. She didn't even realize what she felt was carnal awareness. Desire. No wonder, considering the abuse she'd suffered. He'd wager his favorite horse she didn't trust her instincts.

That was fine.

He trusted his, and the woman standing uncertainly before him was curious but timid. Had she ever been kissed with tenderness?

She still didn't move nor had she opened her eyes.

Flattening a palm at the small of her back, he drew her ever nearer.

"Everleigh, I want to kiss you, but I shan't if it will make you afraid or if you don't want me to."

A lengthy moment passed and, just when he as about to suggest they continue to the nursery, she lifted her mouth.

Humility overwhelmed him that this gentle woman, who had no reason to trust him, would gift him not only with her trust, but a kiss from her luscious lips.

Slowly, so he wouldn't startle her, he lowered his head and barely brushed her lips with his.

She stiffened, then relaxed, a small smile playing around the edges of her mouth.

He kissed her again, this time pressing his mouth to hers a bit more firmly, but making no attempt to deepen the kiss. She wasn't ready for that level of intimacy yet.

"See, that wasn't so awful, was it?"

Her eyelids slowly drifted upward, and wonder shone in her eyes before a mischievous gleam entered them, making the gold shards in her irises glint.

She swatted his arm.

"As if I'd tell you. You're already too full of yourself. I shall admit it wasn't too terribly dreadful."

He chuckled, absolutely enthralled with this playful, bantering Everleigh.

As they continued to the nursery he couldn't keep from asking her again.

"Will you stay for all of the Duchess of Sutcliffe's festivities? Please."

For God's sake, man.

He was all but pleading.

And toward what end?

If she let me kiss her, might she not also let me woo her?

A lot could happen in a December with a determined duke. Wasn't the season supposed to be one of miracles?

Head bent, mouth flattened into a considering line, she pondered his question.

He liked that about her. She thought before she spoke or reacted.

She gave him a small, almost shy smile.

"I shall stay."

6

Late that afternoon, the Duchess of Sutcliffe gathered her guests in the dining room.

At once Griffin sought out Everleigh.

She stood chatting with her cousins and Miss Twistleton.

That Twistleton chit was going to give some man a merry chase. Thank God it wouldn't be him, no matter how lovely she might be. The Breckensole misses weren't easily managed either.

He preferred Mrs. Chatterton's demure presence, especially since he now knew it hid a passionate woman with a spirited disposition and a generous heart.

"Sheffield, I should warn you, my wife has planned couples charades for after supper. I believe the theme is Christmastide traditions." Sutcliffe gave him a conspiratorial wink. "I know your feelings about the game. You might want to join some of the other chaps and I for billiards instead. We'll probably indulge in something a mite stronger than mulled cider too."

Sutcliffe's brandy was legendary stuff.

He followed Griffin's focus to Everleigh nodding at something Miss Ophelia was saying.

"Or mayhap you'll want to participate in the antics after all. My understanding is the ladies also made several kissing boughs." Sutcliffe canted his dark head toward the dining room doorway where a gaily beribboned bundle of berry-laden holy and mistletoe hung suspended from a bright gold ribbon. "Thea fretted that with this many guests, one bough wasn't going to be sufficient. Especially if there were to be enough berries to last till the end of the month."

Griffin furrowed his brow, not altogether keen on taking his turn with the pudding. Nonsensical traditions held little interest for him, but that was probably because his parents hadn't bothered with such trivialities. Truth to tell, they hadn't troubled themselves with their only child much at all.

They'd died when he was at Eton, though he'd rarely gone home for the holiday anyway. That changed when Uncle Jerome assumed guardianship, but, Uncle, a confirmed bachelor—*until now*—hadn't a clue about Christmas falderal either. He'd introduced Griffin to the world by letting him travel with him.

Not a bad trade-off in his estimation.

"I don't take your meaning." Griffin glanced to the head of the table where Dandridge, looking like he'd been made to swallow mothballs, was taking his turn at stirring the fruity goop in the bowl.

Griffin made a mental note to keep his countenance expressionless when his turn came. "What do numerous blobs of berry-covered greenery have to do with me?"

"What he means, Sheffield, is you haven't taken your eyes off Everleigh Chatterton since you entered the room. More accurately, you haven't let her out of your sight since she entered the drawing room last night."

Pennington offered that observation with a hearty slap to Griffin's shoulder.

"I must say, I didn't think she was your type," Westfall said. "Far too starchy and frigid."

The thought of their earlier kiss heated Griffin's blood once more. She wasn't frosty at all. Merely abused and afraid.

"She's not cold, just cautious," he denied.

"*Brrrr*. My ballocks shrivel just walking past her." Smiling wickedly, Pennington gave a dramatic shiver, and rubbed his arms with both hands.

Never before had Griffin had the urge to pop Pennington's cork, but, at the moment, wiping the cocky grin from his friend's handsome face held real appeal. Except, he was certain it would diminish his standing in Everleigh's opinion, and it mattered a great deal what she thought of him.

Eye to eye with Sutcliffe, Griffin folded his arms. "You presume I'd trap Mrs. Chatterton beneath a bough and demand a kiss?"

No need for entrapment. She'd been willing.

God help him if they ever found out she'd already granted him that sweet favor. He'd never hear the end of it. The duke who managed to thaw the Ice-Queen. Sounded like a bad title to a gothic novel.

"She couldn't say no," Sutcliffe said with a furtive half-wink.

Just as a wife couldn't refuse her husband's attentions, damn Chatterton to purgatory.

320

"It's bad luck to refuse a kiss on the cheek, old chap," Westfall weighed in.

For God's sake. Did he truly look so love-struck that his chums had to give him advice on how to woo a woman? He wasn't exactly an inexperienced milksop or a monk in need of instruction.

"You're getting way ahead of yourselves." Griffin wasn't giving anyone else an opportunity to cast speculation around about him and Everleigh. "You do her a disservice as well, and that's beneath you."

To a man, they had the decency to look chagrined. They truly were decent chaps at heart.

Voice lowered for Griffin's ears only, Sutcliffe said, "She deserves a bit of happiness. I don't know all the details, only the bits and buttons Theadosia has shared with me, but Mrs. Chatterton has had a very rough time of it."

Damn, but life was unfair sometimes.

The duchess tapped a wooden spoon against the large bowl sitting at one end of the table. "Can I have everyone's attention, please?"

Griffin nearly shouted yes. Now his friends could leave off interfering in his romantic endeavors.

Gradually the excited chatter trickled to silence.

She fairly beamed, clearly enjoying herself.

"As you know, today is Stir-up Sunday. My father always quoted from the *Common Book of Prayer* before stirring the pudding. As this is the first Christmas James, Jessica, and I shall be celebrating the Yuletide without our parents, I hope you will indulge me as I give the blessing."

Almost defrocked after helping himself to tithes and other church moneys, a disgraced Mr. Brentwood and his wife now shepherded a flock of soldiers and convicts in Australia.

The duchess closed her eyes and bowed her head.

Everyone else followed suit.

"Stir up, we beseech thee, O Lord, the wills of thy faithful people that they, plenteously bringing forth the fruit of good works, may by thee be plenteously rewarded; through Jesus Christ our Lord. Amen."

"Amen," everyone murmured.

Holding the spoon like a magical wand, or perhaps a royal scepter, her grace waved it over the bowl.

"Cook has prepared and mixed the ingredients for our Christmas pudding, and we have the wooden spoon to represent Christ's rib. Everyone will have a chance to stir it. Make sure you stir in clockwise direction thrice, and as you do, make three silent wishes. One is sure to come true. I'll go first to demonstrate."

She closed her eyes and stirred three times. When she opened her lids, her loving gaze met her husband's, and their adoration for each other was so obvious, Griffin felt slightly discomfited, as if he'd invaded a private moment between them.

He couldn't prevent a covert glimpse toward Everleigh.

From beneath her lashes, she observed him as well, but averted her gaze when she noticed his perusal. A rosy hue tinted her cheeks as she followed the others to the table for her turn to stir dessert.

"It'll be the best stirred pudding of all time after we're through," Pennington muttered drolly as he stepped into the queue.

"Indeed." Griffin chuckled. "And I believe the staff will have turns as well."

Pennington arched incredulous brows over his one blue eye and one green eye. "With the same pudding?"

Griffin jockeyed a shoulder. "I dunno.

"Why, rather than a fork or spoon we'll need a teacup to sip it Christmas Day," Pennington said. "I suppose, then, my chances of finding the wishbone is next to none."

"As if you need any more luck, my friend. Besides, I suspect the duchess will have made sure the pudding is full of coins and other charms." Griffin wouldn't mind finding the ring. The finder was said to be certain to be married within a year.

"Yes, well, I'm not having any luck getting Gabriella Breckensole to spare me so much as a smile," Pennington muttered. "I declare she acts affronted each time I draw near, and I cannot imagine what I've done to offend."

Had Pennington at last found a woman who captured his serious interest? Was that such a surprise?

Griffin had as well. His attention strayed to Everleigh once more.

Or maybe, if providence smiled upon him, he would find the ring. Hell, maybe he'd bribe the cook to add a score of rings to the pudding. He almost laughed out loud at the notion. By God, that could have all of the devilish dukes leg-shackled within a year.

Damn, he just might do it. Just to see the flummoxed expressions on their faces when they spooned their pudding.

He shuffled forward a few paces, the enthusiasm of the others creating a jovial atmosphere. To his surprise, he found himself contemplating what his three wishes ought to be.

Not surprisingly, one centered on the beauty who'd befuddled him since they first met.

Guest after guest dutifully stirred the pudding and made their wishes.

The men made quick work of it, laughing or jesting a bit self-consciously while the women took the matter more seriously. Many closed their eyes, and a few of the ladies' mouths moved silently, almost prayerfully, as they made their wishes.

"Where's Sarah, Your Grace?"

Everleigh had made her way to his side and looked around as if she expected Sarah and Nurse to pop out from behind him or from beneath the table's lacy cloth.

"Didn't you bring her with you? Surely she must have her turn as well." Disappointment tinged her voice.

Over her fair head, Westfall waggled his eyebrows at Griffin.

Bloody ponce.

He couldn't tell Westfall to sod off or even give him a cease-your-idiocy glare without alerting Everleigh. He'd not risk her realizing she was the subject of his friends' speculation, even if it weren't malicious.

Instead, he smiled and bent his neck to softly say, "She's a trifle young to understand the meaning, don't you think?"

"Oh, but that's why she needs her chance. Yuletide is a magical time for children. They are so innocent, their wishes so pure." She clasped his forearm. "If you hurry, you can bring her down in time. I'll await my turn until she's here."

How could he resist?

He sketched a half-bow. "I'll return momentarily."

Aware several other males' amused gazes followed him from the room, Griffin took care not to seem too eager. But the minute he was out of their eyesight, he hightailed it to the nursery, and perplexing poor Mrs. Schmidt, scooped Sarah into his arms.

"She needs to stir the pudding and make her wishes," he said, quite out of breath from his sprint up two flights of stairs.

Sarah giggled and clasped his neck as he dashed back down the corridor from whence he'd come mere seconds before.

"I gets a wish, Papa?"

"Three wishes, cherub." He clomped down the first flight of stairs, but slowed his pace to catch his breath on the second. He might have to plant one of his friends a facer if they laughed at him galloping back into the dining room.

He kissed the top of Sarah's head. You'll stir the pudding three times and with each stir, you'll make a wish. Do you understand, pet?"

She nodded, that riot of curls Nurse tried—unsuccessfully—to tame bouncing about her shoulders.

He took a deep breath, and once assured his pulse had returned to a normal rate, sauntered into the dining room. With deliberate intent, he avoided the other dukes' eyes.

Everleigh separated herself from her friends, and, a radiant smile lighting her face, she glided to his side.

He'd barely made it back in time.

Only Jessica Brentwood and Crispin, Duke of Banbridge, hadn't yet stirred the pudding. From the perturbed expression on her pretty face,

Miss Brentwood wasn't succumbing to Bainbridge's fabled charm.

"Did you already stir the pudding, after all, Mrs. Chatterton?" Griffin asked.

She nodded. "Yes, I decided it would be easier to help with Sarah if I did. You go ahead and stir, and Sarah can go last."

"Evlee." At once, Sarah extended her arms, wiggling her fingers.

Without hesitation, Everleigh placed Sarah on her hip, smoothing the child's aster blue gown over her legs.

"Hello, darling." Giving Griffin another smile, she took her place behind him at the end of the short line. "Have you ever stirred the Christmas pudding before?"

Sarah, suddenly shy with all the adults looking at her, shook her head and tucked her cheek into Everleigh's shoulder.

"It's the greatest fun," Everleigh said.

"The pudding has all sorts of delicious ingredients in it: currants, raisins, spices, eggs, brown sugar or molasses, and other tasty things all mixed together. After that, coins and other charms with special meanings are added for people to find in their servings. Everyone takes a turn stirring it, and then on Christmas Day it's served sprinkled with powdered sugar. It's utterly scrumptious!"

When it was Sarah's turn, Griffin pulled a chair before the table for her to stand upon.

Everyone's attention was on the child, indulgent smiles on their faces. Probably each was recalling their own childhood holiday joy.

Everleigh had been right. Sarah should experience this tradition.

Sarah gripped the spoon in her two small hands. She squinched her eyelids shut tight, then popped them open again.

"I gets three wishes?"

Griffin nodded. "Yes."

Eyes screwed tightly closed once more, she stirred once. "I wished a white puppy named Clarence with a green ribbon 'round his neck."

A few swiftly muffled titters followed her sweet declaration.

His gaze met Everleigh's.

They'd forgotten to tell Sarah to make her wishes silently. Well, at least he knew what to get her for Christmas. He'd have to ask Sutcliffe if he knew of any litters in the area.

Sarah stirred the conglomeration again. "I wished my dolly had a new gown."

What about new hair and eyes and stuffing? Or just another doll?

No, Sarah saw Maya through the eyes of love, so she didn't notice the doll's many flaws. If she wanted to put a new dress on the ramshackle toy, then he'd see to it Maya had a new dress.

Her face scrunched in concentration, she stirred a final time.

"I wished Evlee was my mama."

B usy with Theadosia's seemingly never-ending Christmastide activities, the next twelve days passed quickly. Each morning, weather permitting, Everleigh walked with Sarah and Mrs. Schmidt, and more often than not, Griffin joined them.

He hadn't today, and he also hadn't been at breakfast.

Others had also begun taking a morning constitutional. No surprise given the rich foods and lack of occasion to exercise. During summer house parties, guests might play croquet or shuttlecock, practice archery or go riding or boating, but there weren't nearly as many opportunities to be outdoors and stretch one's legs in the wintertime.

Today, Ophelia, Gabriella, and Jessica, arms entwined, walked ahead of Everleigh.

Ice skating was planned for next week, but since she'd never learned how to skate, she'd already decided to stay behind and work on her Christmas gift for Sarah: a new rag doll. A replica of Maya, wearing a crimson and gold striped dress—an exact match to the dress Everleigh was sewing for Sarah.

She'd picked up the material and supplies she needed in Colchester during a shopping excursion Theadosia had planned four days ago so that those who hadn't brought gifts and wanted to exchange them Christmas Day might purchase a few trinkets.

There'd been much whispering and covert tucking of small packages into coats or reticles and brown paper packages tied with strings carried to the carriages by patient footmen, including Hampton. He still looked at her with more interest than he ought to, but he'd not been impertinent again.

Ridgebrook smelled wonderfully of pine and other greeneries. Thea had tossed aside the custom of waiting until Christmas Eve to decorate the house. Garlands, wreaths, and ribbons bedecked the doorways, fireplaces, and mantels. She created a truly festive atmosphere, and, each passing day, Everleigh relaxed a bit more.

Nearly every room bore signs of the holiday, and tonight, again flouting custom, they were to decorate the grand Christmas tree. Smaller trees had already been erected in most of the common rooms, complete with miniature scenes around their bases. For days, in the afternoons and evenings, as one guest or another entertained them with music or songs or even read aloud, many of the others strung popcorn, cranberries, cherries, and currants, or created paper chains for the tree.

Cook had been busy making sweetmeats to stuff in crocheted baskets, and she'd made dozens of pretty cakes and shaped biscuits to hang by ribbons from the tree.

Theadosia's propensity to toss aside custom to entertain her guests and provide them with a Christmastide they would long remember was endearing. She'd forgone no expense or effort to assure them an unforgettable holiday, especially Everleigh.

Everleigh hadn't told Griffin she planned on giving Sarah a gift for Christmas, fearing he'd feel obliged to reciprocate. It wouldn't be proper to accept anything from him, so by being secretive, she saved them both potential awkwardness.

As it was, she was a touch discomfited he hadn't attempted to kiss her again.

She wasn't certain whether she was relieved or vexed. For the first time in her life, she'd enjoyed a man's touch, his warm lips upon hers, and, after that first kiss, she'd even briefly entertained the notion of taking a lover.

If he was the man sharing her bed, that was.

Young and healthy, she was curious to know what all the whispering and giggling was about, and even dear Theadosia had tried to explain that physical intimacy could be wonderful. After Frederick's assault and Arnold's clumsy molestations, until Everleigh had met Griffin—well, until he'd kissed her—she'd thought she could be perfectly content being celibate.

Then again, she'd never desired a man until she met him.

The more time she spent with Griffin, the stronger her yearnings grew, and she feared she'd make a cake of herself one of these days. The wisest course of action would be to leave, but she didn't want to go home now.

Plain and simple, she liked being with him. She enjoyed being with Sarah too.

In fact, Everleigh had even begun to appreciate the comradery of the dukes, though the ten scoundrels teased and harassed one another incessantly.

The storm that had threatened the other day had passed them by, but as she eyed the low-hanging, petulant clouds today, she felt certain their luck was about to change. There'd be snow by nightfall, or she wasn't blonde and that wasn't a doe peering hesitantly from yonder tree-line.

When she could cuddle beneath a warm throw before the fire and read a novel whilst savoring a strong cup of tea, she enjoyed the snow. There'd been so much commotion at Ridgewood every day, finding a quiet niche to read in hadn't been possible.

The only respite she found from the constant tumult was in her bedchamber. A padded window seat ran the full length of the turreted window and also provided an exceptional view of the countryside. Even so, she hadn't spent much time there, except to sew Sarah's presents.

Everleigh hadn't thought she was terribly lonely before, especially with Rayne's company, but there was something to be said for the gaiety of gatherings with friends.

She quirked her mouth at her musings.

Was this the same woman who dreaded assemblies of any sort just a few days ago?

It was the company.

Thea had been true to her word. Except for Caroline that first day, the men and women were nothing like the sots and degenerates Arnold had regularly entertained.

Sarah, her eyes bright and face ruddy from the cold, skipped along the gravel path. Maya, appearing more bedraggled than ever, trailed along the ground as Sarah hopped on one foot, then the other.

"Evlee?"

"Yes, darling?"

"Read to me before I sleeps t'night?"

Everleigh slid Mrs. Schmidt a glance.

Worry puckered the sweet woman's face. She also fretted that Sarah was growing too attached.

"I shall have to check with your Papa, but I think I might be able to. It also depends on what the Duchess of Sutcliffe has planned for this evening. Why don't you go inside now and have your hot chocolate?"

That had become a tradition as well.

Sarah bobbed a little curtsy and clasped Nurse's hand. "You come too?"

Everleigh shook her head and gathered her cloak a bit closer. "Not today. I have some things I need to attend to."

After the mortifying incident with the Christmas pudding, Everleigh had almost ordered the carriage brought 'round to take her home straightaway. She wouldn't have believed a room could grow so completely silent so speedily, but there wasn't a doubt everyone had heard the child's last wish.

Theadosia had hugged Sarah while claiming the spoon and redirected everyone's attention. "Let's all adjourn to the drawing room for a cup of mulled wine, shall we? I have another surprise for you."

That was when she announced the treasure hunt for tomorrow, and, also, since they'd missed exchanging gifts on December 6th, St.

Nicholas's Day, those that wanted to do so, would now exchange gifts on Christmas Day.

"Mrs. Chatterton." Griffin waved at her from the pathway leading to the stables. "Might I have a word?"

He'd no sooner asked than snowflakes began drifting down.

"Snow!" Sarah squealed and stuck her tongue out, trying to catch the fat, fluffy flakes.

"Goodness, child," Mrs. Schmidt fussed. "Let's get you inside before you catch your death."

It wouldn't have hurt to allow Sarah a few moments in the snow, but Everleigh refused to interfere. Sarah was Mrs. Schmidt's charge, and, as Griffin had said, she wasn't a biddable child. Nurse had a difficult enough time reining the child in without others throwing a wrench into her efforts.

The truth was, the cold probably aggravated Mrs. Schmidt's arthritic bones.

Should Everleigh suggest to Griffin a younger, more energetic woman, a governess perhaps, might be in order? It wasn't her place, of course, but Mrs. Schmidt wasn't quite up to snuff, and though she obviously held Sarah in great affection, she was also a bit lax in areas.

Perhaps later, when the house party neared its end, Everleigh might voice her thoughts. For now, she'd keep her own council.

She made her way to Griffin, wearing a shocking red, green, and yellow knitted scarf about his neck. It was quite the ugliest thing she'd ever seen. She tried not to stare, but her gaze kept wandering back to the atrocity.

He chuckled, that wonderful resonance deep in his chest she'd grown to enjoy, much to her befuddlement, and pulled the ends tighter. "Widow Beezely insisted I accept it as a thank you for purchasing a spaniel puppy from her."

Everleigh clapped her hands and practically bounced on her toes. "For Sarah?"

"Yes. I have her in the stables, and the good lads there have agreed to watch the imp until Christmas for me."

"Oh, oh, a *she*?" Would Sarah be terribly disappointed?

"Yes. The males were spoken for, and when I saw this little darling . . ." He grasped her elbow to help her over an uneven spot on the pathway. "Well, you'll see why I had to have her for Sarah."

Inside the stables, she paused for a moment. Smells of hay, horse liniment, manure, and grains filled the warm building. Horses knickered softly every now and again, and a tortious-shell cat padded down the pathway toward them between the stalls. It gave a plaintive meow and another cat answered from the loft above them.

"Claire is down there."

He pointed to a stall at the far end.

"Claire rather than Clarence? Very clever, I must say."

For a man having a child's care thrust upon him, he'd taken to the task of fatherhood with an aptitude many men lacked. He even permitted Sarah to call him Papa, and she couldn't think of another man she knew who would've permitted that.

He grinned, a trifle self-consciously, and lifted a shoulder. "It's the best I could come up with."

"I like it, and I think Sarah will too."

He slid the bolt and pushed the door open. In the corner, sitting on a blanket, was a tiny forlorn, black and tan King Charles Spaniel pup with curly ears. She stood and wagged her tail before toddling over to them.

"Oh, stars above, she's precious." Everleigh sank to her knees, and the puppy clambered into her lap. "I always wanted a puppy as a little girl, but Mama said we couldn't afford one."

Maybe she should get a dog. She'd enjoy the company, especially when Rayne married.

Griffin knelt on one knee beside her, and ran his hand down Claire's back. "With those ears, she reminded me of Sarah."

Everleigh giggled as Claire nibbled her nose and licked her cheeks.

"She's absolutely perfect. Well done, you. Sarah will be ecstatic." She kissed the pup's head. "Don't forget the green ribbon."

Rubbing her face into the puppy's soft fur, she gave him a sideways look.

He touched her cheek then leaned over and skimmed his mouth across hers.

Heaven.

Instinct prompted her to open her lips, and he slid his tongue into her mouth. Not invasive or violating, but in tenderness and gentle exploration.

Nothing else mattered: not the puppy in her arms, the fresh straw she knelt upon, the swirling snow outside, or that she was afraid of men and had vowed never to be vulnerable again.

She simply savored the experience and Griffin. His taste. His essence of soap and starch and something faintly spicy. His hard-muscled thighs pressing into hers, and his lips at once firm but soft, teaching her how to kiss.

After several blissful moments, Claire must've decided she didn't like being ignored, for she nipped his chin.

"Ouch." He lifted his mouth from Everleigh's. "She's punctured me, I do believe."

Everleigh *tisked* as she held the little darling to her neck. "I think you'll live."

"Everleigh."

Griffin cupped the back of her neck, his gaze so penetrating, her heart slowed.

"What is it?"

"Marry me. I have no doubt you'd make Sarah a wonderful mother, and I've never encountered a woman as extraordinary as you."

Marry him?

Was he queer in the attic?

Barely over a week ago, she'd sworn never to wed again. She had far too much to lose by doing so, not the least of which was her independence. He would assume all control of her wealth. All control of every aspect of her life, even her body.

She opened her mouth to tell him just that, but he held up his hand.

"Please hear me out. Please."

Reluctant, battling renewed apprehension, she gave a shallow nod.

"Thank you." He pressed his mouth to her knuckles.

"I know we've only known each other for a short time, but there's a connection between us. You sense it too, I know you do. I realize you aren't ready yet. But I want you to know that I feel something for you. I don't understand exactly what it is, but I also don't want to dismiss it as nothing. It is something powerful and rare. Don't answer now. Just think about it. Can you do that much?"

Gaze lowered, she ran her fingers through Claire's fur.

What could it hurt?

Everleigh wasn't making a commitment or promising to accept his addresses. She wasn't even agreeing to let him court her. The silence grew lengthy. At last she raised her head.

"I shall, under one condition, and you have to promise to accept my decision afterward."

He ran a finger along her jawbone. "All right. What is your condition?"

"You will come to my room tonight and make love to me. I honestly don't know if I shall be able to go through with the act, but I want to know if it's even possible for me to enjoy sexual congress."

She rolled a shoulder as she brushed a fingertip across an eyebrow, both actions to lesson the tension that had her feeling she'd snap like a dry twig if she as much as sneezed.

"If I cannot, then we both know it would be foolish to pursue any sort of a relationship. You wouldn't want a wife who couldn't bear your touch. If I don't find the act as horrific as my singular experience was, then perhaps we can contemplate what a future together might look like."

An uncomfortable minute passed as his dark gaze searched her face. He ran his thumb and forefinger down the bridge of his nose.

"I confess, I'm conflicted, Everleigh. I feel it would be dishonorable to bed you outside the bonds of marriage. You could get with child."

She could.

A grin kicked his mouth up on one side. "Though don't think for an instant that I don't find you desirable. I've had a constant cock-stand since that first night you walked into the drawing room."

"Cock-stand?"

She dropped her gaze to his lap where the evidence of his arousal bulged.

"Oh. I see." Turning her mouth downward, she scrunched her forehead. "I . . ." Gads, but this was awkward. "I thought there were ways to prevent conception."

"There are, but you wouldn't have a complete sexual experience. I would have to withdraw before completion." He set the puppy aside. "Do you understand what that means?"

Good Lord. Here they were kneeling in a horse stall, chatting about sex when at any moment a stable hand might come upon them. She might be known as the Ice-Queen but she'd not have her reputation in tatters.

"I believe I do, and I also believe it is time to return to the house."

She stood and cautiously looked around.

Thank God. They were still alone.

Griffin stood as well.

"What time should I come to your room?"

8

Everleigh paced back and forth, each time she passed the fireplace glancing at the bronze and ormolu clock atop the carved cherry wood mantel.

Half past eleven. And Griffin still hadn't arrived.

A cozy fire snapped and crackled cheerily in the hearth, and candles flickered on the bedside tables and in the wall sconces in readiness for their assignation.

She'd told him to come at eleven o'clock. She pleaded a headache and retired by nine in order to have a leisurely bath and bring her rioting nerves under control.

Now, pacing to and fro in her chamber, snow billowing from the sky as it had for the past twelve hours, she bit her lower lip.

Had she misread him?

Miscalculated?

Been too forward?

He'd said he desired her and had agreed to come to her chamber, so where was he?

A deep sigh escaped her, and after a final glance at the clock, she wandered to the window seat. A pristine, virginal blanket of snow at least a foot deep covered the grounds. At dinner, there'd been talk of sleigh rides tomorrow.

Drawing her knees to her chest, she rested her cheek on them.

What had she been thinking, making such an immoral suggestion? She'd probably shocked Griffin so badly he'd decided he didn't want a woman of her ilk for his wife after all. What man would want someone with that kind of character flaw around a child?

A tear crept down her cheek.

Goose. She wiped it away with the back of her hand.

How she would face him tomorrow, she couldn't imagine, and, in this snow, going home was dangerous. Likely impossible. She'd just have to hold her chin up and pretend she hadn't been a brazen nincompoop.

After a final glance outside, she padded barefoot across the room and extinguished the candles in the sconces. She blew out the tapers on one of the nightstands too, then removed her robe.

Shivering despite the fire, she fluffed a pillow.

The knock was so faint, she wasn't sure she'd heard it.

She paused, head cocked toward the door.

There it was again, the merest scraping.

She flew across the room, her hair billowing around her shoulders Holding her breath, she cracked the door open.

Hair damp, and attired in only a shirt and pantaloons, Griffin stood there.

"Quickly, open up. I should hate to have to explain to Mrs. Schmid what I'm doing fresh from my bath outside your chamber."

Everleigh swung the door wide, and once he'd entered, glanced up and down the passageway, then closed it and turned the key in the lock.

"I didn't think you were coming."

"The chaps decided to ruminate about old times over multiple bottles of Sutcliffe's brandy. It was no small feat nursing my single glass without them catching on. I finally escaped, using a need to look in on Sarah as an excuse."

He gave her a sly wink. "I'm finding having a child has more advantages than I realized."

Now nerves overwhelmed her. She didn't know what to say or do.

Her uncertainty must've shown.

"Come here, darling."

Griffin opened his arms wide, and she rushed into his embrace.

He alone made her feel safe.

"We don't have to do this. I'd much rather my ring was on your finger before we do." He kissed the top of her head.

She wasn't sure she could ever let any man put a ring on her hand again.

"I need this, Griffin."

She wrapped her arms around his solid waist and clung to him, trying to make him understand why it was so important.

"Frederick Chatterton despoiled me, and Arnold could never complete the act. Trust me, he tried many, many times, and took out his frustration with his fists and, at times, a cane. I've never known a man's gentle touch, never experienced passion. I don't know if I can."

She tilted her head back and noticed his smooth-shaven jaw. He'd taken the time to shave too.

"But I think if I am capable, it must be with you. For you do something to me, Griffin. You make me hungry in a way I don't understand."

His eyes had gone flinty and his face granite hard.

"If those two sods weren't already dead, I'd kill them," he said.

"Let's not let them ruin this. I only mentioned them to help you understand why I am the way I am. I trust you, but if I cannot do this, if I displease you in some way, then I have to believe I am flawed. That I really am frigid, and I was never meant to know physical gratification."

He cupped her face, his expression so tender that tears welled in her eyes.

"You are not flawed, Everleigh. And you are most certainly not frigid. I am humbled at the trust you've put in me."

With that, he lifted her into his arms and carried her to the turned down bed. After laying her upon the sheets, he pulled his shirt over his head. His muscles rippled with the motion.

Unlike Frederick and Arnold, he possessed a virile man's form. Broad, sculpted shoulders framed an impressive chest covered with black, curly hair. More muscled ridges grooved his abdomen before tapering to a narrow waist and hips. He didn't remove his pantaloons before lying beside her.

At first, all he did was feather his fingers over her exposed skin. A gentle trailing across her collarbone, a wispy skimming along the inside of her arm. He took his time, speaking soft words of reassurance all the while.

She relaxed and grew accustomed to his touch, each whisper of skin to skin a heady aphrodisiac.

When he grazed his mouth across hers, she was ready for him. Eager to taste him again.

His onslaught against her senses never ceased, but neither did he rush her.

"We have all night, sweetheart."

She wanted him. Now.

He drew the bodice of her nightgown downward until he exposed her breasts.

"So beautiful," he breathed before kissing the taut tip of each.

She gasped and clasped his back, arching into him.

"Griffin."

He chuckled as he nuzzled her neck and pulled her nightgown over her thighs.

"Most assuredly you are not frigid, darling."

Another gasp turned to a groan as he expertly explored her most sensitive areas. She wriggled against his fingers, moaning.

He left her for a moment, and she opened her eyes in time to see him shuck his pantaloons. His manhood strained upward from a nest of thick, ebony curls.

She clutched the sheets, wanting to wrap her fingers around his length.

He returned to her and lifted her shoulders. Half drugged from passion, she was of little help to him as he undressed her. The next moment, he tossed her nightgown aside.

Everleigh scoured his body with her hungry gaze.

He was gorgeous, and he wanted her.

She touched his face.

"I am not afraid, and I don't want you to withdraw. I want to experience it all with you."

With a gravelly groan, he covered her from knees to chest and nudged her thighs apart.

She felt his length at the apex of her womanhood, and it was perfect. She spread her thighs wider and tilted her hips upward, craving him inside her.

Griffin gripped her buttocks, and, face taut as he strained for control, he gradually entered her. Eyes closed, the cords of his neck standing out, he held perfectly still, letting her become accustomed to his length.

Feeling a fullness but no pain this time, she shifted her hips and pleasure flickered. Another tilt brought an answering spark of bliss. A groan escaped her as she wrapped her legs around his, digging her heels into his thighs.

"That's it, darling. Rock your hips. Feel me slide in and out of you."

He thrust into her as she lifted her hips again.

Quicker and quicker she moved, the pleasure taking over.

Griffin held her tightly, expertly playing her body, sending her higher and higher onto a plane of pure sensation. He whispered hoarse words of encouragement and sex to her, and when she thought she couldn't stand it another instant, when she thought she would splinter if she didn't reach the mysterious pinnacle, he reached between them and touched her woman's core.

She screamed as wave after wave of ecstasy burst over her, carrying her along on a tide of sensation. She was barely aware when he stiffened and shuddered against her.

What surely had to be a smile of utter satisfaction curving her mouth, Everleigh at last managed to force her eyes open.

Her gaze collided with Griffin's sexy, passion-drowsy gaze.

He rested his head on one hand, his elbow on the pillow beside her. His other hand curved possessively over her ribs, and one deliciously hairy male leg rested between hers.

Never in her life had she felt so satiated, so relaxed. So wanton.

Never had anything felt so utterly right.

He lowered his head and kissed her shoulder, then gave it a little nip.

"You, my darling, are a tigress."

She giggled and tried to see his back.

"Oh, Griffin, did I scratch you?'

"I prefer to think you left your mark on me." He snatched her hand to his lips. "And not just physically. You've touched my heart too. Branded me for all time."

She blinked away the fresh moisture pooling in her eyes.

"Thank you for this. For giving me a gift I never thought to have."

"*Shh*, no tears and no regrets, sweetheart. It's I who should be thanking you."

Griffin pulled Everleigh into his embrace, her luminous head resting in the crook of his shoulder. He traced little circles on her lower back.

"Does this mean you'll marry me?" he asked.

He'd fallen in love with her.

Probably had that moment in the drawing room when she'd lifted a frightened Sarah into her arms.

Everleigh stiffened, then sighed as she rolled onto her back and slung an elbow over her eyes.

"I said I'd think about it after we made love and I knew if I could enjoy the act."

Disappointment, sharp and jagged, pierced him in the gut. He'd been so sure he'd broken through her defenses. That she'd agree to wed him now. I seemed there was more than just fear of intimacy he needed to overcome.

"One step at a time then, sweet." He caressed her shoulder. "What else are you afraid of?"

She lifted her head, her eyes more emerald than jade in the muted light. The thick cloud of her hair brushed his chest.

"How do you know there is something else?"

Her fair brows pulled together the tiniest bit.

She might be able to put on a bland façade other people couldn't see through, but this remarkable woman's eyes revealed much.

"I can see it in your eyes."

Even now, the shutters that slammed shut when anyone—any man— ventured too close fell into place.

She stared at his chin and spoke softly, haltingly.

"I fear . . . losing my independence. I shan't ever subject myself to a man's whims again. *Ever.* If I marry, my husband has complete control over me. My wealth becomes his. My body becomes his to do with what he will. My children, if there are any, are also his to do with what he wants. As a woman, I have no rights. None."

What she said was true. A woman was at her husband's mercy.

She sank onto the pillow, her back against him and whispered, "That's what I'm afraid of, Griffin. I cannot endure that life again. I cannot."

She curled into a ball, weeping softly.

He pulled her into his arms, his thighs tucked beneath her supple bottom and his chest pressed to her back. He swept her hair away from her neck and kissed the satiny flesh there.

"I would sign a settlement allowing you to retain all of your wealth, and I vow I would never lay a hand on you in anger. As for children, I think they need their mother, which is one reason I want to find a woman who can love Sarah as her own. I believe you are that woman, Everleigh."

"You have more faith in me than I have in myself."

After kissing her neck again, he rose.

"I'd love to stay with you all night, but I shan't risk your reputation. Nor shall I rush you. Wounds such as yours take time to heal."

After donning his clothing, he came around to the other side of the bed and knelt there.

She opened her eyes, the lashes dark and spikey from her tears.

He palmed her damp cheek.

"I've fallen in love with you, Everleigh Chatterton. I shall wait as long as it takes, do whatever I need to do to convince you of that. I'll help you overcome your qualms. My love will heal your fears."

She swallowed, then licked her lower lip.

"You are a good man, Griffin, kind and decent and generous, but I cannot make any promises. It wouldn't be fair to either of us. I need to take things one day at a time. I don't have your confidence. I'm afraid to trust my feelings for you."

"I know." He tucked the bedclothes around her shoulders in much the same manner as he did Sarah. "But *I* trust your feelings, and I have confidence enough for the both of us."

"Humble blighter, aren't you?" She attempted a wobbly smile.

"Go for a sleigh ride with me tomorrow?" Brushing the hair from her face, he paused and ran his fingers through the length before fanning the strands across the pillow. "Sarah's never been."

"Unfair." She hit him with a pillow. "How am I supposed to deny her that fun?"

She didn't look quite so tormented.

He wiggled his eyebrows.

"Madam, when I set out to win a woman's heart and hand, you have no idea what I'm capable of. Erect your ramparts and battlements if you must, but I believe my love will tear them down."

9

The next afternoon, bundled to their noses beneath furs and quilts, three sleighs full of the braver guests pulled into the courtyard that fronted Ridgewood. Jingling bells, the whoosh of the sleighs' rudders, and laughter filled the air.

Under cover of the blankets, Griffin held Everleigh's hand as he had most of the outing.

"Everleigh, the cold weather and these excursions agree with you. Why, you're positively incandescent," Miss Twistleton said, her face radiant as well.

Everleigh only smiled, but Griffin caught the furtive glance she sent him.

Hers was the complexion of a woman who'd been fully satiated and still bore the afterglow.

Miss Twistleton's shiny countenance might be because Westfall had managed to seat himself beside her, the sly devil. Pennington on the other hand, brooded like a woebegone mongrel. Miss Gabriella had taken one look at the sleigh he was in and marched to another, her nose pointed skyward.

Pennington had best turn his attention elsewhere, for that door had slammed shut and was bolted from within.

Sarah, sound asleep and mouth parted, curled against Everleigh's other side, Maya clutched in her mittened hand.

When they reached the mansion, Griffin climbed out first and reached for Sarah.

Everleigh laid her in his arms.

It had been on the tip of his tongue all day to ask if she'd thought any more about his marriage offer, but less than twenty-four hours had passed. He wouldn't rush her. If need be, he'd continue to court her after the house party ended, for he was adamant Everleigh Chatterton would be his duchess.

Everyone bustled into the foyer where much stamping of feet to remove snow earned them a starchy stare from Grover, standing beside three footmen ready to accept the myriad of coats, scarfs, capes, gloves, muffs, and hats from the chilled adventurers.

He raised his patrician nose an inch and announced, "There are an assortment of hot beverages and dainties for your enjoyment in the drawing room. Her Grace begs you to forgive her absence. She's feeling a trifle puny. She'll be present for dinner, however."

"I'll only be a few minutes." Griffin angled toward the stairs.

"I shall walk up with you," Everleigh said. "I'd rather take off my outer garments in my chamber. I need to straighten my hair in any event."

He thought she looked delightful slightly mussed and windblown.

Falling into step beside him, she turned to glance behind her as she removed her gloves. "The poor footmen and Grover are taxed to their limits with this many people."

Griffin shifted Sarah so her head rested on his shoulder.

"True, but they also receive vails from everyone, and with a house party this size, that means a substantial bonus for each of the servants before the holidays."

On the landing they parted; he continued on to the nursery and Everleigh to her chamber.

"Griffin?"

"Yes?"

One hand cradling Sarah's head, he turned back toward Everleigh. She'd paused a couple of paces away.

She bit her lower lip and fidgeted with her gloves.

Were her cheeks still rosy from cold or was she blushing?

He drew nearer and spoke low. "What is it?"

"I . . ."

Staring at the buttons on his coat, she flicked her tongue out to wet her lower lip.

Even though he knew it was a nervous gesture, his body reacted with a surge of lust.

Her attention shifted to Sarah, limp as her ragdoll in his embrace.

"Never mind. It's not important."

Whatever she wanted to say, she was afraid Sarah might overhear, even though the child hadn't so much as stirred for the last half and hour.

"Let me settle her in the nursery, and then we can talk. Do you want me to come to your chamber?"

Risky business that. But if she wanted privacy, her room or his was the best place to have a conversation.

Everleigh gave a short nod. "That's fine."

Twenty minutes later he rapped on her door. Sarah had awakened and fussed for a few minutes when he laid her down, and after she'd drifted to sleep once more, he'd taken the time to go to his bedchamber and remove his greatcoat as well.

When Everleigh didn't answer, he knocked again.

Still no response.

He tried the handle and the door clicked open. Poking his head inside, he looked around.

"Everleigh?"

Curled up on the window seat, one hand tucked beneath her cheek, she was fast asleep, minus her cloak and redingote. Those she'd tossed on her bed.

A potent image of last night, her silken limbs entwined with his, immobilized him for a second. Common sense demanded he leave and let her have her nap.

Bugger that.

Common sense wouldn't win this woman's heart.

After checking the corridor, he closed the door. He sat beside her on the seat, and swept a curl off her forehead. She appeared so peaceful in slumber. He could watch her for hours.

What if his seed *had* found fertile soil in her womb?

Shutting his eyes, he pulled in a deep breath, both exhilarated and appalled at the prospect. Her first pregnancy revealed she was easily impregnated. He was an assling for agreeing to her request. Yet he couldn't regret it, for she'd found she was able to reach fulfillment.

There was nothing for it. She might be carrying his child. He must convince her to marry him, and sooner rather than later.

She stirred, and her lashes fluttered open. Her drowsy smile held something more than sleep.

"I'm sorry. I must've dozed off."

She scooted into a sitting position, resting her back against the window casements before patting her mussed hair. Several tendrils had escaped their pins and curled over her shoulders.

He glanced out the window. It had begun to snow again. They'd returned from sleighing just in time. If the weather pattern held, the Sutcliffes might have guests longer than anticipated.

"I shouldn't have come in," Griffin said. "You're obviously tired."

"Yes, I didn't get a full night's sleep last night," she quipped with a saucy smile and a coy glance.

Now his Ice-Queen was flirting?

What next?

Perhaps she'd also laid awake the rest of last night.

"Indeed." The seductive minx. He hadn't come here to make love to her again, no matter how enticing the idea might be. "But was it worth losing a little slumber over?"

"Oh, very, *very* worth it," she said.

She drew his head to hers and kissed him. "I've wanted to do that all day."

"I'm only too happy to oblige, sweetheart."

He waggled his eyebrows, and she giggled. He'd not deny himself her kisses.

Taking his hand between hers, she linked her slender fingers with his. "Will you come to me again tonight?"

So that was what she'd wanted to ask.

Her appetite had been whetted, and she was eager to practice more. No keener than he was to teach her, but not skulking about in darkened corridors and whispering clandestinely behind locked doors. No, when next she graced his bed, it would be as his wife.

He rubbed his thumb over the back of her hand.

She wasn't going to like what he had to say.

"Everleigh, last night was the most wonderful thing I've ever experienced." He squeezed her fingers. "But because I love you and won't risk impregnating you unless we're married, I must, with deepest regret, refuse."

Her beautiful eyes rounded, and she pulled her hand away.

"Why must we marry? People take lovers all the time. Married people take lovers." She poked his chest, then made a curt gesture with her hand. "Lord knows I witnessed enough fornicating and adultery while married to Arnold."

Undoubtedly witnessed things no respectable woman could ever admit.

Her frustrated gaze impaled him. "You've had lovers. Probably dozens of them, and don't tell me you haven't."

"Not dozens, darling, but I am flattered you think me so irresistible."

She punched him in the shoulder. Hard.

"Arrogant, conceited jackanapes."

Checking the grin that tickled his lips, he rubbed his arm where she'd struck him. By Jove, beneath that cool exterior, her blood and spirit ran hot. This Everleigh would keep him on his toes. What a delightful prospect.

Green sparks flew from her irises, and her anger gave him hope.

She was jealous.

"Maybe I'll take a lover too."

She flung her head back, giving vent to her frustration.

"I'm sure I can find a man to accommodate me."

Over my dead body.

In a way, he was flattered she'd so enjoyed their sexual encounter that she had braved approaching him.

He forced calmness into his tone. "I cannot deny I've been with other women, nor will I apologize for what's gone on before you. However, I shall never knowingly put you in the situation that forced you to marry Chatterton."

"Since when did you get so blasted noble?" she snapped.

He cupped her shoulders and gave her the gentlest shake, forcing her to look at him.

"I'll hear no more talk of you taking a lover. You could end up with someone who would abuse you. What we enjoyed is not typical." No, it had been beyond extraordinary."

"I have only your word on that." Lips pursed, she tormented the tassels of the pillow beside her. "How do I know you're not lying just to keep me to yourself?"

Not ready to concede defeat just yet, was she?

"I'm not, and I believe, deep inside, beyond your disappointment and frustration, you know that. Last night was something unbelievably special and it should be treasured. Even now my child might be growing inside you."

Expression stricken, her mouth parted, and her gaze dived to her belly. She instinctively cradled her womb. Shoulders slumping, she shook her head.

"I thought . . ." She gazed out the window. "It doesn't matter."

Damnation. He hated seeing her so despondent.

"Everleigh, I'll give you all the time you need to grow to trust me. Unless you are with child. Then we would need to wed at once."

Fingering the locket at her throat she thrust her chin upward.

"I've been down that road once already, and I'll be damned, *damned I say*, if I'll do it again."

He could almost hear the ramparts *chinking* higher and higher as she erected self-protective fortifications around herself.

"If I ever marry again, it will be because I *want* to. Not because I *have* to." She pointed a shaky finger toward the door. "You should leave now. Last night was a stupid, stupid mistake. I apologize for imposing upon you."

"Everleigh . . ."

She presented her profile, her Ice-Queen facade firmly in place once more.

"Please don't approach me again. I'm leaving just as soon as the weather permits."

10

Christmas Day. At last.

The past two days had dragged on and on since Everleigh had told Griffin to leave her alone. She hadn't gone down to dinner that night, but instead had cried herself to sleep, something she hadn't done since marrying Arnold.

Her frosty guise once more in place, she kept to the fringes of the activities.

Sarah's two gifts tucked beneath her arm, Everleigh held her emerald empire gown up with her other hand. What had possessed her to accept an early birthday present from Theadosia?

Surely it was the least she could do to thank her dear friend, she told herself.

Maybe she'd wanted to impress Griffin as well?

Why, when she'd made clear her wishes?

She caught sight of herself in one of the corridor mirrors. The gown was truly lovely and befitting the season. It had been a long while since she'd worn anything so colorful, and despite her fragile heart, the gown lifted her spirits a notch.

Evening cloaked the subdued light visible through the windows. And beyond that, snow covered the picturesque landscape. A perfect setting for the holiday.

Griffin must've conspired with Fate to keep her at Ridgewood.

It had snowed intermittently since the sleigh ride, and a good two feet or more of white covered everything. It had been decades since anyone had seen a December with such deep snowfall in Essex. Leaving was nearly impossible, and even though she longed to flee to Fittledale Park, she wouldn't jeopardize a driver's safety for her own selfish wishes.

She'd endured marriage to Arnold for two years; she could certainly abide a few more days here. The company was pleasant, the food exceptional, and Theadosia made sure no one was bored or overlooked. Still, even in a house this large, with the guests confined indoors, unless she stayed in her chamber, she couldn't help but encounter Griffin.

Seeing him across the room hurt like a mule kick to her innards each time, but he'd respected her wishes and hadn't approached her. His gaze never left her though, and the hurt and frustration in his eyes caused hers to get misty more than once.

He was a good man, and he did love her.

She didn't doubt it.

Lying awake at night, reliving the passion they'd shared, recalling his witty rejoinders and the tenderness he showed her and Sarah, she'd come upon a startling discovery.

She might very well love him too.

No. She *did* love him.

Fear had crippled her, warped her emotions, until she didn't even recognize what was before her. Shame infused her as she made her way to the drawing room where the great decorated pine tree stood. She'd used Griffin in the basest, meanest manner. Had their situations been reversed, she'd have thought him a monster for asking to bed her.

Her slippers whooshed on the marble floor as they had that first night. It seemed much longer than just over a fortnight ago.

What if she did carry his child?

An unwed woman ought to be dismayed at the thought, but she wasn't. She'd welcome a child—his child—no matter what.

She paused at the entry to the drawing room. As expected, guests milled about the room and extra chairs had been placed throughout. Candles winked on the grand tree, beneath which were stacked mounds of presents.

"Everleigh! Your gown is stunning." Gabriella grabbed her sister's arm. "Look at Everleigh, Fee-Fee. She's finally out of mourning."

That caused several heads to turn in her direction, one of which loomed above all the others.

Ophelia sent a not-so-covert peek toward Griffin. Everyone probably thought the same thing she did, that Everleigh had set her cap for him.

Appreciation quirked his mouth the merest bit, as his hot gaze trailed over her, and from across the room she could almost hear him begging her to give them a chance.

"Evlee. Evlee." Bum upward, Sarah scrambled down from the settee. She ran to Everleigh and held out her arms. "Up."

Everleigh passed her gifts to Jessica. "Could you please give these to

Mrs. Schmidt for me? They are for Sarah."

The gifts for her cousins and the others had been brought down earlier in the day, but she'd needed to put the finishing touches on Sarah's frock and doll.

"Of course." Jessica smiled, catching the nurse's eye. "You look lovely. Green is definitely your color. It matches your eyes."

Everleigh lifted Sarah. "Hello, darling. Happy Christmas."

"Happy Chris'mas, Evlee. I has a puppy. She has sharp teeth." Sarah twisted, and looking over Everleigh's shoulder, inspected the floor. Her little face crumpled. "I think Papa sent Claire to the nurs'ry."

"I met your puppy. She's adorable, just like you." Everleigh hugged Sarah to her.

She'd miss the little mite.

She felt Griffin's gaze caressing her again as he murmured something to Hampton while accepting a glass of champaign.

Mrs. Schmidt accepted the packages and extended her hand. "Let's go for a walk and check on your puppy, shall we, love?"

A delicate way of saying it was time for Sarah to go to the nursery.

"Papa said I stay up late." Sarah's face contorted into a pout.

"You will, pet. You have more gifts to open." She held them up. "And after supper, you'll have plum pudding!" Mrs. Schmidt said. "Besides, this is Claire's first night in the house. She'll be afraid and lonely, and your puppy will want to cuddle with you."

Everleigh passed Sarah to her Nurse. "I'll come say goodnight to you too. I'd love to see your puppy again."

Sarah stuck her lower lip out. "Promise?"

360

"I promise."

She should've taken the gifts directly to the nursery, and had she been speaking to Griffin, she'd have known what his plans were for Sarah tonight.

She forced a smile as Nicolette approached.

"Everleigh, did you and Sheffield have a falling out?" Nicolette spoke low, but her eyes brimmed with worry.

Everleigh shrugged.

"Not exactly. It just wasn't meant to be."

"Bosh. What utter twaddle." Nicolette slanted her gaze toward him. "He cannot stop staring at you, and you're no better."

"Please leave it alone, Nicolette."

Everleigh didn't mean to sound cross, but neither could she discuss something so painful.

A fleeting look of surprise skated across Nicolette's face before she nodded. "All right. Come sit with me."

She grasped Everleigh's hand and towed her to chairs near the tree.

"I thought we were opening presents after supper?" Everleigh sank onto the gold and cream striped cushion.

"We are, but Theadosia said she wanted to make an announcement."

Just then, Theadosia, wearing a spectacular ice blue gown, floated into the drawing room on Sutcliffe's arm. She positively glowed tonight. As difficult as the past couple of days had been, she still deserved Everleigh's thanks for forcing her out of self-imposed isolation.

She had enjoyed herself—mostly.

Her attention gravitated to Griffin, only he wasn't there anymore.

Swallowing, she lowered her gaze to her clasped hands.

She didn't blame him for leaving. She found it hard to be in the same room with him too.

How she wanted to take those words back. Tell him to not stop trying to win her heart.

Why don't you?

Why indeed? She'd nothing to lose.

Lifting her head, she searched the room. Drat and blast. He was truly gone, and she couldn't very well go in search of him. Not without raising brows. There was also the worry that he might not accept her apology.

She'd never know unless she tried. Her stomach wobbled with excitement.

Oh, and she had to try. She had to, for he was her everything. Nothing mattered but him, not her fears or concerns. Just Griffin and what they had together.

She started to rise when Theadosia clapped her hands. "Please have a seat or find a place you are comfortable standing for a few moments."

Sinking back onto the chair, Everleigh suppressed a frustrated sigh.

"We have an announcement to make." Sutcliffe stepped near and wrapped an arm around his wife's waist.

"Oh, what do you suppose it is?" Nicolette whispered in Everleigh's ear.

"Given the specialness of this day when we celebrate our Savior's birth, we thought it only fitting to tell our dearest friends and neighbors our good news." Theadosia gazed at Sutcliffe with utter adoration.

He lifted her hand and kissed her fingertips. "We are to be parents, come summer."

A chorus of congratulations echoed about the room, not the least of which was the Dowager Duchess's cry of delight.

Everleigh took advantage of the melee to slip from the room. She headed toward the stairs, thinking Griffin might've have gone above to say good night to Sarah.

A movement in the dining room caught her eye.

Griffin?

What the deuce was he up to?

Looking very much like a naughty boy, he was moving the name tags around the table. From just outside the door, an amused smile curving her mouth, she watched him make a complete muddle of Theadosia's seating arrangements.

"I do hope, Griffin, this means you've placed yourself beside me."

He whirled around, one name card grasped between his fingers before a slow smile tinged with mischief arched his lips.

"I was just about to do so."

He set the card down then stood back to admire his handiwork.

"I've been doing a bit of matchmaking." He pointed. "Jessica Brentwood and Bainbridge. Miss Twistleton and Westfall. Miss Breckensole and Pennington—"

"You didn't!" Everleigh rushed forward a few steps. He had indeed. "You wicked, wicked man. Gabriella will never forgive you."

He strode to her and clasped her hand.

"It's not her forgiveness I crave. Everleigh, I rushed you. I tried to force something you weren't ready for. Please forgive me. And if you're never ready to re-marry, I shall accept your decision. I only ask that we remain friends, that I may share your company."

Friends?

Had he been nipping the brandy already? Friends didn't do the naughty wonderful things she yearned to do with him.

"Oh, Griffin. I was looking for you to beg you to forgive me for hurting you. I was wrong. So, so wrong. I love you too, I truly, truly do. I want to be with you more than anything else."

Touching his dear face, she blinked through the joyful moisture blurring her vision.

"It would be the greatest privilege to be your wife." An impulse sprang to mind, and she clasped his hand. "Will you marry me?"

Chuckling delightedly, he crushed her to his chest.

"Yes. Yes! Lord, yes. I shall marry you, you delightfully unpredictable woman."

She tilted her head back, eyeing the kissing bough above their heads. "I believe a kiss is in order."

"Go on, man," Sutcliffe said. "Kiss her. I'm hungry, as are we all."

Everleigh spun around to find the corridor full of amused guests.

Dandridge, grinning ear to ear, pulled his wife to his side and dropped a quick peck on her temple. Ophelia and Gabriella hugged each other. Nicolette eyed Westfall with a considering look. Jessica, Rayne, and Theadosia beamed at one another like they'd planned the whole affair.

Griffin cupped Everleigh's chin, gently drawing it upward.

"Happy Christmas, Everleigh."

And right there in front of everyone, Griffin, Duke of Sheffield gave her a kiss that she nor he nor the other guests would soon forget.

Epilogue

2 September, 1810
Rome, Italy

Everleigh chuckled and shook her head as Claire, her silken ears flapping, raced by in pursuit of the ball Sarah had thrown. Those two never grew tired of that game. The stately Italian villa they'd let for the next month boasted an enclosed courtyard perfect for energetic dogs and almost-four-year-olds.

"Mama, did you see Claire fetch the ball?"

Sarah bent to retrieve the slobbery orb.

"I did, darling." A feathery fluttering in her belly startled Everleigh. She cradled the small mound with both hands. "Well, hello there, precious. Do you hear your sister and Mama?"

The babe moved again.

"Griffin, the baby is moving! Here, you must feel."

She pressed his hand to her tummy. Another flicker caused her to giggle, and a goofy grin divided his face.

"Energetic little fellow, isn't he?" He bent low, murmuring to the small mound. "This is your papa, and he loves you very, very much."

"This is only the beginning." She ran her palms over her stomach. "Theadosia said she could see Amber's entire foot pressed against her belly at times."

His gaze fell on the simple gold band encircling her ring finger. "I wish you'd let me buy you a proper wedding ring, sweet."

She held her hand up, admiring the simple ring. "Not a bit of it. I found this in my Christmas pudding after I asked you to marry me. It's perfect. It was meant to be."

Actually, nearly everybody found a ring that evening, thanks to Griffin's sweet-talking the cook. Not everyone was as pleased as Everleigh had been to discover the trinket.

Wrapping an arm around her shoulders, he drew her near. "You forget, I asked you first."

"Yes, but I turned you down, so it was only fitting that I propose to you, scandalous though it was."

"How about an emerald ring you could wear with this band then?" He caressed her fingers.

"I suppose, if you insist," she teased.

He knew her weakness for emeralds.

She rested her head against his chest. Married seven months already. Their wedding trip had been delayed due to Caroline Chatterton's devious machinations. Somehow, she'd persuaded the local magistrate to open an inquiry into Frederick's and Arnold's deaths.

Probably by bedding the dumpling of a man.

Everleigh hadn't been permitted to leave the country during the investigation, which, after five months, completely exonerated her. Caroline, the fool, hadn't been as fortunate. Seems she'd been cuckolding Frederick with a not-altogether-too-bright fellow of questionable repute, who had taken her at her word when she said she wished her husband and father-in-law were dead. She'd wanted Everleigh dead too, the fellow had confessed, but he didn't hold with killing women.

Ironically, Caroline—fortunate to have escaped the hangman's noose—now sailed for the same penal colony Theadosia's father pastored. Her former lover hadn't been as fortunate.

The postponed honeymoon had worked out well in the end. Everleigh had been able to attend Jessica's and Nicolette's weddings, as well as the dowager duchess of Sutcliffe's marriage to Jerome DuBoise.

Griffin was convinced he'd orchestrated that union, but the Duke of Sutcliffe claimed he'd been responsible.

Sarah paused in her romps to trot over to her new governess, Miss Brimble. Nurse had gratefully retired to a comfortable cottage in Bristol, and Miss Brimble, being several generations younger and the oldest of twelve, proved skilled at managing Sarah.

Maya and Jenny—the name Sarah picked for the doll Everleigh made her—sat serenely on the tolerant governess's lap.

"Let's go for a walk, my dears." Sarah gathered her dollies in her arms, and Miss Brimble stood.

Claire, tongue lolling, had plopped herself at Miss Brimble's feet, but the instant the governess stood, the spaniel leapt to all fours once more.

"Miss Sarah, shall we explore the maze?" She looked to Everleigh for approval, and after receiving a nod, asked, "Shall I hold one of your babies for you?"

Sarah tilted her head and extended both before her, considering them. She passed Miss Brimble Jenny. "Maya needs extra 'tention, so she doesn't get jealous of Jenny."

Was that a hint?

Sarah had been ecstatic when Everleigh and Griffin had told her she was going to be a big sister. Her enthusiasm waned considerably when she learned she might have a little brother, and a jot more when told she couldn't dress the new baby in her dollies' clothes.

As Sarah and Miss Brimble disappeared into the labyrinth, Everleigh turned into Griffin's embrace and hugged him.

"I never thought I could be this happy, Griffin. I love you so much, it almost hurts sometimes." She tilted her head into the crook of his shoulder. "Tell me again when you knew you loved me. I never tire of hearing it."

He pressed a tender kiss to her forehead.

"I knew the moment you scooped Sarah into your arms in the drawing room, and my heart stood still for an instant, that I'd found the woman I was meant to spend the rest of my life with."

About the Author

USA Today Bestselling, award-winning author COLLETTE CAMERON®
scribbles Scottish and Regency historicals featuring dashing rogues and
scoundrels and the intrepid damsels who re-form them. Blessed with an
overactive and witty muse that won't stop whispering new romantic romps
in her ear, she's lived in Oregon her entire life, though she dreams of
living in Scotland part-time. A self-confessed Cadbury chocoholic, you'll
always find a dash of inspiration and a pinch of humor in her sweet-to-
spicy timeless romances®.

Explore **Collette's worlds** at
www.collettecameron.com!

Join her **VIP Reader Club** and **FREE newsletter**. Giggles guaranteed!

FREE BOOK: Join Collette's The Regency Rose® VIP Reader Club to get updates on book releases, cover reveals, contests and giveaways she reserves exclusively for email and newsletter followers. Also, any deals, sales, or special promotions are offered to club members first. She will not share your name or email, nor will she spam you.

http://bit.ly/TheRegencyRoseGift

From the Desk of Collette Cameron

Dearest Reader,

 Thank you for reading SEDUCTIVE SURRENDER SERIES BOOKS 1-3! I hope you enjoyed reading the stories and loved the characters. I also hinted at couples you'll see in upcoming books in the SEDUCTIVE SURRENDER series.

 Fans of heartwarming Regency Romances will also enjoy The Honorable Rogues™ Series and The Blue Rose Romance: The Culpepper Misses Series.

 SIGN UP FOR MY NEWSLETTER on my website www.collettecomeron.com to find out when new books release. I also have a FREE bonus for new subscribers

 Please consider telling other readers why you enjoyed this book by reviewing it. I also love to hear from my readers. Here's wishing you many happy hours of reading, more happily-ever-afters than you can possibly enjoy in a lifetime, and abundant blessings to you and your loved ones.

Collette Cameron

Enjoy the first chapter of

The Earl and the Spinster

The Blue Rose Regency Romances: The Culpepper Misses, Book One

Even when most prudently considered,

and with the noblest of intentions, one who

wagers with chance oft finds oneself empty-handed.

~Wisdom and Advice The Genteel Lady's Guide to Practical Living

1

Esherton Green,

Near Acton, Cheshire, England

Early April 1822

*W*as *I born under an evil star or cursed from my first breath?*

Brooke Culpepper suppressed the urge to shake her fist at the heavens and berate The Almighty aloud. The devil boasted better luck than she. My God, now two *more* cows struggled to regain their strength?

She slid Richard Mabry, Esherton Green's steward-turned-overseer, a worried glance from beneath her lashes as she chewed her lower lip and paced before the unsatisfactory fire in the study's hearth. The soothing aroma of wood smoke, combined with linseed oil, old leather, and the faintest trace of Papa's pipe tobacco, bathed the room. The scents reminded her of happier times but did little to calm her frayed nerves.

Sensible gray woolen skirts swishing about her ankles, she whirled to make the return trip across the once-bright green and gold Axminster carpet, now so threadbare, the oak floor peeked through in numerous places. Her scuffed half-boots fared little better, and she hid a wince when the scrap of leather she'd used to cover the hole in her left sole this morning slipped loose again.

From his comfortable spot in a worn and faded wingback chair, Freddy, her aged Welsh corgi, observed her progress with soulful brown eyes, his muzzle propped on stubby paws. Two ancient tabbies lay curled so tightly together on the cracked leather sofa that determining where one ended and the other began was difficult.

What was she to do? Brooke clamped her lip harder and winced.

Should she venture to the barn to see the cows herself?

What good would that do? She knew little of doctoring cattle and so left the animals' care in Mr. Mabry's capable hands. Her strength lay in the financial administration of the dairy farm and her ability to stretch a shilling as thin as gossamer.

She cast a glance at the bay window and, despite the fire, rubbed her arms against the chill creeping along her spine. A frenzied wind whipped the lilac branches and scraped the rain-splattered panes. The tempest threatening since dawn had finally unleashed its full fury, and the fierce winds battering the house gave the day a peculiar, eerie feeling—as if portending something ominous.

At least Mabry and the other hands had managed to get the cattle tucked away before the gale hit. The herd of fifty—no, sixty, counting the newborn calves—chewed their cud and weathered the storm inside the old, but sturdy, barns.

As she peered through the blurry pane, a shingle ripped loose from the farthest outbuilding—a retired stone dovecote. After the wind tossed the slat around for a few moments, the wood twirled to the ground, where it flipped end over end before wedging beneath a gangly shrub. Two more shingles hurled to the earth, this time from one of the barns.

Flimflam and goose-butt feathers.

Brooke tamped down a heavy sigh. Each structure on the estate, including the house, needed some sort of repair or replacement: roofs, shutters, stalls, floors, stairs, doors, siding...dozens of items required fixing, and she could seldom muster the funds to go about it properly.

"Another pair of cows struggling, you say, Mr. Mabry?"

Concern etched on his weathered features, Mabry wiped rain droplets from his face as water pooled at his muddy feet.

"Yes, Miss Brooke. The four calves born this mornin' fare well, but two of the cows, one a first-calf heifer, aren't standin' yet. And there's one weak from birthin' her calf yesterday." His troubled gaze strayed to the window. "Two more ladies are in labor. I best return to the barn. They seemed fine when I left, but I'd as soon be nearby."

Brooke nodded once. "Yes, we mustn't take any chances."

The herd had already been reduced to a minimum by disease and sales to make ends meet. She needed every shilling the cows' milk brought. Losing another, let alone two or three good breeders...

No, I won't think of it.

She stopped pacing and forced a cheerful smile. Nonetheless, from the skeptical look Mabry speedily masked, his thoughts ran parallel to hers—one reason she put her trust in the man. Honest and intelligent, he'd worked alongside her to restore the beleaguered herd and farm after Papa died. Their existence, their livelihood, everyone at Esherton's future depended on the estate flourishing once more.

"It's only been a few hours." *Almost nine, truth to tell.* Brooke scratched her temple. "Perhaps the ladies need a little more time to recover." *If they recovered.* "The calves are strong, aren't they?" *Please, God, they must be.* She held her breath, anticipating Mabry's response.

His countenance lightened and the merry sparkle returned to his eyes. "Aye, the mites are fine. Feedin' like they're hollow to their wee hooves."

Tension lessoned its ruthless grip, and hope peeked from beneath her vast mound of worries.

Six calves had been guaranteed in trade to her neighbor and fellow dairy farmer, Silas Huffington, for the grain and medicines he'd provided to see Esherton Green's herd through last winter. Brooke didn't have the means to pay him if the calves didn't survive—though the old reprobate had hinted he'd make her a deal of a much less respectable nature if she ran short of cattle with which to barter. Each pence she'd stashed away—groat by miserable groat, these past four years—lay in the hidden drawer of Papa's desk and must go to purchase a bull.

Wisdom had decreed replacing Old Buford two years ago but, short on funds, she'd waited until it was too late. His heart had stopped while he performed the duties expected of a breeding bull. Not the worst way to cock up one's toes...er, hooves, but she'd counted on him siring at least two-score calves this season and wagered everything on the calving this year and next. The poor brute had expired before he'd completed the job.

Her thoughts careened around inside her skull. Without a bull, she would lose everything.

My home, care of my sister and cousins, my reasons for existing.

She squared her shoulders, resolution strengthening her. She still retained the Culpepper sapphire parure set. If all else failed, she would pawn the jewelry. She'd planned on using the money from the gems' sale to bestow small marriage settlements on the girls. Still, pawning the set was a price worth paying to keep her family at Esherton Green, even if it meant that any chance of her sister and three cousins securing a decent match would evaporate faster than a dab of milk on a hot cook stove. Good standing and breeding meant little if one's fortune proved meaner than a churchyard beggar's.

"How's the big bull calf that came breech on Sunday?" Brooke tossed the question over her shoulder as she poked the fire and encouraged the blaze to burn hotter. After setting the tool aside, she faced the overseer.

"Greediest of the lot." Mabry laughed and slapped his thigh. "Quite the appetite he has, and friendly as our Freddy there. Likes his ears scratched too."

Brooke chuckled and ran her hand across Freddy's spine. The dog wiggled in excitement and stuck his rear legs straight out behind him, gazing at her in adoration. In his youth, he'd been an excellent cattle herder. Now he'd gone fat and arthritic, his sweet face gray to his eyebrows. On occasion, he still dashed after the cattle, the instinctive drive to herd deep in the marrow of his bones.

Another shudder shook her. Why was she so blasted cold today? She relented and placed a good-sized log atop the others. The feeble flames hissed and spat before greedily engulfing the new addition. Lord, she prayed she wasn't ailing. She simply couldn't afford to become ill.

A scratching at the door barely preceded the entrance of Duffen bearing a tea service. "Gotten to where a man cannot find a quiet corner to shut his eyes for a blink or two anymore."

Shuffling into the room, he yawned and revealed how few teeth remained in his mouth. One sock sagged around his ankle, his grizzled hair poked every which way, and his shirttail hung askew. Typical Duffen.

"Devil's day, it is." He scowled in the window's direction, his mouth pressed into a grim line. "Mark my words, trouble's afoot."

Not quite a butler, but certainly more than a simple retainer, the man, now hunched from age, had been a fixture at Esherton Green Brooke's entire life. He loved the place as much as, if not more than, she, and she couldn't afford to hire a servant to replace him. A light purse had forced Brooke to let the household staff go when Papa died. The cook, Mrs. Jennings, Duffen, and Flora, a maid-of-all-work, had stayed on. However, they received no salaries—only room and board.

The income from the dairy scarcely permitted Brooke to retain a few milkmaids and stable hands, yet not once had she heard a whispered complaint from anyone.

Everybody, including Brooke, her sister, Brette, and their cousins— Blythe, and the twins, Blaike and Blaire—did their part to keep the farm operating at a profit. A meager profit, particularly as, for the past five years, Esherton Green's legal heir, Sheridan Gainsborough, had received half the proceeds. In return, he permitted Brooke and the girls to reside there. He'd also been appointed their guardian. But, from his silence and failure to visit the farm, he seemed perfectly content to let her carry on as provider and caretaker.

"Ridiculous law. Only the next male in line can inherit," she muttered.

Especially when he proved a disinterested bore. Papa had thought so too, but the choice hadn't been his to make. If only she could keep the funds she sent to Sheridan each quarter, Brooke could make something of Esherton and secure her sister and cousins' futures too.

If wishes were gold pieces, I'd be rich indeed.

Brooke sneezed then sneezed again. Dash it all. A cold?

The fresh log snapped loudly, and Brooke started. The blaze's heat had failed to warm her opinion of her second cousin. She hadn't met him and lacked a personal notion of his character, but Papa had hinted that Sheridan was a scallywag and possessed unsavory habits.

A greedy sot, too.

The one time her quarterly remittance had been late, because Brooke had taken a tumble and broken her arm, he'd written a disagreeable letter demanding his money.

His money, indeed.

Sheridan had threatened to sell Esherton Green's acreage and turn her and the foursome onto the street if she ever delayed payment again.

A ruckus beyond the entrance announced the girls' arrival. Laughing and chatting, the blond quartet billowed into the room. Their gowns, several seasons out of fashion, in no way detracted from their charm, and pride swelled in Brooke's heart. Lovely, both in countenance and disposition, and the dears worked hard too.

"Duffen says we're to have tea in here today." Attired in a Pomona green gown too short for her tall frame, Blaike plopped on to the sofa. Her twin, Blaire, wearing a similar dress in dark rose and equally inadequate in length, flopped beside her.

Each girl scooped a drowsy cat into her lap. The cats' wiry whiskers twitched, and they blinked their sleepy amber eyes a few times before closing them once more as the low rumble of contented purrs filled the room.

"Yes, I didn't think we needed to light a fire in the drawing room when this one will suffice." As things stood, too little coal and seasoned firewood remained to see them comfortably until summer.

Brette sailed across the study, her slate-blue gingham dress the only one of the quartet's fashionably long enough. Repeated laundering had turned the garment a peculiar greenish color, much like tarnished copper. She looped her arm through Brooke's.

"Look, dearest." Brette pointed to the tray. "I splurged and made a half-batch of shortbread biscuits. It's been so long since we've indulged, and today is your birthday. To celebrate, I insisted on fresh tea leaves as well."

Brooke would have preferred to ignore the day.

Three and twenty.

On the shelf. Past her prime. Long in the tooth. Spinster. *Old maid.*

She'd relinquished her one chance at love. In order to nurse her ailing father and assume the care of her young sister and three orphaned cousins, she'd refused Humphrey Benbridge's proposal. She couldn't have put her happiness before their welfare and deserted them when they needed her most. Who would've cared for them if she hadn't?

No one.

Mr. Benbridge controlled the purse strings, and Humphrey had neither offered nor been in a position to take on their care. Devastated, or so he'd claimed, he'd departed to the continent five years ago.

She'd not seen him since.

Nonetheless, his sister, Josephina, remained a friend and occasionally remarked on Humphrey's travels abroad. Burying the pieces of her broken heart beneath hard work and devotion to her family, Brooke had rolled up her sleeves and plunged into her forced role as breadwinner, determined that sacrificing her love not be in vain.

Yes, it grieved her that she wouldn't experience a man's passion or bear children, but to wallow in doldrums was a waste of energy and emotion. Instead, she focused on building a future for her sister and cousins—so they might have what she never would—and allowed her dreams to fade into obscurity.

"Happy birthday." Brette squeezed her hand.

Brooke offered her sister a rueful half-smile. "Ah, I'd hoped you'd forgotten."

"Don't be silly, Brooke. We couldn't forget your special day." Twenty-year-old Blythe—standing with her hands behind her—grinned and pulled a small, neatly-wrapped gift tied with a cheerful yellow ribbon from behind her. Sweet dear. She'd used the trimming from her gown to adorn the package.

"Hmph. Need seedcake an' champagne to celebrate a birthday properly." The contents of the tray rattled and clanked when Duffen scuffed his way to the table between the sofa and chairs. After depositing the tea service, he lifted a letter from the surface. Tea dripped from one stained corner. "This arrived for you yesterday, Miss Brooke. I forgot where I'd put it until just now."

If I can read it with the ink running to London and back.

He shook the letter, oblivious to the tawny droplets spraying every which way.

Mabry raised a bushy gray eyebrow, and the twins hid giggles by concealing their faces in the cat's striped coats.

Brette set about pouring the tea, although her lips twitched suspiciously.

Freddy sat on his haunches and barked, his button eyes fixed on the paper, evidently mistaking it for a tasty morsel he would've liked to sample. He licked his chops, a testament to his waning eyesight.

"Thank you, Duffen." Brooke took the letter by one soggy corner. Holding it gingerly, she flipped it over. No return address.

"Aren't you going to read it?" Blythe set the gift on the table before settling on the sofa and smoothing her skirt. They didn't get a whole lot of post at Esherton. Truth be known, this was the first letter in months

Blythe's gaze roved to the other girls and the equally eager expressions on their faces. "We're on pins and needles," she quipped, fluttering her hands and winking.

Brooke smiled and cracked the brownish wax seal with her fingernail. Their lives had become rather monotonous, so much so that a simple, *soggy*, correspondence sent the girls into a dither of anticipation.

My Dearest Cousin...

Brooke glanced up. "It's from Sheridan.

Printed in Great Britain
by Amazon